TRICK PLAY

TRICK PLAY

Jerica MacMillan

Marycliff Press

Trick Play
Jerica MacMillan
Copyright © 2021 by Jerica MacMillan

This is a work of fiction. Names, characters, businesses, places, events and incidents are either the products of the author's imagination or used in a fictitious manner. Any resemblance to actual persons, living or dead, or actual events is purely coincidental.

ISBN-13: 978-1-956937-03-9

CHAPTER ONE

Cal

She's here.

Awareness of her presence zings through me, even as I flirt with the pretty redhead standing in front of me.

Piper. That's what Kilpatrick called her that time I tried to chat her up after practice a few weeks ago. Once I found out she was his sister, I steered clear.

But that hasn't stopped me from being aware of her anytime she's around. When she comes to our practices, the small hairs on the back of my neck rise, and like a dummy, I push myself harder, hoping to impress her, to claim her attention.

It hasn't worked, though, at least not that I can tell. And who can blame her? I'm second string to her big brother's starting quarterback spot. Who would be impressed by that?

Plus, she probably hates me as much as her brother does, since she actually seems to like her brother. Or at least I assume so, since she watches our practices and cheers for him, meeting up with him afterward.

My sister would never do that. She and I have a … contentious relationship.

But Piper and Kilpatrick appear to be the kinds of siblings who are also friends. Weird. And since I've made no secret of my resentment of Kilpatrick for showing up my senior year as a transfer and taking my starting spot, making it harder for me to get seen by NFL scouts, I'm assuming Piper dislikes me as much as her brother does.

He and his sister both showed up out of the blue at the start of the semester. He was brought along by the new coach—which is a whole other pile of bullshit as far as I'm concerned. I'm still mad about how they forced Coach Hanson into retirement after the way he busted his ass and pushed the whole team the last few years to get us an invite to be a Division I school like the administration wanted. And that's the way they thank him. I guess I shouldn't have been so surprised that my own hard work as the starting quarterback my junior year—in the words of the local sports reporters, the young phenom who carried the team to a Division I ranking—was likewise rewarded by a replacement.

So my attraction to Piper is extremely inconvenient. Her brother is my biggest rival. She probably hates me. And yet I can't shake this awareness I have every time she's around.

I force myself to stop looking at her and refocus my attention on the redhead in front of me—Jenny, I think she said her name was. Jenny's clearly into me with the way she bats her eyes and keeps dragging the tips of her fingers across her chest, subtly drawing attention to her ample cleavage, flicking her long hair over her shoulder or tucking it behind her ear. And I should be into Jenny. She's everything I normally want in a girl—pretty and down to fuck.

But it's the raven-haired beauty with the pale skin across the room that keeps drawing my eyes to her, despite my better intentions.

Not that my better intentions have done anything for me lately.

Look at my living situation. I try to be the bigger person, even going so far as to help my sister patch up her relationship with my best friend—a relationship that they kept secret from me, I might add—and what has that gotten me? An eyeful of my sister grinding on my best friend almost every time I come home since they got back together a few weeks ago. The knowledge that when I leave, they're probably going to fuck on the couch. And Ellie, the little brat, *loves* making me uncomfortable, waiting until I'm all the way in the room before she stops sucking on Simon's tongue, all faux innocence with her,

"Oh, I didn't hear you come in. Sorry, Cal."

Yeah, right. Our house is old and creaky as all hell. No way she doesn't hear me come in when I practically slam the door and stomp around to make sure I give plenty of warning that I'm home.

Maybe I should stop letting my better intentions rule the day. Maybe I should give my baser instincts a shot.

For example, now that I know how much one of my teammates dating my little sister gets under my skin, I can't help but wonder how it would affect Kilpatrick if I started demonstrating my interest in his sister …

Would that mess with him enough to throw him off his game?

If so, I could get more playing time in the lead up to the postseason, not to mention the bowl game we're due to play if all goes well.

With a murmured excuse to Jenny, I slip away from my spot by the breakfast bar and make my way over to where Piper holds court with a few of her friends and some of my younger teammates on the couch. As I approach, she tosses back her head and laughs at something Eli Foster says, and I take advantage of the opportunity to look my fill.

Her long hair is loose, flowing over her shoulders, teasing the tops of her tits. She's got more there than I realized before, since I mostly see her in sweatshirts or jackets that hide her shape above her hips. She's slight, so I figured she'd have small tits, but they're plump and full, begging to be caressed, showing off in her shimmery spaghetti strap tank. It's loose, low cut enough to give a hint of cleavage and skimming over her curves, and I can't help wondering if she's wearing a strapless bra or no bra at all. She's paired the top with curve-hugging shiny leggings that make her ass look slappable.

Not that I intend to caress or slap anything without an explicit invitation. But that doesn't mean I don't think about how good it would feel and how fun it would be, first for its own sake, but second, for the likely effect it would have on her brother.

A broad smile takes over my face just envisioning how mad he'll get when I fuck his sister.

Like she's as aware of me as I am of her, Piper's eyes find mine, the smile still on her face from whatever Foster said that made her laugh.

"Hey, Piper," I say, pitching my voice in that smooth as silk register that has girls handing over their panties in no time. "Can I get you a drink?"

Her mouth twists to one side like she's trying to fight back her smile as her eyes wander down my body and back up again. "Hey," she says on a suppressed laugh, her dark eyebrows rising over her glittering brown eyes. She catches her plump lower lip between her pretty white teeth, and I so want to reach out and free it before covering those lips with mine. But I have a feeling that would be too bold. We've barely spoken. And while she doesn't seem upset by my presence, she's not doing that breathless flirty thing I get from the girls who want me to take them into an empty room and fuck them right away.

That's alright, though. I can still work with the spark of interest evident from her perusal of my body.

"What are you drinking?" I press.

She shakes her head, her smile blossoming again. "Just water for me right now. But I get my own drinks."

I nod toward the kitchen. "Then let me escort you. I know where they keep the bottled water."

Another suppressed giggle escapes her closed lips, but she shakes her head and steps next to me. "Alright, if you insist, McAdam."

That has my brows rising in surprise. "You know my name."

"Of course I do." That irrepressible smile is still on her face. "I come to your practices at least once a week, not to mention your games. Your name is on your jersey."

"Ah, but you made the effort to remember it," I say, leaning in close and almost whispering the words in her ear.

Goosebumps rise on her neck, and my grin is now one of triumph. Yeah, this plan is the best one I've had in ages. It's much better than helping my roommate fuck my sister silly at every opportunity, which I'm sure they're doing right now, actually. I'm not going to be home for a while, and even though they both showed up to this party with me, I haven't seen either one in the last half hour. Ten to one they're already home and naked.

Ugh.

But this plan means I have a high chance of getting with the chick who's held my attention for longer than anyone in quite a while. Not that I have a ban on repeat performances or anything, but some chicks get the wrong idea if you bang 'em too many times, so it's best to keep repeats to a minimum. Plus, it's the chase that's half the fun. Once that's over, my interest wanes pretty quickly.

With Simon and Ellie home already, my options for putting the moves on pretty Piper are limited to an empty room here or going back to her place, wherever that may be. "So do you live on campus?" I ask, trying to figure out the best plan of action for the evening.

She glances at me before turning her attention to the open cooler of ice and water next to the sliding glass door. This is a relatively small party at my teammate Trey's house. He and his girlfriend Brandy like to host their friends pretty regularly. They tend to be smaller gatherings rather than the larger frat parties, though the usual football groupies always find out and show up, and since Brandy's a cheerleader, her squad makes frequent appearances as well. Their parties are always a good time and have the added bonus of never getting out of hand or getting any of us in trouble with the coach. Trey knows how to toe the line between fun and following the rules.

Case in point, instead of a keg, they have open coolers of drinks, plus mixers and liquor on the counter by the sink. The beer and other drinks are mostly for the non-athlete crowd, because our diet plans don't usually allow for that many extra calories. We tend to go for low cal mixers and liquor, instead. I've been nursing a gin and tonic most of the night, but I grab a water out of the cooler, too. Hydration is always a good plan, especially if we're going to exert ourselves later.

As she cracks open her water and takes a sip, Piper narrows her eyes at me. "Why are you asking?"

I shrug and lean against the wall, cracking open my own water and drinking deeply. It's cool and crisp and almost erotic while I stand here trying to figure out the best way into Piper's panties. "Just curious."

Her narrowed eyes flicker over me again. "I live on campus."

I nod, scanning the room, curious if her brother's noticed I'm talking to her yet. Though he wasn't too bothered about her talking to the other players earlier, so maybe he won't care. Yet. I'll make sure he cares before I'm done with her, though.

Piper's voice draws my attention back to her. "Alright, well, good talk. See ya." And she starts to move away.

I jolt upright from the wall and catch up to her before she can go more than a couple of feet. "What's the matter? Why are you running away?"

That seems to be the right thing to say, because she stops and faces me, her shoulders square and her chin tipped up, fire starting to flicker in her eyes. "Excuse me? I'm not running away."

I lift a single eyebrow. "Aren't you, though? I thought we were getting to know each other, and you're about to scamper off." I lean in close and pitch my voice low again. "I promise I won't bite unless you ask me to." Then I grin to show off my teeth.

That has her laughing, which isn't quite the reaction I was going for, but I'll take it. At least she's not leaving.

She crosses her arms, which makes her tits look even more luscious. "Does that line actually work?"

I give her a quizzical look.

She rolls one of her hands. "You know, about not biting unless asked. What makes you think I'd ask you to do anything to me with your mouth?"

Easing closer, I look her up and down, watching the way her eyes focus on my mouth, and let out a rumbly sound. "Well, for starters, the way you can't take your eyes off me makes me think you're attracted to me. You've paid enough attention to me to remember my name, even though we've only spoken one other time, and that was weeks ago."

She scoffs. "Please. I know plenty of names of my brother's teammates." Her eyes meet mine, full of challenge. "And you're his biggest rival. Of course I'd know yours."

I give a slight shrug of ambivalence. "And the fact that you keep looking at my mouth?"

Her breath catches, pushing her tits against my chest. But then she steps back, breaking the contact, looking down and shaking her head, her soft chuckle just reaching my ears over the sounds of everyone else. "Nice try," she says with a smirk, finally meeting my eyes again, though I don't miss the way she keeps glancing at my lips like she can't help herself.

I shrug again, just watching as she takes two more steps backwards before turning and rejoining the girls she obviously came in with. When she glances at me over her shoulder, I give her a wide, knowing grin. She rolls her eyes and turns away, pointedly ignoring me.

That's alright, though. This isn't the first time I've struck out with a girl. And I can't help thinking this isn't so much me striking out as it is her testing to see if I'm really serious.

And I am. More serious than she can imagine.

CHAPTER TWO

Piper

McAdam's eyes feel like a brand on my back, but I resist the urge to turn around again and see if he's really still there, or if I'm just imagining him watching me.

"Oh-oh," Dani, my roommate, says, nudging me with her elbow. "Don't look now, but I think Cal McAdam's decided you're his prey for tonight."

Snorting, I shake my head, refusing to look around for him, no matter how much I might want to. "His prey? Is he a predator?"

She lifts one shoulder and holds her liquor in her mouth as she contemplates the question. Swallowing, she nods. "Yeah. Pretty much. He picks out a girl and stalks her like a big cat before singling her out, isolating her from her group, and going in for the kill."

I raise my eyebrows. "Are you speaking from firsthand experience?"

She snorts and brushes a hand over her plain T-shirt and jeans. I convinced her to go with her black, fitted V-neck tonight, at least. I tried to get her to go for something a little more girly, offering to let her borrow something of mine—it's a party, after all—or at least do her hair and makeup. Our coloring is similar, though her skin is a little darker than mine, and I have some eye shadow palettes that would make her eyes pop if she'd let me. But she declined, opting for pulling her dark brown hair back into her usual ponytail and putting on plain chapstick instead. "Me? The tomboy? Hardly. Cal goes for pretty girls who own things like hair straighteners and makeup."

My brow furrows. "You own makeup."

She gives me a look. "I'm not sure lip gloss and an old tube of mascara my mom bought me in high school really counts."

Pursing my lips, I shake my head. "Whatever. You're hot. Just because you don't wear makeup or own a hair straightener, doesn't mean you couldn't get with someone like McAdam." It's true. She's gorgeous. She just tries to hide it under her tomboy, one-of-the-guys persona, and I've been trying to figure out why since I met her at the beginning of the semester when we moved into our dorm. When I opted for a potluck roommate assignment—not that I had a choice, since I don't have any friends here—I figured I'd end up with another transfer student. But Dani's been here since last year. She just prefers hanging with guys, and her roommate last year moved off campus I guess. Apparently they got along fine as roommates, but weren't exactly friends. I kinda assumed we'd have the same sort of relationship—friend*ly*, but not really friends—but she's been convincing me to come hang with her and her friends the last few weeks. She says I spend too much time cooped up studying and it's not healthy.

Dani almost chokes on her drink at my statement, her eyes sliding to the side where her friend Eli stands next to her, apparently oblivious to our entire conversation. He's a tight end on the football team and the reason we knew about this party. Because my brother sure as hell isn't going to invite me along to a party, even if he doesn't try to make me leave.

In fact, if I were a betting woman, I'd bet that Gray won't go anywhere until after I leave. He takes his older brother duties of keeping an eye on me seriously. Even more seriously now than he did when we were kids, actually.

That's my own fault, though, to some degree. Less than a year out from under everyone's watchful eye, and I almost get expelled from SCU. I'm the reason we're both here, back home in Spokane, attending Marycliff

University. Me, because after what happened in California, my options were extremely limited—namely, go to Marycliff where my parents can keep a close eye on me, or get a job and move out. Gray, because he wanted to help act as a buffer between me and Mom and Dad. See? Serious protective older brother vibes.

Being back in Spokane is working out better for Gray than it is for me. He's the starting quarterback of the newest Division I football program, getting lots more press than he would've gotten back in Ohio, where he'd been recruited out of high school, even if he would've been the starter there too. Because here, how good the team is doing is even more impressive since it's a relatively small school with a new coach and a new starting quarterback.

I should be happy he's here. He's the reason our parents didn't force me to live at home. If not for him, I wouldn't be able to go to any parties at all. But I can't help thinking he's trying to keep an eye on me just as much as Mom and Dad.

"Anyway," Dani says, oblivious to my wandering thoughts. "My point is, Cal McAdam has his eye on you tonight. Rumor has it that it's worth letting him catch you, as long as you know it's just a one-time thing."

"Noted." But despite whatever rumors might be floating around about McAdam's sexual prowess, I have no intention of letting him catch me.

For one thing, that guy's got trouble written all over

him.

For another …

Well, that's reason enough right there, isn't it?

My goal is to stay out of trouble, keep my head down, and graduate as fast as possible. I already escaped this town once. I'm determined to do it again. And I'm still kicking myself over the fact that I got dragged back here so soon after my first escape.

And while, yes, I'm aware that I'm responsible for vandalizing the Alpha Nu house, those actions were triggered by a guy a lot like Cal—pretty, popular, able to get any girl he wants. And for a time, he wanted me.

Too bad I didn't know what that really meant. If I had, I wouldn't have gotten myself into the mess I'm in now.

So no. I won't be going anywhere near McAdam, not even if he keeps talking to me in that deep, sexy voice that I'm sure makes straight women everywhere cream their panties.

But despite me dismissing Dani's claims that McAdam has his eye on me, I can't deny that his eyes seem to be tracking me for the rest of the night. Or the way my blood heats every time I catch him looking at me. Or the relief I feel when he leaves without taking another girl with him.

None of that matters. Nope. Not a bit. Because I'm definitely not going there.

* * *

Huddled against the mid-November wind, I keep my head down as I walk across campus, keeping my pace brisk, because I'm *cold*. I didn't realize it would be this cold when I left my room and only put on my lightweight fleece. But the wind cuts right through it, making me shiver.

So I don't notice the wall of giant men off to the side of the walkway except as a barrier between me and my destination—Kent Hall, where Anthropology meets every Tuesday and Thursday.

The professor is full of fascinating stories, none of which have anything to do with what's on the test. Which makes attending class feel almost like a pointless exercise, but hey, it's ninety minutes twice a week dedicated to reading the textbook so I know the answers to the questions that actually will be on the test. And if I get through with the reading for Anthropology, I can always bust out the textbook for my Poli Sci class, because Dr. Presley doesn't pay much attention to what any of us are doing as long as we're not being disruptive.

It's not until a voice calls my name that I slow, lifting my head and looking around, the wind whipping my hair around my face. I foolishly wore it down today.

And here's another poor choice—stopping at the sound of my name. Because while the voice sounds familiar, it belongs to someone who I definitely don't want to see.

Cal McAdam.

I cross my arms and cock my hip, adjusting my backpack on my shoulder as I watch him jog up to me in easy strides, his normally tousled blond hair covered by a beanie that I'm irrationally jealous of, his Marycliff Football jacket pressed against his broad torso by the wind. He just looks so *warm*. And part of me wants to snuggle up next to him, let him wrap those strong arms around me and block the wind with those shoulders. But no, no, that's a terrible, terrible idea. I mean, the warmth and windbreak would be lovely, don't get me wrong, but knowing it would only encourage him makes it bad. Except I stopped to let him talk to me, which is all the encouragement he seems to need.

"Hey," he says, his perfect lips curling in a sinful smile that I *know* he's perfected over the years with the sole aim of turning girls into a messy puddle of arousal. He's several inches taller than me, but since my brother's a giant, I'm used to guys towering over me. I'm almost eye level with his mouth, and I can't help thinking how easy it would be to kiss him. All I'd have to do is lift my face, maybe press up on my toes, and he'd only have to bend a little bit.

But I blink rapidly, dispelling that image from my mind. The cold must be messing with my brain, because kissing Cal McAdam is nowhere on the list of possibilities. Even if I wanted to date somebody—which I absolutely don't have time for since I'm currently taking twenty-one credits, much to my advisor's dismay, so I can try to get out of here sooner than later. Since my parents forced me to withdraw from SCU mid-spring semester, I'm way behind. My entire goal in high school was to get out of this town and explore the wider world. That hasn't changed. But even if I had time to date, I definitely wouldn't date someone like Cal.

At least that's what I keep trying to tell myself, because with him standing in front of me smiling like that, I'm having a hard time remembering all of those things.

"Hey," I return, my tone deliberately flat and unencouraging.

Which only makes his smile grow bigger in his tan face, his cheeks a little red from the cold wind. Uh-oh. Is he one of those guys who thinks a girl's disinterest is a challenge to be conquered? I can't decide if that makes me dislike him more or worried I won't be able to resist for long.

His ocean blue eyes roam over my face as he stuffs his hands in his pockets. "You headed to class?"

I nod, turning as I check the time on my phone. "Yup. And if I don't hurry, I might be late. Good to see you!"

He jogs a couple of steps to catch up with me. "Where you headed? I'll walk with you."

I glance at him, fighting back a smile. "What if I'm going in the opposite direction of where you need to go?"

"I've got time," he answers with a shrug.

"I don't, though." I do my best to make my voice as firm and discouraging as possible. "I've got a full class load, and it's freezing out here, and I don't really feel like making small talk with a random dude bro on my way to class. So thanks for the offer, but I'll pass."

"What about later?" he asks, as persistent as ever. "I can get you a hot chocolate after class to help you warm up."

I shake my head. "I have another class after this one. Back to back until dinner."

"Dinner, then," he offers, still full of confidence despite me shooting him down twice already. "Anywhere you want. My treat."

I toss him an amused look, almost tempted to say yes, the possibilities of where I'd want to have dinner ticking through my mind. "I mean, you're asking me on a date, so I'd hope it'd be your treat." But I shake my head. "I can't." It's Thursday. That means weekly dinner with my parents. Even if I wanted to say yes to Cal, I can't. I speed up, the door to Kent Hall only a few feet away, and wave over my shoulder. "Thanks, anyway."

Once I'm inside, out of the wind and the cold and away from the weight of Cal's gaze, I stop and take a deep breath. That was close. Because I know the next thing out of his mouth would be an invitation to dinner tomorrow night, or whenever I am available. And then I'd have to just … tell him no. And for some reason, whether it's the sad puppy-dog look he pulls off far too well that I did my best to ignore or the effect that smile of his has on me, I'm not sure if I could make myself do that.

But guys like Cal lose interest quickly. Even if he sees me as a challenge right now, I only have to resist or stay busy—which isn't difficult, given my schedule—long enough for him to move on to more receptive targets.

And that thought doesn't at all make me sad or disappointed. Not even kind of. Because, like I keep reminding myself, I don't have time for any guy, and especially not a guy like Cal.

CHAPTER THREE

Cal

I stand frozen to the spot where Piper shot me down, not once, not twice, but three times. In a row. What is going on?

Simon bumps my shoulder with his fist, a chuckle underlying his words. "Dude. What was that?"

I shake my head, wondering the same thing. "I'm not sure." I mean, it's not like this is the first time a girl's turned me down. It's not. But it *is* the first time in a while. And none of the girls who turned me down before stared at my mouth with the kind of naked hunger I saw on Piper's face. I stare at the door where she disappeared, ignoring the wind trying to freeze off the tip of my nose, and try to figure out what went wrong.

Is this another test? Or is she really not interested? But if she's not interested, why would she even stop to let me catch up to her. And she looked at me like she wanted to kiss me. I wasn't imagining that. So what's stopping her from letting me buy her a hot chocolate?

"She's Kilpatrick's sister, you know," Simon says next to me, and I finally turn away from the door and fall in step beside him as we head toward the student center to grab lunch, which is what we were doing when I saw Piper hurrying past. My nose is starting to run from the cold, and Simon's cheeks are red against his normally tan skin, his shoulders hunched against the wind.

"I know." Which is part of her appeal, really, but I'm not about to admit that to Simon.

His dark eyes narrow, his brows lowering. "Dude."

I stop and look at him, forcing him to stop too. "Seriously? *You're* going to lecture me about dating a teammate's sister? You? Of all people?"

If I thought reminding him of the fact that he hooked up with my sister behind my back would tone down the censure, I was apparently wrong. Because all he does is shake his head, not an ounce of repentance on his face. "Just be careful, man. Kilpatrick and his sister actually get along. And you're not his friend. It's not the same situation at all."

I snort, but keep my thoughts to myself, because I'm supposed to be cool with Simon and Ellie being together.

And it's not that I'm *not* cool, it's that I still think him dating Ellie is a dick move. And even though I want to say that he's right, Kilpatrick and I aren't friends, so me dating his sister isn't any kind of betrayal, that would just make me sound bitter and like I'm not okay with Simon dating Ellie. And, okay, maybe I am a little bitter, but I'm trying not to be. I spent the entirety of my high school football career trying to keep my asshole teammates *away* from my baby sister. It wasn't the whole team, but a group of guys thought it was hilarious to flirt with her because they knew it would piss me off. She's got this happy, sunshiny naïveté, and she didn't know they were insincere, mocking her and talking about her in the locker room, how she'd look sucking cock and how they wanted to corrupt her, even going so far as to put together a betting pool to see who could fuck her first, and the winner got a bonus if he took her virginity.

I did my best to keep her as far away from my teammates as possible after that. When I left The Dalles to go to college, I was relieved that she'd finally be relatively safe. A couple of the younger guys I was friends with promised to look out for her and make sure she didn't get with any of the douchebags who were part of the pool. And I made sure not to let anything similar start with my teammates here, never letting her meet anyone if I could help it. Which was easy enough when she was still in high school. But then she decided to come to Marycliff too—which I can't really blame her for because our parents said they'd cover whatever scholarships wouldn't if we chose Marycliff—and I had to work harder to keep her at arm's length, which wasn't helped by our parents constantly badgering me to make sure she was happy and safe and making friends. How could I keep an eye on her and make her stay away at the same time?

But all my efforts blew up in my face. My sister is convinced that I've spent the last eight years basically hating her. And she still got with my roommate and best friend.

And while I know that Simon's not like those guys on my high school team, the imperative to keep her away is so deeply ingrained by now that it's hard to just … stop.

But the alternative to being okay with them dating is both of them hating me for coming between them, and I'm really not okay with that. So I suck up the fact that my best friend is dating my baby sister and hope that they'll stay together forever. Then Simon would be my brother-in-law, and that actually sounds pretty cool, as long as I can just pretend that they're in a weird, sexless marriage that's an extension of what I'm pretending is their current weird, sexless relationship.

Except my sister insists on making out with him in front of me as often as possible—which is her way of getting back at me for being an unmitigated asshole to her for years—so there's no way I can pretend that for long.

Still, Kilpatrick knows we're rivals. He shouldn't be surprised that I give zero fucks about his opinion. And it's not like he can retaliate by dating my sister. She's happily taken.

Suddenly, Ellie and Simon being together just got a whole lot better.

* * *

After lunch with Simon in the cafeteria, we part ways. He has a class to get to, and I have some time to kill before my three o'clock. Normally I'd relax in the student center or head to the library to get some work done, but instead I'm watching the clock, wanting to time it so I can get a hot chocolate and get back over to Kent Hall by 1:20, so I can be waiting for Piper to get out of class.

Maybe she doesn't have enough time to go with me to get a hot chocolate, but that doesn't mean I can't still buy one for her.

Fortunately, the campus coffee shop line is blessedly short, the lunch rush having passed and the between-classes frenzy not having started yet. I debate getting whipped cream on Piper's hot chocolate but decide against it, because then the to-go lid wouldn't fit. I splurge on a coffee for myself as well and head over to the door where Piper disappeared. The campus tower chimes the quarter hour as I walk over, so I know I'm not too early or too late. Perfect.

So I wait.

And wait.

When the clock chimes the half, I start to get antsy.

Did I miss her? Did she go out a different door? Maybe she has another class in the same building. Should I go inside and check?

But if I do, will that make me look like a stalker?

Sighing, I swallow down the last of my cooling coffee, her cup of hot chocolate barely warm in my hand now that I've been holding it for twenty minutes, and admit defeat.

At least for today.

CHAPTER FOUR

Piper

After my encounter with Cal on Thursday, I'm thankful the team has an away game this weekend so I don't have to worry about whether or not to meet Gray afterward. Which also means I get to avoid seeing my parents twice in a week, so double win. Good god, what if Cal approached me in front of my parents? I can't decide how they might react, actually, but either way it would be bad for me. Either they'd tell me he seems like such a nice boy and how it would be good for me to socialize a little and let him take me out for dinner. Or they'd completely freak out that a guy is paying attention to me, especially one as pretty as Cal, because that's what got me into trouble at SCU. My money's on the second one.

Because if I hadn't gotten involved with a boy, then he wouldn't have been able to snap naked pics of me without my knowledge to share on his frat's secret server where they apparently shared nudes of any girls they fooled around with—and not a small amount of revenge porn. And if that hadn't've happened, then it wouldn't matter that when we reported it to the university, they swept it all under the rug, refused to hold either the frat as a whole or the individual guys accountable for their actions and tried to get me to sign a gag order that wouldn't allow me to report the revenge porn to the police. And by the time I did make the police report, Brent had already broken up with me for my "breach of trust" of looking at his phone and discovering the secret porn server, so I no longer had access to the evidence, and the police couldn't or wouldn't do anything either.

And don't get me started on that whole "breach of trust" bullshit. Because, come on, if you don't want people discovering your illegal porn server, maybe don't leave your phone unlocked and open to it in plain view for me to see? With a freshly uploaded picture of my tits? That you clearly took while my eyes were closed during sex not five minutes before that?

The only reason I didn't break up with him first was because I was trying to keep him on the hook long enough to get him in trouble.

So when allllll of the powers that be declined to do

anything to those assholes, I decided to serve justice myself.

Except apparently the whole house has video surveillance "for security purposes"—if security means making sure you get as much footage of naked chicks getting fucked by frat brothers as possible—and they caught me sneaking in and stealing all the cables and controllers for their TVs and video game consoles, plus every game I could get my hands on, and their modem as the cherry on top.

It was petty as fuck and not nearly enough justice for what they'd done, but it was the best I could do on my own. They love their TV and video games, so having them disabled and stolen would've made them upset for at least a little while. Yeah, sure, they could replace all that shit without too much trouble, but it would take time and effort.

Except I got caught. Campus police came to my dorm room, recovered everything that I stole, and then *I* got in trouble.

I guess in this case the fact that the school doesn't often involve the real police worked out in my favor, because I apparently stole more than a thousand dollars worth of equipment, so I would've been charged with a felony. Though if they'd held the frat responsible for their behavior in the first place, I wouldn't have felt the need to sneak in and steal stuff …

But I guess that's neither here nor there at this point.

My parents made a deal with the dean that I would

withdraw instead of being expelled, and now I'm here. At Marycliff. With no time for boys, especially the ones that are too pretty for my own good. Because boys only lead to trouble.

So I avoid practice the next week. When Gray texts to ask if I want to meet him after practice for dinner on Wednesday, I tell him I'm too busy. He sends me back a sad face emoji. But I wonder if it's not for the best for him too. Shouldn't he be hanging around with his friends and having a good time instead of constantly making room for his little sister to tag along? Maybe I should just stop going to his practices all together. And his games. Gray needs his own space to live his own life without me dragging him down or cramping his style.

At least that's the excuse I tell myself, because I'm refusing to admit that I'm really avoiding the pull of Cal McAdam's piercing blue eyes and sexy, model-perfect smirk.

Instead I keep to my well-worn paths between classes and my dorm room, watching out for Cal so I can avoid him like I did after Anthropology last week when he was lurking outside the door to Kent Hall with two cups in his hands, obviously the hot chocolate he'd offered to buy me. I felt a tiny stab of guilt when I reversed course and went out the door on the other side of the building, taking the long way to my next class and arriving two minutes late and out of breath, but it was worth it to save my sanity. And possibly my education.

And that's the only reason I'm here at Marycliff—to

finish my degree in political science, apply to a law school far, far away, and get out. So I fill all my free time with studying, only watching movies with Dani when I need a break.

"Ugghhh," Dani complains when I suggest another movie on Wednesday evening, flopping down on the couch next to me and giving me her *I mean business* face. "No. Not after the movie marathon all weekend and every other night this week. That's too many movies. I'm tired of being cooped up in this room, and you need to get out and breathe some fresh air. Let's go do something."

"I get plenty of fresh air," I protest, ignoring her suggestion of "doing something."

She quirks an eyebrow. "Oh? When?"

"Between classes. I'm outside walking every day. And since I'm taking so many classes, it's like an hour of power walking a day when you add it all together."

She rolls her eyes and shakes her head. "That doesn't count."

"Why not? Of course it counts. I'm moving, I'm outside"—I count my points off on my fingers—"that's both exercise and fresh air."

"But it's not relaxing"—she shoves at my shoulder, almost knocking me over—"or taking care of yourself or having fun."

"And what would qualify, in your exalted opinion?" I ask with narrowed eyes, though I'm pretty sure I already know the answer. Her usual idea of "doing something" and "having fun" is hanging out with her friend Eli and his roommates and friends. Which is fine, except that Eli's a football player. And I'm trying to *avoid* anywhere the football team congregates, because there's a chance that McAdam will show up. And while I need a break from studying, and Dani's right that getting out of the room would be good, I'm not sure it's worth the risk.

"Well …" She glances at me out of the corner of her eyes. "Eli—"

"I knew it!" I slap my hands on my thighs then point a finger at her. "I knew you were going to suggest going to his place."

"So?" She shrugs. "He's my friend. I like hanging out with him."

"Uh-huh. And how is hanging out and watching Eli and Jackson play video games better than watching a movie here?"

"For one thing, I'll be playing video games too. You could try it. You might have fun."

I give her a skeptical look, and she just shrugs, standing and grabbing her favorite black hoodie from the back of the wooden dining chair we picked up at a thrift store for cheap. It's supposed to be extra seating, but it's been turned into a spot to dump jackets and bags.

"You're going dressed like that?" I ask as she pulls the sweatshirt over her head, fixing her ponytail and redoing her thin elastic headband to hold back the wispy hairs pulled free by putting on her sweatshirt.

A frown mars her un-made up face as she looks down

at her jeans and shapeless sweatshirt bearing the white silhouette of a man holding a barbell above his head and the words KR Strength & Fitness. "Yeah. What's wrong with this? It's what I always wear."

I sit forward on the couch. "It's fine for rolling out of bed and going to class at eight in the morning. But it doesn't do your body any favors. You're about to go hang out with a bunch of guys. I'm just saying you should wear something that shows you off more."

Rolling her eyes, she scoffs. "First off, it's Eli and Jackson. Eli and I have been friends for years, and Jackson is too shy to approach a girl, even if he did possibly find me attractive. Number two, they see me as one of the guys. Showing up in some girly outfit would make them think I dropped the barbell on my head doing overhead presses and suffered a brain injury. So yes, I'm absolutely wearing this, and you can't say a thing to change my mind."

I close my mouth before I can point out that maybe Eli or Jackson would see her as more than just one of the guys if she tried to get them to see her as a girl, but I think she likes things the way they are. And even if I think she might have more than just friendly feelings for Eli, if she's not ready to acknowledge them, who am I to push the issue? "Fine," I grumble, "Point made."

"You should come," she says, grabbing her keys and phone and putting them in the kangaroo pocket of her sweatshirt.

I give her a dubious stare that only makes her shrug

again. "Suit yourself," she says, turning for the door.

"Wait." I scramble off the couch, looking around for whatever I might need to bring with me to play video games at my roommate's best friend's house. "I'll come."

Dani smirks, her hand on the doorknob. "Great. Grab a sweatshirt and let's go."

Giving in, I grab my Marycliff sweatshirt, keys, and phone and follow her out the door.

When we park in front of Eli's house, I take in the cars overflowing their driveway. "I thought you said it would be just Eli and Jackson."

"Oh, well …" she hedges, giving me another sidelong glance. "Eli might be hosting a tournament of sorts, and the whole football team might be invited."

"Dani!" I screech, whacking her arm. "Why didn't you tell me?"

She shrugs, unfazed. "I didn't think you'd come if you knew. But you need to unwind. What's the big deal? You hang with your brother and half the football team anyway. I don't understand why you're suddenly avoiding him, and by extension everyone else you know here."

I mumble something about giving my brother space, but Dani's not buying it. "He's never acted like having you around is bad, ever. In fact, the opposite is true. He always seems genuinely happy to see you."

"Yeah, you're right," I admit grudgingly.

"Okay, soooo …" She gestures at the front door. "Let's go, get signed up on the roster, and have some fun."

"You realize I'm going to be eliminated in the first round," I tell her as we climb out of the car.

She beeps the lock and falls in step beside me. "Who cares? The point is to have fun. Do your best, have some fun, get some space from the constant grind of classes and everything." She stops me and puts her hands on my shoulders, her chocolate brown eyes earnest as they meet mine. "You can do it. I believe in you."

Laughing, I swat her hands away, and she grins at me. "See?" she says. "You're on the right track already."

CHAPTER FIVE

Cal

I load up my plate with the high protein snacks and sliced vegetables that Eli and Jackson have set out. Since this has somehow become a team activity and we all have tailored nutrition plans to follow, the food and drink choices are mostly designed to fit into that. Mostly.

I cast a longing glance at the bowls of chips they put out for the normals who were lucky enough to get an invite and the pan of brownies someone's girlfriend made. Maybe I can have just a tiny square?

The front door opens and closes, bringing in a gust of cold November air, and I turn to see who's arrived. All thoughts of calorie counts and wondering if it's worth giving up a treat later for a brownie now fly out of my head when I see who's arrived.

Piper's here, shivering in nothing more than a Marycliff hoodie and a pair of dark gray leopard print leggings, her cheeks and the tip of her nose pink from the cold.

There's a loud cry of greeting from various parts of the room, and something suspiciously like jealousy worms its way through me when I see Eli stand and bound to the door to greet her. Except he only nods at Piper while leaning in to hug the other girl I just noticed is with her.

Kilpatrick lifts his hand in a wave from his spot on the couch, but he's next up to play *Mario Kart*, so that's the only greeting Piper gets.

Perfect.

Time to make my move.

I step away from the table, and like I hoped, the movement catches her eye so she looks at me. I lift my chin in a nod of greeting, and the pink in her cheeks deepens as she quickly looks away.

Now that's an interesting reaction.

Putting on my most charming smile, I scoop up the clipboard from the couch that Eli's using to coordinate this tournament and bring it over to Piper and her friend. "Here. Don't forget to sign up," I say as I hand the clipboard to Piper.

She looks between me and her friend, who wears an amused expression as she waits for Piper to take the clipboard from me.

"Yes!" Eli agrees, gesturing to the clipboard. "Find an empty slot and write your name. We're just getting started, so you'll have to wait a bit before it's your turn." He keeps going in his happy puppy dog way, filling the girls in on the rules for the tournament and the snack options for while they wait for their turn.

I take advantage of the moment to examine Piper, who seems to be studiously ignoring me, which only serves to turn my deliberate smile into something involuntary. She thinks that's enough to discourage me? She clearly doesn't know me at all. A situation I mean to remedy as soon as possible.

"I haven't seen you around lately," I murmur as she's forced to move past me to follow Eli and her friend to the table laden with food.

She stops, her head whipping in my direction, hair flying, her eyes jumping all over my face. "Have you been looking for me?"

I give a careless shrug. "I've been keeping an eye out for you, yeah."

Her eyes narrow, and she crosses her arms. "Why?"

Taking a chance, I run a finger down her arm. "I wanted to buy you that hot chocolate like I offered the other day."

"Didn't you already do that?"

When my brows jump up my forehead, her eyes go wide, like she's just realizing what she said.

"So you *do* usually come back out the door you go in

before Anthropology. And you saw me waiting and ... went the other way?" That should be enough to make me leave her alone, and maybe normally it would be. But I need her help to distract her brother so I can get more playing time. I'm not going to give up that easily. Besides, it's obvious she's attracted to me. I'm not sure why she's resisting the pull.

Her mouth opens and closes like a goldfish, and it's adorable seeing her this flustered. Before she can come up with a response, I lean into her space, enjoying the way her eyes flicker down to my mouth and then my chest. Yeah, she's definitely into me. "Why are you in denial about our obvious chemistry?" I ask, my voice pitched low so she can hear me, but no one else can. They're all wrapped up in watching the race going on, shouting encouragement and smack talk by turns. No one's paying attention to us.

Her mouth snaps shut, her lips pursed, and if she was adorable flustered and unsure, she's fucking hot with that fire in her eyes. "I'm not."

I raise my eyebrows again. "You're not in denial? Glad to hear it. So why don't you let me take you out after we're done here."

She rolls her eyes. "I meant that I'm not attracted to you."

"No?" I ask softly, and her eyes dilate until they're almost black as they focus on my lips.

She shakes her head, but it's a weak denial, and we both know it.

"Prove it."

She blinks, leaning away from me ever so slightly, a frown pulling the corners of her lips down and her brows drawing together. "What?"

"Prove that you're not attracted to me." My pulse kicks up like it does before a game. When Eli said he wanted to host a *Mario Kart* tournament for the whole team, I thought it sounded silly. I have homework I need to get through, plus new plays to study, game tape to watch … the list is endless. But then the team captains declared it mandatory, and since my goal is more playing time, I have to appear to be a team player. Which means going along with silly video game tournaments. Simon came without grumbling and brought my sister along, who's so happy to be included and excited about the whole thing that I feel kinda bad for keeping her at arm's length for so long, even if it was for her own good. But when she's not sticking her tongue down my roommate's throat in an effort to punish me for being a dick to her, she's actually pretty fun.

But now? With this little dare between Piper and me? Today just got a whole lot more interesting.

"How am I supposed to do that?" she asks, exasperation clear in her voice.

"Hang out with me today. Sit next to me. Don't avoid me. If, by the end of the day, you can stop staring at my mouth every time I speak"—her eyes lurch up to mine, but can't manage to stay there when my lips quirk in another involuntary smile—"then I'll concede that you're not attracted to me, that you aren't wondering how well I'd kiss you, and leave you alone. And by the way"—I drop my voice another half octave for good measure—"I'd be the best kiss of your life."

Her eyes meet mine again, the frown disappearing to be replaced by laughter. "So modest."

I shrug, unrepentant. "I know my strengths."

She purses her lips—I can't stop staring at her mouth either, and I'm not too proud to admit it—and studies me, trying and failing to keep her eyes on mine. I try—I really do—I try not to smirk. But I can't help it. Because she's already failing miserably.

"So if I win, you'll leave me alone?"

That gives me pause, because leaving her alone derails my plan completely. But what are the odds of that actually happening?

I nod.

"And what do you get if you win?"

A thrill of excitement surges through my veins. She's actually going to do this. "You go out with me."

She arches one eyebrow. "When you say 'go out,' what do you mean, precisely?"

"A date," I clarify. "Dinner and maybe a party or something. We can determine the specifics together."

"Just one date?"

I let out a soft chuckle. "I doubt you'll be able to stop at just one, but yeah, for the purposes of this bet, one date."

She rolls her eyes again. "Fine. I won't avoid you

today, and if I can't maintain my non-attracted status, I'll go on a date with you. One." She holds up a finger to drive the point home.

"Deal."

She sticks out her hand to shake on it, and when I clasp my hand around hers, I'm almost surprised we can't see sparks flying into the air. Her eyes widen at the contact, and I know she feels the chemistry threatening to bubble over between us too.

Yeah, today just got a lot more fun. And I can't wait to take her out on a date.

CHAPTER SIX

Piper

I am in big trouble.

I knew coming here was a mistake as soon as I walked in the door and caught sight of Cal McAdam. He seems to dominate any space he occupies with his broad shoulders, tapered waist, and thick thighs. And it's not just his body. His face is almost too perfect, the slight bump of a healed break on the bridge of his nose the only thing marring the perfection of his high cheekbones, square jaw, and full lips.

I tried to ignore the tingles racing over my skin as he made his way over to me all sleek and fluid like a panther, to pretend I wasn't painfully aware of his presence as he handed me the clipboard, but he's one determined sonofabitch.

He wouldn't just let me sign up and hang with my friend—who promptly abandoned me to Cal's tender attentions while she went off with Eli—*noooo*, he had to go and force me into some kind of bet about me being attracted to him.

Gah!

And he's been glued to my side ever since, walking me over to the table, handing me a plate, finding us a place to sit together where we're close enough to see the TV and far enough away that we can still talk.

I'm uncomfortably aware of the way Dani keeps throwing me glances and grinning like I've struck the jackpot by being cornered into spending the day with Cal, who I've increasingly begun to think of by his first name. Gray has also given me a few quizzical glances, like he can't figure out why in the world I'd be sitting with Cal at all. I just give him a shrug in return, because he's across the room and I'm not going to shout the particulars of what's going down between Cal and me for all the world to hear and also, I don't think I'd tell Gray anyway. I'm not sure exactly how he'd react, but I don't think it would be positive. His rivalry with Cal isn't very friendly. They barely seem to tolerate each other.

Which is yet another reason I should really be staying as far away from the boy as possible instead of letting him pull my chair closer as I munch on tortilla chips and salsa, Lit'l Smokies in a tangy barbecue sauce, and a brownie.

It's not exactly the dinner of champions, but I'm not that hungry yet.

Cal's plate is loaded down with various vegetables plus skewers of chicken and beef, but he keeps looking longingly at my food.

"Do you want some?" I ask, pointing to my plate after at least the fifteenth time he's stared at my chips as I picked one up and brought it to my mouth. At first I thought it was part of our bet where he just stares at me hungrily all evening in order to get me to crumble and admit I'm attracted to him too—which, I have to admit, wouldn't be the worst plan he could come up with, dammit. But the longer it goes on, the more I'm convinced that for at least right this moment, he's more interested in my food than me.

He shakes his head, straightening in his chair and picking up a carrot stick, biting into it with a snap of even white teeth. "No, I'm fine," he says after swallowing, but it's clear he's lying.

My lips pull to one side as I fight back a smile. "You're a terrible liar, you know that?"

His eyes raise to mine, and that damn smirk of his pulls up one corner of his lips. "Oh, yeah? You're a pretty shit liar yourself."

When I don't respond to that barb, he shifts in his chair again, leaning closer to me—close enough that his breath fans over my neck. I should've kept the hoodie on to protect me from this kind of thing, but my hair was going down the neck, and I felt suffocated under the thick layer of fabric, so I took it off a few minutes ago. I'm kicking myself for that decision now. I should've just suffocated.

"Just admit that you're attracted to me," he whispers, "then we can start planning our date."

"If I do that, are you going to stop staring at my food like a starving orphan from a Dickens novel?" I ask, trying to sound completely unaffected by him. I'm not sure I really pull it off, though.

He chuckles, the sound sending heat pooling low in my belly. God*dammit*. Whyyyy does he have to be so effortlessly sexy? I really should just admit that I'm attracted to him. I'm really just delaying the inevitable at this point.

"Probably not," he says. I guess he's honest, at least. Which, if I were keeping track, would be a point in his favor. But I'm not keeping track. Nope nope nope.

"Why don't you just have some chips or something?"

The groan he makes is far too sexy for my sanity. "I wish. It's not on my meal plan, though, and I don't want to get in trouble with the nutritionist. I've been on thin ice lately as it is. I'm trying to be a good boy."

I toss him a smirk. "Somehow I find the idea of you as a good boy to be completely ridiculous."

His blue eyes darken, that smirk drawing up the corners of his mouth. "Oh, baby, you have no idea."

My breath catches, and my entire body erupts in flames. Poof. Just like that, I disappear in a cloud of smoke.

Except I don't. That would be too easy and put me out of my misery. Instead I gulp. Audibly.

Cal leans in so his face is only inches from mine. "You're going to lose our bet, and when you do, I'm going to show you exactly how bad I can be."

I'm in so much fucking trouble.

So. Much. Trouble.

* * *

"Hey, Piper," Dani says as she makes her way around the couch and the bodies of football players littering the floor. "I need your help with something."

I pop out of my seat, setting my plate with only a few crumbs, a dab of salsa, and a half eaten brownie on it on my chair, only too happy for a chance to escape Cal and his smoldering gaze and heated promises. "Sure. What do you need?"

She gestures into the kitchen with her head, and I follow behind. But once we're in the kitchen, she grabs my hand and tugs me down a hall and into a bedroom, where she shuts the door behind us.

I glance around at the clothes scattered on the floor, the rumpled bed, and the football gear in the corner. "Uhh, you need my help in one of the guys' bedrooms? Why?"

She rolls her eyes, her hands on her hips. "What's going on with you and Cal?"

A flush creeps up my face, but I pretend like I can't

tell. "What are you talking about? Nothing's going on with me and Cal?"

She huffs. "Yeah, right. He's barely taken his eyes off you since we got here. And he bought you hot chocolate or something? Why didn't you tell me?"

I wave a hand, trying for airy indifference. "It was nothing. It's not what you think.

Dani's not buying it, though. "Bullshit," she says succinctly. She points a finger at the door. "You weren't here last year, so you don't know how he operates. I do. Eli was on the team last year too, and I was around just as much then as now. Tell me what happened."

Shrugging, I bite my nail and look away. "I bumped into him on the way to class one day, he offered to buy me hot chocolate since it was cold and I hadn't dressed warm enough. I declined. When I left class, he was waiting at the door to Kent Hall."

Dani's eyes grow wider as I recite my tale, and she whacks my arm. "Dude. You have to tell me these things."

It's my turn to roll my eyes. "First of all, I don't, actually. Second of all, there was nothing to tell. Nothing happened."

"Ouch," she says, a flicker of genuine hurt in her eyes that makes me feel bad.

"Look, Dani—" But she cuts me off with a wave of her hand.

"No, you look. I know we're potluck roommates and not BFFs or anything, but I thought we were friends."

"We are," I insist. Sighing, I rub my forehead. "That's not what I meant. I'm sorry. I just don't like being told what to do. It's nothing personal. My auto reaction to being told I *have* to do anything is to say, 'No, I don't.' As far as Cal goes, literally nothing happened. I saw him waiting before I got out the door, turned around, and went out the other side of the building."

"Dude," Dani says, her voice heavy with disbelief. "You had one of the hottest guys on campus flirting with you, and you ran the other way?"

All I can muster in response is a shrug. She shakes her head slowly. "So what's the deal today?"

I bite my nail again, really not wanting to answer.

"Piper," she says, her voice a mixture of cajoling and warning that shouldn't work, but somehow it does.

Dropping my hand, I sigh in frustration. "Fine. We somehow made a bet that if I can make it through the day without staring at his mouth or admitting I'm attracted to him, he'll leave me alone. But I can't do it by avoiding him."

Dani's eyebrows climb her forehead. "And?"

"And what?"

"And what happens when you lose?"

I choke on a laugh. "*When* I lose? Thanks for the vote of confidence."

"You *can't* stop staring at his mouth. I've looked over at you like fifty times and at least half those times you're watching him eat, looking like you'd rather be eating him."

"Uhh, no. I think you have me mistaken for him."

She scoffs, crossing her arms. "Oh, come off it. *You* think he's hot. *I* think he's hot. Hell, your brother probably even thinks he's hot. It's just a fact—water's wet, snow is cold, and Cal McAdam is hot as fuck."

Normally something that sounds so much like a slogan or a weird football cheer would make me laugh, but instead I huff out an aggrieved sigh, stomp my foot, and roll my eyes. "Fine. He's hot. Happy?"

Dani nods, a smug smile on her face. "Yes. Now what happens at the end of the day when it's clear you haven't won?"

"I go on a date with him," I mumble, but not so quietly that Dani can't hear me. She hoots with laughter, clapping her hands.

"Oh my god, that's perfect."

But before she can go into why, exactly, this ridiculous situation is 'perfect,' we're interrupted by a knock at the door.

Grabbing her arm, I shush Dani with a hiss.

A female voice calls out, "Dani? Is Piper in there with you?" The door opens, revealing the familiar face of a girl. She lives on the same floor as Dani and me, and I think she's dating one of the football players, but I don't know her very well. Emily? Ella? Ellen?

"Hey, Ellie," Dani says.

Ellie—that's her name—smiles at us both, then settles her gaze on me. "Hey, Piper. You're up."

At first I don't know what she means, and my

confusion must be obvious on my face. Which is no surprise, really, since I apparently broadcast my every emotion, because Dani can tell I'm attracted to Cal as easily as Cal himself can. And if Dani can see it, I can't just blame it on Cal's overweening ego.

Ellie hooks her thumb over her shoulder, her dark brows pulling together. "For the video game? It's your turn."

"Oh, right. Of course." I force a laugh, and Ellie smiles at me, looking me up and down, this time more like an exam.

"So you're spending the day with my brother, huh?" At my confused look, she clarifies, "Cal? My brother? He's saving you a seat on the couch. You guys are in the same round."

"Oh, uh, yeah. I didn't realize he was your brother."

She leans in close and lowers her voice to a conspiratorial whisper. "Let me know if you want any embarrassing details about him. I've got all kinds of ammunition."

At my surprised laugh, she beams at me, then holds the door open and gestures for Dani and I to follow her.

Dani throws me a bemused look as we trail behind her to the living room where Cal's waiting for me, just like Ellie said.

As I accept the controller from him and sit down, I glance around, noticing Ellie curled up next to the massive guy I saw with Cal that day he tried to buy me hot chocolate. That must be who she's dating. She gives me a finger wave, and when Cal clears his throat, I give him my attention.

He nods to the TV, a smug grin on his face. "Pick your character."

I settle on Kirby, and Cal chuckles. "I figured you'd pick Princess Peach."

"Oh yeah? You think I'm a princess?"

His eyes dip to my lips, and I just know he's about to say something suggestive, but he doesn't get the chance, because Eli shouts, "Three, two, one, go!" And the race is on. Cal picked Bowser, and he's apparently in it to win it, throwing himself all over the place as he goes around curves, using every attack to try to keep me behind him.

But he has no idea that I have a competitive streak a mile wide, especially when I already know I'm going to lose at something else. And as much as I hate to admit it, I'm definitely going to lose this bet. So I'm determined to at least beat Cal at *Mario Kart*, dammit.

CHAPTER SEVEN

Cal

Piper throws her body against me hard enough to jostle my thumb off the controller. When I glance at her, she looks almost entirely unaware of me, her face set with a grim determination I wouldn't have expected to see from a girl participating in a football team video game tournament.

But what do I know? I haven't been paying attention to any of the other girls here. Maybe they're all just as fiercely competitive as Piper is. Or maybe it's a family trait, because I know I've seen that expression on her brother's face before, usually during a tough game. Except I don't find it sexy on her brother, but on Piper …

A wide grin stretching across my face, I refocus on the game. She wants a fight? Then I'll give her a fight.

A few adrenaline-filled minutes later, she squeaks across the finish line right in front of me, the screen declaring her the winner, and she stands, lifting her hands above her head in a victory pose. "Yussss!" She faces me, her smile fierce and triumphant. "In your face!" And then she proceeds to do a victory shimmy right in front of me, and while I normally wouldn't appreciate losing or having the person who beat me rub it in with a dance, in this case I'll make an exception.

Leaning back on the couch, I spread my legs and watch. When she finally stops, still smug and lit up with well-deserved pride at winning, she looks at me, her gaze tracking down my body and back up again before meeting my eyes. "Well?" she says, the single syllable wrapped in challenge.

I lift an eyebrow and gesture at her to continue. "Keep going. I was enjoying the victory dance. Feel free to come closer if you want to. It's worth losing if this is the consolation prize."

She stares at me for a long moment, her grin fading, her chest heaving, and I wait for her to say something, do something as her eyes drift to my mouth. My lips quirk in a grin. I can't help it. She's dying to kiss me, and while this would be easier on both of us if she'd just admit it—because the feeling is really fucking mutual—this kind of foreplay is more fun than I've had with a girl in I don't even know how long. Maybe ever.

When she finally gives in to me, I know we'll be explosive.

Eli calls out the names of the next people up, and Piper tears her gaze away from me, turning and leaving the TV area abruptly. Eli gestures for me to vacate the couch so the next round has access to the TV. Gotta keep things moving, or this tournament will never end, even though it looks like I'm out. I have no complaints, though. Because now I can focus all my attention on Piper.

Standing, I stretch, looking around to see where she scampered off to. I don't see her in the main area, but her roommate nods toward the kitchen. Dunno why she's on my side instead of her friend's, but I'm not complaining. Ellie gives me a thumbs up from her spot in Simon's lap. And yeah, I'm just going to pretend that doesn't make me want to throw up in my mouth.

Piper's leaning one hand against the counter, her back to me and her head down, a half empty glass of water in front of her. I step up behind her, close enough that she could lean back against me if she wants. "Ready to admit defeat?" I whisper in her ear.

She startles, straightening and forcing me back a half step so her head doesn't clock me in the mouth. Then she turns slowly, her narrowed eyes meeting mine. "I'm sorry? I'm pretty sure that I just beat you."

I chuckle, soft and almost menacing. "That's not what I'm talking about, and you know it." The thrill of the chase sings through my blood. I love that she's pushing back like this, especially when we both know how this will inevitably end.

Her nostrils flare, her lips tightening, but her eyes drop to my mouth.

"See what I mean?" I say softly. "You're doing it again."

"What am I doing?" she asks, breathless.

"Staring at my lips. I can kiss you now if you want. That way you can stop wondering."

Her eyes jerk to mine, dark with desire, but with an edge of defiance. "If you kiss me now, then I don't have to go on a date with you."

She's trying to negotiate. Interesting. Does that mean she knows she's already lost?

I consider her for a moment, taking in the way her eyes wander over my face, continually straying to my lips and then back to my eyes. She wants me to kiss her. And I want that too. But I'm not ready to give up the possibility of a date. "If you kiss me and don't like it, then sure." I shrug. "I'll let you off the hook."

Her body sways toward mine, and I force myself to be still. She needs to verbally agree to the change of terms. And she needs to admit defeat. "But just so we're clear," I say, "you letting me kiss you means you're admitting you're attracted to me."

She huffs out a breath, pulling back. "Are you serious right now?"

I nod once. "Admit you find me attractive. Ask me to kiss you. And if you can convince me you hate it, then no date."

Another huff, and her arms come up like she wants to cross them, but there's not enough space between us to make that happen, and with the counter behind her, she can't back up either, so she drops them back to her sides. "I have a feeling there's no way I'd manage to convince you I hate your kiss."

One corner of my mouth lifts. "Oh, I'll be able to tell if you're lying."

She rolls her eyes. "Fine."

I raise my brows. "Fine? What does that mean?"

A put-upon sigh. "Fine, I admit it. I find you attractive. As my roommate put it, you being hot as fuck is as much of a fact as gravity. The sky is blue, water is wet, Cal McAdam is hot. You win."

I grin, enjoying this impromptu exposition on my hotness, plus the tidbit that she's discussed me with her roommate. "And?"

She rolls her eyes again and jiggles her whole body in the most delightful way, even though I know it's a sign of frustration. I kinda like frustrating her like this. Deciding to pursue her is the best decision I've made in a long time.

She mumbles something.

"What was that?"

Her cheeks are pink, and when she draws in a deep bracing breath, her tits almost touch my chest. "Please kiss me," she says quietly, but clearly, each word perfectly enunciated.

"It would be my pleasure."

CHAPTER EIGHT

Piper

I try. I really, really try to resist. To remain stiff and unresponsive. But when he brushes his soft lips across mine in a tentative graze, the gesture more question than demand, my resolve starts to crumble.

He pulls back and looks at me, his blue eyes going dark, and his hand cups my jaw, tipping my face up at a better angle, and this time when his lips touch mine, it's less question, and more command. And despite my innate contrariness that makes me resist commands, my desire to resist him chips away with each press of his soft, warm lips against mine.

When he parts his lips, taking mine with them, I'm lost.

Why was I so hellbent on resisting this again? To get out of going on a date with him? And why was that a bad idea? He kisses me like he knows all the secret ways to bring me pleasure. Going on a date seems like a really good plan, actually.

His tongue sweeps into my mouth, tasting me, seeking out mine. And I give him exactly what he's looking for, unable to resist anymore.

He crowds me back against the counter, his hand leaving my jaw, sliding down my back to cup my ass, his hand hot and firm through the thin fabric of my leggings. His thigh nudges between my legs, other hand flexing on my hip, urging me to rub against him. And I do. God help me, I do.

When he pulls back—which happens far sooner than I'm ready for, dammit—his chest is heaving, and it's clear he's just as affected as I am. He rubs his nose on my cheek, nips at my earlobe, and whispers, "Let's go."

Releasing my grip on his hair and shoulder, I slide my hands to his chest and push back enough so I can look him in the eye. "Go where?"

He lets out a groan, harsh and tortured. "Anywhere. Your place, my place, hell, a bedroom here. I don't care. Let's just *go*."

Before I can answer, he claims my lips again. No soft, questioning prelude this time. Just masterful dominance, his tongue in my mouth, his hands on my ass, his taste, his scent, his body, completely surrounding me. Overwhelming me.

He pulls me away from the counter, ending the kiss with the clear goal of taking me somewhere, his fingers tangling with mine.

But I stop, rooted to the spot. "I can't." The words are barely more than a hoarse whisper.

He freezes, every line in his body pulled tight, like a bow ready to release an arrow. "Why not?" All that cocky arrogance is gone, wiped away by that kiss along with my better judgment.

I gesture weakly toward the living room. "I'm still in the tournament."

"Forfeit." That arrogance comes back into his voice, sparking my will to resist.

"No."

He narrows his eyes at me, and I lift my chin. Shaking his head, he reels himself back to me by our connected hands, his free hand sliding behind my back, holding me close. "Fine. We'll stay until you lose, and then we'll finish this somewhere else."

It takes everything in me to shake my head—because finishing what we just started somewhere else sounds like a fantastic idea right now—but I manage to. "Can't. Homework." He's reduced me to single words. I can't even string together simple sentences right now, like *I can't. I have homework.*

He sucks in a breath, his nostril flaring, and his firm chest pressing against mine. A muscle ticks in his jaw, and his lips are pressed in a flat line. He's annoyed at my resistance, which he clearly thought was a thing of the past. "You have homework all night?"

I jerk my head in a quick nod. "Yeah. Lots of classes. Lots of homework."

His eyes narrow. "You owe me a date."

My breath leaves me on a sigh. "I know. But I can't tonight. I still have lots of reading to finish."

"Tomorrow, then." It's not so much a request as a demand. But …

"I can't tomorrow either."

"Dammit, Piper—"

I place my hands on his chest, hoping to placate him with my touch. I'm not sure why I think it'll work. He clearly thinks I'm just trying to get out of the bet I so clearly lost. I mean I was practically wrapped around him by the time he ended the kiss, and I let him kiss me again. I definitely responded, so there's no use claiming I didn't like it.

"I have plans tomorrow."

But that doesn't appear to be the right thing to say. His eyes are hard, and he's clenching his jaw again. "Cancel them."

"I can't. I have dinner with my parents every Thursday night. It's not optional." From the way he studies my face, narrowed eyes, his lips still pressed together in a firm line, I can tell he's not sure if I'm lying or not. "You can ask my brother if you don't believe me."

His eyes widen a fraction at that, and then he relaxes.

"Sorry. Fine. I believe you. We have an away game this weekend, so I guess I'll have to wait until next week to collect."

Somehow that's more disappointing than it should be. "I guess so."

"Give me your number," he demands, reaching in his pocket to pull out his phone. He unlocks it and hands it to me. I should put up a fight, if for no other reason than because of the high-handed way he just expects me to do what he tells me, but I don't. After typing in my number, I hand his phone back. He taps at the screen, and a second later, my phone vibrates on the counter. He gives me a hard look, then dips his head for another fierce, thorough kiss. "No more excuses," he tells me when he pulls away, moving back and putting space between us. "See you next week."

And just like that, he turns and walks away.

I take a moment to compose myself in the kitchen, finish my water and collect my phone, then return to the living room. But when I do, he's gone altogether.

And I don't know whether I should be relieved or disappointed. So somehow, I'm both.

* * *

Gray picks me up to take me to dinner at our parents' on Thursday, which isn't unusual. We often ride together. I just normally meet him at practice. But I'm still avoiding practice right now, though I couldn't exactly say why. I made out with Cal in Eli's kitchen and we're going out on a date next week, so it seems silly to avoid Gray's practices just to avoid Cal. But here we are.

"Hey!" I say when I climb into the passenger seat of his car. "How's your week been?"

He glances at me out of the corner of his eyes, waiting for me to fasten my seatbelt before putting the car in drive and pulling away from the curb in front of my dorm. "Fine. How was yours?"

"Good. Busy. Lots of homework."

Another side eye. "Oh yeah? That why you haven't been at practice lately?"

"Yup." I mean, that's not the *only* reason, but Gray doesn't need to know that. "You know how it goes. We're getting close to the end of the semester, so everyone's piling on the work."

He hums noncommittally. "You didn't seem too busy last night."

I throw him a confused look, but he stares steadfastly at the road, not even glancing at me. "It's good to take breaks. Dani was invited to Eli's get together, and she asked me to come. So I did. Is that a problem for you?" He's never made a big deal about me being at football team events before.

He grunts. "I don't have a problem that you came yesterday, no. I do have a problem with who you spent most of your time with."

"Oh my god," I mutter under my breath, not even bothering to hold back my eye roll. "Are you serious right now?"

This time he does look at me, and yes, he absolutely is serious.

I just roll my eyes again.

He turns onto a side street in a random neighborhood and pulls over in front of a house, slamming the car in park and turning to face me. "Piper, I'm serious. McAdam isn't a guy you need to be spending time with."

"Thanks, *Dad*. Your objection is noted."

Apparently that's not good enough, though, because instead of putting the car back in drive and taking us to Mom and Dad's house, he stares at me, his jaw clenched. "He fucks anything that moves."

Ohhh, we're onto the *convince Piper she's too dumb to know when someone's bad news* portion of the evening. Or maybe it's *convince Piper she's not special by attracting this boy's attention*? Hmm. It's a toss up.

I put on my most thoughtful and intrigued face. "*Anything* that moves? Really? Interesting. I guess it's good to know he's not into necrophilia."

Poor Gray just looks confused and horrified. "No. What? Why would you say that? And that's not supposed to make him sound interesting."

I shrug, still keeping up the pretense that I don't know what he's trying to do. "Well, it sounds like you're saying he's pansexual, which I happen to find interesting."

The horror has left Gray's expression, and now he's just stuck on confused, his forehead all wrinkled and his mouth hanging open. "I didn't say that at all."

It's tough, but I manage to stifle my laughter. Sometimes it's so easy to wind him up. I place a finger on my lips. "Wait. Hang on. Are you trying to tell me he's put the moves on you? Because that might be a deal-breaker for me."

"*That's* your deal-breaker?" Gray's almost shouting now, and I roll my lips between my teeth to keep from giggling. "Not the fact that he can't be trusted and is obviously trying to use you."

Not gonna lie, that stings. "Ohhh, that's what you're trying to say. He's just using me." I nod, like I understand everything now. "Got it. There's no way a guy could just, y'know, be interested in *me*, after all. Hot guys are only ever interested in me to use me for their own nefarious purposes. Thanks for clearing that up."

Gray lets out a frustrated sigh. "That's not what I said."

But I don't let him finish his defense. "You know, Gray, it's fine. Don't worry about it. I'm a big girl. I can take care of myself."

"Yeah? Then why'd you end up back here where Mom and Dad can keep a closer eye on you. And why'd I transfer here to be a buffer for you if you don't need any help from anyone?"

I jerk my head back, hurt by the unexpected blow. Tears come to my eyes, and I blink them away before they can fall, looking out the window so Gray doesn't see how affected I am.

Gray's had my back since we were kids, and he's a

good big brother for the most part. I get that he thinks he's protecting me by trying to warn me about Cal, and maybe I shouldn't have given him shit just now, but I also don't want him to think he gets to dictate who I do and don't date.

Nodding, I look down at my hands in my lap and clear my throat. "Sure. You're right. Maybe I'm not so on top of things. Obviously I do need a babysitter. That's why you're here, right? That's the point of these weekly dinners—so everyone can check up on me, the family fuckup." I glance at him before looking away again. "I might be a fuckup, but I'm not an idiot."

"I never said you were," he says softly.

When I don't respond, he lets out another frustrated sigh. The blinker clicks in the silence of the car, and he pulls away from the curb. We don't talk the rest of the way to Mom and Dad's house, and even though I try my best to act normal, I'm quiet and subdued all through dinner, answering the standard questions about school and classes when asked, but not volunteering anything extra.

Gray does a better job of acting normal, but he studies me more than usual, seeming to weigh all my answers extra carefully. I don't know if it's because he's looking for clues that I'm more involved with Cal than he thinks or because he feels bad for what he said in the car, but either way, I pretend not to notice.

Until Mom asks her favorite question. "Have either of you met anyone interesting lately?" That's her way of asking if either of us has a new boyfriend or girlfriend.

"Nope," Gray answers, looking at me. "I don't have a lot of time between classes and football."

Mom purses her lips. "You really should make time to socialize," she says. "It only gets harder as you get older, you know." Then she turns to me. "What about you, sweetie?"

This question is always dicier for me, given my history. For Gray, it's hopeful. They want him to meet a nice girl and have a stable relationship. Me? Anyone I'm willing to date is automatically suspect. Brent did a great job of screwing me over in so many, many ways. I wonder if he's proud of what a total and complete wanking asshole he is.

I offer a polite smile and shake my head. "No one for me either. I don't have football, but with my class load, I don't have a lot of time for much besides studying."

I can feel Gray's eyes on me, and I meet his glare with a cool look of my own. We have our own little staring contest in the middle of dinner.

"I do hope you're making time for friends, though," Mom says. Dad clears his throat, and I wait a beat for him to object before responding.

As much as I hate to be the first to look away, I break off the staring contest with Gray and look at my mom. "I am. My roommate and I do things together, and I've made a few other friends in my building. I'm not a complete hermit, don't worry."

Mom reaches over and pats my hand. "I'm your

mother. It's my job to worry." She cuts a bite of her chicken. "I'm glad you're getting out some, though. I know you want to graduate as soon as possible, but when we agreed to let you live on campus it was because we all wanted you to have a typical college experience. And part of that means socializing and making friends."

"I know, Mom." I force another smile, because smiling is better than screaming, and that's what I really want to do by the end of every one of these dinners. They're always a minefield of jabs and reminders and making sure I'm walking the tightrope of being the good little girl I always was growing up. There's extra pressure, now, though, because of what happened last spring. I think my parents still don't know what to make of what happened, or don't understand how it could've happened. Because I was the good girl growing up—honors student, involved with clubs and activities at school, had friends, the usual amount of adolescent drama and boyfriends, but nothing crazy. Certainly no encounters with the police or the school disciplinary system.

So they're still trying to wrap their heads around how that all went up in smoke, how I ended up both a victim and a perpetrator in two separate instances. And they're blaming it on either too much freedom too soon or a boy, hence their requiring me to go to Marycliff since it's in my hometown and having these weekly dinners and the regular probing into my social life.

Since Gray's here, it makes it seem like standard

parental curiosity. But we all know that with me, it's more than that.

Once we finish, Mom offers ice cream for dessert, but Gray shakes his head and holds up his hands. "Can't, Mom. It's not on my meal plan."

Mom purses her lips like she thinks that's ridiculous but leaves it alone. Standing, I shake my head, too. "Sorry, Mom. Not tonight. I need to get back to campus and finish up a paper for tomorrow."

Mom wraps me in a hug, and I close my eyes, letting myself be transported back in time two years when Mom-hugs were simple gestures of affection and didn't carry worry and fear and latent frustration with me as well. Once Mom releases me, my Dad gives me a hug too, his shorter and more perfunctory, but nice all the same.

My parents care about me. I know they do. But turning into the black sheep before I even turned twenty has been rough.

Gray says his goodbyes, and we both retrieve our jackets from the front closet. Another round of hugs and goodbyes later, we're out the door, and even though the night air is cold, I can breathe easier.

Once we're in his car, Gray starts it, but makes no move to drive. "Look, Piper," he starts, but I wave him off.

"It's fine, Gray," I say quietly. "Don't worry about it."

He's quiet for a beat, and I hope he'll just let it go, because I don't want an apology or an explanation about what he said on the way over. All I want is to be treated like I'm not an undetonated bomb from a long ago war, liable to go off at any moment. That's better than any apology and light-years better than an explanation that does nothing to acknowledge harm.

"I don't think you're a fuckup," he says at last, putting the car in reverse and backing out of the driveway.

"Then stop treating me like one."

CHAPTER NINE

Cal

By Sunday, I'm regretting more and more how fast I left Piper behind on Wednesday. I knew if I'd stayed, I wouldn't be able to keep my hands off her, not after what passed between us in the kitchen. And I also knew she wasn't ready to take things beyond that. Hell, getting her to agree to a date was a hard-won victory.

But she's not much for texting. Or she genuinely is that busy. I honestly can't tell which it is, and the only person I know who could answer that question would probably rather punch me in the throat than give me any information about his sister.

In fact, he's been glaring at me at every opportunity

for the last few days. A smug grin comes to my face at the thought. My evil plan is working already.

Does he know I kissed her? Or is he just mad that I sat with her for half the evening? If it's the first one, then I'm going to have to step up my game, because he's not nearly mad enough if he knows about our kitchen make out session. But if he's this pissed from me sitting next to her?

I have to fight down the urge to laugh like Dr. Evil from *Austin Powers* as I pack my gear into my car. Simon nods at me over the back of his truck, and I lift my chin in response. "You goin' to see Ellie?" I ask, already knowing the answer. I just want to confirm that I'll have the house to myself for a while.

Part of me still wants to punch the grin off his face when he says, "Yeah. She's got her room to herself for a few hours."

"TMI, dude. T. M. I."

Simon just laughs, which doesn't help anything. But it does make me pull out my phone and try texting Piper one more time.

Me: Back in town. When are you free this week?

Because if I'm this riled up about Simon banging my sister, how much worse is Kilpatrick gonna feel when I seal the deal with his? He actually hangs out with his sister willingly. And I'm pretty sure he hates my guts.

Driving home, I fantasize about Kilpatrick exploding at me and getting yanked for the season because of his behavior. That's the ideal option. The other possibility is him choking enough times that Coach Reese pulls him and makes me the starter, but that seems less possible and more likely to cause problems. For one, Coach loves Kilpatrick for some reason. Thinks the sun shines out of the dude's ass. So he'd have to choke really bad a lot of times for Coach to change the lineup. And if he does that bad, then we might lose our spot in the Poppy Bowl, and no one wants that.

So the goal is to get him to fight me. Or try to fight me. I need to make sure I look like the innocent.

One thing at a time, though. First, I need Piper to schedule our date.

* * *

One bonus about Simon not being home—and I'm not going to think about where he is, who he's with, or what they might be doing—is that since I got Pigged this weekend, it makes it easy to pass it off to him right away.

This game has been going since my freshman year. One of the seniors that year wanted the team to have a mascot, and for some reason he thought a teacup pig was the best choice. Why? I have no idea. I guess he figured goats are overdone, or that a pig would be easier to take care of or something.

Of course, Coach Hanson was against the idea. He said we didn't need the distraction and that we were all a bunch of jackasses who could barely take care of ourselves, much less another living creature. So Collins, the starting quarterback and one of the team captains that year, bought a little stuffed pig, and he took one of the jerseys from the stuffed bears they sell at games and in the campus bookstore and put it on the pig. We named it Piggy, because we're very creative, and Piggy became our interim mascot. Except the schedule Collins made where everyone took care of it for a week to show that we could handle the responsibility of taking care of another creature devolved quickly into a weird spin on the game Hot Potato.

Piggy started showing up in random people's lockers or duffel bags between practices and games. Or he'd be waiting for you on the squat rack when it was your scheduled leg day.

Yesterday Piggy was hidden at the bottom of my locker when I got back from the shower after the game, his now-dingy little snout peeking out of my clean clothes.

The rules of Pigging have developed over the last few years. You can't get caught Pigging someone. If you get caught, you have to keep Piggy for longer, and you can't try to give it to the person who caught you. If you know who had Piggy last, even if you didn't catch them Pigging you, you can't Pig them back immediately. The idea is to spread it around the whole team. Whoever ends up with Piggy at the final game has to keep Piggy until the next season, which means I'm safe at the end of this year at least. You can't Pig a senior the last week of the season or postseason, because they're not coming back.

I kept Piggy the second half of my sophomore year until practice started up again the next August. It was a relief to get rid of him that first practice back.

Living with Simon means that it's easy to pass Piggy along right away, and even though he'll know I did it, he won't be able to give him back.

Creeping into his room, I wince as the floorboards creak once I'm over the threshold. Which is ridiculous. He's not home. He won't be home for hours. I could stomp in here like King Kong and it wouldn't matter. I don't know why I'm trying to be sneaky or stealthy. Habit, I guess. When you Pig someone in the locker room, you have to be quick and quiet so they don't catch you, hoping the other guys don't give it away with their giggling. I've gotten caught a few times since it started, but not at all this season or last.

I wrinkle my nose at the evidence of Ellie spending time in his room as I scan for a good hiding spot for Piggy. I really need to get over my hangup about them. I know it. But seeing one of her cardigans hanging over the back of his desk chair and a stack of her books sitting on his nightstand makes it obvious that they're in here banging at every opportunity. And regardless of who she's dating, I don't want any reminders of my sister's sex life. At least no bras are dangling from the lampshades.

As I tuck Piggy under the corner of Simon's pillow, my phone vibrates in my pocket. A jolt of adrenaline shoots through me. Could Piper be texting me back?

I pull out my phone as I leave Simon's room, careful to leave the door cracked as much as it was before I entered, and a strange lightness fills my chest at the sight of Piper's name on my screen. While I'd like to tell myself I'm only this excited because it means I'm a step closer to regaining my spot as the starting quarterback, I'm not in the habit of lying to myself.

The idea to do this was a mix of anger at Simon dating my sister, a desire to get back at Kilpatrick somehow, and also because Piper's fucking hot and I wouldn't mind getting with her anyway. After that kiss last week? That part's quickly climbing the priority list and edging out the revenge fantasy. Or it was last week. Then this weekend when she never responded to my text and I had to spend more time with her brother, the revenge fantasy started winning again.

With her finally responding, well, hot Piper is in the lead again. I can't wait to get my hands and tongue and other body parts on her. In a more private location. If I weren't holding my phone, I'd rub my hands together in anticipation.

But when I unlock my phone to actually read her text, that lightness bursts, my stomach plunging.

Piper: This is a really busy week

That is not the answer I was expecting.

Narrowing my eyes, I open up my contacts and tap on her name. I have an easier time convincing people to see things my way over the phone than I do over text. A fact that my sister has caught on to, so now she won't take my calls if she thinks I want something. She sends me to voicemail and texts me back. Or pretends her phone is dying or she can't get a signal. Little brat.

Piper, however, is unaware of those ridiculous tricks. Or maybe she just wants to talk to me, because she answers on the second ring. That thought makes me smile.

"I'm in the middle of writing a paper," she says by way of greeting.

"Take a break."

She blows out a frustrated breath. "It's due tomorrow."

"Doesn't mean you shouldn't take a break. Let me take you to dinner. You'll be refreshed when you get back to your paper."

"Dani and I have already ordered dinner," she says. "Taking a break with you would mean I don't have time to finish my paper tonight, plus I have five chapters to read by tomorrow."

I grunt, mulling over my response. I'm not sure I'm going to be able to win this one if she really has that much work to do. "Did you put off all your homework until tonight just to have an excuse not to see me?" I ask before I can think better of it.

She lets out a disbelieving chuckle. "Wow."

"Wow?" I'm pacing the living room, my rising frustration not letting me sit still. "You're the one who seems like she's trying to get out of a bet."

"Oh my god, Cal. I hate to be the one to break it to you—actually no, no I don't. I'm *thrilled* to inform you that the world does not in fact revolve around you, your desires, or your schedule. I'm taking twenty-one hours this semester. I literally have a paper, project, or test due every other day from now until finals week. I'm busy."

My jaw works as I mull that over, both annoyed and turned on by the attitude she's throwing my way. And annoyed that I'm this turned on. I usually like chicks who are upfront about what they want—and what they want is me. We have mutual amounts of fun and pleasure, and then we go our separate ways. It's easy and drama free.

And now I've gone and entangled myself with this chick who can't seem to decide if she wants me or not. Or, that's not true. She definitely wants me, but she's trying to deny herself for some reason. Maybe it's because she knows her brother and I don't get along.

But I feel like bringing him up right now would backfire on me.

I let out a slow breath, trying to decide on the best tactic. But before I can say anything, she sighs again, this time sounding more resigned and less frustrated.

"Look, I promise I will go out with you. But tonight's not gonna happen. Thursday is always booked. Pick another night, and I'll make it work."

Tamping down the swoop of elation her words evoke, I pick, "Tomorrow."

"Tomorrow?" she squeaks. "How about Tuesday?"

I'm not gonna back down on this, though. "You told me to pick a night and that you'd make it work. You just said that." I've been waiting for days. I'm not willing to wait a second longer than absolutely necessary. "Besides, if you *literally* have something every other day, and you have a paper due tomorrow, that means your next major thing shouldn't be until Wednesday."

She sighs again. "Fine. Tomorrow it is. My last class ends at four, but I have a bunch of reading to get through. Pick me up at six, and no keeping me out all night."

"I promise to have you back at a reasonable hour." It's not ideal, but I can make it work. I'll just have to make the most of the time I have. And if it's not enough to get through everything on my list, I should at least be able to make it good enough for her to want an encore.

She huffs out a laugh. "Okay. See you tomorrow, then."

CHAPTER TEN

Piper

I'm stupidly nervous as I get ready for Cal to pick me up for dinner. I should be reading. I should be able to pick out an outfit, put it on, and get homework done while I wait. Instead, I'm flipping through my hangers agonizing over what to wear.

It's not like this is a *real* date. I lost a bet. A stupid, stupid bet, over how attractive I find him.

Pausing with my hand on a hanger—this dress is hot, but it is way too cold outside to wear it—I let out a sigh. Bet or not, it feels like a real date. Because why would he want to go out with me if he's not attracted to me? Even if Gray's right about Cal—that he just sees me as some kind of challenge—that's really not the worst thing in the world. I go out with him, I put an end to the chase and let him catch me, we both get whatever this is between us out of our systems, and we move on with our lives.

Then he won't be a distraction for me anymore. I get a release from this tension that's only gotten worse since that evening at Eli's house.

I see no problems with this plan.

Okay, since I'm admitting this is a real date, I feel more justified taking time to pick out an outfit—I finally settle on a slinky knit sweater dress that clings to my curves—style my hair—soft waves flowing around my shoulders—and do my makeup.

When I come out of the bathroom, Dani gives me a wolf whistle fit for a football stadium. She stands and clasps her hands next to her face. "I'm so proud of you," she says wistfully.

Laughing, I reach for my jacket. Cal's already texted me to let me know he's waiting in the parking lot as agreed. "For going on a date?"

She nods. "Yes. And on a weeknight, no less. I'm surprised you didn't tell him you have too much homework."

"I tried that," I tell her, busying myself with putting on my jacket and making sure I have everything I need.

"Well, I don't know what he said to make you change your mind, but whatever it is, I'm glad. All work and no play makes Jack a dull boy, you know."

"Yes, I've seen *The Shining*, too. I'm aware. But even if

I didn't go on a date, I'm pretty sure I wouldn't end up chasing you through the halls with an axe."

Dani cocks her hip and raises an eyebrow. "You sure about that?"

With a laugh, I nod. "For one thing, I like *you*. If I were chasing anyone with an axe, I'd hope you'd be on my side." She looks thoughtful as she contemplates that answer. "For another," I continue, "I'm not isolated and alone. I have you. We go out sometimes."

Her thoughtfulness turns to doubtfulness. "While I appreciate the vote of confidence, I'm not sure I'm enough to keep you sane. I mean, Jack Nicholson had his family with him ..."

Shaking my head, I turn and head for the door. "Well, since I'm going on a date, I think we can lay that fear to rest, okay?"

"Fine. I'll give you that one. Oh, wait!" she calls out when my hand hits the doorknob.

I turn, eyebrows raised, wondering what else she has to say. But she doesn't have anything to say at all. She disappears into her room and comes back with two little boxes in her hands. It's not until she's right in front of me that I realize they're condoms. "Whaddaya think? Regular or Magnums?"

"What?"

She wiggles the boxes. "You made out with him. Did you get a good feel for his size? Or here." She picks up my hand and slaps both into my palm. "Just take both. That way you're prepared no matter what."

"You think I'm gonna put out on the first date?"

"*Pfft.*" She crosses her arms and cocks her hip again. "Please. Why wouldn't you? I mean, if he's a total asshole, then sure, don't. Obviously. But you've already kissed him." She holds up a finger, clearly about to start ticking off her points. "And you clearly liked it, or we wouldn't be here, right?" She waits for my nod before holding up a second finger. "But it's Cal McAdam. He's not known for his long-term relationships. If you don't bone him tonight, you'll miss your chance. And since your parents yanked you back home in April, you lived with them all summer, and you've been a hermit all semester, I'm assuming it's been quite a while." A finger goes up with each thing she lists until she's run out and throws her hand in the air. "Have fun, that's all I'm saying. And if you're prepared to have fun, then so much the better."

Laughing, I tuck the packages into my purse. "I'm just used to the guy supplying the condoms."

She shrugs. "I mean, in an ideal world, they'd all be Boy Scouts, yeah. But this is the real world, Piper. Bring your own condoms, and then you know you're covered."

"Or he is, at least," I deadpan.

Dani's snort of laughter is the last thing I hear before closing the door. At least someone is rooting for me. Even if it is just my crazy roommate who's perfectly content to push me to get dick from the hot, popular football player when she's unwilling to put herself out there in the same way.

My nerves ratchet back up as I make my way down

the stairs, my ankle boots clacking on the laminate floor of the stairwell. I stop at the door to the lobby, one hand on the bar to push it open, and force myself to take a deep breath. And another.

"Excuse me," a voice says behind me.

"Oh. Sorry." I turn and offer a smile to a girl I recognize with wavy lavender-pink hair. Autumn, I think her name is. She lives on the other end of the hall from me with that other girl who was at the party with the giant left tackle. Cal's sister. They both know Dani, but I've kept my distance, though now that I'm face to face with her and she's giving me a warm smile, I can't remember why. I've shut myself off from everyone this semester, kept myself holed up in my room or the library, only making rare exceptions to do things with my roommate. Because … at the beginning of the semester that felt smart. But now it just feels lonely.

She pauses before leaving, taking a minute to examine me. "Deep breaths," she encourages.

I blink and offer a confused smile. "I'm sorry?"

She chuckles. "You look nervous. Breathe deep. From your belly. Like this." She places one hand on her own stomach and sucks in a breath through her nose, making her hand move, then she lets it out very slowly. I mimic her, almost unconsciously. We breathe together a few more times, and I do feel strangely calmer.

"There," she says, offering me a sunny smile. "Better, right?"

I return her smile. "Yes. Thanks."

"Big date?"

Chuckling, I look away and tuck a strand of hair behind my ear. "Something like that."

She presses her back to the door, her hands behind her, and starts to open it. "Focus on whatever it is you want, and let it come to you," she advises, sounding like some kind of new age guru. Then she shrugs. "And if at some point tonight, you realize this date isn't what you want at all, leave."

"Oh, it's that easy, huh? Just up and leave?" I step through the door she's holding open for me.

"It can be. You're in charge, after all. It's your life. No need to waste it on crappy dates with boring guys or assholes."

"What if all the not-boring guys are assholes, though?"

She turns and studies me for a moment. "Maybe you need to reevaluate why you're only attracted to assholes?"

And with that parting shot, she heads for the door.

I follow her out more slowly, contemplating what she said. Am I only attracted to assholes? And if I am, what do I do about that?

Stepping into the cold November air, my breath immediately condenses into puffs above my head. And then it stops altogether.

Because Cal's standing there, leaning back against his car, his thick, muscley thighs clad in dark wash denim that molds to the shape of his quads, bulging just above his knee as he props himself up, his unzipped black leather jacket held closed by the weight of his hands in his pockets. Good god. Something about a hot guy in a leather jacket just really does it for me. I want to feel the softness of that leather as I brush it aside and slip my hands through that opening to feel the shape of him beneath it, the scent of the leather mixing with his cologne. Will I get to do that later?

Or should I take Autumn's advice and bail?

No.

The objection rings through me, low and resonant as a church bell. No, I don't want to bail. I want to see where this night can take us. I can reevaluate whether or not I'm only attracted to assholes—and whether or not Cal actually is an asshole—later.

Because right now, Cal's looking at me like he wants to eat me up.

And I'm looking at him like I want to let him.

CHAPTER ELEVEN

Cal

Holy fuck.

I've mostly seen Piper bundled up against the cold or in casual hangout clothes. All dressed up and ready for a date?

My mouth goes dry, and I almost swallow my tongue as my eyes track up the long lean length of her legs clad in black stockings, the hem of a red dress swishing a few inches above her knees. Her open jacket lets me see a plunging V-neck that gives a tantalizing view of her cleavage, the fabric of the dress molding to her tits and nipping in at the waist.

But swallowing my tongue would be a tragedy of epic

proportions. Because if I did that, how would I lick every inch of that fit little body?

God, deciding to pursue her is the best idea I've had in a long time. Maybe ever.

She offers me a smile, her red lips curling at the corners. It's the smile of a woman who knows exactly what kind of effect she has and is happy—no, *thrilled*—about it.

I can't say I have any complaints.

While I may have enjoyed the challenge of the chase she's presented so far, I like sexual partners who have some experience. I know there are guys who get off on pursuing wide-eyed virgins who exclaim over the size of their dicks because they have no frame of reference. Not me. It doesn't take a lot to impress someone who doesn't know what good is.

I like variety, and I like someone who knows what they like. What they want.

And something tells me Piper is just that kind of woman. The kind who's unashamed of her desire and isn't afraid to ask for what she needs.

I'm already half hard just from watching her walk down the steps of her dorm.

As she approaches, I straighten, meeting her with a smile and an obvious once-over. "You look beautiful," I tell her, simple and honest.

She smiles prettily, showing her teeth this time. "Thank you, so do you."

I chuckle at that and arch an eyebrow. "I look

beautiful?"

She nods. "You have to know you're pretty."

My other eyebrows joins the first, high on my forehead. "I'm pretty?"

With a laugh, she shakes her head. "Yes. You're pretty. Very." Her eyes drop to my lips.

"I don't think anyone's called me pretty before."

Her eyes meet mine again, her smile wide. "Maybe not to your face."

"Is that a good thing?"

She makes a sound of amusement in her throat. "Well, I don't think I've ever been offended by being called pretty. Sounds like a compliment to me."

Leaning in until my mouth is only an inch from hers, I wait for her smile to fade a little so I can kiss her. "Well, then. Thanks."

"You're welcome," she whispers.

I brush my lips across hers. It's barely a kiss, but she gasps at the contact. And I can't stop at just that brief hint of a touch. Not when she reacts like that.

My hand goes to her hip, my fingers flexing as my lips seal to hers and part, my tongue seeking just a tiny taste of her.

But again, once she responds, I'm lost to sensation. Lost to her. She tastes of mint, like she just brushed her teeth, and that fact is somehow ridiculously endearing.

She brushed her teeth. For me. Just in case of this.

Forcing myself to stop, I pull back with a crooked grin, enjoying the way she's looking up at me, her lips still parted, her eyelids heavy, her hands gripping the open halves of my jacket.

She seems to come back to herself slowly, blinking rapidly, her hands loosening their grip, her mouth closing, then curving up into that self-satisfied smile again.

I release my hold on her hips and step back to open the door for her. She tosses me a grin as she climbs in, and I can't help smiling back as I close the door behind her.

Once I'm in and we're all buckled up and on our way, I glance at her. "Are you hungry? Or do you just want to go back to my place?" After that kiss, I'm ready to skip dinner and get right to the good part of this date. Our chemistry is incendiary, and I'd be happy to skip dinner entirely if it means I get to spend the evening feasting on *her*. Simon and Ellie are probably still home, but I can text him and tell him to get out. I've made myself scarce for them plenty over the last few weeks. It's time for them to return the favor.

Piper just laughs. Not a cute giggle or a soft chuckle or anything. No, she guffaws, throwing her head back, peals of laughter ringing through the car, which makes me chuckle as well despite the fact that it's an obvious no. Normally girls try to be all flirty and giggly. But she's not putting on any kind of show for me. She's just being herself. I like it.

She shakes her head. "No, I'm not going straight to your house. You promised me a date. That was our deal. I'm holding up my end of the bargain. A quick fuck and whatever leftovers happen to be in your fridge is not a date."

I give her a crooked grin and a shrug. "You can't blame a guy for trying."

"I can, actually," she murmurs, her smile more subdued, but still present. "You're gonna have to work harder than that to get into my panties."

"I've never been afraid of hard work," I tell her, my tone dark and heavy with promise.

"Good."

Fuuuuuuck. This chick.

Yeah, she's making me work for it. But that just means the reward is gonna be that much sweeter in the end.

* * *

"Oooh, fancy," Piper says when we pull up in front of the restaurant.

I cast a glance her way as I unbuckle my seatbelt. "You've been here before?" The outside of the restaurant is unassuming—a squat faded brick building with an old, wooden door and a small sign bearing its name, The River Garden. It doesn't look like much from the outside, but the food is delicious and expensive, and it has a great view of the river out the picture windows on the back of the building. Nothing anyone would call fancy, unless they've actually been inside.

It's a splurge bringing her here, but I still have enough saved up from working at my dad's doctor's office filing charts over the summer that I can swing it. Since my parents help with the tuition and living expenses my sizable scholarship doesn't cover—provided I'm pre-med and work for my dad over the summers—all my summer earnings are just spending money for extras like this.

She spares me a glance as she reaches for the door handle—apparently she won't be waiting in the car for me to open her door. "I grew up here. This is where my date took me before Junior Prom." Then she opens the door and climbs out before her words even have a chance to sink in all the way.

Dang. I was hoping to impress her with my choice of restaurant. She seems like the type who enjoys hidden treasures, which is exactly how I think of this place. Unassuming and maybe even a little scruffy on the outside, but a sparkling treasure within, like those rocks my sister was obsessed with as a kid. Geodes.

Climbing out of the car, I lock it and jog around to catch up with her, hooking her pinky with mine.

She glances at me out of the corner of her eye, the amused smirk she seems to wear most of the time when we're talking still in place. "Aww," she says, half mocking. "Are you bummed I ruined your surprise?"

I lift one shoulder. "Maybe a little."

That provokes another quiet laugh. "At least you can admit it." She glances between me and the door, standing back to let me open it for her. "I'm surprised you didn't go for Luigi's, honestly."

With my hand on her lower back, I guide her through

the door, following close behind her. Her shoes make it so I only have to bend a little to talk directly into her ear. "That seems too obvious. Everyone goes to Luigi's. It's the campus date spot. I thought you'd prefer something a little more off the beaten path."

She turns her head, her eyes clashing with mine. They're wide and dark in the low light of the restaurant, her face so close that we're breathing the same air. I could kiss her right now. Again. But the restaurant might not like an R-rated dinner show. Because I'm not sure I could keep it less than that.

Her eyes bounce back and forth between mine, but she doesn't say anything as the seconds tick by. Then she lets out a breath and turns away, taking the last steps to the hostess stand. "Good call," she says over her shoulder, a forced lightness in her tone.

Yeah, it was. A slow smile stretches my lips. I've got her pegged, and I don't think she likes that. But I'm thrilled by that little admission, the same thrill that comes from shooting off a beautiful pass or calling the perfect running play. It's only a first down, but it means I'm a step closer to a touchdown.

And I can't fucking wait.

CHAPTER TWELVE

Piper

I'm grateful for the brief reprieve of following the hostess to our reserved table. Though it's not much of a reprieve with Cal right behind me, so close I swear I can feel his body heat scalding my back, the spicy smell of his body wash or cologne enveloping me. And the walk to our table is woefully short. The River Garden is a small, intimate place. The kind couples choose for a nice night out. The kind of place you can't get into without a reservation. The French-inspired menu changes seasonally, and it's always delicious. I haven't been here in ages, though it's always been a treat.

The fact that Cal picked this place over the more

obvious choices is … disconcerting. I figured he was more flash and show, but this choice seems to reflect more depth than I gave him credit for. Especially since he chose it with me in mind. Not to impress, but because he thought I'd like it.

I wasn't prepared for him to care about *me*, and not just getting me into bed. And now I'm more confused than ever about his endgame. Because this is just a game, or at least that's what I thought.

The hostess pulls out my chair, and I slide into it, glancing at the lights twinkling on the trickling water below. Since it's November, the dams are mostly closed, and the water is low. Nothing like the rushing spate in spring when the ice melt from the mountains fills the waterways.

Somehow that seems like what's going on between Cal and me. Right now the dams are almost closed, our chemistry and attraction little more than a trickle flowing between us. What would it be like to open the dams wide? Let it all flow through?

More importantly, what will happen if I don't? If it's all building up on the other side, will everything explode without some kind of release?

I steal a glance at Cal as I spread my napkin in my lap. His blue eyes watch me closely, waiting for me to react or give a verdict or … I don't know what, exactly. But he's clearly waiting. Waiting for me to make the next move. Give him the go-ahead. He already suggested skipping dinner. And when he leaned in close behind me and whispered in my ear?

I close my eyes against the fresh wave of heat and arousal that washes through me. I almost turned and pushed him back out the door, taking him up on his offer to skip dinner.

But no. That's not how this is going to go. For one thing, I need to make sure that he's trustworthy enough. After letting my pussy do the thinking last time, I need to make sure I won't find pictures of my tits on the internet after getting with Cal. He doesn't seem like the type to do that, but then again, neither did Brent, and look where that got me. I'm not going to make that mistake a second time.

But I'm also ridiculously attracted to him. And it's clear he's not going to stop pursuing me until he gets what he wants. The quickest and easiest way to keep him from becoming a huge distraction is to find out exactly what he wants and let him have it—provided it's something I'm willing to give.

Sex? Sure.

But I'm not opening myself up to the possibility of being featured in nonconsensual porn again.

That means no sex in a frat house. And no letting a casual hookup have a phone handy.

Now that I'm looking at Cal, he offers me a smirk and picks up his menu. "I've never been here before," he offers. "My roommate told me about it when I was looking for a place. He said it's really good, and good for conversation. Which, if you know Simon, is saying a lot.

That dude barely talks."

Smiling at Cal's choice of small talk, I pick up my own menu. "Oh yeah? That must make living with him pretty easy, at least. Unless you prefer having someone who talks all the time."

He snorts, glancing up at me. "It was nice for a long time. And then he started dating my sister. So now I'm plagued with her presence half the time, and if she's not at our place, he's at hers."

"Having the house to yourself sounds nice, though. And as long as he's good to your sister, what's the problem?"

He sets his menu down and stares at me until I look up. "Would you like it if your brother were dating your best friend?"

Laying my menu back on the table, I stop and think about that, one corner of my mouth curving upward. I shake my head and pick my menu up again, trying to decide between the duck and the ravioli. "I don't think you'll like my answer."

He snorts. "Please. You'd really be okay with it if your brother dated your best friend?"

I shrug, deciding on the duck. While the mushroom ravioli sounds really good too, I get duck even less often. "My best friend is in California. So if she were dating Gray, she'd be here, which would be good in my book. Plus, Gray's a pretty cool guy most of the time. I like my friend. I like my brother. I wouldn't be mad about them liking each other." I raise one eyebrow. "I take it you don't feel the same way. So it must be your sister who you don't like, because I'm guessing your roommate was also your friend and not just a random guy you live with."

His lips press together in a firm line, and his eyes flick between me and my menu. "You decided what you want to eat?" The question is gruffer than normal, lacking the polished charm he usually gives me.

"I have," I say carefully, setting my elbow on the table and leaning my chin on my hand. "Have you?" How fascinating that when the conversation turns to him and his sister, he clams right up.

He grunts, his eyes back on his menu. Then he sets it aside, his hands rubbing his thighs under the table, his shoulders tight under his navy blue dress shirt. Finally he expels a breath. "It's not that I don't *like* my sister," he starts, but just then our waitress approaches.

I fight back a smile at the tight set of his mouth, his nostrils flaring as the waitress asks for my order before turning to Cal. By the time she gets to him, he seems to have regained his lost equilibrium. He's usually so smooth that seeing that side of him is … entertaining.

When the waitress leaves, I sip my water and watch him, wondering if he'll continue our earlier conversation. But he doesn't, instead going for safer topics like classes and majors. Discovering that he's pre-med somehow doesn't surprise me. Nor does his goal of playing football professionally. He's got high-achiever written all over him.

"What about you?" he asks, after filling me in on the

NFL draft pick process. I knew some of that from Gray, but Cal seemed excited to talk about it, so I let him, enjoying seeing another side of him. His excitement is infectious, and it's clear he wasn't lying earlier when he said he's not afraid of hard work. Though anyone trying to play a professional sport would have to be willing to put in the effort. "What are your plans after college?"

I shake my head, adjusting in my seat as the waitress sets our dishes in front of us. We both murmur, "Thank you," and pick up our silverware. Cal waits patiently for me to take a bite before looking at me expectantly again.

"Law school, most likely. Get out of Spokane, though I'm not sure where I'm planning on applying exactly yet. I just know it won't be here. We'll see, though. Right now I'm just trying to play catch up."

Cal's eyebrows jump. "Catch up from what?"

Oh, right. Ugh. I don't want to get into that right now. "Not everything transfers easily." It's almost true. I know other transfer students who've had difficulty with transfer credits because there's not an exactly parallel class offered here or something. It seems to happen more with classes in your chosen major.

Cal seems to accept that answer, though, nodding and cutting another bite of his steak.

"How is it?" I ask, nodding to his plate. That was my third choice. And discussing our food seems far safer right now than continuing to discuss my transfer. Because the next question is almost always, *Why did you transfer?* And we're definitely not going there. Not tonight.

Probably not ever.

His eyes brighten and a slow smile curves his lips as he cuts another bite. "It's really good. Tender. Delicious. Wanna try a bite?" He holds up his fork, a bite speared on the tines, offering it to me.

My mouth pulls to the side as I consider him, his wicked little grin, and the bite of food. I mean, he's willing to share his food. That makes him less likely to be a complete dick, right?

I lift my hand to reach for his fork, but he pulls it back and tsks. "Let me," he says, his voice low and velvety. His gaze zeroes in on my lips, a spark of hunger lighting his eyes that has nothing to do with food, igniting an answering spark of desire between my legs. Just his attention on my mouth makes my skin prickle with awareness.

Ohhh. We're playing this game, are we?

He raises his gaze to my narrowed eyes. Do I want to let him feed me?

The zing of arousal I feel at the prospect seems like my body is saying yes.

Fuck it. Why not?

I lean forward, and his eyes widen, his nostrils flaring as he brings the fork to my lips. It's quiet enough in here that I can hear the sharp hiss of his breath as I close my lips around the fork, my eyes never leaving his. A surge of power at the effect I have on him rushes through my veins, heady and fizzy like good champagne.

Pulling the bite off the fork, I straighten, barely aware

of the food in my mouth for the sparks that are flying between us.

Holy fuck. I think I'm going to go up in flames. And I can't find it in me to regret it.

CHAPTER THIRTEEN

Jesus. I think I might come in my pants.

This chick.

She doesn't back down from a challenge. At first I didn't think she was going to let me feed her. I almost caved and handed her the fork. But then she leaned in, and holy shit. Holy fucking shit.

Her eyes hold mine, a hint of challenge in their depths as her lips part, letting me slip the fork between them, all plush and red and delectable.

Closing around the tines, pursing slightly as she pulls the morsel into her mouth, curling in a wicked smile as the fork pulls free.

Fuuuuck.

I don't know how I'm going to last the rest of dinner. God, what if she won't come home with me afterward?

I'm going to have to spend the rest of the night fucking my fist, the image of her letting me feed her playing on a loop in my head.

Just a few minor tweaks, and it's her on her knees letting me feed her my cock.

What I wouldn't give to make that a reality.

Clearing my throat, I shift in my seat, and when I risk a glance at her again, she's smiling. That knowing, self-satisfied smirk. She knows exactly what she's doing to me.

She returns her attention to her plate and cuts a bite. "Would you like to try mine?" The fork comes up, a small chunk of meat speared on the end. I look from the fork to her dark eyes dancing with amusement. And heat. She's loving this kind of foreplay.

"You're going to make me take it from you, aren't you?" I ask quietly.

Her chin dips once in a nod.

I run my tongue over my teeth, considering, then shake my head. "No, thanks. I'm good with my steak." And I place another bite in my mouth, the perfect balance of seasoning, grill char, and tenderness.

She scoffs. "It's gonna be like that, is it?"

Smirking, I shrug. "Guess so."

The rest of our conversation sticks to shallow subjects—classes, which professors to avoid if you can, football—but underneath is this simmering tension, like a steel band tightening around us, drawing us closer together. She's still resisting its pull, but me? I can't wait to find out what happens when there's no escape for either of us.

Once I have her underneath me and writhing in pleasure, it'll be easy to get her completely under my spell. I'll get everything I've wanted all semester—the hot chick I've been lusting after for weeks *and* my starting spot back. Staring at her as we eat, I can't restrain the smile that curves my lips. Because finally, everything is coming together.

* * *

"Did you save room for dessert?" the waitress asks as we're finishing up with our dinner.

I meet Piper's eyes. "What do you think?"

Shaking her head, that sweet little smirk pulling at her mouth, she says, "Not for me. I'm stuffed."

With a smile for the waitress, I ask for the check.

Piper's keeping her attention on her plate, scraping up the last bits of sauce and rice with the edge of her fork. Studiously avoiding my gaze from the looks of things.

I put my hands in my lap and lean forward, ducking a little to try to catch her eye. "Where should we go next?"

She spares a glance for me, but won't hold my gaze. "Oh, hmm." She wrinkles her brows and shakes her head. "You know, I really have to get some homework done.

You should probably just take me home."

Narrowing my eyes, I consider protesting, but I don't. Not yet, at least. While she may have a lot of homework—she mentioned that she's taking way more hours than a reasonable person should—that response sounds far too stilted. She's definitely avoiding me now.

Maybe everything's not going my way as much as I thought a few minutes ago. I guess it's my own fault for cornering her into a date with a bet. But maybe I could use that to my advantage? No way am I ready to throw in the towel that easily.

Sitting back in my chair, I shake my head. "Nah. I don't buy it."

Her eyes snap to mine. Success.

"You don't buy it," she repeats.

I shake my head again and reach for my water glass, turning it around. "Nope. I don't."

"Did you miss the part where I said I'm taking twenty-one hours this semester? Or did you forget when I told you that I had a test, a paper, or a project due every other day for the rest of the semester?"

Raising my glass to my mouth, I study her cool composure. "No," I say after I set my glass down again. "I didn't miss or forget either of those things. But I think you made a point of telling me about both of them so you'd have an excuse to duck out of our date early. I agreed not to keep you out all night, and I won't. But it's"—I check the time on my phone—"barely after seven. It hardly counts as late. And you agreed to dinner and another mutually agreed upon activity. So where should we go next?" I know where I want to go next—my bedroom—but she's not going to go for that right now.

Her eyes have narrowed to slits. Then she lets out a huge sigh and sits back in her chair, abandoning the pretense of scraping all the remaining bits of food off her plate to avoid my eyes and returning my gaze with a defiant glare of her own. "Fine." She holds up a finger. "One activity."

I let my eyes drift down to her cleavage and the hint of her waist visible over the table then back to her eyes and give her my most charming smile. "Then we better make the most of it."

I don't push my luck until we're back in my car, though, the heat blasting to take the edge off the chill in the air. Pulling out my phone, I pull up the app for the local movie theater. "So what's it gonna be? You wanna go see a movie? We could go get drinks somewhere? Or …" I glance at her, wondering if she'll fill in any options while imagining the fun we could get up to in the back of a darkened theater. Or in the bathroom at a bar. I figure if I get a good orgasm out of her, she'll be willing to go back to my place for more. My fingers and tongue can be very persuasive.

She grins and shakes her head. "I just turned twenty last month, so getting a drink is out."

I feign shock. "You don't have a fake ID? And I thought your brother liked you."

Laughing, she shakes her head. Normally I don't

really care that much about making a girl laugh—or maybe it's that I don't usually have to try very hard—but every time I get her to laugh, it feels like a reward. A hit of dopamine that makes me want to keep going, keep searching for the next way to get that reward again. "My brother likes me fine," she says. "But I've learned my lesson. I know better than to tempt fate."

"Oh?" I lean toward the center console, wanting to be closer to her, to invite intimacy and the sharing of secrets. "It sounds like there's a story there."

Her smile fades. "There is. But not one I'm sharing tonight."

Part of me wants to probe, see if I can get at whatever darkness lurks behind the smile she hitches back up her face. But what am I going to do? Solve her problems?

I'm not the guy people go to for solutions. Never have been. Especially not women. Unless the problem is a lack of orgasms. Or that they haven't slept with every football player on the team. Those are problems I'm well-known for helping solve.

This, though? Whatever makes Piper not want to tempt fate? I'm no good for those kinds of problems. Hell, fate's already smacked me down a time or two as well, and I haven't managed to recover yet. Though if I play my cards right tonight, I'll be on my way to fixing that.

"Well, I know one place where you can get a drink anyway."

She raises her eyebrows. "Oh yeah? And where's that?" Her tone betrays amused skepticism, like she can see right where this is going. And smart girl that she is, I'm sure she can.

I grin widely. "My place, of course. It's comfy. Quiet. And fully stocked."

Her eyes flicker over my face, lingering on my mouth before dropping to take in the rest of me. She lets out a breath, but shakes her head. "I'm not sure that's a good idea."

Leaning in again, I lower my voice. "What can I do to convince you that it is?"

She giggles, then reaches over and pats my arm. "Nothing," she whispers.

Trying to ignore the disappointment at her words and the way my body reacts to just that brief touch, I readjust in my seat again. "Well, I guess that leaves a movie." I wiggle my phone at her. "Lady's choice."

She accepts the phone, her lips pressed together as she looks at the screen. "Everything's already started, and the next showing isn't until late."

"You're just trying to get out of this. I'm warning you, I won't accept this as paying up on our bet if we don't do some kind of activity."

She lets out a bark of laughter. "I'm not," she protests. "I swear."

I spread my hands. "Well, unless you have an idea, I'm not sure what else to suggest. Unless you want to go park somewhere and make out?" I wouldn't mind that option. Who knows where making out could lead? The appeal of the movie was getting to sit somewhere in the dark with her. I don't even care what movie as long as I can move the armrest out of the way and have that tight little body pressed to mine. At least making out in my car abandons all pretense of watching a movie.

"So those are my choices?" she asks. "Park somewhere and make out in your car. Go to your place to get drunk and have sex. Or stay out later than I want to watch a movie?"

I hold up my hands, widening my eyes in faux innocence. "Whoa. Who said anything about having sex? I didn't." She gives me a look that says *cut the bullshit* more eloquently than words, and I can't help but laugh. "We could watch a movie at my house and not drink. I have practice tomorrow, so even if I have a drink, it'd be one, so I won't be getting drunk. And if you did, I wouldn't have sex with you. I don't need to get a chick drunk to get her into bed."

She looks me over again, all skepticism and suspicion. "If we go to your house"—she sticks her finger under my nose when my lips curl into a smile—"I said *if*."

Nodding, I fight back my smile, but it takes everything in me not to let it out again.

"*If* we go to your place, I get to leave when I want?"

"I mean, I don't think it's fair if you step one foot inside and then declare yourself ready to go. We can just hang out and talk. But when you're genuinely ready to go home and not just trying to screw me out of the date you owe me, then yeah. Of course." Though I plan on using every tool at my disposal to get her to stay as long as possible. I'm sure she's aware of that without my having to spell it out, though.

She studies me for another long moment, and I hold my breath waiting for her answer, more worried than I'd like to admit even to myself that she might turn me down. She has before. And I'm not sure how much farther I can push this bet thing. I have the feeling I'm reaching my limits. If she doesn't agree to come home with me tonight, I don't think she ever will, and continuing to push it will just make me look like a creepy weirdo.

"Fine," she says on an exhale, sending a jolt of adrenaline shooting into my veins. *Success.* "Your place it is. But if you try to pull this 'you owe me a date' bullshit again after this to try to convince me to stay, I'm going to call Gray to come pick me up and kick your ass in the process."

Chuckling, I put the car in reverse and back out of my parking spot. "Got it."

This just officially turned into a no-lose situation.

CHAPTER FOURTEEN

Piper

Part of me thinks that taking me to his house was his plan all along, and everything else was just pretense. The fact that he suggested skipping dinner and going straight there is solid evidence to back up that supposition.

For all my bluster and protest, I'm tense and excited and my pulse is pounding out a rapid drumbeat between my legs. He mentioned watching a movie, but I'm not sure I can even bother to keep up the charade.

As long as his phone stays safely out of reach, we might as well just head to his bedroom.

In fact, that seems like the quickest way to end this

date. Though, if I'm being completely honest with myself—if not with Cal—I'm not sure I want the date to be over so soon. While I *do* actually have homework—just because my paper isn't due until the day after tomorrow doesn't mean I don't need to work on it—this reprieve from the usual grind has been refreshing. And entertaining. And the way he kisses me …

Once he starts kissing me, my veneer of resistance will dissolve like cotton candy in a summer rain. And I'm pretty sure that he knows that as well as I do.

The blessedly short drive to his house passes in a sexual tension-filled silence. My nerves are all drawn so tight, you could play them like a harp. From the way Cal keeps sending me glances so hot I'm surprised my clothes haven't burned away and clenching his hands around the steering wheel as he refocuses on the road, I know he's just as affected as I am.

It's been ages since I felt this kind of chemistry with someone. It makes what I had with Brent look like a sad Wish knockoff. At the time, I thought we had great chemistry, all light and fun and flirty. Until he dumped it in the toilet, of course.

While there's definitely fun and flirting with Cal, it has an edge to it. A little bit dark, a little bit dangerous, like cliff diving or bungee jumping, where there's an adrenaline rush, and a slight amount of risk, but ultimately, with the proper precautions, no real danger.

Brent was a snake in the grass. What looked like a pretty summer meadow turned out to be filled with poison.

Cal is … well, I'm not sure what Cal is, exactly. While he definitely has the smooth, practiced moves and arrogance of a player, there's an undercurrent of sincerity. At least with me.

Or maybe I'm just taken in by another pretty face, and this will also blow up spectacularly if I'm not careful.

Which is why I'm going to be careful.

Someone as … experienced as Cal isn't going to want a relationship. That's where I went wrong with Brent. I fell for the line that he wanted to try a relationship for the first time. I know better now. And Cal hasn't fed me any of that bullshit.

Maybe that's why he seems more sincere. There's no mistaking his intentions. He's attracted to me, he wants to have fun, my initial resistance only provoked the competitor in him, and here we are.

While this is fun, it's not anything to get hung up on. So we'll skip the movie, have our fun, and both return to our regularly scheduled lives. Perfect.

As soon as I come to my decision, Cal parks in the driveway of a cute little one-story brick house with an arched entrance over the door. A few leaves cling to the trees in the yard, fluttering in the breeze, barely illuminated by the porch light glowing from under the archway and a single street lamp across the street.

When he turns off the car, the silence feels almost suffocating. I glance at Cal. He's staring at me.

I arch an eyebrow and smirk, needing to get back to a

comfortable place for both of us. Something about being here feels significant in a way it has no right to. We're college students. One-night stands are perfectly normal and acceptable. I mean, maybe I don't have a storied history of engaging in them, but there's a first time for everything. And given that Cal admits that he only does casual relationships, who better to have my first one-night stand with? This really isn't a big deal, and neither of us needs to make it one.

His low chuckle slides over me, turning down the tension a notch or two. Enough that we can speak, at least. "My roommate's not home," he says quietly, like speaking too loud would be offensive somehow.

My smirk turns into a grin. "That's good."

Leaning over the console, he slides a hand behind my neck and pulls me close. His lips touch mine, and I inhale sharply as warmth spreads through my body from every point of contact.

Sweet baby Jesus, if just his fingers on my neck and his lips on mine is this good, what will it be like to have him all over me?

This might be the shortest, most tame kiss we've ever shared, but it's incendiary.

He pulls back, his eyes dark, nostrils flaring, jaw tight. "Let's get inside." He practically grinds the words out, like he's restraining himself from barking out orders. Or yanking me into his lap and fucking me senseless in the driver's seat of his car only a few feet away from his front door.

At my nod, he throws his door open and climbs out, every movement efficient and purposeful. And I'm left sitting like a rag doll, watching him in his jeans that show off his biteable ass and thick thighs and that sexy leather jacket that clings to his broad shoulders. The dark smirk he gives me as he crosses in front of the headlights that haven't switched off yet is almost enough to make me orgasm on the spot.

I am in the best kind of trouble.

I've barely popped the door open, and he's there, holding out a hand to help me out of the car. I let him this time, enjoying the grip of his strong, capable fingers wrapped around mine. Once I'm out of the car, he doesn't let me go, instead sliding his fingers between mine and walking me to his front door.

I almost bury my face in his neck and inhale, but I don't. Not yet. That can wait until we're inside, at least. If I did that, I'm not sure what kind of beast I would unleash. He seems like he's barely able to restrain himself as it is.

Once we're inside with the door closed behind us, all bets are off. I pull him to me by our joined hands, my free hand gripping his jacket and giving it a yank.

He resists just enough to let me know that he can, but lowers his head, releasing my hand to slide an arm around my waist. I wrap my hand behind the thick column of his neck, the short hair at the nape like velvet under my fingertips, and pull his mouth to mine. Or pull myself up to him. I'm not really sure how it happens exactly, just that it does, and this time, he doesn't hold back.

His arm cinches around me as his tongue slides into my mouth, and I open willingly, letting him take control of this kiss, even if I'm the one who started it.

His other hand smooths down the soft fabric of my dress, cupping and kneading my ass for a moment, before descending down the back of my thigh. When he reaches the hem, his hand starts its return trip, this time underneath, the heat of his palm so immediate through the thin fabric of my stockings.

I press myself into his body, sliding my hand under his jacket, relishing his firm chest and the bunch and flex of his muscles as he explores my body.

He lets out a groan like a man in pain when he reaches the top of my stockings and finds bare skin between the elastic tops and my lace cheeky panties. He draws back and looks down at my face, his fingers still tracing over my skin under my dress. "I thought we were going to watch a movie," he rumbles, the words all rough and gritty like sandpaper.

"Is that really why you invited me over?" I ask, my voice far too breathy for my taste, but from the way his cock twitches against my belly, he seems to like it.

Another groan, and his mouth falls to my neck in an open-mouthed kiss, sucking lightly at my skin. "So that's a no to the movie?" he clarifies, his breath cool on my overheated skin.

"No movie."

"Thank fuck," he murmurs, his mouth on mine again. But only for a brief moment, because the next thing I know I'm getting scooped up like a bride and carried down the hall.

A laugh bubbles out of me, and Cal gives me a grin I can only describe as rakish. He shoulders his way into a room and kicks the door shut behind him. For a brief moment, I'm weightless, and then I crash onto a plush mattress that barely even bounces under my weight.

Cal glares down at me as he removes his jacket and tosses it at a chair. It misses, but he either doesn't know or doesn't care, because his eyes never leave my body. "I gotta see what you've got on under this fucking dress," he mutters, and I'm not sure if he's talking more to me or to himself.

Sitting up, I unzip my booties and barely manage to kick them off before his hands are on my knees, spreading them apart so he can kneel between them, his hands bunching the fabric of my dress up to my waist. He glances at my face once, quickly, and when I smirk back, his jaw clenches and his chest inflates as he draws in a deep breath before looking down to see what he's revealed—lace burgundy panties and the tops of my black, nearly opaque, stockings.

"Jesus fuck," he mutters, his fingertips tracing lightly over the center seam of my panties, stopping just short of the gusset.

I lift my hips almost involuntarily, and he gives me a wicked smile before brushing a knuckle over my own seam. "That what you want?" he asks.

With a jerky nod, I press into his fingers, wanting more.

"Say it," he commands. "Tell me what you want."

My eyes go wide, but he simply holds my gaze, his own body pulled taut as he waits. I don't mind initiating or helping direct the action as necessary, but I've never had anyone command me to verbalize what I want before giving it to me.

When he starts to pull his hand away, I let out a wordless cry of protest that causes his lips to curl up in an infuriatingly sexy smirk. Jesus, this guy and his endless repertoire of smirks.

"I want you to touch me," I manage to say, the ache between my legs coming out in the rasp of my voice. "Please."

His eyes glitter with triumph and desire, and he brushes his fingers between my legs again. "Here? You want me to touch you here?"

When I nod again, he tsks. "Words, Piper. I need your words."

"Yes," I breathe. "I want you to touch my pussy."

His eyebrows jump, but he rewards me by sliding his fingers under the edge of the lacy fabric that's barely a barrier anyway and tracing my puffy lips that have been slick and aching for what feels like hours already.

"You're so wet for me, Piper. So fucking wet already." He watches his fingers as he dips one just inside me and continues tracing all the slippery contours of my center, around my inner labia, up and over my clit, back down again. Exploring. Playing, with no obvious goal in mind at this point, other than to torment me with his fingers while he torments me with his words. "I'm surprised your dress doesn't have a wet spot on it, because you've soaked through your panties already. Not that they're much protection anyway." He meets my gaze, his pupils almost fully dilated with arousal, only a thin band of icy blue still visible. "Did you wear these for me, Piper? Were you hoping I'd see them?"

I make a wordless sound, and he tuts again. "Answer, or I stop."

"You're such a fucking bastard."

He grins at me, completely unrepentant. "That's not an answer."

"I don't know," I say as he brushes my clit again. But then his touch disappears. "Fine!" I shout. "Yes. Are you happy? Is that what you wanted to hear? Yes. I wore them thinking you might see them."

One finger sinks inside me. "Was that so difficult?" he asks, sounding almost reasonable except for the ragged edge to his voice. "I like them. And the stockings. You're a walking wet dream."

I almost laugh. And if he'd said that to me under any other circumstances, I would've. But with two of his fingers sliding in and out of me slowly and his thumb brushing my clit, I can't bring myself to take his words as anything other than a compliment. And from his tone of voice, dark and rough as it may be, he meant it as one.

When he withdraws his hand, I let out a cry of protest that he silences with a kiss. "Don't worry, baby," he whispers in my ear as he pulls my dress higher up my torso. "We're just getting started."

CHAPTER FIFTEEN

Cal

'm not sure what's come over me tonight. I've never done this before—making a woman explicitly tell me what she wants. Sure, I've asked if they want me to do things, but this is another level.

I know what Piper wants. I can read her desire in every line of her body, every tremble, every hitched breath. The way she presses herself against my hand.

But hearing her say it? Making her give me the words?

It ratchets up my arousal several levels.

Holy fuck. I'm gonna explode if I don't dial it back a notch or two. Because I'm sure as hell not ready for this to be over yet. Hell, we both still have our clothes on. I haven't even seen her tits yet.

Reaching down, I give my aching hard-on a firm squeeze, trying to back myself down from the edge.

But when she whimpers at the loss of my touch and looks up at me with hazy, lust-drunk eyes, any good it did is immediately wiped away.

"Don't worry, baby," I tell her, my voice rasping like my throat is made of gravel as I reach for her again. I can't keep my hands off her, not with her whimpering for my touch. "We're just getting started." I have plans for this chick, this body. Big plans. Plans that may not all be possible tonight, but I'm sure as hell gonna do my best.

I lift her dress up, revealing her perfect tits cupped in lace and satin that matches her panties. With a soft groan at the erotic picture she presents—between the stockings, lacy panties that reveal as much as they cover, and matching bra, she could easily be a pin-up model—I dip my head and trace my tongue around the edge of her bra cup.

She shifts and writhes beneath me, her legs restless, but with how I have her dress bunched, she can't move her arms much. Smiling against her skin, I take a little bit longer than I was originally planning, dragging my mouth up to her collarbone, drawing out the torturous anticipation before lifting my head and pulling the dress off, the material still warm from her body.

Her dark hair falls around her shoulders, mussed from lying on the bed and my not-too-gentle undressing, and Jesus fuck, she's gonna kill me. She looks like a fucking sex demon here to suck me dry. I've always thought there were worse ways to go, though, so I waste no time stripping off my shirt, undoing only enough buttons so I can pull the whole thing up and over my head.

As I toss it in the corner, she gets up on her knees, her cool hands brushing up my abs and over my pecs to my shoulders, her eyes following their path until her fingers meet behind my neck, stroking the hair at the base of my skull. My hands fall to her hips, settling perfectly on those ripe swells, pulling her closer and covering her mouth with mine once again.

And just like every other time, our kiss just seems to make the flames glow brighter, hotter, and I'm starting to rethink how this night might go. I'd originally planned to make her come at least once with my mouth or my fingers before fucking her. But we might need to have two or three rounds. At least. And that's just tonight. Because I don't know how long I can torture myself by drawing this out. I don't think I have that much control.

Her lips are delicious under mine, and the way she meets each thrust of my tongue only makes me more excited to see how enthusiastic she'll be once things really get started. Sliding my hands down over her ass, I grip her upper thighs, pulling her up and around my waist and once she's hanging on, I brace my arm along her spine to lay her back without losing contact at any point.

Once she's on her back, I only have to make a slight

adjustment and I can grind my aching cock into her hot little pussy. It's nowhere near enough. My fucking jeans are still in the way, and I hate them more than anything right now. But I haven't taken them off on purpose. As a reminder that no matter how much my dick is begging to be enveloped by her, I need to make sure she comes first.

But I can't help rocking against her just one more time.

She turns her head to the side, breaking the kiss, her chest rising and falling under mine, her heart pounding in time with mine. "Fuck," she breathes.

"Yes, ma'am."

Chuckling, she turns and meets my eyes as I drop more kisses down her sternum, hooking the edge of a bra cup with a finger and tugging it aside so I can run my tongue over and around her hard pink nipple.

She presses her chest up, wordlessly asking for more with a soft hum of pleasure.

But that's not good enough.

"Say it," I command, blowing softly over her nipple, making it draw up even tighter.

"You're a bastard," she mutters.

I grin. "I am. But if you want me to keep going, you have to say it. Tell me what you want me to do to you."

Relaxing her back, she stares at me with solemn dark eyes for a moment. Then she lifts her head, her hand coming up and tangling in my hair, bringing my face close to hers. "You want me to tell you what I want you to do to me?" she asks, her voice a deadly whisper.

"Yes. Tell me."

Her delicate nostrils flare as she stares into my eyes. "I want you to quit fucking around and demanding that I articulate everything before you do it again. I want you to suck on my nipples, then fuck me with your fingers while you suck on my clit until I come, and then I want you to put a condom on your dick and fill me up until I scream with pleasure."

I can't breathe. Holy shit. She just … *fuuuuuck*. This chick.

"Is that explicit enough for you?"

I nod, my scalp stinging with her grip in my hair. Somehow that only adds an edge to all of this.

"Good." She releases her hold on me and rests her head on the bed again, her back arching up for a moment and her hands disappearing behind her back. When she pulls her hands out, she pulls her bra straps off her arms and flings the lingerie somewhere, leaving her topless and waiting for me to do what she just told me she wanted.

Dipping my head, I hold her gaze as I circle her nipple with my pointed tongue once more.

"Good boy," she says, practically cooing.

Oh, I'm a good boy, am I? We'll see about that.

I suck her nipple between my lips and then press the edge of my teeth against it. Gently at first, then progressively harder until she gasps, her eyes wide as she looks at me. I scrub my tongue over the tip quickly, then release that nipple so I can give the other the same treatment.

This time when I bite down, she lets out a low, throaty moan. And fuck. Maybe I am a good boy. If this is the reward I get—her moaning and rubbing herself against me—I'll take it.

Dragging my mouth down her belly, I pause to nip at her ribcage, her hip, the skin just above her bare mound, before settling on my knees on the floor. I tug her panties down, slowly at first, because while she might want me to stop teasing, I'm not quite that obedient, then all at once when they get past her thighs. With my hands on her hips, I yank her closer to me, then press her legs back and apart, revealing her dripping pussy to me for the first time.

Christ, she really is going to be the death of me.

She wiggles against my restraining hands, clearly desperate for my mouth. And if that weren't enough, she says, "Cal," in a warning voice, all stern and sexy as fuck.

But like I said, I'm not that obedient.

I rub my nose up her inner thigh, starting just above her knee, stopping less than halfway up. "Hmm?"

"Please." This time it's a broken plea.

"Please what?" I barely recognize the dark edge of my own voice. But if she's going to beg, I want her to beg properly.

"Pleeease," she draws out. "Lick me. Touch me. Fucking *do* something."

I trail my tongue up her other thigh.

She lets out a choked laugh. "Eat my pussy, Cal." This

time it's all command.

"I dunno, Piper," I whisper against her inner thigh, close enough that I can feel the heat of her pussy on my face, but not so close that there's any chance of accidentally touching her there. "I kinda liked it when you were begging."

"Fuck you."

"Mmmm, yeah, that's the plan."

Another choked laugh. Another wiggle of that sweet ass. "Please eat my pussy," she whispers. "Please, Cal. Please."

"Good girl," I breathe over her wetness just before swiping over it with my tongue.

Her hips jerk like I just gave her an electric shock, and then she moans as I lick her again, slower, and she relaxes into me.

"That's it," I tell her. "I've got you." And with the point of my tongue, I trace my way along every nook and cranny of her pussy, lingering on her clit for a moment before pulling away.

She moans, and I kiss her thigh. "I've got you, baby," I tell her again. "I'll give you what you need."

Keeping one hand on her thigh, I pull the other away, rubbing it over her, spreading her juices all around. She's obviously more obedient than I am—that or she's unwilling to change positions and risk me stopping or changing the sensation, because even though I'm not holding her open anymore, she doesn't move her free leg at all.

I ease one finger inside her, loving the way her body welcomes me, hot and slick and easy. She presses her hips into my hand in response with a soft moan.

"You ready for more?" I ask, gliding my finger in and out.

"Fuck. *Yes.*"

Palm up, I slide in two fingers, slowly, even though she takes them with no trouble. But watching my fingers gradually sink into her is so fucking hot that I pull them out and do it again. Her moan is louder this time. And when I curl my fingers and find that slightly rougher patch on the front wall of her pussy, she curses.

Grinning, I keep it up and trace her clit with my tongue in slow circles, watching the way her body undulates for me. Her pussy is already fluttering around my fingers, and when she comes, it's going to be explosive.

I can't fucking wait.

I suck her clit between my lips, scrubbing it with my tongue as I increase the pace with my fingers. With a wordless shout, her whole body curls up, her hands gripping her thighs, her fingers digging into her flesh just above where one of my hands still holds her leg back. Her pussy contracts rhythmically around my fingers, but I don't let up. Not yet.

She's groaning and growling and cursing, and I keep fucking her with my fingers, stroking her clit with my tongue, until she reaches between her legs and shoves my face away.

"Enough," she shouts. "I can't take anymore. Stop stop stop."

After one last lick that has her legs jumping, I pull away and ease my fingers out of her.

"Jesus Christ," she says in a hoarse voice, her hands covering her face. "Holy shit."

Standing, I wipe my chin with one hand, then lean over and kiss her lips. She cups my cheeks in her palms and kisses me back, not at all shy about tasting herself on my tongue.

I'm already undoing my pants and shoving them down as fast as I can. Because if I don't get inside her right away, I'm gonna blow my load all over her belly. And while the thought of marking her has a certain appeal I don't want to examine too closely, that's not how I want this to go. I might be gunning for multiple rounds, but she's already tried to duck out early. If I want more than one round, coming all over her doesn't seem like the greatest way to convince her to stay longer.

No, I need to follow up that orgasm with one where she's stretched around my dick.

Not gonna lie, I want that for me too. I want her pussy milking my cock the way she did my fingers. I can come all over her belly and tits next time. Because there sure as fuck is gonna be a next time.

CHAPTER SIXTEEN

Piper

I can barely move after the orgasm that I thought would never end. And while that sounds really great, the hypersensitivity of being forced to come in overlapping waves gets to be too much.

Plus, I want to see that dick. And I want to feel it inside me.

Cal's moving around even as he's kissing me, and if he's going to make me tell him everything I want him to do to me in explicit detail, then I'm not going to be shy about shoving him away when I want to see what he's up to.

Once his tongue's out of my mouth, I wriggle back far

enough so I can sit up in time to see him straighten and shove his pants and underwear down all at once. His chest is mostly hair free, and I don't know if he grooms it that way or if he's just naturally hairless, but he's got the most delicious treasure trail leading to an even more delicious treasure. His cock juts out from his torso, thick and proud in its nest of dark blond hair.

And I want to touch it.

But when I reach for it, he catches my wrist in his hand. So I use my other hand, and he doesn't have time to catch it before my fingers circle his girth and give him a squeeze. His cock jerks in response, and I can't help smiling. When I look up to meet Cal's eye, he's practically glaring at me, a muscle in his jaw ticking.

So I do what any self-respecting girl would do with a big, muscley guy staring down at her with his cock in her hand—I swipe my tongue over his cock head, picking up the salty taste of his precum.

He groans. "Fuck, Piper. Fuuuuck. I need a condom."

After one more lick—turnabout is fair play, after all—I release him. "What are you waiting for?"

He gives me another baleful glare, and then moves to his dresser, kicking his pants out of the way in the process. "Fuck."

But this curse sounds like one of frustration, not the sexy curses he's been muttering since we got here. He tosses the condom box down. "Empty."

I make grabby hands in the direction of the door, where my jacket and purse ended up. "Hand me my purse."

He cocks an eyebrow at me, a sexy grin growing on his face as he does what I ask. His body is a work of art, golden skin stretched taut over chiseled muscles that bunch and flex in delightful ways as he bends to scoop up my purse and hand it to me.

When I pull out the small boxes of condoms, he chuckles in delight, swiping one out of my hand—Magnums, of course—and bending to kiss me, quick and hard. "I have *never* been more attracted to you than I am right now," he says before straightening and tearing into it.

He makes short work of sheathing himself, and then he hooks his hands under my knees and pulls me closer, the tip of his cock lining up with my entrance.

"Do it," I whisper. "Fuck me. Now."

"No please this time?" he asks, the cocky little shit.

"You really need me to beg again? When you know you're dying to get inside me?"

The tip of him nudges my opening, and he releases my legs to prop his fists on the bed on either side of me.

I raise my face to his, and he closes the last fraction of an inch, his lips parting mine as his cock slides into me, stretching my swollen tissues in the most delicious way. He swallows my groan as he gives me his own. Stilling when his hips meet mine, he raises his head, staring into my eyes as he withdraws ever so slightly and rocks into me.

"Fuck, Piper," he whispers, his tone reverent.

Too reverent. This isn't supposed to be tender and sweet. It's supposed to be sexy and rough and *over* once we're done. There's no room here for whispers and caresses. Just flesh slapping flesh as we ride each other to our separate pleasure. I've got mine. It's time for him to get his.

I curl my lips in a deliberately wicked smile. "Yes, that's the idea." And I squeeze my internal muscles around him, pushing my hips into him.

He groans again, his eyes falling closed, but he's powerless to resist this, rocking into me again. Still achingly slow, small movements, like he's afraid of really letting loose. I know he's been dying to get inside me since we kissed in front of the dorm. And for some reason he's still holding back. Is this more of his kink where he makes me tell him what I want?

Licking my lips, I force my brain to form words. "Fuck me, Cal. Hard and fast. Fuck me like you mean it."

At first I think that might've been a miscalculation. Too goading, maybe? Because he stills, his eyes flashing with something dark when they meet mine. Then he growls, one hand sliding under my ass and lifting my hips an inch, and then he pulls back almost all the way and slams himself back into me, driving all the air from my body, leaving room only for him. Again. And again. Still slow, but getting faster with each stroke.

"Like that?" he demands through clenched teeth. "That how you want me to fuck you?"

My answer is little more than a grunt, because that's

all I can manage when he's fucking me so hard, and with the way he angled my hips, each stroke plows over my G-spot. It's almost too much, but I can't back away. Can't resist. Can't do anything but take it.

"Yeah," he mutters. "Fuck yeah. That's what you want. I told you I'd give you what you need. Fucking take it. Take it deep and hard and rough. Fuck." He growls again, punctuated by muttered curses, his hips pistoning faster, and holy shit. Oh fuck.

Oh fuck oh fuck oh *fuck*.

My muscles pull tighter with every stroke, my entire being focused on the few inches between my legs and the drag of his cock in and out of me, and I'm going to come again. I didn't think I could after that. I didn't know my body could ever respond like this.

And then it hits me, a tsunami barreling into me, carrying me along in its wake, almost painful it's so intense.

And Cal just fucks me through it, keeping it going, and I don't know how much more I can handle before my body just breaks apart under his relentless fucking. When he slams into me and stays there, grinding into my hips, it's almost a relief. His fingers dig into my ass, pulling me tight against him even as he pumps a few more times, wringing out the last of his own orgasm before slumping over me, holding himself up on one elbow, breathing like he just sprinted the length of a football field.

"Fuuuck," he groans after a moment, raising his head to meet my eyes. "You're gonna fucking kill me with this pussy," he says, his fingers sliding over me and making me shudder as he grips the base of the condom and pulls out.

I let out a sharp burst of laughter. "I'm gonna kill you? What about you? God, I thought I might explode from the way you were drilling into me."

He gives me a cocky smile before heading for the door. "You asked for it."

Covering my face with my hands, I chuckle weakly. Because he's right, I asked for it. "I didn't say I was complaining," I call out, not sure how far away he is.

I hear a faucet turn on and off again a moment later, and I sit up as he strolls back into the room, still half hard. He slides onto the bed, adjusting the pillows so he can lean back against the wall behind him. Resting his arm out to his side, he pats the bed next to him. "Come here. Let's chill for a bit, and then we can go again."

Standing, I let out an incredulous laugh and run my fingers through my hair. "I'm not sure my vagina can take getting battered like that twice in one night."

"I'll be gentle next time. Promise."

I make a noncommittal hum, because the idea of next time is far too appealing considering this was supposed to be one and done. "Where's the bathroom?"

He gestures at the door. "On the right. It's open. You can't miss it."

Feeling strange walking around a stranger's house in the nude, I pick up Cal's shirt and slide it over my head. He chuckles, but his expression when I glance at him over my shoulder is anything but amused. Oh no, it's the look of a man who's hungry for seconds.

Their bathroom is surprisingly tidy. After seeing the frat house bathrooms, I formed a very low opinion of boys left to their own devices. Apparently my parents' insistence on us cleaning our bathroom led me to believe that everyone learned that bathrooms shouldn't be disgusting. But the guys of the frat shared no such background, I guess. At least not the guys Brent shared a bathroom with. Their sink always had stray globs of toothpaste all around it, splatter on the mirror, various body and grooming products overflowing the counters, a variety of hair types—stubble, pubes, etc—lying around on the floor. Musty towels. Puddles of unknown origin dotting the floor. (Were they water splashed out of the sink or shower? Or something else? No one ever seemed to know the answer to that question.) Don't even get me started on the toilet area. Gag. Walking through it was a minefield best avoided if possible.

But the pedestal sink in this bathroom is clean and free of clutter. A wall-mounted toothbrush holder next to the mirror holds their toothbrushes, and I'm assuming the toothpaste and everything else is hidden in the medicine cabinet. The towels hang neatly on a towel bar. The shower curtain is closed, but a quick peak reveals a clean shower-tub combo with body wash and shampoo clustered neatly in a corner. Still, I approach the toilet with some trepidation. But there are no puddles, no invisible sticky nor yellow spots on the white tile floor.

Cal's room might be cluttered, but at least he's not a pig. And he may have some justification for his cockiness with women. And I *might* find it a little bit cute.

Ugh. I'm not supposed to actually like this guy. I don't have time for that.

As I finish up in the bathroom, I stare at my reflection in the (spotless) mirror, and give myself a mental lecture. We had our fun. We lived up to our agreement with regard to our bet. Now it's time for me to go home, go back to my life of studying and classes and homework, and finish reading the last article for my paper that I need to write. Depending on how long that takes me, I might even be able to get started on the first part of it, which means I'll have less to do tomorrow.

With a firm nod, I take a deep breath, and pull open the door, only to practically jump out of my skin.

"Oh!" says the girl on the other side of the door, her eyes flying wide in shock as she takes a step back. "I'm sorry! I didn't know anyone would be in here."

My initial shock fading, I realize I recognize her. She was at the video game tournament. I rack my brain for her name. Dani's friends with her, and I saw her roommate before leaving tonight. "Ellie, right?"

She smiles, her expression going from almost scared to warm and welcoming. "Right. And you're Dani's roommate. Piper."

"That's me." Her eyes track over me, and suddenly I'm *veeerrry* conscious of the fact that all I'm wearing is Cal's shirt. I cross my arms over my chest, not that it does anything to hide the fact that Cal and I obviously just had sex.

Ellie's cheeks are pinker now. "Well, again, sorry. I needed to grab a book I left in Simon's room, and I accidentally left my favorite lip gloss in the bathroom earlier, so I was going to just try to grab it too."

"Ellie," Cal's voice rumbles, and he doesn't sound happy.

She jumps and turns to face her brother. Because Jesus Christ, I just fucked her brother. My cheeks heat. How long has she been here? How much did she hear?

"Hey, Cal. Sorry. I needed my textbook." She holds the book in question in the air and wiggles it back and forth. "I have a test tomorrow."

Cal crosses his arms over his naked chest, but I notice he at least put on sweatpants. Good god, it's not fair how sexy he looks in fucking *sweatpants*. "You could've texted. We agreed that I got the house tonight."

She lifts her chin. "I did. It's not my fault you were too … ah … busy to see it. You're usually glued to that thing. I'm surprised you didn't check it as soon as you finished." Her eyes cut to me, but just for a second. "Look, I'm sorry. I wasn't trying to barge in. Like I said, I just needed my textbook, and I hoped to get my lip gloss."

I step into the hallway and ease past her. Cal gives me an apologetic look, and I just offer him a quick smile as I slip through the door behind him and close the door as quietly as possible before collapsing against it. It's bad enough   bumping   into   your   one-night-stand's housemates. I really didn't need to get into anything with his sister who's also an acquaintance and lives on my floor.

Gathering myself and forcing away my embarrassment, I find my panties, bra, and dress—my stockings never came off—take off Cal's shirt, and start getting dressed. After a few more annoyed-sounding exchanges between Cal and Ellie that I hear the tone more than the words, Cal opens the door and eases into the room. He takes one look at me and stills, then lets out a heavy sigh. "You want me to take you home?"

CHAPTER SEVENTEEN

Cal

At Piper's nod, my gut sinks. I knew this was likely to happen, especially when she didn't really respond to my suggestion of a round two, but I thought I might have the opportunity to convince her.

Thanks to my little sister, all chance of that has evaporated. Piper's dressed and picking up her shoes and coat and gathering the remaining condoms to stuff back into her purse.

Fucking Ellie forgetting her shit, knowing that I had a date tonight and that I'd called the house until at least midnight. And fucking Simon for bringing her back here like it's no big deal. Like I don't clear out for them on the regular. You don't see me sneaking back home for shit I forgot while they're fucking in Simon's room. What if we'd been in the living room? Or the kitchen? What if she'd come home while I was the one in the bathroom?

We're going to have to have words about this. Just because I haven't done this before doesn't mean I won't again. I glance at Piper where she's bending over to zip her boots up to her ankles. If I get my way, this will become a regular occurrence. Because if anything, tonight only made me want her more.

But I've pushed my luck as far as it'll go tonight, and I know when to admit it's time to back off.

Pulling a long sleeve T-shirt out of my drawer, I yank it on, then grab a sweatshirt. I sit on the bed next to Piper to pull on my socks, leaning over to her and kissing her shoulder.

She turns to look at me, wariness and surprise warring in her face. But she kisses me back when I lift my lips to hers, her tongue tangling with mine for a second before she pulls away, standing and putting her coat on.

Another pang of disappointment echoes through me. I'd thought maybe she'd change her mind—or let me attempt to change her mind—when she responded like that. Tonight was electric, and while I'm not usually one to drag things out with a chick, after that, I'm willing to make an exception. Especially since being with her not only means more of *that* kind of sex, but should also mean I'll be starting again once her brother loses his shit.

But no. She's clearly determined to leave. *Don't take it*

personally, I tell myself. *She said she has lots of homework and can't stay out late.*

Rifling through my coat pockets, I find my keys and phone, and sure enough, I have two unread texts, one from Simon and one from Ellie, both telling me she needed to pick something up and to stay in the bedroom until she texted with the all clear.

I guess they tried at least. Stifling a sigh, I straighten and offer Piper a closed-mouth smile. "Ready?"

She nods and picks up her purse, holding it in front of her like a shield as she goes through the door I hold open for her.

The drive back to campus is as silent as the drive from the restaurant to my house, but it feels different. That silence was thick with anticipation and excitement. This one just feels … final.

When I stop in front of the dorm's entrance, I put the car in park and lean across the console, catching her before she can open the door. With my fingers under her chin, I bring her in close for another of those soul-shattering kisses.

After we break apart, she sucks her lower lip into her mouth, like she's savoring the taste and feel of me on her lips, her eyes opening slowly to meet mine, and all it does is make me want to kiss her again, suck that lip into my own mouth, see how she'd react if I nipped it with my teeth. She liked when I used my teeth on her nipples and nipped and sucked my way down her body. I want to find out where else she'd like my teeth, where she prefers only my lips or tongue. But I won't get to map that out tonight.

"What's your schedule the rest of the week?" I ask before she can completely come back to herself and run away without agreeing to another meetup. I'll be damned if I don't get another taste of what we had tonight.

"Um." Her eyes narrow as they peer into mine, like she's searching for something, some deeper meaning or ulterior motive. "Look, Cal—"

I blow out a breath and sit back in my seat. "Seriously?"

She huffs and crosses her arms, leaning against the door to face me. "What?"

I roll my eyes at her. "Is this the beginning of the 'let's just be friends' speech? Or the 'I'm too busy for a boyfriend' one?" I shake my head. "It doesn't even matter, really. Because it's complete bullshit. You can't tell me you don't want a repeat performance."

At least she has the decency not to deny any of it. Dropping her eyes, she picks at a piece of fuzz on her dress. "I *am* busy," she insists quietly.

"So am I. I have a full course load and a demanding major, so it's not like I'm just taking easy classes, either. I have plenty of homework on top of football."

She nods and spreads her hands in front of her, her shoulders climbing to her ears. "So you get it. You see why this can't be more than this between us."

"I see no such thing," I respond, eyes narrowed. I'm not going to let her slip away this easily. Not when I've had her demanding I do filthy things to her body and moaning on my cock. That's too good to give up without even trying. Plus, seeing her repeatedly is the best way to cement the other part of my plan. "I'm not proposing anything serious or overly time-consuming. You had fun tonight. Admit it."

Her cheeks color, and she fights the smile that's pulling at her lips. "I admit nothing."

I shake my head. "You're impossible."

"And that's why you like me." She's lost the fight with her grin, and it's taken over her face.

"I admit nothing," I fire back at her. She's right, though. I do like her.

She snorts, shaking her head. Then she sucks in a deep breath. "This was only supposed to be once."

Who said that? I know I didn't. I don't ask that question, though. "You really want to let it go at one time? When it was that good?"

She rolls her lips between her teeth and inhales deeply, her tits pressing up against the neckline of her dress. After holding her breath for a beat, she releases it in a gust. "Fine. I'll text you on Wednesday after I turn in my paper."

"Perfect." I reach for her hand and tug her closer so I can kiss her again. "I look forward to it. If I don't hear from you by the end of practice, though, I'll be calling."

Her nostrils flare. "Deal."

* * *

I'm going over some notes for my biochem class when Simon gets home a while later. Alone, thank god. Ellie doesn't sleep over very often, which might be out of some latent sense of respect for my feelings, but is more likely because it's still the football season and our morning workouts are earlier than Ellie's first class. She doesn't want to have to wake up that early to get back to campus. And since we have all away games through the end of the semester, no weekend sleepovers either.

Simon surprises me by dropping his jacket and backpack just inside the living room instead of going to his room. Crossing his arms over his chest, he stares down at me, his eyes narrowed.

I sit back, my laptop still perched on my legs, my textbook open next to me, and take in Simon's posture. It's not often he graces me with one of his lectures, but I recognize the warning signs.

"Can I help you?" I ask when he just continues to stare at me for a moment.

His jaw works like he's rolling the words around in his mouth before spitting them out. "Kilpatrick's sister?" is all he asks, though, the two words a bit of a disappointment after all that build up.

I quirk an eyebrow. "Yup," is my equally verbose reply.

He snorts, sounding like a frustrated bear. Or at least what I imagine one would sound like. I don't actually have any in-person experience with bears. Just nature documentaries my parents occasionally insisted we watch for family movie nights and nature shows in middle school science class. Though my seventh grade biology teacher was much more likely to show us videos of deer attacking people. I never really figured out why that genre featured so heavily in her class, but any time we had a sub or she decided to show a video, nine times out of ten, it was something like *Deer Attacks!* Or *When Deer Attack 2*. Or *Top Ten Most Insane Deer Attacks*.

She was kinda strange, to be honest.

But no one would ever compare Simon to a deer. He's way too big, for one thing. And no antlers. He'd be closer to a moose, if we're going with *Cervidae*. They're big. Keep to themselves unless provoked.

And something I've done seems to have provoked him, because he's still glaring at me, apparently expecting more than a one word answer.

Sighing, I spread my hands. "What do you want me to say?"

"Do you actually like her?" he demands. "Or are you just fucking around to get back at Kilpatrick for transferring here and taking your starting spot."

My jaw clenches, and I force myself to take deep breaths. Simon's my friend. A fact I've had to remind myself of more often than normal lately, because he's really been pissing me off. He's supposed to have *my* back. Literally, when we're talking football. But instead, he's guarding Kilpatrick more often than me, and that seems to be bleeding over into our time off the field as well.

"Dude. Are you accusing me of fucking a girl as some kind of revenge plot?" I set my laptop on my book and lean forward, propping my elbows on my knees. "Is that really where you're going with this?" I mean, I kinda am, to be honest. But I don't need Simon's holier-than-thou attitude trying to make me feel bad about it. Kilpatrick's a dick. He deserves to be taken down a notch or two. And elite sports is cutthroat. How is it my fault if me fucking his sister distracts him enough to make him lose focus so I get a chance to regain what's rightfully mine?

It certainly doesn't hurt that I *do* actually like Piper. Maybe my decision to pursue her was motivated by getting at her brother. But she's intriguing. Hilarious. And our chemistry? It's off the charts. At this point, Kilpatrick getting mad I'm boning his sister is more of a bonus than a primary motivator. I'd want to see her again regardless.

Simon spreads his hands. "I notice you didn't deny it."

Snorting, I shake my head and stand. "Fuck you, man." I close my laptop and gather my things. If Simon's going to be like this, then I might as well study in my room. "Yes, I actually like her. That make you feel better?"

He stares me down for a second before stepping aside and letting me leave the living room, but he follows me into the hall. "Yeah, actually, it does. She lives on Ellie's floor, you know."

I pause in front of the bathroom, casting him a glance

over my shoulder. "No, actually. I didn't know. They friends?" Does it make a difference to me if they are? I mean, it might make things awkward, but Ellie's already screwing my friend, so it'd serve her right.

Simon shrugs. "More like acquaintances. She knows Dani, Piper's roommate, better than Piper. Says Piper tends to keep to herself and spends most of her time doing homework."

Even though I just decided I don't care if she's friends with my sister, I can't help feeling relieved they're not close. I nod in response to Simon's statement. "She's taking a lot of classes. Trying to graduate early or something, I think."

That has Simon raising his eyebrows in surprise. "And she's making time for you?"

"Fuck off," I tell him again, this time more good-naturedly. This is more normal for us, so I tag on my standard response. "I'm awesome."

Simon chuckles, placing his things inside his door. "Seriously, though," he says before I can disappear into my room. "As awesome as you are, be careful. She seems …" He trails off, his brows drawing down like he can't quite come up with the right end to that sentence.

I lean into my bedroom door and set my things on the desk, then prop my shoulder against the wall and wait for Simon to figure out what he's trying to say. But instead, he just shakes his head. "Just be careful, man. That's all I'm saying."

I give him a mocking salute. "Sir, yes, sir."

He flips me off.

Laughing, I head into my room and close the door.

But my space feels different now, which is why I was studying in the living room. The scent of sex lingers in the air, and all I can think about is the way Piper looked spread on my bed, the way she felt all tight and clenching around my cock, the way she cried out my name as she came again and again.

Yeah, maybe I did go after her to get to her brother. But no amount of warning from Simon could keep me away now.

CHAPTER EIGHTEEN

Piper

I force myself not to text Cal until after I turn my paper in on Wednesday afternoon.

But his patience runs out before mine. When I get out of class, there's a text from him waiting on my phone.

Cal: Told you I'd text if you didn't text me first. Do I need to come find you?

An irresistible smile pulls at my lips and a lick of heat races down my spine as I walk out of the classroom, stepping out of the flow of traffic to text him back.

Me: Maybe. What would you do if you did?

"Bring you hot chocolate," says a familiar voice behind me.

Whipping around, there's Cal sitting in a cluster of chairs in an alcove, a cup from the campus coffee shop in each hand. He stands, that self-satisfied smirk on his face that drives me crazy. How does a guy manage to look so arrogant and so sexy at the same time? I can never decide if I want to slap him or kiss him when he smirks at me like that. He steps away from the chairs, his dark gray joggers clinging to his thighs, and I have to swallow not to picture him naked. I know what he looks like naked now, so it isn't hard to imagine the way his muscles move beneath his skin with such athletic grace.

This is why I made myself wait. I knew that if I made any sort of contact, he'd try to see me. And if he tried to see me, he'd succeed, and we'd end up naked and sweaty somewhere. Which would mean scrambling to finish my paper. And I needed to finish my paper.

This boy is dangerous for my grades, and therefore dangerous for my sanity.

If I let him distract me, I'll be lucky to catch up and graduate on time, much less graduate early like I'm planning. I'm still trying to convince my parents to let me take summer classes. My scholarships only cover the two main terms. And I was lucky enough to get those, given how I left SCU. But since my parents managed to smooth everything over and the university allowed me to withdraw and transfer instead of officially disciplining and expelling me, I was able to get the scholarships I would've qualified for had I gone to Marycliff as a freshman. We just said that I'd had to withdraw due to "personal issues," which is code for anything from severe mental health problems to being the victim of a crime.

The latter case is true. Even if that crime wasn't prosecuted.

Much as I'd like to forget any of that ever happened, the reality of where I am now makes that impossible. And no matter how much fun sex with Cal might be, I need to stay focused so I can eventually move away (again) and move on.

I accept the hot chocolate with a smile, trying to seem as normal as possible. "The hot chocolate you offered to buy me."

He taps his cup against mine. "I'm nothing if not persistent."

"That you are," I say with a chuckle before sipping the rich beverage. The coffee shop here does make good hot chocolate.

He steps back to his chair and lifts his backpack, easily tossing it over one shoulder. "Where are you off to now?"

"The library."

"What an exciting life you lead, Piper." Smiling, he gestures for me to lead the way, falling in step next to me, his hand brushing mine for a second before he hooks his pinky in mine.

When I glance up at him, he gives my little finger a

squeeze.

"What about you?" I ask, wondering if he intends to just sit in the library and watch me study. "What do you have next?"

"Practice in an hour. So I'm all yours for the next forty-five minutes."

Another wave of heat washes over me. "All mine, huh?"

The look he shoots me is incendiary. "Mmhmm. All yours."

I swallow down the words riding the lust flowing through my body. *Let's go back to my room* is trying to claw its way out of my mouth. But I shouldn't. My plan was to go to the library and text Cal from there, assuming we'd get together tonight. For dinner. Or after dinner. Not now.

"I have to study," I say, my voice hoarse. "I have a test tomorrow and another paper due on Monday. I need to find sources."

"Okay," he says amiably, like he wasn't just trying to melt my clothes off with his eyeballs. "I'll help."

I let out a laugh, bracing myself for the gloomy cold as we head out the door. "You'll help?"

He throws me another grin, just as heated as the last one. "I can be *very* helpful."

I'm not sure how he makes offering to help me find sources for a paper into a double entendre, but he absolutely does.

At a loss for how to respond, I make a noncommittal

hum as I swallow more of the hot chocolate. Something about the gesture is unbearably sweet. Sweeter than the hot chocolate itself.

And more than anything, that feels dangerous.

* * *

Cal claims a table for us, surprising me by pulling out his own laptop and books, for all the world looking like he's going to study as well.

He returns my surprised look with a bland expression. "What? You thought all I did was play football and stalk you to give you hot chocolate?" He gives a derisive snort. "I told you I'm pre-med. I have homework too, thank you very much."

I hold up my hands in a gesture of surrender, fighting a grin. He doesn't bother holding back his own, though, his gaze heavy as he watches me get out my own laptop and notebook so I can write down the call numbers of the books most likely to have information I need.

Eventually, though, I glance up to find him engrossed in his work, and I finally relax enough to concentrate on mine.

All he does is glance up at me as I come and go from our table, assembling a stack of books that I want to look through to see if they have enough useful information to be worth checking out, or if it's easier to just snap pics of the important paragraphs to reference later and write down the bibliographic citation in case it actually makes it into my paper.

But the next time I get up, Cal stands too, making a big show of stretching. I give him a quizzical glance, but don't wait to figure out what he's up to. I have limited amounts of time and a lot to accomplish. I don't need the distraction of Cal's sweatshirt riding up and showing off the band of his boxer briefs, a strip of skin, and the treasure trail that I know leads to a delicious destination.

Nope nope nope. Definitely don't need that distraction.

But Cal follows me, catches up, tangles his fingers in mine, and tugs me away from the shelf I was headed toward. "What are you doing?" I hiss at him as he pulls me off to the south side of the building, away from the windows and the stairs and the central traffic area, as far back and away as we can get, back to the farthest corner. He spins me in front of him, his mouth sealing over mine, and he presses me back into the corner. At my gasp, his tongue sweeps into my mouth, stealing any objection I may have tried to voice.

Because as much as I absolutely *should* object for all the reasons already stated, I can't bring myself to. I want his tongue in my mouth, his body pressed to mine, his already hard dick digging into my belly as his hands grip my ass and hoist me up so we're lined up better.

He drags his mouth away from mine to draw a line of searing kisses over my jaw and down my neck. "Fucking hell, Piper," he whispers into my skin. "You're such a fucking tease."

I gasp, partly from his words, and partly from the nip of his teeth on my collarbone. He immediately soothes the sting with his hot tongue. "Am not," I manage weakly.

He chuckles, the sound dark and almost ominous. "The fuck you aren't. Wiggling this tight little ass in front of me as you go back and forth, back and forth, getting books, bending over and giving me the briefest glimpse of your tits down your shirt as you set the books down, your ass swaying away from me again a second later." He kisses me hard and fast. "Fucking tease."

His tongue fills my mouth again, and even though I only want to surrender to his kiss, I struggle against him and push him away, my brows pulled together. "I told you I needed sources for a paper," I start to protest, but the words die on my lips as soon as I see his smirk.

"You did, yes. Doesn't fucking matter. I've wanted you since you left my bed the other night. I couldn't wait until after practice tonight to see you again, so I came to find you, and you're making me watch you in the library. You're the fucking worst, Piper."

As he complains, it dawns on me that he's enjoying this, the teasing, as he calls it, the challenge. The chase. Yes, he's caught me already, but I'm still not making it easy on him. And it flashes through my brain that maybe I should, maybe I should just capitulate quickly, make it so I'm not a challenge, the chase is over, and he's won. Then he'd get bored faster, and I could go back to my normal schedule, the distraction resolved.

But I can't. Much as the sensible part of me screams at

me to give in, take him to my room, have an afternoon quickie and study later, I just can't.

This is too much fun.

"Oh?" I put all the coy innocence I can manage into my voice. "Is it *hard* for you to watch me study?"

He rocks his hips, grinding his dick into me, making me gasp. "Yes, Piper. Yes, it's fucking *hard*." He rocks his hips again, and the feeling that rockets through me is more than just arousal. It's triumph. Elation that I reduce this big, cocky athlete—the guy who was, apparently, king of the campus before this year, the guy who can get any chick he wants—to this. To begging. To complaining that I'm a tease. To pulling me into dark corners of the library to make out and dry hump against the wall.

"What are you going to do about it?" he demands.

I let out a shocked laugh. "What am *I* going to do about it? I fail to see how this"—I reach between us and give him a firm squeeze, making him groan—"is my problem."

"You're the reason I'm like this," he mutters, his lips on my neck. "It's your fault. You should take care of it."

I hum thoughtfully, like I'm considering it. I'm not, though. No way. We're not having sex in the library, out-of-the-way corner or no. "And what do you propose I do about it?"

"You could give me a blow job." The words are clear as day, whispered directly into my ear, then he sucks my earlobe between his lips, making me shiver when he scrapes his teeth over it.

But I'm already shaking my head, no more teasing in my tone. "No, Cal. No. I'm not doing that."

He pulls back, surprise on his face, the haze of lust still there, but fading to the background as he examines me. "Really? We won't get caught. I promise."

I refuse to look to closely at the fact that his confidence is likely from experience with back corner library blow jobs and shake my head again. "Really. I can't …" I just shake my head once more. I don't want to get into why I'm too terrified to break the rules, even if the idea of giving him head here feels deliciously illicit. I can't risk another disciplinary action. Even if the university wouldn't expel me for getting caught going down on a guy in the library, my parents would for sure make me move back home. Maybe take back my car. Keep me on an even tighter leash. It's not worth the risk.

He eases back, concern pulling his brows together. Then he tips my chin up with his fingers and brushes his lips over mine, the kiss tender and light. "Okay," he whispers, followed by another peck. Then he puts space between us, standing with his hands on his hips, an obvious tent in his pants that makes me grin.

His eyes flash, a potent combination of lust and danger. "You owe me, though."

I let out an incredulous laugh, straightening my shirt and running my fingers through my hair. "Oh, I do, do I?"

He nods, that cocky smirk in place. "Sending me to practice rock hard with blue balls? Yeah, babe, you owe me."

At my arched eyebrow, he chuckles, then reaches for me, pulling me close and wrapping his arms around me. "How about this. I'll text you after practice, and we can finish what we started."

"Alright," I whisper into his chest. "I think I can handle that."

CHAPTER NINETEEN

My ears perk up when I hear Kilpatrick's voice saying, "Hey, monkey butt. What are you up to tonight?" The juxtaposition of the insulting term with the clear affection in his voice has me stopping in my tracks, holding onto the towel wrapped around my hips as I make my way from the showers to my locker to get ready to meet Piper.

I don't normally hear Kilpatrick call anyone names, though, so I can't help wondering who he's talking to.

Taking the long way back to my locker, I find him holding a phone to his ear. When he sees me watching him, his amiable expression turns into a scowl. Returning his scowl with one of my own, I nod at Martinez and Johnson and then slide onto the bench next to Simon, who's already tying his shoes and ready to head out.

He jerks his chin at me. "What are you doing tonight?"

I give him the same scowl I gave Kilpatrick. "Trying to see if you get the house to yourself?"

He chuckles, finishing with his shoes and standing. "Just wondering if you want to grab dinner."

Standing as well, I pull up my underwear and reach for my joggers. "You don't have plans with Ellie?"

"Sure. But you could join us for dinner if you want."

"Because there's nothing I love more than being the third wheel with my sister and best friend," I deadpan. "No thanks."

Simon just shrugs and pulls on his sweatshirt. "Suit yourself. Does that mean you're not coming home?"

Shaking my head, I finish pulling on a T-shirt, followed by my own sweatshirt. "Nah. I'm meeting someone."

Simon looks all around the room, then leans in close, his voice low. "You getting together with Piper again?"

"So what if I am?" I avoid his gaze as I say it, gathering my things, but when I meet his eyes, I don't see the judgment I expect. It's something more like concern mixed with a question. "You gotta problem with that?" I push, knowing I sound like a dick, but I can't help it. He's pulling the protective older brother routine as if he even knows Piper beyond seeing her around a few times, and it grates on me. Especially given that he *knows* I'm an actual protective older brother where my sister is concerned and he didn't let that stop him. Why should his misplaced vigilance about someone else's sister stop me?

He just holds up his hands, taking a step back. "Nope. If you really like her, then you should keep seeing her. Do what you think is best and all that."

I snort. "Thanks, Dad. I appreciate the permission with a side of backhanded guilt."

He shrugs off my sarcasm, and we head out together, Kilpatrick largely forgotten as I pull out my phone and find a text from Piper.

Piper: The room is mine for a few hours. Come over as soon as you're done. Text me when you're on your way, and I'll meet you at the door.

Simon's snort makes me aware that I'm not alone. Not yet. He glances at my phone, then up at my face. "You two kids have fun."

"Alright, Grampa," I shoot back. "We will."

All I get is a laugh as Simon heads toward the parking lot, while I turn in the opposite direction and start for the dorm. Grinning, anticipation thrumming through my blood, I text Piper back.

Me: On my way.

* * *

I walk to Piper's dorm with my hands in my pockets to disguise the semi I'm sporting just from thinking about her. From remembering how she felt the other night, the way she was grinding on me in the library earlier, what it'll feel like when she has those pretty lips wrapped around my cock.

After Ellie's untimely interruption the other night and Piper's insistence that she needed to leave, we didn't have time to get to that particular activity, but I fully intend to tonight.

My dick thickens and lengthens just thinking about it, and I adjust myself as I go, uncaring who might see.

She meets me at the door as promised, pushing it open and letting me inside, but she's surprisingly not alone. Another chick is with her, dressed in a shapeless sweatshirt, her hair pulled back into a ponytail. She looks familiar …

When she jerks her chin up in the same way guys nod at each other, it clicks. She hangs out with Foster a lot.

"Dani, right?" I say, returning her nod.

She gives me a cheeky grin. "Yup. Hey."

"Dani's my roommate," Piper interjects. "She was just keeping me company while I waited."

"Sounds like a good friend." I don't want to be a dick, but I also don't want to stand in the tiny lobby of their dorm talking to Piper's roommate.

Dani seems to get the idea, though, because she flashes me another grin before turning it on Piper, this one knowing, her eyebrows waggling in corny amusement. "Well, I won't keep you crazy kids any longer. I'll check in when I'm ready to come home if I haven't heard from you first." She fishes her keys out of her kangaroo pocket. "Our girl's got homework, so don't jeopardize all her time," is her parting shot to me before she waltzes out the door.

"You have an assortment of guard dogs, don't you?" I say to Piper as she leads the way to the stairs.

She casts a glance over her shoulder, a confused smile on her face. "What are you talking about?"

I gesture behind me. "Your roommate. *My* roommate. I'm assuming your brother, too."

Scoffing, she shakes her head. "Don't mind Dani. She's harmless. Well, I mean, she's actually really strong. But I've never seen her try to hurt anyone before. She's actually pro-whatever this is."

I wrap an arm around Piper's waist and crowd her against the wall, my back to her front, grinding my hard dick against her perky little ass, thoughts of anything besides getting her naked again falling away. "Whatever this is between us? I'd say it's something worth exploring, wouldn't you?"

Her breath comes faster, her cheeks turning pink as she glances up and down the stairs, looking for anyone coming from above or below. But then she pushes her ass back against me, and I have to bite back a groan so it doesn't echo up and down the stairwell.

"Definitely," she answers, one hand clutching the arm

wrapped around her waist, the other propping her up against the wall. "I thought that's what we were doing, after all."

"I dunno, Piper. You seem to keep trying to push me away. To put up roadblocks. Sometimes I wonder what exactly you want." The chase was fun at first, but I want her to admit that she wants me. That she feels something like what I'm feeling—a desire for more. More time together, especially if we can both be naked, but studying in the library with her was surprisingly enjoyable. I got through a lot of my own homework, I got some eye candy while I worked, and we dry humped in the stacks. Sure, I was hoping for a blowie, but semipublic sex acts seem to be a no-go for her. Which is mildly disappointing, because there's a special thrill from having a chick go down on me in the library, the illicit juxtaposition of serious and sexy making me get off even faster, but nowhere near a deal-breaker.

Her glazed brown eyes meet mine. "This really where you want to have this conversation? Right here, right now?"

With a rumble in my chest, I back away enough that she can pull away from the wall, but I don't relinquish my hold on her. "How far is your room?"

She gestures up. "Third floor. Not far from the staircase."

I swat her ass. "Let's go, then."

The look she gives me is pure spite. Then she climbs the stairs even slower than before, putting an extra sway in her hips with each step.

This time I don't hold back my groan, and there's no mistaking the evil grin curving her lips as she gets a few steps above me, where her profile is almost—but not quite—hidden by the distance. She wants to give me a show? Fine. I *love* shows. Especially sexy ones put on by girls for the express purpose of turning me on.

Taking my sweet time, I follow her up the stairs, enjoying every fucking step, my eyes glued to her ass, completely unaware if anyone else passes us.

When we finally reach her floor, she pushes the door open and holds it for me. Rather than taking the last few steps two at a time like I want to, I maintain my leisurely pace. Two can play this game.

But when I reach her, I yank her against me with one hand, the other tangling in her hair and pulling her head back so I can give her a punishing kiss.

It's quick and hard, and she gives as good as she gets, all teeth clashing, tongues tangling, hands gripping. I fucking love it. My cock jumps, straining to bury itself inside her. Somewhere. Anywhere.

"Where's your room?" I pant when I rip my mouth from hers.

"That way." She gestures weakly behind me, and I break away, letting her pass me to lead the way. This time I don't let her put distance between us. Or slow walk us the last few feet.

This time I wrap my arm around her, cinch her to my side, and speed walk us closer to our destination.

When she tries to slow us down, I growl.

But she just laughs. "Cal, stop. This is my door. We passed it."

I release my breath in a huff and let her go, following her back two doors, leaning against the wall as she unlocks the door and pushes it open. Once we're both inside, I flip the deadbolt and strip off my sweatshirt.

She looks at me, eyes wide, her tongue darting out to swipe over her lips. "Oh, we're getting right to it, I see."

"Is that a problem?" I grip the hem of my T-shirt and pull it up, not all the way, just enough to give her a peek at my abs.

She blinks a few times, seeming unable to decide whether to look at my face or my stomach. Eventually my stomach wins, and she steps closer, her hands reaching for my waist, pushing my shirt up more. Grinning, I oblige and pull the shirt off entirely, dropping it on top of my sweatshirt.

After toeing off my shoes, I step into her touch, loving her hands running up and down my torso, exploring in ways she didn't on Monday night. Much as I'm enjoying it, I want to enjoy her as well.

She makes a soft sound of annoyance when I start tugging her top up, because she has to stop touching me long enough for me to get it off. But her hands immediately go back to my sides, and mine fall to her tits, plumped and pretty in a light pink cotton bra. It's not the sexy lacy thing she wore for me Monday night, and while I appreciate nice lingerie, it's what's inside the package that matters more than the wrapping for me.

I give her tits a gentle squeeze, dipping the fingers of one hand inside the cup to find her nipple already hard and waiting for me. Her breath hisses through her teeth as I squeeze it between my fingers, rolling it around, and I smile at her responsiveness.

But I'm impatient, or I've just been waiting too damn long, and she's made no effort to explore below my waistband.

Still rolling her nipple between my fingers, I flatten my other hand over hers, stilling it, then drag it down, down, down until her fingers curl around my aching cock.

"That's better," I mutter as she strokes me through my clothes. And it is. Better. But it's still not fucking enough.

"I want you to suck me," I whisper, dragging my thumb across her lips. "I want to see these pretty lips wrapped around my cock. Will you do that for me?"

She inhales sharply, her eyes dragging up to mine. She starts to nod, but then stops, the lust clearing from her gaze for a moment, her hand stilling on my dick. I thrust against it almost involuntarily.

"What's wrong?"

She shakes her head. "Where's your phone?"

I wrinkle my brows at the non-sequitur, but drop my hand from her face, reach into my pants pocket, and pull out my phone.

She takes it from my hand and steps back, forcing me to let go of her nipple as she releases my cock. Turning it over in her hand, she finds the power button and presses down on it until the thing turns off, tosses it on the pile of clothes at my feet, then grabs my hand and pulls me into her bedroom.

I don't even have time to wonder what just happened, much less formulate an actual question, before she's dragging my pants down to my knees, her hand stroking my cock, her hot breath fanning over the head.

"Are you watching?" she asks, gazing up at me through heavy-lidded eyes. "You ready?"

"Take your tits out." It comes out as a command instead of a request, and with the way she's been acting today, I'm not sure if she'll do it, or if she'll put on a parka just to be contrary.

But she does what I ask, pulling them out to sit on top of the cups, propped up like an offering for me, creamy and round and tipped with those perfect pink nipples. Maybe she's in as much of a rush as I am. Maybe she just didn't want to relinquish her hold on my dick yet. Whatever her reason for doing that rather than just taking off her bra, I don't fucking care. This chick is absolutely perfect.

Made more so when she lifts my dick and gives a long, slow swipe of her tongue from base to tip, swirls her tongue over the crown, and closes her lips around it.

"Fuuuuck," I grind out, my glutes tightening with the desire to thrust farther into her mouth.

She plays with my slit with the tip of her tongue, giving another swirl and a hard suck as she dives down my length.

"Jesus Christ." I force myself to hold still and let her work me over. Some chicks like it rough, like it when I hold their heads and fuck their mouths, but I don't know Piper well enough to try that without asking. And she seems pretty happy with the way things are going, and I'm not about to do anything that might ruin it. So I do nothing but force my legs to hold me up, wishing I had something to hang onto, to sag against, because her hot little mouth working me over, her tits sitting there like an offering for me, the way she looks up and makes eye contact every so often—it's enough to take me to the brink. Make me weak. And I wouldn't have it any other way.

As her head bobs, pausing to suck and work my cockhead with her tongue every so often, she continues to explore me with her hands, caressing my thighs, cupping my balls, one intrepid finger stroking my taint.

My balls draw up tight when she does that, and I try to pull away. But she follows me.

"Piper." I breathe her name like a curse. "Fuck, babe. You're so fucking hot. Your mouth is amazing, but I need to feast on your pussy now."

Those seem to be the magic words, because in a flash, my dick is wet and cold in the open air, and she's yanking her pants off and crawling onto her bed, legs open and waiting for me.

With a wolfish grin on my face, I kick my pants the rest of the way off and go to make good on my promise.

CHAPTER TWENTY

I don't know what it is about him that has me acting like this—brazen, wanton, shameless. Climbing on my bed and spreading my legs as wide as I can, waiting for him to, as he so eloquently put it, feast on my pussy.

After the way he wrung that earth shattering orgasm out of me two nights ago? I'd be stupid to turn down a repeat performance.

Thank fucking Christ that he doesn't bother with the teasing and making me tell him what I want this time around. No, this time he simply gathers my thighs in his arms, his biceps flexing as he yanks me close, his fingers digging into the insides of my thighs, and he buries his mouth in my aching cunt.

He even has me thinking differently. His tongue and his dick and his words have apparently rearranged my brain. I've always found the word cunt distasteful. Vulgar. But with him? It feels decadent and fitting.

His groan vibrates through me, and I arch against him, riding his face as he spears me with his tongue then sucks on my clit.

He's not taking his time anymore. No, he's eating me like a starving man. No tender ramp-up. No slow build. Just ferocious, almost angry, *feasting*. There's really no other word for it.

It's amazing and terrifying, and I'm barreling toward my orgasm so fast I don't know what'll happen to me when I reach it.

Then the fingers of one hand release me, while the others seem to grip me harder. Suddenly his fingers lance inside of me in one hard stroke, his hand turning so he can stroke deep inside me.

"Let me feel you come," he growls against my clit. "Let me suck all the pleasure out of you. Give it to me, Piper. Let me have it." Then he sucks my clit deep, his fingers pistoning and rubbing and working me hard.

And I explode in a wave of heat and light and pleasure, all my breath forced out in a scream.

"Fuck yeah," he mutters. I hear him tear open a condom package before arranging my legs, hooking an arm under one knee, and then his cock enters me in one hard thrust. "Fuck. Yeah," he repeats, each word punctuated by his cock drilling into me. "That's my girl. Coming hard all over my face." His eyes meet mine, practically navy blue. "You got another one for me? You gonna come all over my cock?"

All I can do is moan in response, and he gives me a feral grin. "If not now, then later for sure. We're exploring, right, Piper? We're fucking exploring until your roommate's ready to come home. I want to explore all the ways I can make you come. All the ways I can make you scream. You like the sound of that? Because I fucking do." He pounds into me harder the longer he talks, and I don't think I am going to come again. Not right now anyway. And that's fine with me, especially since I apparently have hours of orgasms ahead of me.

And right now, I can't say I have any complaints.

* * *

Sometime later, after fucking me into oblivion, stroking my body and making me come with his fingers while he recuperated, then going for round two that lasted longer than I thought possible, I'm lying mostly on top of Cal in my twin bed, one of my legs tangled between his, my face on one of his pecs as he rubs the base of my head, down my neck, and over my shoulders.

It's almost hypnotizing in its consistency.

He lets out a low rumble, the sound vibrating under my ear. "Fucking finally," he mutters.

"What's that?" I ask in a drowsy voice.

"You're finally relaxed. All it took was four orgasms plus a twenty minute massage."

I start to lift my head, but his hand gently presses my face back to his chest. "That wasn't an invitation to get tense again," he murmurs, and I chuckle against his skin, his flat nipple perking up as my breath blows across it.

"What are you doing next week?" he asks after several moments of him stroking down my spine.

"Hmm?" I mumble sleepily, trying to get my brain in gear. We should figure out food soon. I'm getting hungry. But I'm so satisfied and boneless and relaxed that thinking about anything sounds like too much trouble. How'm I supposed to know what I'm doing next week if I can't even figure out what to do about dinner?

He lets out a soft chuckle. "Next week is Thanksgiving. Are you going to be in town?"

"Oh. Right. Yeah. Since the dorms are closed, I'll be staying at my parents'." Not my ideal way of spending the week off, but it's not like I have any better options. Besides, everyone else will be gone anyway. It'll be a good opportunity to show my dedication to school and that I'm able to keep up with my punishing class load by finishing up my last projects and papers that'll be due the week before finals, plus get a jump on studying for finals.

At least Gray will be around for part of the time. He pulls some of the focus off me, high achiever that he is. Mom and Dad prefer to focus on their perfect child when they can to distract from the disappointment I've become.

Story of my life, really. Gray was always the one who

did everything right—good grades, star athlete, prom king, the whole nine.

Growing up in that shadow didn't leave me a lot of room to shine, so I mostly didn't bother to try. He already excelled at everything. What was left for me?

So I did enough to get by and spent my free time with my friends. Not that any of it was Gray's fault. He didn't try to outshine me at every opportunity. He encouraged me to do things I like and excel at my own pursuits. He never tried to get me to follow in his footsteps. He didn't care if I didn't study hard or go out for athletics. But I had to do something to look good on college applications, and one of my friends decided to go out for debate. So I joined her, and then my junior year, I ran for class president. I won student body vice president my senior year, and that combination of debate and student government experience landed me my sweet scholarship to SCU. My ticket out.

College was supposed to be my chance to do something different. Be my own person, out of the long shadow cast by Gray that plagued me through high school even after he left. I was still Gray's little sister, after all, even after he'd graduated and gone to Ohio. All the teachers knew him more than me, and while they treated me fine as long as I didn't buck their perception of how I should be too much, not being like him was still a surprise for many people. He was beloved, after all. Who wouldn't want to be like him?

But I was going to California, where no one knew him.

Or if they did, it was as a member of a rival football team, and no one made the connection between him and me unless I made it for them. And that suited me just fine.

And then Brent happened.

And here I am. Back in Spokane. Back in Gray's shadow, only worse this time. This time my parents are even more concerned. Because this time, I've got a serious strike against me, which means an even bigger hole to dig out of.

Cal's voice under my ear brings me out of my reverie. "I'll be in town too. For the first part. Simon—my roommate—his parents are having us over for an early Thanksgiving on Wednesday because we have an away game on Friday." He pauses, his hand making another pass down my spine. "We could hang out some. Before I have to leave. If you want."

My breath leaves me in a combination of sigh and … I'm not sure what feeling. "That … yeah. We could do that." It's maybe not the greatest idea, to be honest. It's one thing to fool around here and there when no one needs to know where I am or who I'm with. I mean, Dani knows, but she doesn't care. As long as I'm having fun, she's happy for me.

But explaining who I'm with to my parents? To Gray?

That might be an issue.

Cal's hand stills on my back. "We don't have to," he says, displaying an uncharacteristic amount of insecurity. Normally he'd try to boss me around or offer some stupid bet to get me to agree to it. But instead, my hesitation has him backing off.

"No. I want to," I reassure him quickly. "It's just … my parents will have questions."

"And?" His voice is lighter, amused. "Can you not tell them the truth?"

I push up to sitting, and this time he lets me, his eyes straying to my naked tits for a second before coming back to my face. And I can't suppress my smile, grateful for the distraction. "You really haven't gotten enough yet?"

His mouth hitches up in that familiar cocky smirk. And suddenly things are back on their normal footing. His eyes flick toward his crotch, where his dick is already growing. "What do you think?"

My laugh is equal parts incredulous and happy. "I think you're almost ready for round three."

He pushes himself up so he's sitting against the wall, then reaches for me and drags me into his lap. "And what about you?" he asks, his hands roaming my skin. "You up for round three? Or would you prefer to suck me off and let me come on your tits."

"Are those my only options?" I ask with a coy smile.

He lifts one shoulder in a shrug, his grin growing wider. "I mean, I'm open to suggestions, but those are my top two."

His hands on my hips drag me slowly back and forth on his now fully-hard cock, the head bumping my clit each time.

"Not so rough this time," I whisper, my head falling back between my shoulders. "Be gentle."

Leaning forward, he captures one of my nipples in his mouth, laving it slowly with his tongue, sucking lightly, a sharp contrast to the way he usually sucks my tits. He normally sucks hard and deep, biting down enough to lend an edge of pain to my pleasure. But not this time—as though he's using this opportunity to show just how gentle he can be.

He moves to my other nipple, giving it equal treatment, his hands sliding to my ass, spreading my cheeks apart, his fingers brushing lower until he can dip one fingertip into my cunt, circling my opening slowly, never actually penetrating.

Somehow that makes me ache even more.

I let out a low moan of distress, grinding on his dick harder, trying to jerk my hips back to plunge his finger inside me.

But his hands prevent me from moving enough to do that, and he lifts his head, his cocky grin wiped from his face. "You ready for me, baby? You ride me, then you can set the pace, alright?"

At my nod, he leans down and grabs another condom from the strip he brought with him. When I first saw it, I figured he'd probably overestimated his stamina, and now I think he might've overestimated mine.

I scoot back on his thighs, freeing his cock so he can roll on the condom, but he surprises me by reaching between my legs first, his finger circling my opening again before slipping inside me, drawing out and spreading my wetness all around. He does it again and again until I'm grinding on his hand, and when he pulls away at last, he rubs my juices all over his cockhead, then rolls the condom on. "We want to be all nice and juicy if we're taking it slow and easy this time," he whispers.

Then his hands are on my hips again, and he's pulling me forward, sealing his lips to mine. I rise up, and he drags the head of his cock all over my slippery cunt until the head notches in my opening. With matching groans, I slide down his length, slow, slow, so slow. Agonizingly slow as he stretches my already aching tissues yet again.

It's sharp and sweet and almost unbearable, and I'm glad that I'm in control right now. I pause when I'm fully impaled, sucking his tongue, gripping his neck, enjoying the way his hands still roam my body. He's touched me literally everywhere today, and he still can't stop touching me.

I've never had a guy seem this crazy over me before. Sure, I've had chemistry where it felt like we couldn't get enough of each other, but it wasn't like this, where we've been naked and touching for literal hours today and each touch still feels like we're covering uncharted territory. Like he's starving for my skin.

Not just sex. Not just skin. But *my* skin. Sex with *me*, specifically.

Having this effect on someone is heady and intoxicating, and it's almost enough to make me lose sight of what's important.

Almost.

Because as delicious as this is, it can't last. There's no

way. Something this intense has to burn out quickly.

And despite asking to see me again, I'm under no illusion that this is some kind of serious thing for Cal. This is casual. We have crazy chemistry. We both get some stress relief out of it. So I might as well have fun.

And as nuts as it sounds, after Monday night, I was able to focus better after I got home, and writing my paper yesterday was a breeze.

So if some recreational sex makes studying easier, I'd be stupid to turn it down.

"You think too much," Cal mutters against my lips. "It's not time to think right now." One of those big hands slides down my spine, kneading my ass. "It's time to feel."

He thrusts up into me, slow and easy, and I roll my hips in response.

He's right. I do think too much. Especially the last few months.

That's why being with him is so nice. I don't have to think so hard. I just have to do and be and feel.

When my orgasm hits, it's the lapping of a gentle wave, rather than the overwhelming surge of a tsunami. And I'm grateful for the lessened intensity, especially since Cal's not there yet, though I can tell he's getting close.

Despite his promises to be gentle, his thrusts get harder, faster, even from below, and his grip on my hips turns almost harsh.

But I don't care anymore. I want to watch him find his

release, knowing he got that pleasure from my body. That I'm the one with this power over him. Maybe not forever, but for now.

And right now, that's enough.

CHAPTER TWENTY-ONE

Cal

I'm not used to this antsy feeling creeping over me on Sunday night. It's been days since I've been inside Piper, not since Wednesday's marathon in her dorm room, and I'm getting withdrawals or something. I can't remember ever feeling this way about a girl before. It's more than just general horniness, because my desire is specifically for Piper. No one else holds any appeal. And I kinda resent the fact that I haven't seen her in four days, because apparently Thursdays are always out, and it's not like I can change my football schedule.

I'm home—somewhat recuperated—and Ellie sleeping over with Simon for the week certainly doesn't help my mood. I mean, I can't blame Ellie, really. Or Simon. They want to be together. I get it. But it only serves to highlight that I can't see Piper as often as I want to. And that would be every damn day if I could make it happen. Hell, if I could have her stay over, I would. But I know better than to ask. She's made it clear that she wants to keep me at arm's length, even if that drives me fucking crazy. Plus, it's ridiculous to be this hung up on her already given we've only been on one actual date.

Which is fine. I mean, it's not. But it's fine. We'll get there. Hopefully. Maybe.

Or not.

But having Ellie all up in my space nonstop making googly eyes at my roommate, and what's worse, him doing the same thing back? I need to get away from here. And it's only day one. I'm not sure how I'm going to make it until this weekend when we'll be in Colorado. Of course that'll put me back in this same place of feeling antsy without Piper.

It's a no-win situation.

At least there are still practices and workouts the rest of the week to provide some distraction. And Trey and Brandy are hosting a team Friendsgiving on Tuesday night. Ellie will come with Simon, of course.

I wonder if Piper's been invited?

She normally comes to team events, and she's in town. But I'm not sure if her brother or her roommate invites her.

I've been waiting to reach out to her, half hoping

she'd contact me first. She hasn't yet, and part of me really wants her to. Wants to know that she's as into this as I am. She dodged the question entirely last week, saying the stairway wasn't the place for the conversation. And by the time we got to her room, I was too distracted by giving her orgasms to remember to ask again.

When we're together, it seems like she is. But maybe she can take or leave the sex. Whereas I'm addicted to it. Addicted to *her*. Because it's never been like this with anyone else. I made the conscious decision not to get involved in serious relationships a couple years ago when I decided that I was going to try to go pro. Relationships take time, and when things get shitty, as they almost always do, it's a distraction I don't need.

I still feel that way, to be honest. Which is why I'm not trying to have a serious relationship with Piper.

I just like spending time with her. And the way she feels wrapped around me. The way she sighs my name. The way she begs for me to pound into her harder, faster, more.

Aaaand now my dick is getting hard. While my roommate and my little sister snuggle on the other end of the couch.

Gross.

Standing, I shove my hand in the pocket of my sweats and hold my dick off to the side so it's not leading the way.

Simon pauses the movie and throws me a questioning look.

I wiggle my phone in the air and gesture at the TV. "Keep going without me. I gotta take care of something."

He narrows his eyes, looking me up and down, but just nods. I don't even look at Ellie to see what her reaction is.

Once inside the safety of my room, I give my dick a squeeze and pull up my texts with Piper.

Fuck waiting for her to come to me. At this rate, that might take too long.

I thought I was clear last week that I'm not looking for anything serious. I thought we were on the same page at the time. But maybe that's the problem? Is she wanting more than I'm prepared to give?

Would I be willing to be her boyfriend to get at her brother? My plan was just to fool around with her long enough for him to notice and get pissed. And the fact that I actually like her is great. But … I'm not sure if I could even handle a relationship.

I know I look good on paper—pre-med, bio major, good family, star athlete, blah blah blah. But I see the way Simon is with Ellie. He goes out of his way to do things that he knows make her happy. Sappy shit that makes me want to gag, largely because my sister is the recipient, but I think I'd feel that way even if he were dating some other random chick.

Dude's whipped.

He's happy, so whatever, but it's the truth.

Whatever. I'm not going to bring it up. If she wants more than sex from me, she can broach the subject. No need to add complications to something that should be simple and straightforward. And if that means I'm always the one texting her for a booty call, well, I guess that's the way it'll be.

And if she decides she's not interested anymore, well …

I just hope that doesn't happen anytime soon, because I'd be super bummed.

I mean, I'd get over it and find someone else. Or many someone elses. Eventually. But I'd be bummed for a while, too.

Me: Hey, babe. What are you doing tonight?

Hopefully the answer is me. And for some reason I expect her to answer right away. She has before, after all. But this time … I wait. And wait. And wait.

Disappointed and frustrated, I toss my phone on the bed next to me and lean back, lifting my hips to push my sweats and underwear out of the way and lifting my shirt high on my chest, letting out a sigh of relief when my cock is finally free.

Gripping myself at the base, I give myself a slow stroke. I'm not so much jacking off as just idly stroking my cock, hoping that Piper texts back before the urgency to come, to get some relief for my aching dick, becomes too much. I'd rather come *with* her rather than because of memories of her, but at this point, I'll take what I can get. And what I can get might just be my hand and the memory of her touching me, sucking me, fucking me.

The images flashing through my brain—memories of our times together here and in her room, fantasies of things I still want to do with her but haven't yet had a chance—are too much, and soon my dick is leaking precum, and I'm using it as lube, my hand shuttling faster, my hips lifting as I fuck my own fist, wishing it was her.

Biting back a low groan, my dick jerks in my hand as I come on my belly in thick spurts.

And then my phone rings. With a rueful chuckle, I reach for whatever's handy to clean myself up. But there's nothing, so I take off my shirt and use that as I answer Piper's call.

"Hey, babe. I was just thinking about you."

"Oh, yeah? Good things, I hope."

"*Very* good things." I put as much sex into my voice as I can so there's no mistaking my meaning.

"Oh." She sounds a little breathless now, and the grin on my face stretches wider as I ball up my shirt and toss it in my laundry hamper. "Wow. Um, okay. Thanks?"

I puff out a laugh and pull my pants back up. No need to have my dick hanging out right now. "You're welcome. What are you up to? You busy?"

She hums thoughtfully, and my brows wrinkle together in consternation. That doesn't sound like a good sign. "Depends on your definition of busy," she says at last.

Blowing out a breath, I stand with one hand on my hip, letting my head drop back between my shoulders.

Why is everything with this chick a battle of wits? And a battle of wills? I just want to fuck and have fun. With her, specifically. Is that really so much to ask?

"I was wondering if you wanted to go somewhere and hang out. I'm stuck at home with my sister and my roommate until we leave on Thursday, and I need a break. I was hoping you'd be bored and looking for something to do too, but based on your answer, I'm gonna take that as a no. Call me if you want to hang out. Or don't. Whichever."

I really don't mean for my frustration at everything to leak out at Piper like that. I'm supposed to be all charm and seduction with her. That's my plan, right? Use her to get under her brother's skin enough to throw him off his game? Hopefully in practice so that Coach subs me in *before* the game even starts so our chances of making the playoffs don't get fucked up. Though if Kilpatrick gets so in his head that he screws up royally in a game and then Coach puts me in and I save the day, I wouldn't mind that either.

The sound of Piper's sigh stops me from ending the call immediately. The edges of the phone dig into my hand as I squeeze it, waiting.

"Look, Cal, it's not ..." She makes a sound of frustration that eases some of the tension in my body, and I almost smile. Almost. "It's not about you, okay? It's ... it's just not a good night for me to go anywhere."

"Don't tell me you're busy doing homework." I try, and mostly fail, to put a teasing edge into my voice.

But she chuckles softly anyway. "Would you believe me if I said I am?"

"Actually, I would." I sink down on the edge of my bed, rubbing my palm down my thigh. "I'm just not sure why you'd decide to do homework *now* when you have all week and over the weekend while I'm out of town to do it, and we could have some fun instead."

"Because I know what your idea of *fun* entails, and we can't do that here, and you already said your sister and roommate are home. Based on the last encounter I had with her at your house, I'm not sure you really want me there with them either."

I grunt, because that's a fair assessment. "We could just, I dunno, go see a movie or something. Wander around downtown and see what bars have good bands playing. Something. Anything. We don't even have to have sex." I hate sounding desperate, but the truth is, I am. Desperate to get away, desperate to spend time with her, even if I can't be inside her.

She lets out a sharp laugh. "Oh, we don't, do we? What happened to not wanting anything serious?"

I shrug, even though she can't see me. "Since when is going to a movie or bar hopping anything serious?"

Another noncommittal hum. "Good point, I suppose. And as tempting as that sounds—and believe me, it does—I'm still going to have to pass." Then, softer. "I'm sorry, Cal. I really am."

"It's alright," I answer, just as softly. Because what else am I supposed to say?

"I'll call you later," she promises, but I don't really believe her.

"Sounds good."

I stare at my phone in my hand for a stupid amount of time after we hang up, wondering how I got so hung up on a chick—any chick, but especially this one—that I offered to hang out without expecting to get any.

CHAPTER TWENTY-TWO

Piper

At nine o'clock on Monday morning, with my mother's far too cheerful face poking through my bedroom door, I can't decide if I'm grateful for my past self's wisdom in turning down Cal's invitation or regretting that I didn't have some fun when I had the chance.

"Rise and shine, my little Pipette!" Mom chirps at me.

Groaning, I wave a hand in her direction.

"Oh, don't be like that," she scolds, but still in that same chirpy, cheery voice. "It's already nine. Don't want to sleep the day away. And besides, if it were a normal week, wouldn't you be up by now anyway?"

"But it's not a normal week, Mom," I grumble. "It's a vacation. And I was up late working on my next paper."

"Well, don't work too hard," Mom says, like she and Dad didn't just tell me the other day that I need to be sure to commit myself to my studies, especially since I'm taking so many classes to try to catch up. It's a constant barrage of *try your hardest but don't work so hard, you'll make yourself sick.* And while I do believe they come at it from a place of genuine love and concern, the constant contradictions are exhausting. Like, I don't actually need to be reminded to work hard, thanks. And if you want me to work hard, why are you griping at me about getting a head start on my paper due early next week? And the project due the day after?

This semester is almost over, and I just have to keep my head above water for a little longer, and then it'll be finals, which honestly feels like a cakewalk after the second half of this semester, because it's one or two things a day for a few days and then I'm done. And then it's Christmas break, which I'm approaching with the same mix of relief and dread that I've been feeling about Thanksgiving break. Relief for the obvious reason that it's a break from classes and school, but dread because I'll be here, under my parents' watchful eye, waiting for me to fuck up again.

"I made waffles for breakfast," Mom says, backing out of the doorway. "Come and eat before they get cold." With that, she closes the door behind her, leaving me in blessed silence once again. At least until I hear her knocking on Gray's door across the hall. "Rise and shine!" comes through muffled, but clear enough.

At least I'm not the only one getting this treatment. Everything's more bearable when there's someone else suffering with you. I'm not exactly sure why Gray is here and not staying at his place, though I suspect it's to give me moral support, and I'm grateful for it.

Gray's always been like this. The shield.

I was the one with the wild ideas, cooking up harebrained schemes, and he was the voice of reason, getting me to maybe tone down the danger enough that none of us would get seriously injured or killed, and protecting me from trouble as much as he could. Claiming responsibility, or at least sharing in it, when we did get in trouble for the crazy ideas I came up with. Cleaning up my scrapes without telling Mom and Dad that time I almost fell out of the tree.

I'd climbed too high, then got scared when I looked down and saw how far down the ground was. In my fear, I grabbed a flimsy branch too hard, it broke, and I slid several feet down the tree before catching myself. Terrified, I clung to the tree until Gray climbed up after me, close enough that he could touch my leg, his calm voice guiding me down until we both reached the ground.

He helped me home and snuck inside to get Band-Aids and washcloths that he got wet from the backyard spigot, cleaning up the scrape on my cheek and my raw palms and forearms.

By the time we went in for dinner, Mom and Dad had just looked me over with a resigned sigh and asked if I was okay, then told Gray he needed to watch out for me.

"He did," I always insisted during these conversations. "He helped me. It was my fault I scraped my arm and my cheek."

"Well, be more careful."

And that about sums up our whole family dynamic. Do everything. Take risks. But be careful. And Gray, look out for your sister.

And the first time that Gray wasn't around to look out for me, I screwed up my life so bad that I got yanked back home and Gray transferred here to be the model big brother he's always been.

Which is … great.

But also stifling.

Because when do I get to just be me? Don't I get the chance to learn from my own mistakes? I have no intention of repeating what I went through with Brent. And while maybe Cal seems like him in some ways—the pretty, arrogant, douche vibe comes to mind—he's also nothing like Brent.

Cal has goals other than partying and smoking pot, though it's clear that he enjoys a good time, too. And after our conversation last night, I'm coming to realize that Cal likes spending time with me, and not just in the bedroom. He just wanted to hang out. And he could've called so many other people—most of the football team is still in town, for one thing—and instead he called me. And he's been meeting me with hot chocolate after at least one class a day since we went out.

Maybe our little bet that started everything off was a weird way to pursue a girl, but A, it worked, and B, it also shows that he was interested in *me* and not just any girl. In fact, I don't think I've seen him look at another girl since that first party where he escorted me to the cooler and I turned him down cold.

When he told me to call him if I wanted to hang out, or not, whichever, something in my heart shriveled. He sounded so … dejected. And sad. It made me want to tell him I'd meet him at his place in twenty. Except …

I know how my parents would act if I said I was meeting a boy. And when Gray finds out I'm spending time with Cal?

I let out a deep sigh just thinking about it as I pull on a sweatshirt and slippers and head to the bathroom before going downstairs for breakfast. Gray's already warned me off Cal once before, when nothing had really even happened between us.

Now?

I know Gray thinks he's looking out for me. But he doesn't know everything, after all. And I think he's wrong about Cal. Or maybe he doesn't see the same side of Cal that I've seen. I don't doubt that Gray dislikes Cal for a reason.

But Cal's been interested in me for a while. If anything, me being Gray's sister should've scared him off already. And it didn't. So despite his insistence that he doesn't want anything serious, his behavior says otherwise.

Which is great, on the one hand, because I honestly don't like the idea of him fucking around while we're seeing each other. But on the other, I don't really have time for anything serious right now either. Not with my class load.

Gray tromps down the stairs behind me in sweatpants and a ratty T-shirt, dropping into his usual chair across from me at the kitchen table. Mom's still bustling around the kitchen, cleaning up the detritus from waffle making. Since it's a Monday, Dad's at work already. He's currently designing a custom mansion of someone's dreams.

It's all very hush-hush, and he and Mom both had to sign an NDA, so all I know is that he's working for someone famous and demanding, since he couldn't take the week off like he normally does. But this is nothing new. He's been doing high-end residential architecture since I was a kid, once he made the leap out of working for a commercial firm. Most of his work has had the name of the owner redacted from the pictures I've seen.

Mom's schedule has always been more flexible. As the interior designer, she'll have her hands full with this project later, once construction is finishing up. She works from home when she's not on site, and she mentioned last week that she's cleared her schedule for the week, which means she'll be home all the time with no appointments or shopping trips taking up her time.

Hence the fancy breakfast.

A stack of four waffles sits on a plate in the middle of the table, a small carafe of syrup and a dish of butter next to it. Gray grabs one first, scraping a small amount of butter over it. I have no nutrition plan I'm required to stick to, so I'm more generous with both the butter and the syrup on mine, making a big deal about it when I take a bite. "Wow, Mom. These waffles are soooo good. And drowning them in butter and warm maple syrup makes them even better."

Gray narrows his eyes at me, fully aware of what I'm doing. "Shut it, monkey butt," he hisses.

"Make me, buttface," I hiss back.

"Now, kids," Mom says. "I thought you would've outgrown the name-calling by now."

"You know we only do it with affection, Mom," Gray says, putting a nearly dry piece of waffle in his mouth. "You don't have to make breakfast like this every morning, you know," he says around a full mouth. His tone is light, but I know he'd actually like Mom to lay off. Since we're both home for the holiday break, she's been going nuts. She made brownie sundaes for dessert last night after dinner—to celebrate Gray's big win, she said. And now waffles this morning.

Since Gray has to count calories, this has to be hell on his nutrition plan. But Mom would get her feelings hurt if he turned her down and skipped dessert or had an egg white omelette for breakfast like he probably does on his own. And with the team's Friendsgiving tomorrow night and our early Thanksgiving dinner on Wednesday, he's probably going to be way over his calorie counts for the week.

Leaning closer, I kick him under the table. "Hush up," I hiss, trying my best to be nearly inaudible. "If she wants to make delicious food every day this week, you can just eat smaller portions, or make use of the extra calories to power your winning game or something."

Mom comes over and smooths a hand through my hair, placing a kiss on top of my head. "Thank you, Piper. I'm glad you appreciate my food."

"I do, Mom. Your food is the best part of my week." I'm not even lying. While the helping of lectures and advice that come with dinner aren't my favorite, my mom's a fabulous cook.

"I appreciate your food, too, Mom. But too much fat and carbs throws off my nutrition plan."

Mom waves a hand, dismissing that like it's nothing as she puts the last of the dishes in the dishwasher. "You're a growing boy. You need good food. Your coach should understand that."

Gray glares at me, and I just smile in return.

With a soft snort, he shakes his head, a smile creeping up his face too.

After breakfast, Gray changes and leaves for his morning workout, stopping to give Mom a quick kiss on the cheek.

Maybe I should start up a morning workout routine. At least for the break, just to give me something to do.

But is it really worth going for a run just to get out of the house? A quick peek out the front window confirms that no, it's definitely not. The sky is varying shades of gray, the bare tree branches whipping in the gusts of wind blowing past, and every so often a smatter of rain that sounds like hail hits the glass.

Definitely not good weather for running.

Which means taking myself up to my room to study. Yaaaay.

When I return to my room after a lunch break, I let out a defeated whimper at the sight of my textbooks, notebooks, and laptop still in a jumble on my bed the way I left them an hour ago.

I can't do this for a whole week with nothing to distract me. I'm already losing my mind, and it's only been a couple of days.

With a sigh, I pull out my phone and open my texts, contemplating my last exchange with Cal. I said I'd call, but what if he's still at the gym? Or in the shower? Or ...?

A text is better. Obviously. Cal's weird with his preference for actually calling. And it's not like we don't text. We do. The evidence is right in front of me.

And I'm stalling. I don't even know why I'm stalling. Cal's my only hope of distraction right now.

With a deep breath, I type out a quick message and hit send before I can second guess myself any more.

Me: Help! I need a distraction, stat. I've been studying almost nonstop since I got home because there's

literally nothing else to do, and I can't take it anymore.

I stare at my phone as the seconds tick by, fidgeting with the cracked corner of my case, waiting, waiting.

With a low sound of frustration, I flop myself back on the bed. He's probably not feeling like a prisoner trapped in his room. Which isn't entirely fair. I'm sure my mom would love it if I'd come down and do something with her. I'm sure she'd offer to take me shopping or ask if I want to help her bake a batch of cookies. And if last spring hadn't happened—if Brent hadn't happened—I'd probably take her up on that. But that shifted our relationship into this awkward hell of my own making. Now any time I spend with either of my parents consists of them gently probing to see how I'm doing, acting like I'm some fragile creature who might break at any moment.

And it's exhausting. I have to act normal while trying to make sure I'm adequately reassuring but not call out what they're doing, because that will be met with either outright denial or a *Can you blame us?* type lecture, and I've had my fill of both of those.

I love my mom. And I really do wish that I could just go down and say, "Hey, let's go to Ulta and try out new makeup," or, "I'd love some new throw pillows for my dorm room." And then we'd make a day of hitting her favorite home decor stores and all the available makeup counters, and when we'd get home, Dad would pretend to scold us about spending us into the poor house before asking to see our haul.

But even if we went to those places, it would lack the carefree attitude we would've had this time last year. And if I bought new makeup, Dad would ask who I was planning to wear it for, as though wearing it for myself isn't good enough anymore. There has to be some ulterior motive, some *guy*, and remember what happened with the last guy?

And that's why texting Cal is risky, even though it feels like my only option. I need to get out because I'm suffocating. But if they find out I'm seeing a guy, any guy, but especially this guy who really doesn't like my brother, it'll be a whole thing, and the concern will become more overt, and as much as I hate the subtle probing, the overt concern often takes the form of severe restrictions on my freedoms. And while yes, I'm legally an adult, I don't have the finances to support myself, so I can't just tell them to fuck off and leave me alone.

But it might not matter anyway. Because Cal's not texting me back. And it's possible that playing hard to get for so long has actually worked.

I should be happy about that.

But I'm really not.

CHAPTER TWENTY-THREE

Cal

I'm just getting out of the shower at the gym when my phone buzzes with a text in my nest of clothes on the bench. Piper's name flashes on the screen, and a surge of triumph and lust rushes through my blood.

She texted me.

She made the first move. For once.

About fucking time.

I can't text her back right away, though. For one thing, I'm in the middle of the fucking locker room, and while right now my lower body is hidden, I'm already half hard just from seeing her name and the words *Help! I need a distraction …*

And she knows I'm good for a distraction any time she needs one.

My shit-eating grin is irrepressible, and I keep my head down so no one else wonders why I'm walking around like I own the place. I mean, I should have the right to do that anyway, but I don't need questions right now. Especially if her brother's still around.

Hang on, why don't I need questions? If Gray finds out his sister's texting me to be her booty call, that's exactly what I want, isn't it?

So why does that feel so shitty all of a sudden?

Smile—and boner—fading, I finish toweling off and wrap the towel around my hips to head back to my locker, resolutely ignoring any bad feelings that seem to be bubbling up out of nowhere. Piper texted me. That's a good thing, and I'm going to focus on that.

I make short work of pulling on a clean pair of joggers and a T-shirt, wanting to get out of here quickly so I can find out when Piper wants her distraction delivered.

But before I can make it out, Coach Miles, the quarterback coach, steps into the room and nods at me. "McAdam. Come see me in my office before you go."

"Yessir," I bark automatically, hiding the twinge of disappointment that I won't be able to text Piper back immediately. Or better yet, call her. Her low, smoky voice has a way of making everything better.

But maybe Coach Miles has good news for me? It's unlikely, but you never know.

Pulling on a sweatshirt and stuffing my feet into my shoes, I grab my bag and head over to the coaching offices, knocking on the open doorframe on my way in.

Coach Miles looks up from his clipboard and gives me a perfunctory smile, carving the smile lines deeper into his face, the grooves running from his bushy mustache down to his chin. Dude's as old as the hills, and just as timeless. He was old when I was in high school, and even though Coach Hanson's retired, Coach Miles is still here, chugging along. I guess I should be grateful that he wasn't forced out—or worse, fired—when they brought Coach Reese on. I hate to admit it, but Reese has been good for us. Even if he brought that asshole Kilpatrick and several new coaching staff with him. At least Miles is still here.

"Glad to see you're finally pulling your head out of your ass," he says, gruff and to the point as ever. The man's never been one to mince words.

"Uh, thanks?"

He glares at me through his faded blue eyes. "It wasn't a compliment. You've been a shit all season. And you're finally coming around. I want to see you for extra practice this afternoon. Go get something to eat and be back here in an hour."

"Yessir."

With a wave of his hand, he dismisses me.

Shit. I was hoping to see Piper sooner rather than later, but I guess that won't be possible.

Still, at least I can call her and let her know what's going on. With a smile, I hit her name on my contacts list, more confident than ever that we're on the same page.

* * *

Three hours later, tired but horny and wired, I pick up stray books and papers and pile them neatly on the coffee table, straighten the remote controls, put the video game controllers in the entertainment center, and check the time on my phone every two point five seconds to see how much longer before Piper will get here.

I have the house to myself since Simon took Ellie to his parents' house for dinner. It's her first time meeting them. They're nice people, so I'm sure they'll love her. Pretty much everyone loves her, to be honest. She's funny and smart and knows how to impress parents. It comes from working her ass off to impress ours, despite the impossibility of that task. Well, it's really Dad more than Mom. He has Expectations, with a capital E, and I know Ellie thinks they worship the ground I walk on, but that's just because I've managed to give good lip service to Dad's plan for me, which was to be the best at everything and become a doctor. So I study my ass off and maintain a 3.5 GPA, which still isn't quite good enough for Dad. I should be graduating at least *magna cum laude,* or what's even the point, right? But I've never been as good in class as I am on the football field. And my performance there hasn't been good enough this year either with the arrival of Kilpatrick showing me up. I think Dad's secretly glad about that, though he hasn't said it out loud, because he thinks it means I'll have to let go of my dream of going pro, go to med school like he wants, and come home to work with him in his practice.

But my parents aren't here, thank god, and thanks to Simon's parents wanting to meet Ellie, neither are they. Which means I'm free to have Piper come over without worrying Ellie might show up to get her favorite pen she forgot in Simon's room. She doesn't need a pen at a meet-the-parents dinner. Not one of her super special hand lettering pens, anyway.

Speaking of, she left one of her brush pens and a notebook of fancy paper on the couch. She's always been a doodler, and then she really got into calligraphy and hand lettering after I left for college. I actually didn't realize what a big deal it was to her until she declared her graphic design major. Now my house is littered with all her artsy accoutrements. Even though her final projects are all rendered on the computer, she does a lot of sketching by hand to test new concept ideas. Scooping up the pens and paper that's only allowed to be used with those pens, I take them to Simon's room. He can keep track of them for her. I don't need that kind of responsibility for Ellie's things. She's very particular about them, which I learned the hard way a couple weeks ago when I made the mistake of tearing a page out of one of her notebooks to jot down a note and she went ballistic on me. Won't be making that mistake again.

I'm freshly showered and freshly shaved, dressed in jeans and a navy blue henley that clings to my upper body just enough to look good but not so much that I look like a douche, and I force myself to stop in the doorway of the living room and survey the space instead of moving constantly. I'll sweat through my deodorant if I keep moving like this. I've already had a solid workout this morning plus this afternoon's passing practice. I don't need to burn more calories. Although, given the way my time with Piper usually goes, I'll be doing that anyway.

Still, no need to work up a sweat just yet.

I check my phone again. It's only been a minute since the last time. Still nothing since she texted that she was heading over.

I don't know where her parents live, so I don't know how long it'll take her to get here.

Thankfully, the doorbell rings.

Blowing out a breath, I open it to Piper standing on the other side, her dark hair loose around her shoulders, eyeshadow shimmering under the porch light when she blinks, glossy lips pulling into a smile as I look her over.

"Hey," she says, her voice husky.

My own lips curve in an answering smile. "Hey. Come on in." I stand back and gesture her inside.

She slips off her coat, revealing a slinky top that spills over her tits and nips in at her waist, giving a hint of what's beneath. She's paired the top with wide leg pants that mold to the curve of her hips before draping to the floor. And since I've seen those curves and mapped them with my hands, I know exactly what they look like. But that fact doesn't at all detract from my appreciation for the artful arrangement of clothing over her body.

I'm trying not to just rip her clothes off like an animal at the first sight of her, even though that's really what I want to do.

I wanted that last night, and she stayed away despite my best efforts.

She said she needs a distraction and something to keep her from getting bored. I'm happy to provide that outside of the bedroom as well.

Taking her coat, I hang it on one of the hooks in the hall. Simon and I don't use them much, but Ellie always hangs her coat there when she comes over, which is all the time lately. And even though I went from ignoring the hooks to being annoyed by them because of Ellie's coat so frequently hanging on them, now I'm grateful they're here so I have somewhere to hang Piper's coat.

Good god. Listen to me. Waxing about fucking coat hooks in my hallway. Because of a girl. What have I become?

With a mental shake of my head, I clear my throat and gesture toward the kitchen. "I made dinner. You hungry?"

Her grin changes into something between amusement

and warmth. "You cooked for me?"

I shrug like it's no big deal. Because it's really not. "Well, I cooked for me. But I made enough for you to eat too since you were coming over. Did you eat already?"

She shakes her head and precedes me to the kitchen, which gives me the opportunity to ogle her ass swaying in front of me, the fabric of her pants swishing as she walks.

"It's nothing fancy," I say, passing her once we're in the kitchen to reach the stove. I take the lid off the skillet and plate the chicken breasts I made, spooning sauce over each one, then scooping a helping of broccoli onto each plate. I set the plates on the dining table Simon's mom insisted we needed. We hardly ever use it except as a place to dump stuff, but I cleaned it off after I got home from practice in anticipation of Piper coming over.

She looks between the plate and me, her lips twitching.

"What?" It comes out rude. Gruff. Demanding. Which isn't what I wanted, but with her looking at me like that, like I'm a curiosity, it has my hackles up. I didn't cook for her to make fun of me.

She shakes her head and rolls her lips between her teeth, looking down at her plate and tucking her hair behind her ear. "Nothing. It's just ..."

My brows pull together. "What?" This time's a little more modulated. Less rude, at least.

She shakes her head again, picking up the fork from

the napkin I'd set out already. "I don't think a guy's ever cooked for me before, is all," she says at last.

"Okay." I draw out the word, not quite sure where she's going with this. I cook fairly often for Simon and me. I'm not sure what the big deal is here.

She glances up at me, her red lips pulling into a smile that she quickly tries to suppress, one shoulder lifting in a shrug. "You just made such a big deal about this being casual, and then you invite me over and cook me dinner?"

"So? Would you prefer I ordered pizza or something?"

Another shrug. "I mean, that's what most guys would've done. Cooking for someone is generally considered … romantic. Something more serious, anyway."

I narrow my eyes at her and pick up my own silverware, aware of an uncomfortable tightness in my chest. "It's not that big of a deal," I insist. "You need to eat. I need to eat. I'm going to be eating tons of stuff I'm not supposed to tomorrow and the next day. I'm saving calories for that. Ordering pizza wouldn't work for that. And besides," I add after a moment, my voice lower, darker, "eating here is easier than trying to go out somewhere. The distance to my bed is a lot shorter, for one."

That has a short burst of laughter coming out of her, and the set of her shoulders seems to relax. "There's the horny football player I'm used to."

I grin at her, feeling better too, like we're back on familiar footing. "Never went anywhere, babe. Just had a hard practice today, and I need some sustenance before I make you scream."

I don't miss the way she shifts in her seat at that. "Better hurry up and eat, then," she murmurs, and I couldn't agree more.

CHAPTER TWENTY-FOUR

Cal spends dinner making small talk, asking me about what I have left to get through before finals, what I'm planning to do over Christmas break, if my class load next semester is just as punishing. And the whole time, his eyes stray to my mouth again and again. I can't help doing the same—staring at his lips each time he takes a bite or licks a stray bit of sauce from the corner of his mouth.

He's right that chicken and broccoli isn't particularly fancy. But with the balsamic sauce he made with it? It's delicious, even if it is his way of skimping so he has room for more calories tomorrow and the next day.

As soon as I finish my food, he pulls my plate away, stacking it on top of his, grabbing our glasses by the openings between his strong, capable fingers and taking them to the sink. Then he's behind me, taking my hand and guiding me to my feet. He backs me against the kitchen table, my ass on the edge as he drags his lips up the column of my neck to the point of my jaw, his breath hot on my skin. Then his teeth capture my earlobe. "Up on the table," he commands, his voice deep with every expectation of obedience.

"Say please," I retort, but it comes out less sassy and more breathless.

He smiles against my neck. "Please," he says, the single word full of indulgence. Like he knows I'd do it without the pleasantry if he pushed, but he doesn't feel the need to prove his mastery over my body. At least not right now.

His hands fall to my ass, helping ease me up onto the table, his hips in the cradle of my thighs. He grinds against me, the movement somehow both slow and rough. Almost desperate.

But he's still fully in control.

He kisses me, his mouth owning mine, his tongue sliding between my lips and tasting me, coaxing me out, as though I need any kind of coaxing.

When he pulls away, his eyes are dark blue, his lids heavy. "Lie back," he whispers, his hand slipping up between my breasts and exerting just enough pressure to emphasize what he wants from me.

I give him a dubious look. "Why?"

He gives me a cocky smile. "I want to eat you for dessert."

A surprised laugh splutters out of me, but my thighs tighten around his hips, and I pull him close enough that I can rub against him.

A low sound of pleasure rumbles in his chest. "See? You like the idea. Just listen, and I promise I'll take care of you."

I'm about to do as he asks, the arrogant little shit, when I realize I need to not get carried away just yet. "Where's your phone?"

He raises an eyebrow, his voice equal parts amused and confused. "In my pocket. Why?"

Reaching between us, I start trying to work my hand into one of his pockets, but he pulls my hands away and retrieves the phone himself. "What are you doing?" he asks.

Instead of answering, I take the phone from his hand and power it down, then set it well out of reach. I mean, he could still get to it if he really wanted to, but I'd notice at least.

"Want to make sure we can't be interrupted?" he asks with a smirk.

I grin back, grateful for the plausible excuse. "Of course." I rub my hands up his chest, wrapping them behind his neck and pulling his mouth to mine.

"What about yours?" he murmurs against my lips, peppering them with tiny, nipping kisses.

"Hmm?"

"Your phone. Shouldn't you turn it off too?"

I blink. "Oh. Right. Good point." My phone is still in my chair where it was stashed under my thigh during dinner. He retrieves it and holds it out to me, waiting patiently while I turn it off and set it next to his.

"Now," he says, that dark commanding edge back in his voice, "lie back."

I lean back, the table hard under my elbows, but I stay propped up enough so I can watch.

He picks up my feet one at a time and unzips my ankle boots, dropping them on the floor. Eyes glittering, Cal slips his hands under my top, the calluses on his fingers making me shiver as they brush over the skin on my belly. He undoes the fastener on my pants, the zip making a soft sound, then he hooks his fingers in the waistband and starts inching my pants and underwear down, down, down, his eyes never leaving mine as he slowly drags them all the way off my body, my hips lifting at the right moment almost of their own accord.

He settles on one of the chairs and places my legs on his shoulders, that cocky grin that turns me on way more than it should playing over his lips.

"You ready?" he asks, his hands sliding up and down the outsides of my thighs.

Everything about this feels deliciously naughty. Decadent. Sinful.

I nod, wondering which version of Cal I'm going to get at first. Will he be restrained, teasing, making me beg?

Or is he going to go full savage and devour my pussy with his whole mouth? Which do I want more?

Do I even have a preference?

When he leans closer, his hot breath fanning over my mound, I decide that in fact, I do not. I just want his mouth on me, his tongue on my clit, those magical fingers inside me. I don't care how he does it, as long as he does it.

His tongue parts my folds, tracing all my dips and valleys with the tip of his tongue. Not slowly, but in no hurry either.

"I've been dying for this pussy for days," he says after a moment, a groan of satisfaction riding the words.

"Oh yeah?" I ask, a note of challenge in my voice.

His eyes dart to mine, narrowing slightly. One eyebrow arches. "You don't believe me?"

I give my best approximation of an unconcerned shrug considering I'm lying on a kitchen table with my pants somewhere on the floor and my legs over a hot football player's shoulders. Boulder shoulders is the term that comes to mind whenever I see him, even with a shirt on. He's a little bulkier than the standard build for a quarterback, but I have zero complaints, especially as my calves rest in the cradle made by the dent between his traps and delts, the soft cotton of his henley making me extra aware of the fact that he's still fully clothed.

"You're not acting like someone who's been dying for my pussy," I murmur.

His eyes flash, something almost feral moving in their

depths, and his jaw clenches. I'm poking the beast, and I'm not at all sorry.

Without another word, his mouth is back on me, and there's nothing leisurely or gentle about it. His tongue spears into me, moving in and out, then he licks all the way up with the flat of his tongue. His eyes never leave mine as he sucks my clit into his mouth, giving me the edge of his teeth until I cry out. His eyes crinkle at the edges, and I know he'd be smirking if his lips weren't busy.

Two of his fingers thrust into me without warning, but I'm so wet and ready that the invasion is welcome even as I grunt at the suddenness. Curling his fingers, he immediately finds my G-spot, and I'm already reduced to a shivering, shuddering mess as my orgasm races toward me with the force and speed of a bullet train.

Even as my pussy spasms around his fingers and I shriek at the intensity, he doesn't let up, doesn't back down for a second. Not until I'm shoving at his head and pushing on his shoulders with my feet. "Enough. Enough. Stop."

With one last shudder-inducing lick, he stops, standing and sucking his fingers. The fingers that were just inside me. Fuck. Me. This guy. And even though I'm halfway to another orgasm, I'm grateful for the reprieve, my chest heaving as I suck in huge gulps of air. "Holy shit," I mutter, staring up at Cal's smug face, that feral look still lingering in his eyes.

"That proof enough for you?" he practically growls.

"Uh-huh."

He grips my ankles and wraps my legs around his hips, the seams and rivets of his jeans scraping against my thighs as he grinds into me, leaning over and kissing me. When I arch up into him, rubbing my tits on his chest, he slips his hand behind my back, holding me close as he plunders my mouth with his tongue.

"I'll break the table if I fuck you here," he murmurs against my lips, and I can't help smiling.

"That might be kinda fun, though."

With a chuckle, he straightens and pulls me to sitting. "Maybe when I have time to get a replacement before my roommate gets home."

Before I can respond, he ducks his head, his hand still holding my wrist, and plants his shoulder in my belly, hoisting me off the table fireman style, my head dangling down his back before I even know what's happening.

"Hey!" When I smack his ass in protest, he just laughs, a deep rumbling sound that vibrates through his back and into my chest. "For the record, this isn't what most girls picture when they think of being swept off their feet."

His hand smacks on my bare ass with just enough force to sting before it turns into a caress. "Are you complaining?" he asks, amusement still bubbling in his voice as he carries me down the hall and through a door.

Then the world tilts again as he dumps me onto the bed. I brush my hair out of my face, fully aware that my death glare is somewhat ruined by the fact that I have no pants on. "About you going all caveman to cart me off to your room?"

And then he yanks his shirt off, distracting me with all his golden skin stretched over the bumps and grooves of finely honed muscles. I get up on my knees, unable to stop myself from reaching out and touching him, sliding my hand up his abs and over his pec.

Another laugh rumbles out of him, his hands at his waist. "Yeah, I didn't think so."

Narrowing my eyes, I give him a hard pinch on the nipple. "I do, actually. Carrying me over your shoulder isn't sexy. I don't appreciate it."

He shoves his pants down, his cock bumping into my belly, hot and hard. His arm goes around me, yanking me against him, his hand traveling to my ass. He slaps it, making me jerk my hips forward, and my eyes fly up to his.

His lips brush mine in a quick kiss. "Really? You're mad about me carrying you over my shoulder?"

I shrug, fighting down my smile. "Not mad, exactly, but I mean, it's not my favorite thing ever."

"Alright. Noted. I'll only do it if I want you feisty and riled up."

I let out a shocked laugh. "Should I call you Gronk, then?"

"Baby, you can call me whatever you want, as long as you let me inside that sweet little pussy," he murmurs, and then his mouth is on mine again, his tongue in my mouth, and any response I might've given is swept away.

It's good, though, actually, him ruining the romantic

atmosphere of cooking me dinner by carrying me off like a caveman. Because otherwise I might think there's more to this than there is. He's been clear. I've been clear. We're both on the same page that this should stay casual. No complications. No need for romance. Just this—hot, sexy, and fun. And Cal's nothing if not fun. And sexy. And ohhh …

He pulls my top off before laying me back, then he rolls on a condom and climbs over me, that beautiful dick of his stretching me open in one smooth slide. His hand grips behind my knee, pulling my leg up to his side so he can get deeper. We let out matching groans of pleasure.

"Yeah, baby, that's what I've been needing," he whispers before kissing me again.

And I have to remind myself that he just means my pussy. Not me. This is just sex.

That's it. And that's fine. And that's all I have time for.

And maybe if I tell myself that enough times, I'll manage to believe it.

CHAPTER TWENTY-FIVE

Cal

There are a handful of cars already parked outside of Trey and Brandy's house when Simon, Ellie, and I park and get out. We all came together, since we're all staying at the same house this week and going to the same place. It just made sense.

Or at least that was Ellie's argument when I blinked in surprise that she assumed we'd be going together. I'd assumed we'd be coming separately. Simon and I were each assigned a different dish, after all.

Brandy doesn't take Friendsgiving lightly. Which is why she and Trey are the ones hosting it. That and they have a big enough rental that we can all squeeze in.

Almost the whole team is coming. A few guys who live semi-close went home for today, since it was our rest day for the week. Tomorrow is a regular practice and workout, Thursday we're traveling to Colorado, and then it's the game on Friday night. Simon, Ellie, and I are lucky enough to get a "real" Thanksgiving with Simon's family tomorrow, but for most of the team, this is the only Thanksgiving they'll get. So it's a big deal every year.

Trey and Brandy hosted last year, too. Next year it'll have to be someone else, though, because Trey, like Simon and me, is a senior. So's Brandy, actually. As one of the cheerleaders, she'll be going with us to our game. And Thanksgiving is important to her, which is why she's been the one to handle everything since she and Trey started dating.

Rain falls on us in inconsistent, splattering gusts blown by the wind. Ellie ducks her head and hurries to the front door as fast as her little legs can manage, Simon and I bringing up the rear at a more sedate pace like we're her bodyguards or something. Bodyguards carrying a grocery sack full of frozen dinner rolls, per Brandy's request. Apparently that's about all she expects me to be able to handle, not that I'm complaining.

Ellie rings the doorbell, but Simon nudges her aside so he can open the door. "It's alright," I hear him murmur to her. "They know we're coming."

The door opens into the already crowded living room, and a general cheer goes up when everyone sees we're here. Trey comes from the kitchen at the back of the house, greeting Ellie first, rubbing his big brown hands together at the sight of the pie in her hands. "Apple, right? Homemade?"

She nods, grinning at his gleeful expression.

"Brandy's in the kitchen. She'll tell you where to put it."

Ellie casts a glance at Simon and me, then makes her way to the back of the house while Trey greets us, nodding at the bag in my hands. "Rolls to the kitchen too. She'll relax knowing those are here. She's about to get the mac and cheese in the oven. That's the last important side that's missing. If you didn't come through, I was going to have to go out and scour the open grocery stores for whatever they have left because it's too late to make them ourselves."

Grinning, I hold the bag out to him, but he holds his hands up. "No, man. You were in charge of rolls. If you wanna stay on her good side, you deliver them your own self."

"Thanks, man. I'll hand them off myself, then."

He and Simon fall into conversation about the offensive line—Trey's the center—and things they need to watch out for when facing off against our opponent this weekend. We've all been watching game tapes religiously this week. I'm doing my best to stay focused, but it's hard when I know the odds of me getting any playing time are slim to none.

Unless …

I hadn't noticed Kilpatrick or Piper when I walked in,

but maybe they're hiding in the kitchen?

When I get there to hand off the rolls to a grateful Brandy, there's no sign of either one. "Just so you know, I had to go to three different stores to get enough of these, since you had very specific brand requirements."

She flashes me a grin, tossing her long box braids over her shoulder. "I appreciate the effort. Any old grocery store rolls won't do. They have to be Sister Schuberts." She leans in close, lowering her voice to a conspiratorial whisper. "It's my Aunt Sara's secret recipe."

Chuckling, I tuck my hands in my pockets. "Not so secret if they're just grocery store rolls."

Shrugging, she opens the freezer and stuffs the whole bag in. "They're what she uses when she needs to save time or energy. Homemade rolls are the best. But these are a close second."

"My mom's secret recipe is a frozen deep-dish apple pie that she puts in her own pie plate. She takes it to all the potluck type parties she has to go to and graciously accepts everyone's compliments."

Brandy turns back to the bubbling pot on the stove. "See? You know how it is. And anyway, I put myself out enough for you Philistines, making my family mac and cheese recipe and the turkey and organizing all of this. The least you can do is bring the good rolls." She flashes me a grin when I chuckle, then points at a cooler full of ice tucked against the end of a counter. "Help yourself to a water. Gray's in charge of the rest of the drinks, and he's not here yet."

"Thanks, Brandy," I say, and she waves me off.

At least that's one question answered. If Kilpatrick's not here, then neither is Piper. Before she left my place last night, rubber-legged from satisfaction, she mentioned she'd be here. And the knowledge that I'd see her this afternoon is the only reason I haven't given in to the urge to text her today. But my ability to hold off is quickly wearing thin. If she's not here soon, I might just have to text her to find out when she will be.

Just then the front door opens and closes, letting in a gust of cold, wet air and raising a cry of greeting from everyone once more. And when I turn to look, my eyes clash with Piper's. She's grinning, accepting greetings from everyone, helping her brother carry in boxes of soda and beer.

The door opens and closes again, and her brother's gone, presumably to get the rest, so I take advantage of the opportunity to greet her without his interference.

"Hey," I say, moving in close and grinning at her. I want to kiss her, but I'm not sure how she'd feel about that, especially with the way her eyes keep darting around the room behind me. "Let me help you with those," I say instead, taking the boxes out of her hands.

"Oh, um, thanks," she stammers, following behind me. Trey's already grabbed the boxes that Kilpatrick set down and taken them to the kitchen, ripping open the flimsy cardboard and adding them to the cooler full of ice.

When he sees me, he nods, his eyes darting to Piper behind me. He raises his eyebrows, but otherwise doesn't acknowledge that me helping Kilpatrick's sister is maybe a little strange since it's well-known that he and I don't get along.

Once we've deposited our drinks into Trey's capable hands, I pull her into the doorway leading to the hall, needing to give her a proper greeting without an audience. Sure, yeah, I want everyone here to see us together, especially her brother. But first I need her to myself. Just for a second.

She grins up at me like she finds my behavior amusing. And I give in to the urge to kiss the smile right off her face.

Rising up on her toes, her fingers stroke the back of my neck as she meets my kiss, giving as good as she gets. With my hands on her hips, I'm careful to maintain space between our lower bodies despite the fact that I want to grind her into me, turn my semi into something more. Something that would demand taking care of.

But we're not here for that.

Ending the kiss, I can't help smiling at the way her eyelids flutter open. "Hey," she says, the breathless quality of her voice sending a spark of satisfaction straight through my middle.

"Hey."

Her smirk matches mine. "So it's like this, is it?"

I shrug. "Guess so."

I'm not sure if she's referring to the kiss, the fact that I pulled her into as much privacy as we can get without being ridiculously obvious, or the fact that I'm willing to do this where others might see. Even though he's keeping his eyes turned toward the cooler and the drinks he's loading into it, Trey could see us if he turned his head, and Brandy only has to look away from the dish she's slicing sweet potatoes into to see what we're up to.

Kilpatrick's voice douses me with cold water. Or at least Piper's reaction to it does. She yanks her hands away, jumping back like I've burned her. She steps fully into the kitchen, tucking her hands into her pockets, meeting my narrowed eyes. "Uh, th-thanks for helping with the drinks," she stammers, turning and heading out of the kitchen.

A second later, I hear her voice joining in the general conversation in the living room. Kilpatrick glares at me, arms crossed, chest puffed out, nostrils flaring. Trey looks between him and me, one eyebrow raised in question. I shrug my answer and head out of the kitchen.

"Stay away from my sister," Kilpatrick growls as I walk past.

I turn, holding my hands up, planting my douchiest smirk firmly on my face. "Sure, sure. I can't promise she'll stay away from me, though."

He surges toward me, an almost incoherent question on his lips, but Trey's big palm slaps his chest, holding him back. "Leave him alone, Gray," he says quietly. "He's just trying to get a rise out of you. And you're giving it to him."

Kilpatrick subsides, or at least he stops coming at me enough that Trey's hold loosens, even if it doesn't completely relax. "I mean it, McAdam. She's not some groupie for you to mess around with. Leave her alone." Kilpatrick grits out.

Shrugging, I turn to the living room, making a big show of looking around for an empty seat before parking myself right next to Piper in her spot on the floor, leaning in close and bracing my arm behind her. It's subtle, casual, but clear I'm staking a claim.

She glances at me, her eyebrows drawn together, but turns back to the conversation she's having with one of the underclassmen and the girl he brought with him. Jacobsen? Jensen? Something with a J. He's deep on the defense bench. We don't have a lot of overlap, so I don't know him well enough to remember his name.

As the conversation progresses, Piper leans against me, more comfortable with me here with her, accepting my presence, my claim. I participate in the conversation, tossing in my two cents when appropriate, but my attention is mostly split between paying attention to the growing crowd in the room and the *Lord of the Rings* marathon that's on TV. My mom loves these movies, so I've seen them a few times over the years. We're somewhere in the second one, and I'm half watching so I don't miss my favorite scene when the Ents destroy Isengard.

There's a change in the air before that happens, though, and Piper stiffens beside me, pulling away. Looking around, I see her brother glaring at both of us. Raising my eyebrows, my eyes never leaving his, I reach out and pull Piper against me, making it clear to anyone watching—and specifically to Kilpatrick—that Piper and I are clearly comfortable enough with each other to touch casually like this. Like a couple. Now, I wouldn't go so far as to use that word to describe whatever we are to each other, but he doesn't need to know that. Right now he just needs to see that Piper and I are something to each other, and no amount of warnings from him will change that.

Except Piper stiffens, pushing away from me. "Stop it," she hisses, drawing my attention away from her brother at last. She's looking between him and me, her brows drawn together. "What are you doing?" she asks in a low voice.

"Spending time with you. What does it look like?"

She rolls her eyes and huffs. "It looks like you're in a dick swinging contest with my brother, and I am not here for that. Back. Off."

Holding up my hands in surrender, I scoot away from her, giving her the space she clearly wants, refocusing on the movie. After a moment, my frustration bubbling over, I get up, because I can't stay next to her and not touch her. Not just because I want to rub it in her brother's face that she lets me touch her—and I do want to do that—but also because I just have to touch her when she's near me. Period. Whether there are people watching or not.

Needing to move, I pick my way to the kitchen and grab a bottle of water from the cooler, cracking it open and sucking part of it down. "Need any help, Brandy?" I ask after a moment.

She glances at me over her shoulder, her eyes amused. "How are you with carving a turkey?"

"Uhhh."

"That's what I thought," she says with a laugh. "Trey always gets all nervous. His dad carves a perfect turkey, he says, and he feels like he's butchering it. Plus he gets all squeamish about popping the legs out. Says it reminds him too much of the sound of a knee going out."

I shudder at the thought.

She chuckles again. "Yeah. Just like that." She shoos me away. "Get outta my kitchen. I got it. If I need help, Trey knows his way around. You'd just be asking me seven thousand questions and getting in my way."

"Fair enough." My eyes immediately find Piper when I look over the overflowing living room. She glances my way and holds up her phone, jiggling it back and forth at me.

I pull mine out and find a text from her.

Piper: Sorry. I just don't want to rub Gray's nose in anything.

Unfortunately, I do. But I'll respect her wishes. It's enough that Gray knows now, at least as far as I'm concerned.

Me: You're forgiven. But I expect you to make it up to me later.

Her eyes widen and find mine when she sees my response, and I give her a sexy smile. "Tonight," I mouth.

Her cheeks turn just a little pink, and the girl she's talking to looks around, her eyes landing on me, clearly putting together that something's going on between us.

Good. If some random chick can figure it out, anyone with eyeballs surely can. And that's all I need.

Glancing around, I see there's an empty spot on the couch next to my sister, so I go and claim it, ignoring her squawking protests.

With a rumbly chuckle, Simon picks her up and deposits her on his lap. "Better?" he asks her.

Huffing and glaring at me with annoyance, she nods. "Yes. Now Cal won't elbow me in the head, at least."

Simon drapes his arms around her and resumes his conversation. I poke her knee. "You having fun?"

She widens her eyes and looks around the room, laying a hand on her chest dramatically. "Moi? Are you actually *speaking* to me? In a room full of your friends and teammates?" She leans forward, perching on the edge of Simon's leg so she can place the back of her hand on my forehead. "Are you feeling alright? Do you have a fever? Do you need Tylenol?"

I swat her hand away, rolling my eyes. "I'm fine. Stop it. I can't talk to my sister?"

She leans into Simon, who adjusts her casually, her eyes narrowed as they bore into me. "You never have before."

I scoff. "I've talked to you plenty of times."

"Not in front of your friends you haven't. Not even at the other parties and things I've been to with Simon and you. You'll talk to him. You'll talk to other people in front of me. But you still never acknowledge me. So you'll have to excuse me if I'm a little surprised."

I think over the few weeks since she and Simon told me about their relationship and got back together. I mean, I know I didn't really talk to her at parties before that. Or when I did, it was to try to make her leave, which I readily admit was a dick move. I thought I was trying to keep her safe, out of the way of asshole frat dudes and my teammates who can sometimes be just as bad. But Simon's right. She's safer here with us where we can keep an eye on her. It helps that she's dating one of the biggest guys on the team. And while he's not naturally violent, dude knows how to grapple and take someone down if need be. That's literally his job on the football field.

Shaking my head, I pat her foot. She's taken her shoes off and just has her rainbow striped socks on. "Sorry, El. I feel like that's almost all I say to you these days. I'm trying to be less of an asshole. I swear."

She grins, nudging me with her toes. "You are. It's a work in progress, though. I get it." She follows my gaze to where Piper's sitting and talking to someone else. "Sooo …" Ellie says, trying to sound sly.

I look at her out of the corner of my eye. "Sooo … what?"

Chuckling, she shakes her head. "You and Piper. How's that going? I thought you guys were becoming a thing, but now you're over here and she's over there, but neither of you can keep your eyes off each other. What's up?"

It's my turn to chuckle and shake my head. "It's fine, Ellie. Don't worry about it."

I should know better than to think that would deter my little sister, though. Her eyes dart between Piper and me a few more times. When Piper stands, Ellie pushes herself off Simon's lap. "I'm parched," she announces more loudly than necessary. "I'm going to go get a drink. Anyone want anything? No?" And without waiting for an answer she heads for the kitchen. While I'm sure she'll get herself a drink, I'm equally sure she's going to corner Piper, and even if I tried, I don't think I could do more than delay the inevitable, so I just watch my sister go after my … whatever Piper is to me.

CHAPTER TWENTY-SIX

Piper

I'm not really sure what's going on between Cal and Gray when I push Cal off me. I just know that I feel like some kind of object in their game, and I'm not okay with that. But when I push Cal away and tell him to stop, the flash of hurt in his eyes is unmistakable. Sure, maybe he is trying to prove a point to my brother, but my rejection of his attention makes him unhappy on its own, separate from whatever their deal is.

I know they're not friends. That much was clear when Gray warned me away from him the first time. But I think that's more to do with the fact that Gray's the starting quarterback and Cal clearly wants that position. And who can blame him? I imagine Gray would feel the same if the situation were reversed. That doesn't make Cal a bad guy, though. And he's been nothing but generous and charming with me. Even when I thought he was a little over the top at that first party where he tried to pick me up, I never thought he was an asshole.

All of his gestures, from the hot chocolate between classes to cooking me dinner at his place last night, have been sweet and romantic, despite his protestations to the contrary. I can't really blame him for wanting to make sure the other guys know I'm taken. I wouldn't feel great if there were a bunch of single women here trying to get his attention. Not that there are a bunch of guys trying to get my attention, but Cal quashed that possibility before it even had a chance to start. He couldn't have been more clear if he'd pissed a circle all around me.

I feel Cal's eyes on me frequently, especially after our text exchange. *You'll have to make it up to me later*, he'd said, and I can't help a little shiver of anticipation about what exactly that might mean. It won't be unpleasant, I know that for sure, not with the heated stare he gave me while mouthing, *Tonight*.

And ever since, I've been wanting this Friendsgiving to hurry up and be over. Not that I'm not having fun. I am. It's just … a lot.

I spend most of my time holed up in my room or the library doing homework, with the exception of football games and practices and the rare party Dani convinces me to come to with her. And all of them are football parties because she's best friends with Eli Foster, the tight end. Sometimes I wonder if there's more to their relationship than the platonic friendship she insists is all they have, but so far I haven't seen anything concrete to prove my theory that they both secretly like each other.

Needing a break from sitting on the floor, I stand and stretch, making my way through the kitchen to the guest bathroom in the hallway. It's occupied at the moment, so I pull out my phone and check my email while I wait, debating whether or not to send another text to Cal while I have a second. Maybe I can get him to divulge how he'd like me to make things up to him later. And maybe I can convince him to duck out early with me, though I'm not sure how to make that happen exactly since I came with Gray. Maybe he drove? Did his roommate drive separately? Hmm.

"Oh. Hi. There's a line?"

I look up to see Ellie entering the hallway, not at all fooled by the faux surprise in her voice.

Grinning at her, I tuck my phone in my pocket. "There is. But I feel like you followed me back here to talk, not because you need to pee."

She shrugs, returning my smile, no trace of remorse in her face. "Can't it be both?"

Laughing, I tuck my hands behind me and lean against the wall. "What can I do for you?"

Not bothering to hide her assessment of me, she looks me up and down. "What's going on with you and my brother?"

My eyebrows fly up. "Not beating around the bush at all, are we?"

Another shrug. "What would be the point of that?" She points to the bathroom door. "I'm not going to stop you from peeing when they're done as some kind of interrogation technique, so that means I only have a few minutes." Eyeing me again, she rolls her hand in a *get on with it* motion. "So? Answer the question please."

I look away, tucking my hair behind my ear and crossing my arms, not really sure what the answer is to that question. "We're …" I shrug and level a look at her, raising one eyebrow. "You really want to hear that I'm banging your brother in our mutual spare time?"

Her cheeks turn pink, but she doesn't flinch. "I mean, I don't need details or anything. But it seems like there might be more than just that. Am I wrong?"

My continued silence seems to be all the answer she needs, because she nods like she understands completely. "Well, just let me know if you ever need any help knocking sense into him. He can be a big dummy sometimes, and he's not the most observant about things he doesn't think impact him."

I sputter a little, choking on my laughter, and she grins at me. But the bathroom door opens, revealing a pretty girl I've seen around but haven't talked to. She smiles at us both. "Dish session in the hallway?"

Ellie giggles. "Something like that."

And I slip into the bathroom before it can go any farther. I don't really need to dish about Cal in the hallway. Especially not with his sister. I like Ellie well enough, but that's just awkward. Even if she weren't related to Cal, we don't know each other that well. And dishing with friends feels strange when it's not with Shelby, my roommate from SCU. She was the one I always dished with about Brent, and I haven't tried to cultivate the kind of relationship we had with anyone at Marycliff. I should call her, actually. Especially since I'm on break and have all this free time. Frowning, I realize it's been weeks since we've spoken at all, and then it was just when I texted a meme I saw that made me laugh.

I finish up in the bathroom, my mood sour now that I've realized how far apart I've grown from my best friend. We spent so much time together last year, and now …

Now I'm a thousand miles away wrapped up in an overloaded class schedule, tons of homework, and a hot football player who monopolizes the small amount of free time I've allowed myself.

But if she's not reaching out to me either, I guess there's not much I can do but call her and do my best to stay in touch. And let the friendship go if it's clear she's not interested.

Maybe I should make more of an effort to get to know people here. Dani's great, but extending my network of friends would make the next few years less painful. Especially if I can't keep up my current class schedule.

When I open the bathroom door, Ellie's still waiting in the hall. She looks up from her phone with a smile.

Then she thrusts her phone into my hands. "Here. Type in your number. We can hang out while the guys are away or something. And ..." Glancing behind her, she leans in close and lowers her voice. "I know what it's like when your brother isn't enthusiastic about who you're dating, so if you ever want to talk ..." She looks pointedly at her phone, and with my recent thoughts about making more of an effort to make friends swirling in my head, I quickly type my number in the open contacts screen.

"I know it's not exactly the same situation," she continues when I hand her phone back to her. After she taps on the screen a few times, my phone alerts in my back pocket. "There." Another big smile. "Now you have my number. Like I was saying, our situations aren't identical. For one thing, our brothers don't seem to get along like, at all. Whereas Cal was just mad I was dating one of his friends. He never wanted me around anyway, and it seems like your brother actually likes you and vice versa." Her cheeks turn pink again, and she waves a hand like she's swatting away a swarm of gnats. "Sorry. I'm babbling. Just ..." Her dark eyes find mine, earnest and sincere. "Seriously. Text me. Let's do something."

I give her a reassuring grin. "I will. Are you going to be here all week?"

Her shoulders slump. "No. I'm going home tomorrow. My mom insists I have to be there for Thanksgiving. She says at least one of her children has to come, and it's not like I'll be doing anything here. Staying with Cal and Simon for a few days was only barely okay."

She brightens, heading into the bathroom. "But I'll be around for a lot of Christmas break. Your parents live in town, right?" At my nod, she beams. "Great. We'll find time to get together. Ooh! Maybe we can have like a double date at Cal and Simon's! That would be so fun. But we'll talk about that later, because I seriously have to pee."

She closes the door on my laughter, and I turn back to the living room, feeling lighter than I did a few minutes ago. When I reclaim my spot on the floor, Cal catches my eye from the couch, then bends his head over his phone.

My phone is already in my hand when it vibrates with his text a few seconds later.

Cal: My place. As soon as we can get away.

An irrepressible smile creeps across my face, and when I glance up, he adjusts in his seat, his blue eyes sparkling with heat and promise.

"Okay," I mouth back.

Giving me a tiny nod of acknowledgment, he returns his attention to the conversation with the guys next to him, and a moment later Ellie comes out and settles back on Simon's lap.

Despite what Ellie said in the hallway, he doesn't seem to have a problem with her being with his friend. He makes room for her as best he can in the crowded space, including her in their conversation and acting totally normal.

Maybe her suggestion of a double date could be fun after all. It sounds really relationship-y, but would that really be so bad? I know I've been saying I don't have time, but it seems like over the break I would …

I guess the biggest issue is whether or not Cal would go for something like that. And for some reason, the idea that he wouldn't makes me inexplicably sad. It shouldn't, because this thing between us isn't serious, and double dates—couple friends—are the trappings of serious relationships, right?

But if it were to become serious, would that really be so bad?

* * *

I'm still floating from the mind-altering afterglow of Cal-induced orgasms when I quietly make my way into my parents' house late that night. We'd both ducked out and taken an Uber back to his place so that Simon and Ellie could drive his car home. We took advantage of the empty house for a while, being as loud as we wanted until the unmistakable sound of Simon and Ellie getting home had me stuffing his comforter into my mouth to muffle my shrieks as he pounded into me from behind, driving me into the mattress with each thrust, and I can't get enough. Somehow trying to stay quiet just made everything hotter.

Creeping up the stairs, I'm careful to skip the creaky step, not wanting to disturb my parents who are surely already asleep since it's almost midnight. I'd texted Mom and Dad that I was hanging at a friends' house again, so I'd be home late. The nice part is, it's not technically a lie. Or at least it's even less of a lie than it was when I told them yesterday that I'd be hanging with a friend from the dorms who's staying in town with her brother for Thanksgiving break. Cal and I are certainly friendly, and after this afternoon, it's clear that Ellie wants to be friends, so … The fact that I wasn't hanging out with her at all either time is immaterial. We're all happier with the small subterfuge. I get screwed senseless with multiple orgasms each round—and holy shit, I didn't even know that was possible, and Cal is insatiable—and Mom and Dad don't have to worry needlessly about me being involved with a boy who'll make me go nuts and do something illegal again.

The situation is entirely different this time. For one thing, my expectations of Cal are exceedingly low. I thought things with Brent were more serious than they were. With Cal, we both know that it's not serious, despite the lingering ache from the ideas Ellie planted in my brain earlier. It's not worth getting my hopes up that this could be anything more than it is. And for another thing, I'm extremely careful that Cal doesn't have access to any cameras while we're together. He doesn't seem like the kind of guy who'd snap pics of me without my knowledge and post them online, but I didn't think Brent seemed like that either, so … better to be safe than sorry.

No illegal porn means no need to get revenge when

the system won't do anything.

But Mom and Dad would worry unnecessarily, so it's better if they just don't know.

I usually have the house to myself this late at night. With his practice and workout schedule, Gray goes to bed earlier than I do as well, and it's nice to have an hour or two of quiet time all to myself where I don't have to worry about what anyone else is thinking about what I'm doing.

But when I get to the top of the stairs, I'm surprised to find Gray standing there, arms crossed over a threadbare Ridgeview High School T-shirt, his jaw ticking, his brows pulled together in an angry frown.

Stopping in my tracks, I look him over. "Hey, Gray," I whisper, trying to keep my tone light. "What are you still doing up?"

He scoffs. "What do you think I'm doing? I'm waiting up for you."

I skirt around him to my bedroom door, unsurprised when he follows me. "Okay. But why?"

I set my phone and keys on the corner of my dresser, opening a drawer and pulling out clean PJs.

Gray waits until I've placed the clothes on my bed before answering my question with one of his own. "Where were you?"

"At a friend's house," I answer, sitting on my bed as well, because apparently I won't be changing right away. Fine by me. My shirt still carries the lingering scent of Cal, and I'm okay with not taking it off immediately. Though I think I'd prefer to watch a few episodes of *Derry Girls* before going to bed over having a stilted confrontation with my brother.

His jaw ticks again, his lips pressed in a flat line. "A friend's house," he repeats.

I nod slowly. "Yes, Gray. A friend's house. You know—friends? Those other people who aren't related to you that you enjoy spending time with?"

"Which friend?" he demands.

And I'm officially done with this interrogation. Rolling my eyes, I stand. "None of your business, Gray. Don't you have practice tomorrow? Or a morning workout? Shouldn't you be in bed?" I poke him in the side until he starts budging toward my open door.

But he stops in the doorway, glaring down at me. "You were with *him*, weren't you?"

I raise an eyebrow. "You're going to have to be more specific."

His eyes go wide in shock. "Is there more than one? Seriously?"

Rolling my eyes again, I huff. "Gray. Are you asking if I was having a threesome? And do you really want the answer to that question?"

He makes a choking sound, glancing all around like he's trying to figure out which way is up and which way is down. Then he shakes his head, planting his hands on his hips in a fair imitation of Dad when he's in full lecture mode. "Piper, he's not a good guy."

"Says you."

"Yes." He nods. "Says me. I've spent a lot of time with

him. And if he's sharing you around—"

I hold up my hand and cut him off. "Nope. Stop. Right there. Number one, I'm not anyone's property to be shared. I'm not a cake. If *I* choose to sleep with more than one person at a time, that's one hundred percent my business. I didn't realize you were such a prude. And number two, given that I'm not anyone's property, that means you don't actually get a say in who I do or do not spend time with, including your teammates that you don't get along with particularly well. Good night, Gray. Get some rest. You're clearly overtired if you think that waiting up for me to lecture me is going to get you anything positive."

He takes a step back in response to me grabbing the door and starting to close it on him, but stops it with a hand, and unfortunately he's big and solid enough that I can't outmuscle him. "Did it ever occur to you that he might be using you?"

Giving up on using the door to shove him out, I rub my forehead with a sigh. "Using me for what? Sex? That's kind of mutual."

Gray makes another choking sound that makes me smile, but I hide it behind my hand, straightening my face before meeting his eyes. "No," he finally says. "Using you to get at me."

I roll my eyes. It's an involuntary reaction to the ridiculous arrogance of that assertion. "Right. That's right, Gray. It must be about you. Because a hot guy couldn't possibly be interested in me on my own. Sure,

I'll text him right now and call everything off."

"Really?"

I could seriously slap that hopeful look off his face. I content myself with throwing my hands in the air and scoffing. "No, Gray. I'm not going to break up with a guy I'm not even really dating just because you think he could only be interested in me to get at you. *Good night*, Gray."

"This isn't over, Piper," he says as he steps into the hallway, letting me close the door behind him at last.

"Fantastic," I mutter, frustrated that my dumbass brother has ruined a perfectly good afterglow. Sighing, I flop down on the bed. If this is the way my brother reacts to me hanging out with a guy, I'm glad I've kept it from my parents. I can't even imagine how bad their reaction would be.

CHAPTER TWENTY-SEVEN

Piper

I get to find out their reaction the very next day, when my brother decides to spill all my beans at our family Thanksgiving dinner.

"So, Piper," he says, and I know from his tone of voice that this isn't going to be good.

"Yes, brother dear," I say in my most saccharine voice.

He rolls his eyes.

"Kids," Mom puts in, a clear warning in her voice.

But Gray ignores her, the asshole. "Which friend were you with last night?" He places a bite of turkey in his mouth, looking at me expectantly as he chews.

"I told you already," I say, trying to give my words just enough of an edge to get him to shut up without tipping off Mom and Dad that something's up that they should be more interested in. "One of my friends is staying with her brother for the break, and we hung out for a while."

Gray's brows draw together like he's pondering my response. "What's her name again?"

"Ellie," I answer, my voice clipped. I glare at him, trying to force him to drop this conversation with the power of my mind.

Mom and Dad look back and forth between us, their brows wrinkled in identical expressions of confusion. "Piper texted us last night that she'd be out late with her friend," Mom says.

"It's just interesting," Gray says, his attention seemingly focused on the food he's scooping onto his fork. "Because Ellie and her boyfriend stayed at Trey and Brandy's house for at least an hour after you disappeared." He glares at me. "I also noticed that your *friend's* brother left at about the same time as you. Do you know anything about that?"

The question is asked with such faux innocence, such malicious planning, that all I can do is gawp at him, my mouth opening and closing.

How could Gray do this to me? Didn't he come here to help shield me from Mom and Dad's over-attentiveness in the wake of what happened at SCU? Why would he throw me under the bus like this?

"Piper?" Dad asks. "What is he talking about? If you weren't with your friend, where were you?"

I swing my attention to Dad, glancing between him and Mom as I scramble for an answer.

But before I can say anything, Gray answers for me, driving the nails deep into the coffin of what freedom I've managed to hang onto. "She was with Cal, the second-string quarterback who's had it out for me since I showed up at the first team meeting back in August. He hates me. And he'll do anything to take my place as the starter. Including, it seems, screwing my sister to get into my head." He pulls his napkin out of his lap and wipes his mouth before standing. "I just thought it would be good if everyone knew the truth." He skewers me with a significant look before leaving the room.

I stare after him, moving to stand, but Dad's flinty voice stops me. "Sit down, Piper. You have some explaining to do."

Turning back to face my parents, I notice that the color has drained out of Mom's face, and she's holding one hand over her mouth, pressing it to her lips like she's trying to stop herself from releasing a flood of words she won't be able to take back.

But I stand anyway. "I'm not sure what else there is to explain," I say, my voice unfortunately hoarse, not steady and firm like I want it to be. "I thought the point of me living on campus was so I could have as normal of a college experience as possible. That includes dating, right?"

"Piper," Mom says around her fingers. "Yes, but—"

"But nothing," I interrupt, much to my father's displeasure if the flash of irritation in his gaze is anything to go by. "Either I get to have a normal college experience, or I'm your prisoner, disallowed from having a social life. Which is it?"

We stare at each other in stony silence for a moment. "Well," Dad says at last, "it seems the latter, since you can't seem to make good choices."

But before he can finish whatever else he was going to say, I'm leaving the room, unwilling to listen to him. I'm twenty years old. I won't be held prisoner by my parents.

Taking the stairs two at a time, I head straight for Gray's room, banging on his door once before shoving it open. "What is your fucking problem?"

"What's *my* fucking problem?" he spits, anger making him swell to his full height like he's trying to intimidate me. Ha. I know too much about him to find that intimidating. Plus, I know Gray would never hurt me. Not physically, anyway.

He steps closer, but I hold my ground, uncowed. "My fucking problem is you hellbent on self destruction."

That has me faltering slightly. "I'm not—"

He cuts me off with a sharp chop of his hand. "Cut the bullshit, Piper. I'm trying to *save* you. You won't listen to me, so maybe you'll listen to Mom and Dad." He points at me with one shaking finger. "You forced my hand. I told you to stay away from him weeks ago. And then you show up at *my* teammates' house at *my* invitation so you can spend all afternoon with him hanging off you and eye fucking you only for you to leave with him as soon as possible without offending Trey and Brandy. And you have the audacity to ask what *my* problem is?" He pounds his chest for emphasis. "What's *your* fucking problem?"

I step back, blinking in surprise at his vehemence, his anger. "What? That's not …" I shake my head, searching for the right words. "He's not whatever you've decided," I say quietly. "He likes me, Gray. And I like him. Besides, it's not like we're running off to get married or something. We're barely even dating. We're just … enjoying each other's company."

He scoffs, loud and angry. *"Enjoying each other's company."* He makes air quotes with his fingers, mocking my choice of words. "Is that what we're calling it now?"

Lifting my chin, I cross my arms. "We're fucking. Is that what you want me to tell you? He comes to my dorm, or I go to his place, and we fuck. A lot. And it's fan-*fucking*-tastic. The best I've ever had."

Another scoff. "Like you've been with *so* many guys."

"How would you even know?" I ask. "You've been gone."

"And look what happened at the first taste of freedom you got!" he shouts, throwing his arms wide. "You almost torpedoed your college career before it began. Because you were fucking some guy! Some asshole who couldn't treat you right, and when you didn't get justice through official channels, you decided to take it into your own hands, getting yourself in trouble in the process, forcing Mom and Dad to come riding to your rescue. Of *course* they're worried about you. Of course *I'm* worried about you. I came back here so I could look out for you, make sure this didn't happen again, and it's like you're determined to fuck your life up before you even have a chance to get started. What the fuck, Piper? What are you doing?"

My arms are still crossed, but my chin has dropped. I take another step back, swallowing hard, fighting down tears, finally understanding my family's view of me. "Right," I say. "Of course. You're right." I sniff, hating that I need to, but I can't help it. My voice is all watery, my throat tight from the tears fighting to get out. But I won't let them. "I'm the screwup hellbent on destroying my life as quickly as possible. By fucking some guy. I'm not, I don't know," I throw my hands up, looking all around the ceiling like I'm searching for possibilities, "a normal twenty-year-old who made a mistake almost a year ago. Nope. That's impossible. I'm just the family fuckup, doomed to always fuck up if I'm ever allowed any amount of freedom or ability to make choices. Sure. Okay. Yeah." I nod some more. "Thanks for clearing that up for me, Gray. And here I thought you came back to support me. Turns out you're just here to babysit me. What was the plan for next year? Are you gonna give up your chance at the draft to babysit me for the rest of college? And what about when I graduate? You gonna move me in with you? And how's that gonna work when I'm a competent adult? Hmm?"

He deflates, his anger leaking out of him. "Piper, no, come on. That's not—"

An angry, unnatural laugh breaks out of my chest. "That's not what? That's not the plan? That's not what you meant? Save it, Gray. You've made your position on my competence perfectly clear. Unfortunately for you, the legal system says otherwise. So I'll just get out of everyone's hair, alright?"

He follows me into the hall, stopping in my doorway where he watches me pull my suitcase out of the closet and start throwing clothes in it. "Piper, stop. What are you doing?"

"Leaving," I say firmly without sparing him a glance.

"Where are you going?" he asks as I yank my phone charger out of the wall and stuff it in my backpack along with my laptop, charger, and the books I brought with me.

"Somewhere else."

Mom and Dad are standing at the bottom of the stairs, but I ignore them as I drag my suitcase past them. My mom follows me out to my car, my coat in her hand. I accept it with a muttered, "Thanks," and put it on. It's too damn cold not to have it.

She stops me with a hand on my arm as I pass her to get to the driver's side. "Piper, we don't want you to be a prisoner. And we don't think of you as the family screwup."

I let out another low, angry chuckle. "Coulda fooled me, Mom. You've spent the last six months watching me like a toddler in a knife shop." Sniffing, I cross my arms and look away. "You're acting like I'm a criminal for spending time with a guy."

"A guy you lied to us about," she puts in calmly.

"Can you blame me?" I ask, looking her straight in the eye, my eyebrows raised. "When *this* is the reaction I get?" I throw my arm wide, gesturing at my father and brother standing in the open doorway watching Mom and I talk. "What about any of this invites disclosure? If I weren't here, I wouldn't be telling you that I'm spending some of my free time with a guy. I've been seeing him for weeks, and you just now found out about him. The only reason Gray knows is because he's seen us together. It's not that serious, so it hasn't seemed worth mentioning. Or do I have to tell you about every single person I interact with now? Is Gray subject to the same scrutiny, or is this special just for me?"

"That's not fair, Piper. Gray didn't—"

"Gray didn't make a mistake and date the wrong person. Gray didn't have porn posted of him without his permission. And Gray didn't have the university and law enforcement both tell him that there's nothing they can do and he should just be more careful who he sleeps with. Well, I am being careful, Mom. And I don't appreciate the double standard, or being treated like I'm the one who did something wrong."

"Well, you did get in trouble for breaking and entering and theft," Mom says on a sigh. "It's not like you did *nothing* wrong."

My eyes bug out of my head, and I choke on my outrage. "I hardly think that walking through an unlocked door is breaking and entering, especially when one of the brothers actually said hi to me shortly after I walked in. As for the theft, they got everything back. And stealing their modem and other forms of electronic entertainment was supposed to be poetic justice. They could've easily replaced everything. I did no lasting damage. And in the end, they weren't even out the money it would take to replace everything. But they *violated* my trust, my privacy, my autonomy. They took all that from me. And received nothing. No retribution. No punishment. No justice. So yes. I did that. I decided to serve justice on my own in whatever small way I could. Can you really blame me?"

"Piper ..." Mom begins, her voice a combination of conciliation and censure.

But I'm done. I really can't handle more of this right now. "I have to go."

Ignoring further pleas, I climb into my car and pull

away, working hard to hold back the tears that have been threatening for far too long. I can't fall apart. Not yet. Not until I'm somewhere safe.

Once I'm out of the neighborhood, I pull into a gas station and text Cal that I'm on my way over. Without waiting for his reply, I start heading that way. I doubt he'll have any objection. Worst case, if he's not there and waiting for me, I'll text Ellie. Either way, I'm heading to the same house.

CHAPTER TWENTY-EIGHT

Cal

Piper: I'm heading over to your place. Hope that's okay.

Me: Of course. See you soon.

I frown at Piper's text. She'd said that she was having dinner with her parents tonight and wouldn't be available, so I wasn't expecting to hear from her. We don't have a chat-every-day kind of relationship, after all. And I definitely wasn't expecting her to stop by.

"Everything alright?" Ellie asks as she comes back from the kitchen with a glass of water and cuddles up to

Simon on the other end of the couch. We've been back from his parents' house for almost an hour and decided to watch a movie and relax for a bit. Simon and I are heading out tomorrow morning, but I packed earlier so I wouldn't have to worry about it last minute since we weren't sure how late we'd be at his parents'.

"Yeah, everything's fine. Piper's on her way over."

Simon shoots me a look, part surprise, part censure.

"Shut up, dude," I tell him, making him snort. "I didn't invite her. She just texted and said she was coming over. And besides, you have *your* girlfriend here tonight."

Ellie holds up a finger. "One, I've been staying here all week, so that's not exactly surprising. And two, since when are you calling Piper your girlfriend?"

"I'm not," I grumble. "You're missing the point."

She puts her hand under her chin, a coy look on her face. "Am I, though?"

I ignore her in favor of staring at my phone in case Piper texts again. But she doesn't. About ten minutes later, there's a knock at the door. Simon pauses the movie while I answer it, surprised to see Piper's hand wrapped around the handle of a suitcase.

"Hey," she says, her voice wavery.

"Hey," I return, my brows drawing together, my eyes flicking between her and her suitcase. "What's going on?"

"Um ..." She clears her throat, and a tear slips down her cheek. She wipes it away with a furious brush of her hand, sniffing hard and clearing her throat again. "Sorry," she says, "I know ... I'm just ..."

"Piper?" Ellie says from behind me. "What's wrong? Are you okay? Cal, invite her in. Why are you making her stand crying in the cold?"

"What? I'm not—"

But Ellie completely ignores me, elbowing past me and reaching for Piper's suitcase. "Come in, come in."

Ducking her head, Piper follows Ellie inside, glancing at me as she passes.

I close the door behind her, taking the suitcase from Ellie and dragging it to my room. When I'm done, I find them in the kitchen. Ellie has Piper seated at the table, and she's plying her with drinks. "Do you want tea?" Ellie asks as I enter the room. "We have, umm …" She pauses as she searches our cabinets for tea. "I could've sworn they had *some* kind of tea." Closing the cabinet, she turns back to face Piper. "I could text Autumn. She's the queen of teas to help with anything. And then I can send Simon to the store to get whatever it is."

Piper lets out a soft, spluttery laugh, taking off her coat and draping it over the back of her chair. "That's okay, Ellie. I don't need tea. I appreciate the offer, though."

"Water, then? Or …" Ellie darts a glance at me, then at Simon who's lingering in the hall behind me. Lowering her voice, Ellie leans in close to Piper. "I know where the secret cookie stash is. I can liberate one for you."

My eyebrows shoot up. There's a secret cookie stash? I glance over my shoulder at Simon, who just gives me a bland look.

"I don't need cookies. I'm … I just …" She raises her eyes to me. "I didn't know where else to go."

"It's fine," I tell her. "You can stay here. Do you want to …" I finish the sentence by tipping my head toward my room.

She nods, the chair scraping against the vinyl floor as she scoots back. "Yes," she breathes. "That sounds good."

Ellie watches me wrap my arm around Piper and lead her to my room, and I can hear her and Simon murmuring to each other in the kitchen behind us, but I don't really care what they're saying. All my attention is focused on Piper right now.

When we get into my room, she sighs and sinks onto my bed, kicking off her shoes. She offers me a tentative smile. "Thanks. I had a fight with my parents. I needed to get away."

I sit on the bed next to her and rub a hand down her back. "Do you want to talk about it?" I'm not really sure what the protocol is here.

But she shakes her head, and I have to hold in my sigh of relief. I'm not good at this kind of thing—the talking and the caring and the "boyfriend" type duties. Which is why I've never really tried to be anyone's boyfriend.

And that's not what I'm doing here, either. Not exactly. But she clearly needs someone, and for whatever reason, she decided to come here. Because she didn't have anywhere else to go. All her friends are home for break. The dorms are closed. It makes sense.

Before I can say anything else, she turns to me and

cups my cheek, bringing my mouth to hers. Her lips are soft, tasting of salt. I kiss her back, but don't move to deepen it. I'm not sure what she's looking for from me, but whatever it is, I'll do my best to provide it.

She pulls back from the kiss, her eyes flicking back and forth between mine. Then she stands and faces me, edging over my lap. With her hands on my shoulders, she presses me back, climbing over me. This time when she presses her lips to mine, I open for her.

This is new and different. I don't think I've ever comforted someone with sex before, but if this is what she wants, I definitely have no objections.

She settles over my hips, pressing down on my quickly hardening cock, grinding against the bulge in my jeans.

When my hands slide to her hips, reaching around to grip her ass, she moans into my mouth, pressing harder, moving more. I push my hips up, and holding her tight to me, I flip us over so I'm on top, propped over her on one arm, gently brushing her hair out of her face.

She looks up at me with impossibly wide eyes, dark, deep pools of sadness. "Are you okay?" I whisper.

In answer, she pulls my face to hers with a hand on the back of my neck. Alright, then. No more questions. No more talking, except for whispered words of need and pleasure.

"Take your shirt off," she requests, and I do, following it quickly with my pants. While I'm undressing, she pulls off her clothes, but I stop her before she can unhook her bra, reaching behind her to do the honors myself.

Once her tits are free, I take my time worshipping them, plumping them with my hands, enjoying the way they fit perfectly in my palms, sucking on the tips until they're tight, shiny peaks, and she's arching into my mouth with every pass of my tongue, every pull of my lips.

When I finally put on a condom and sink into her depths, it's achingly slow and tender, which seems to be exactly what she needs right now.

And as I move, my tongue exploring her mouth, her body moving in time with mine, both of us perfectly in sync, the phrase *making love* keeps pounding away in my brain, no matter how much I try to ignore it.

I've never made love to anyone before. It's always just been sex. Fucking, banging, screwing. Simple physical release. And before this, I would've said that's what Piper and I had too. Sure, yeah, it's been consistently with her for the last little while and I haven't had any desire to find anyone else. Why would I when the sex is so fantastic between us?

But this is different. More. And even as my hips move faster, the soft sounds she makes deep in her throat as I swallow her cries spurring me on, a hard shell inside me seems to be cracking open with each thrust, revealing a soft center I've never wanted to acknowledge.

I snap my hips faster, pounding into her harder, as though I can hold off the realization and keep it at bay with brute force, trying to turn what this is back into what it used to be, relishing the way she squeezes me in her slick heat as she comes, shuddering around me, her orgasm triggering my own.

But there's no getting away from the truth of tonight after we clean up and settle into bed with me spooning around her naked body, holding her close and doing my best to soothe her with my skin on hers since that seems to be what she wants—what she needs—right now.

I care about Piper. I'm falling for her. I've never quite understood why people called it that—falling for someone. But nothing else describes the dizzying loss of equilibrium I'm feeling as the realization sinks its roots into me.

But once I relax into the sensation, it settles, a soft cloud buoying me. Closing my eyes, I drift off to sleep secure in the idea that Piper means something to me, and if she's here with me in my bed as a refuge from whatever storm has knocked her off course, I must mean something to her too.

CHAPTER TWENTY-NINE

Piper

I wake to a kiss on my forehead. Then another on my lips. All at once, awareness of where I am and who's kissing me comes rushing in. Cupping his cheeks, I pull Cal close for another kiss.

He chuckles against my lips, brushing his over them once more before gently disentangling himself and pulling away. "Sorry, babe. Much as I'd love to stay and indulge in another round, I can't. I gotta go. But I didn't want to just leave without saying goodbye and making sure you're okay."

Blinking my eyes open, I gaze up at his pretty face, noticing that he's already dressed and ready to go, a pair of duffle bags sitting next to the door. He gives me a soft, almost regretful smile. "You can stay here for as long as you need." He holds up a key and sets it on the bedside table. "Here's my house key. Don't lose it. Help yourself to whatever's in the fridge or the cabinets. We'll be back on Sunday. I'll text when we get there, okay?"

With one hand holding the sheet over my chest, I sit up. All I can do is nod, stunned by everything that's happening. Am I dreaming? Because this doesn't feel entirely real. I wasn't quite sure of my welcome when I texted out of the blue announcing my impending arrival last night. I mean, he's usually up for sex, so I didn't think he'd turn me away in a text. But when I showed up at his door with a suitcase in tow and tears on my face ... well, that's a bit of a different situation than our usual booty calls.

But not only did he—with the help of his sister and roommate—welcome me in and make me feel like this was a safe place for me to land, he responded to my every unspoken request, not prying for information about what drove me to his door in this state, instead doing his best to comfort me with his body and his warmth. And now he's offering to let me stay here, in his house, sleeping in his bed, without him being home, expecting nothing in return?

A fresh wave of tears prickles behind my eyes, but I do my best to fight them back. I cried last night, letting a few tears fall silently after he fell asleep, and I don't want to cry anymore right now. I can already tell that my eyes are puffy this morning. But Cal doesn't seem to notice or care as he examines me with clear affection on his face.

His thumb brushes my cheek, gathering a stray tear that I couldn't hold back. "Are you gonna be alright?" he asks softly.

I nod. "Yeah," I croak, clear my throat, try again. "Yeah. I will. It's just …" I shake my head. "Last night sucked, and you're being so nice, and …"

He lets out a soft chuckle. "Did you expect me to be a dick?"

Looking away, I lift one shoulder. "No. I mean, I wasn't sure what to expect. We don't exactly have a sleep-over-at-each-other's-place kind of relationship, and here I am showing up with a suitcase in tears, and you just calmly let me in, no questions asked, and now you're telling me I can stay through the weekend?" I spread my hands, palms up. "It's just more than I could've hoped. And I'm a little emotional at the moment. So, tears." I wave at my face with one hand.

He slides his big, calloused hand over mine, squeezing gently. "You don't have to explain yourself to me. I mean, if you want to talk, I'm here. Well," he glances at his phone, "I mean, I have to leave in five. But metaphorically. You can text or call or whatever. Unload everything in a voicemail if you want to call while I'm in the air so you give me all the info I need but don't have to field any questions right away." He gives me a crooked grin, and I can't help smiling in return.

"Has anyone told you that you're pretty great?"

He laughs, leaning in for one last kiss. "I tell myself that every day."

"Somehow that doesn't surprise me at all," I say on an answering laugh.

His gaze softens. "I really do have to go. But I think this is the first time that I haven't wanted to."

I squeeze his hand and let go. Sighing, he stands, lifting one bag over his shoulder and picking up the other, he pauses with his hand on the doorknob. "Talk soon, okay?"

At my nod, he leaves, the door closing quietly behind him. I hear quiet voices in the hall, the baritones of Cal and Simon plus a higher one that can only be Ellie. Climbing out of bed, I pull on my leggings and a discarded T-shirt of Cal's before heading out of the bedroom.

I make it out just in time to wave at Cal as he heads out the door. The look he gives me is tinged with longing, like all he wants is to come back in and climb into bed with me again. Which is probably exactly what he's thinking, because we usually have two rounds minimum when we get together with multiple orgasms for me, and while last night was fantastic and exactly what I needed, we each only had one orgasm.

But he pulls the door closed behind him, and I'm standing in the hall with just Ellie, who turns and faces me with her hands layered over her chest, her face the real life version of a heart eyes emoji.

"You two are so precious," she gushes.

I level a look at her, because I'm not in any position to handle gushing or dissecting my relationship with her brother right now. Especially after last night and the shift I felt deep in my softest places when he wrapped himself around me and held me close while he fell asleep.

She immediately straightens her face and drops her hands. "Okay, fine. We won't talk about Cal. Or whatever happened last night that had you landing here. Instead, let's talk about today. And tomorrow. And the two days after that." She crosses one arm over her torso, propping her elbow on her fist and her chin on her other hand. "What are your plans?"

I can't help laughing at the way she turns on a dime. "Umm, I really don't know." Yawning, I rub one eye and turn toward the bathroom. "First I have to pee. Can we discuss it after that?"

"Of course." She waves me toward the bathroom. "I'll make coffee. And then I'll tell you my plans, and you can decide from there, okay?"

I give her a somewhat bewildered nod and head into the bathroom. Once done, I find her in the kitchen, the coffee pot gurgling as she cuts a bagel in half and pops it in the toaster. She turns as soon as that's done, leaning back against the counter as she faces me. I'm worried she's going to give me the heart eyes face again, but she seems to pull herself together.

"So," she starts, sounding very businesslike, "today is officially Thanksgiving, and I think I mentioned the other day that my mother has decided I must return. I was actually supposed to go home yesterday, but Simon's parents had the three of us over for an early Thanksgiving dinner for the guys, and I finally managed to convince my mom that I couldn't possibly miss that, that it would be a horrible social faux pas to miss my first Thanksgiving with my boyfriend's family when I was specifically invited." She pulls out the carafe and pours herself a mug of coffee, setting another mug on the counter and gesturing for me to help myself. Then she grabs a jug of creamer from the fridge, jiggling it at me in silent question after pouring a healthy splash in her mug.

Grinning, I nod, and she sets it on the counter while I fill my own mug with coffee.

The toaster pops, and she hisses at her burnt fingers as she pulls the bagel out and drops it on a plate before buttering it. "You want one?" she asks.

"Sure."

She passes me the bag, and I pull the cinnamon raisin bagel apart with my hands and pop it in the toaster.

"Anyway," she continues, "that makes today my third Thanksgiving this week. But if I don't go, it'll be a whole thing. Wanna come with me?"

I turn, surprised, not realizing this was where she was heading with this conversation. "Seriously?"

She nods emphatically. "Hell, yes. Having you along would be fantastic, actually. I've been dreading going home. I mean," she tilts her head from side to side, "arguably it should be better than Fall Break considering I've actually declared a major so my dad won't be on my case about that. And my grades are good, barring any major disasters with finals, so they can't gripe at me about that. But my dad will surely find something. Probably harp on me taking so long to declare a major and how I need to make sure I get any and all prereqs taken care of as soon as possible so I'm not too far behind." She rolls her eyes and shakes her head. "Anyway, I'm sure there'll be something. But he tends to tone it down if there's a guest. Not completely. He'll still find something. I mean, how else will he entertain himself if he doesn't have me to pick at?" I'm not sure what to say to that, but apparently an answer isn't required, because she waves the thought away. "Sorry. Welcome to my pity party." She does a half curtsey that makes me laugh, and she comes up smiling back at me. "Whaddaya say?"

"Your parents won't mind me showing up without advance notice?"

She shrugs. "I already texted my mom and asked if it'd be okay for me to bring a friend, and she said of course. Actually, when I told her I'd found out today that a friend was going to be alone on Thanksgiving, she texted back that I should be sure to invite you before I even finished typing the second part of my message asking if it would be okay."

I chew on the inside of my cheek. "A friend, huh? So you didn't tell them about Cal and me?"

A mischievous grin breaks out on her face. "Well," she says slyly, "since neither of you will admit to what exactly there is between you, no, I didn't tell them that you're anything to each other." She shrugs again. "Besides, you live in my dorm. You have my number. We're friends."

The toaster popping covers my surprise at her easy declaration of friendship. She pulls out a plate for me and slides the butter over to me.

"Um, alright," I say as I spread butter over the toasted bagel. "That sounds good. I'll come."

She claps and says, "Yay! Great. Okay. I'll let my mom know you're officially in, that way she can make sure to have the air mattress ready for you. It's not the greatest, I know, but it's better than the floor for sure. And this way you won't be moping around my brother's house all alone or having to deal with … whatever else." She looks up from her phone, examining me. "It's alright on your end for you to come, right? You won't make everything worse by leaving town for a few days?"

I shake my head. "No, I mean, not any worse than it already is. I'll text my mom and let her know so she doesn't worry, but I need some space to figure out how to deal with everything that happened. Besides, I haven't been out of town in far too long, so this'll be a nice change." I pause, taking a bite of my bagel. "So, um," I say as I swallow, "where are we going exactly?"

With a laugh, Ellie leaves the kitchen. "The Dalles, Oregon," she calls over her shoulder. "I'm surprised you didn't know that already." Her head pops back through the doorway. "Cal never told you where he's from?"

Shrugging one shoulder, I give her a lopsided grin. "It never came up."

She cackles. "I'm sure it didn't."

CHAPTER THIRTY

Cal

Me: We made it. <Selfie in the hotel room> Team meeting in 10, so I'll text again later.

Piper: Okay. I'm at your parents' with Ellie. We're about to eat. Hope everything goes well.

"What's up?" Simon asks when he notices me staring at my phone, surprise probably written all over my face.

"Uh, it appears that my sister got Ellie to go home with her for the weekend."

Simon chuckles. "That surprises you? She's been moaning about having to be home by herself all week.

Plus, she's been angling to get Piper alone so she can grill her about you two since she found out there was a you two." He spreads his hands. "I don't know why you didn't see this coming."

I glance at him before sitting down on my bed in the hotel room. "I guess I just didn't think about it."

He snorts and shakes his head. "Of course you didn't."

"What's that supposed to mean?"

Shrugging, he opens his bag and puts his shaving kit in the bathroom, going through his usual routine of settling into a hotel before the team meeting downstairs. "Just that you don't pay much attention to your sister."

"Jesus Christ," I mutter.

He smirks. "You don't. We all know it. I'm not giving you shit, just stating facts."

"Fine. I guess I don't."

"Because if you did," he continues like I didn't just agree with him, "you'd know that Ellie has your entire future with Piper all planned out. Starting with couple dates and game nights once football season is over."

"Please tell me you're joking."

He shoots me a look that lets me know that no, he is not joking. Sighing, I drop my head back on my pillow. "It's not like that with Piper and me. We're not …"

"A couple?" he supplies.

I lift a hand and let it drop back on the bed. "I guess." But that doesn't feel right. It doesn't sit right with me to deny that she's more to me than a booty call. Especially after last night.

Simon sits on his bed and levels a look at me. "For real? She shows up at your door when she's upset and just got in a fight with her family, and you're gonna sit there with a straight face and tell me that you aren't in a relationship with this chick?"

"Fuck you," I grumble, and he just laughs.

"Come on. Time for the meeting."

* * *

We return to the hotel after our game on Friday, tired and elated from our win, running on adrenaline and endorphins. I even got some playing time. I didn't start, and it wasn't until the fourth quarter. Apparently Kilpatrick tweaked something in his shoulder, and Coach would rather baby him to make sure he can play for the most important games that are still to come. But at this point, I'll take what I can get.

Coach's parting words when we get back to the hotel are, "Don't stay out too late. And don't get yourselves in trouble. I don't have it in me to bail you out of jail this far away from home, so if you end up there, you'll have to get yourself out and find your own way home." With that, he and the other coaches file off the bus, leaving us to follow behind them and figure out our own plans.

A loud groan goes up from Lancaster when he picks up his duffle and notices the little stuffed piggy snout sticking out of an end pocket. "Fuck, man. I've already had Piggy five times this season. Isn't it someone else's turn?"

Laughter ripples through the team. "Don't leave your bag where anyone can get to it," Gardner shouts back at him, and Lancaster tosses Piggy at him.

"Nice try," Johnson says, picking up Piggy and handing him back. "That's not how you get rid of Piggy. And anyway," he gives the stuffed pig a little pat, "be careful with Piggy. He's getting old. We don't need him to get all dirty. Remember what happened the last time he needed a bath?"

Foster cracks up. "You got stuck with him for the rest of the year because he wouldn't dry in time for you to pass him off before the end of the season."

Grumbling, Johnson and Foster and the rest make their way off the bus, plans for the best ways to celebrate starting to circulate among the team.

I'd normally be down to go out and have a few drinks, maybe find someone to take the edge off the usual post-game horniness running through my veins. But tonight is different. Piper has made things different. I wouldn't have picked anyone up before what happened Wednesday night, but I still would've gone out for drinks at least. But Wednesday night caused another shift, a resettling, an adjustment in what I want and how and when and with who.

I'm horny, and if I can't be with my woman in person, then I at least want to exchange sexy pics and get off with her.

Simon glances over at me as we head into the hotel, the guys around us talking loudly, looking at their phones, comparing notes on the best places to go according to their preferred referral sites. He gives me a knowing grin. "I'm going to go with …" he gestures vaguely at Trey and some of the other offensive lineman. "Wherever they're going. Catch you later."

I lift my chin in acknowledgment. "Cool. Have fun." Simon rarely goes out when we're on the road, and never without significant encouragement from me, so I know he's doing this to give me some time alone in the room. Which probably means that when he gets back, I'll need to go for a walk or something to return the favor. And I'll just pretend that I don't know he's sexting with my sister.

But for now, I'll take advantage of having the room to myself.

I strip down to my boxer briefs when I get back, grateful to be out of my game day suit, and settle onto the bed. Palming my growing erection, pulling the fabric taut to show the outline of what I wish I could give Piper, I snap a few pics, adjusting the angle and how close I am to the light to get the best shot. I don't send it yet. But I have it at the ready so I don't have to adjust lighting and compose the shot on the fly.

Me: Hey babe. What are you up to?

I lazily stroke myself as I wait for her answer, getting stupidly excited about sexting with my … with Piper.

I don't think I've ever been excited about sexting before. I mean, sure, I've had chicks send me nudes, and who doesn't like seeing a nice pair of tits? But it's never had this edge of anticipation, this thrill. It's not just the prospect of release, but it's the connection with her that makes it better.

Piper: Ellie and I are watching a movie.

A fine thread of disappointment winds through me. Of course she's doing something with my sister. She's at my parents' house keeping Ellie company for the weekend. I shouldn't be surprised. I *know* that she's not still lounging in my bed in my house just waiting for me. But that's the image I have of her in my head regardless.

Me: Can you get some privacy for a little bit? Or would that be weird?

Piper: I mean ... probably. Why? What did you have in mind?

I send her the best shot. It's not a true dick pic. Not yet. I mean, yeah, my dick is in it, but it's not uncovered.

Piper: OMG. Warn me before you send that kind of thing. Your sister is sitting right next to me trying to see what we're texting.

I slap my forehead and cover my face with my hand.

Me: Well go somewhere else. Don't let her see. I don't creep on Simon's texts with her. That's weird.

Piper: Lol. She left.

Me: Good. Send me a pic of what you're wearing.

She sends a selfie of her unmade up face, her hair loose, an oversized T-shirt covering her upper body.

Me: Now take off your top and send another.

I continue lazily stroking myself while I wait for her response. When it takes her a few minutes, my excitement grows, my dick getting harder, my hand moving a little faster. She has fantastic tits, and getting a pic of them to keep on my phone would be epic. Especially if she's not wearing a bra …

Piper: No

That has me stopping short, pushing myself up to sitting, my aching dick abandoned and neglected while I stare at the two letter response. No? Why not? I type and delete multiple variations of that question, not sure how to ask what I want to know without coming across like a demanding asshole. Texting doesn't exactly allow for a lot of nuance. And I'm not trying to be demanding, even if my last request maybe came across that way. But she tends to like it when I tell her what to do in bed, and if it's something she's not comfortable with, she never just gives me a flat refusal. We talk, adjust, accommodate. So her no, just no, catches me off guard, and I want to know what's going on, what I can do, how we can adjust, but it's hard to communicate that in text.

Finally, I give up and call her. I'd rather hear her voice anyway. I figured sexting might be safer noise-wise since she's with my sister at my parents' house, but I'm good with phone sex if she's willing to do that instead.

She answers on the third ring, which seems weird, because isn't her phone in her hand? We were literally just texting.

"Hey." Her voice is short. Curt.

My brows draw even closer together. "Piper? What's wrong?"

She sighs, a long, slow release of breath. "Nothing. It's just … I don't … do that."

"Do … what, exactly?"

"Send pics. Topless pics. I don't … I don't send nudes."

"Ever?"

"No."

"Umm, okay." I mean, we all have boundaries. And this hasn't really been an issue before now, so … okay.

"Okay?" She sounds almost relieved.

"Yeah. I mean," I let out an awkward chuckle,

"what'd you expect? Me to get mad and demand nudes or else?"

"Not … exactly. I just … I don't know."

"Baby." I soften my voice, going for as reassuring as possible. "You're fucking hot, so you have nothing to be ashamed of. But if you're not comfortable sending topless pics, I'm not going to get mad or try to pressure you. I just miss you and thought it would be fun to have some long distance sexy time."

"Okay," she says, her voice equally soft. Almost inaudible. Then she sniffs. Is she crying?

"Are you okay? Is everything okay? Has going to my parents' been awful? What did Ellie tell them about us?"

She lets out a soft laugh, like my concern is endearing and amusing. "Yes, I'm fine. Everything's fine. Ellie didn't tell them anything about us. She said I was a friend from the dorm who she just found out would be alone on Thanksgiving and your mom insisted she invite me."

"That sounds like my mom," I say with a smile.

"It's actually been pretty great. Ellie's really happy I'm along to help deflect your dad's attention, though from what I can tell he's mostly thrilled that she's actually picked a major. I take it that was a serious point of contention?"

"Ha. You have no idea." I tuck my dick back into my underwear and stand, grabbing a pair of shorts out of my duffle bag. Whatever this conversation is, I strongly suspect it won't become phone sex. Not after that reaction. I don't know if it's whatever happened with her parents, the fact that she's at my parents' house with my sister, or something else entirely, but the uninhibited sexy woman I'm used to in person is very much absent on the phone. She's reserved right now, almost shy.

"Right." I can hear the smile in her voice, and that brings an answering smile to my face. "So how'd the game go? Your dad said he tried to find live coverage of it somewhere, but couldn't. We watched a few highlights online, but it's not at all the same as being there, or even getting to watch it on TV. You guys won, though?"

"Yeah. I finished out the game, actually. We ran an awesome blitz and scored the touchdown that cemented our win. It was close before that, with only a three point lead, but we got to breathe a little easier after that. Not that we let them score again, of course. But if they had, it would've been okay."

"Gray didn't play the whole game? Is he okay?"

Right. Of course she's worried about her brother. I'm somewhat irrationally wounded that she isn't at least able to be excited for me first. What do I expect, though? Sure, she comes to me when she's upset about something, that's great, but he's still her brother. I'm just the guy she's screwing.

"Yeah," I say, unable to keep the flatness out of my voice. "He's fine. His shoulder was bothering him on his last few plays, so Coach subbed me in just to make sure it's nothing serious. We want him in peak playing condition for the postseason, after all." A little sarcasm leaks in on the last sentence.

Piper sighs. "Sorry. It's just weird for Gray not to finish the game unless he's injured. I didn't mean to rain on your parade. I'm glad you got an awesome play. Were there scouts there, do you know?"

Mollified by her apology, I try to let go of my hurt feelings. Maybe I was wrong about the shift in our relationship that I thought we both felt the other night. Maybe it was just me. "Rumor has it."

We chat for a few more minutes, and by the time we're done, I'm not sure how I feel. My adrenaline-fueled horniness hasn't been sated, but it's more of a subtle background noise now, and somehow getting myself off without Piper at least on the phone with me doesn't hold much appeal.

So I text Simon, find out where he is, and head out. If I can't celebrate the way I'd really like, I can at least bask in our victory with my teammates.

CHAPTER THIRTY-ONE

"Alright," Ellie says as she exits the freeway, heading back toward campus. "Let's stop by the dorm and take in our things, then we'll head over to Simon and Cal's place to see the guys and get your car."

"Sounds good." This weekend has been surprisingly relaxing. Ellie's actually pretty low key when she's just hanging out and not trying to get me to say that her brother is my boyfriend. Cal and I haven't even had that conversation other than way back when we first started spending time together when we said we'd keep it casual. As far as I know, that's still what Cal wants.

Except he called you after his game, a voice in my head

reminds me. *And you've been texting with him all weekend. And he was the first place you thought to go when you were upset.*

Still. That all may be true. But without any definitive agreement between him and me, I'm not confirming or denying anything to Ellie. When I finally laid all that out to her, she stopped pushing, which was a relief. And then we just got to hang out, eat junk food, watch stupid old movies, and basically have an extended sleepover.

After the stress of the last nine months, it was just what I didn't even know I needed. We also managed to get homework done, though I didn't get quite as far ahead as I'd planned when I expected to be at my parents' with only my brother for company for the week.

Speaking of, my phone vibrates in my hand with another call from Gray, but I send it to voicemail, just like I have every other time he's tried calling yesterday and today. He didn't try at all between me leaving Mom and Dad's Wednesday night and his game on Friday, which I should be grateful for, but somehow only makes me more angry at him. He didn't know where I ended up that night, and apparently doesn't really care. So much for the whole protective older brother coming home to make sure I stay out of trouble schtick, huh?

Part of me wants to answer and say those words to him, but the rest of me knows better. For one, I don't want to get into a shouting match with my brother on the phone while Ellie's driving us back to campus. For another, it wouldn't actually change anything.

Surprisingly, a voicemail notification lights up my phone a moment later. He hasn't left a message the other times he's called, though he has texted with a terse demand that I call him back, which I've ignored.

Ellie glances between my phone and me at the stoplight. "Your brother again?"

I nod.

"He left a voicemail?" It's a question, but it sounds more like a statement. She can obviously see the notification lighting up the car in the dim early twilight of late November.

"Yeah."

"You gonna listen to it?"

I look down at my phone again, even though it's dark now. "Not sure yet."

"Do you want to talk about it?"

"No." The answer comes out hoarse, and I clear my throat, forcing down my anger and frustration. Time and space has made it easier to ignore, but it hasn't done anything to diminish it. I'm not honestly sure what will.

An apology, maybe. That would be a start, anyway.

When Ellie parks her car in the parking lot by our dorm, she does a little happy dance in her seat for scoring a spot so close to the front. But before climbing out of the car, she lays her hand on my arm and looks me in the eyes, her face suddenly serious. "If you ever do want to talk about what happened, I'm here, alright? I get crazy family dynamics and disappointing expectations."

I quirk an eyebrow, but she nods, her face earnest. "I'm the black sheep. Cal's the golden child. Since he wasn't around, it was less obvious, but I promise that's the dynamic. I'm the flighty, silly one who can't make up her mind. He's focused and serious and Going Places, TM."

I can't help laughing at the way she phrases that. Then I let out a sigh and shake my head. "That's not exactly the dynamic with my family. I mean, kinda, I guess. Gray is also Going Places, TM, and coming back here probably helped with that, but that wasn't the whole reason he came home." I sigh again, looking down at my hands, not wanting to get into all the shitty details. I alluded to having trouble in California my freshman year and transferring here, but I didn't get into why. Ellie was clearly curious, but she didn't pry. Just like she's not really prying now. She's just … trying to be a friend. And maybe I should share, but I'm too tired and emotionally wrung out to go there right now.

Shaking my head, I blow out a breath. "I'm the screwup. And there's no telling what crazy stupid thing I'll do next." I wave my hands around to show how ridiculous I think that is, and Ellie watches me, her mouth pulling down at the corners, her face troubled.

She tilts her head, looking me over. "Aren't you taking like a bajillion classes this semester?"

I bark out a laugh. "Yeah. Something like that."

"And you're doing well in all of them?"

Swallowing, I nod. "So far, yeah."

"How does that make you a screwup?" she asks, genuinely puzzled.

With a shrug and a sigh, I shake my head again. "That's me trying to make up for the screwing up I did already. But somehow it isn't enough. I'm not sure anything will be."

Ellie squeezes my shoulder, and I offer her a small smile. "Well, you're enough for me. And that's all that matters."

When I laugh, she grins at me, and mood sufficiently lightened, we climb out of the car and wrestle our things across the parking lot and up the stairs to our separate rooms. She waves when we part ways at the top of the stairs, promising to come get me in a few minutes.

When I get to my room, Dani's already there. She jumps off the couch in our living area and throws her arms around me. Laughing at her exuberance, I drop my backpack and return her hug.

"You're back," she says, rocking us back and forth. "I missed you. So fill me in," she says as she releases me. "Did you do all your homework for the next week plus study for all your finals while you were at your parents' house?"

"Ha. Not hardly." I fill her in on the fireworks of the week, from hanging with Cal at the start of the week to ending up at his parents' house all weekend with his sister.

When I finish, Dani's eyes are wide. "Wait, wait, wait," she says. "I have so many questions. First, I thought you and Cal weren't serious."

"We're not. Or we weren't. Or …" I trail off and shrug.

"Okay," she says. "Let's put a pin in that. It sounds like you and he need to have a whole conversation about *that*." She waves her hands in big circles in the air around me, and I giggle, because Dani isn't usually this animated.

She gives me a crooked grin. "Sorry. I was hanging out with my sister back home. She's a lot more lively than I normally am. It rubs off. But back to you."

I shake my head. "No, not back to me. Fill me in on your break really quick. Ellie's coming to get me soon, because we still have to go to her brother's house and get my car."

"Uh-huh," Dani says with a knowing look. "Get your car, huh? And you're not going to spend *any* time with a certain football player we happen to know?" She bats her eyelashes at me, all innocent inquiry.

Laughing, I toss a throw pillow at her. "I mean, why deny the obvious truth? But seriously, how was your break? You were saying you might get to see Sean. Did you? How'd that go?"

Her expression sours. "Oh, him. Yeah. I saw him. But, ugh." She shakes her head. "I don't want to talk about him. He's …" She looks up, searching for the right words, then shakes her head. "He's a big, dumb *boy*." She spits the word like it's the most insulting term she can come up with.

Reaching out, I pat her shoulder in commiseration. Sean was her high school boyfriend, and they kinda got together again over the summer, and she'd hoped for some kind of reprise over Thanksgiving, but clearly that didn't work out. Before I can ask for details, though, there's a knock at the door, and I know it's Ellie.

I point at Dani. "You'll fill me in when I get back, right?"

She waves me off. "Go see your man. Figure yourselves out and then *you* fill me in when you get back."

Laughing, I grab my jacket and open the door to Ellie's smiling face. She waves at Dani. "Hey! How was your break?"

They exchange a few pleasantries, and it strikes me how much I've been isolating myself this whole semester, insulating myself from the world with classes and homework, giving excuses more than going out with anyone who invited me, with the notable exception of Dani, who just decided one day that she wouldn't take no for an answer anymore, especially after she found out I was watching my brother's practices when I wanted to take a break.

And why? I mean, I know why I'd decided to take a break from boys. My parents weren't the only ones worried I'd end up in the same place I did last spring. But why did I put that all on myself in the first place? I'm not the one who decided to post pics of girls without their permission or knowledge. I'm not the one who made it a bet, a game, a dare. And I'm not the university who decided a written warning not to do it again—the equivalent of a finger wag from an overly indulgent parent—was sufficient.

While I maybe could be forgiven for doubting my ability to pick a guy who isn't a douche—though for all his obvious douchiness in the beginning, Cal's actually turned out to be pretty great, on balance—why did I decide not to even give the girls who only wanted to be my friend a chance?

Dani already knew Ellie and Autumn from last year. She's hung out with them a few times and invited me along, and I always declined, only going with Dani to football parties, because Gray would be there, so it seemed safe.

Can I really blame Gray for wanting to protect me from myself? Didn't I want him to do that for me too? That's why I filled my free time with him and his friends instead of finding my own.

I don't even know what I was thinking anymore. The girl who made those decisions feels like a different person than I am now. And I'm not really sure when or how that changed exactly, except when Cal bet me I couldn't kiss him without liking it, claiming a date as his winnings, I didn't have a choice but to get out of my own way.

Only my brother and my parents didn't get the memo that I'd put my self distrust to bed, and they haven't come around to trusting me yet.

I should listen to Gray's voicemail. And call him back. And then figure things out with my parents. But that can all wait. First, I'm going to see Cal, because I've missed him more than I've allowed myself to admit. And I want to see him before I deal with any of the other stuff.

CHAPTER THIRTY-TWO

"The girls are on their way over," Simon says from my doorway.

I look up from my textbook, having resigned myself to catching up on homework today instead of spending time with Piper. He laughs when I straighten up as his words rearrange themselves in my brain until they make sense. "Really?"

His face is full of indulgent amusement. "She didn't text you?"

Grabbing my phone, I check the screen and shake my head, my brows drawing together. "No, she didn't."

With a shrug, Simon leaves. "Maybe she doesn't want

to see you after all," he says as he walks away.

"Fuck you," I call after him. As usual, he laughs.

It doesn't take long for the girls to get here. Ellie knocks on the door and lets herself in. "We're here," she calls out in a singsong voice. I block out Simon's rumble of pleasure as I poke my head out the door, trepidation and happiness warring in my chest.

Piper didn't mention she was coming over. I mean, I assumed she'd stop by at some point since her car is still here. But maybe she just wants to get it and leave. Maybe she didn't even come inside with Ellie.

But she's there, standing in the entryway in front of the closed door, tucking her hair behind her ear as she looks me over like she can't get enough of me.

A grin stretching across my face, I straighten to my full height, my chest swelling with my inhale. "Hey, babe. Come here."

She returns my smile with an almost shy one of her own, walking slowly toward me, her eyes scanning my body once more. "Hey," she says softly, her eyes darting to Simon's now-closed door. I'm just going to block out the fact that Simon and my sister are on the other side of that door, because I'd much rather focus on Piper here in front of me and how I'd really like to greet her.

When she's close enough, I hook my arm around her waist and pull her against me, stepping back into my room and closing the door behind us. Then I back her against it, dropping my mouth to hers. She presses against me, her fingers sliding over my shoulders and around my neck, holding me in place as though I'd want to go anywhere else.

My tongue slides past her lips, seeking hers. She sucks on it briefly before sliding her tongue against mine, and I groan into her mouth, pressing my hips into her belly.

"God, I've missed you," I whisper when I tear my mouth away, panting like I've just run wind sprints.

She rubs herself against me with a soft moan. "I've missed you too."

"Good."

I pull her away from the door, sitting down on my bed and pulling her over me. I need her. On top of me, surrounding me, welcoming me home. I've been aching for her since I left her here on Thursday morning. It feels like an eternity ago, even though it's only been a few days. How is it that since I met her, time has seemed to move both slower and faster? It feels like we've known each other forever, and yet when I'm with her, our time together is always over far too soon.

Peeling down her leggings, I barely wait for her to kick them the rest of the way off before sliding my hand between her thighs, finding her wet and ready for me already. She gasps into my mouth when I push two fingers inside her, finger fucking her until her fingers dig into my shoulders.

Then I lay back on the bed and urge her up my body with my hands on her ass. "C'mere, baby," I whisper. "Let me taste you."

She strips off her top, a slinky, soft tee with a wide

neck that tends to fall off her shoulders, her bra following it until she's naked and ready for me. There's an awkward moment where she maneuvers her legs so she's straddling my face, giving a self-deprecating laugh as my arms and her legs get tangled together.

But then I'm staring up at her soft, wet pussy, her scent surrounding me, and with my hands gripping her ass, I pull her down to my mouth. She gasps at the contact, her fingers going to my head, tangling in my hair.

I take my sweet time savoring her, running my tongue over every inch of flesh I can reach, dipping inside her a few times before focusing on her clit. I start slow, drawing circles around it, watching her body undulate over me.

Her hand tightens in my hair, and the sting of my scalp somehow makes this even better. My dick twitches when she slides her other hand up her torso to pinch her own nipples. I groan into her pussy, so fucking turned on I think I might come in my pants just from this.

When I suck her clit between my lips, she jerks, her thighs flexing and squeezing around my face, her hips moving gently. With my hands still firmly holding her ass, I encourage her to move as much as she wants.

She's gasping and cursing and pinching her own nipples with both hands and holy fuck I need to be inside her. But I want her to come first. I want to watch the waves of her orgasm crash over her like this before I make her come again on my cock.

It's become something of an obsession, seeing how many times and how many ways I can make her come each time we're together, and it never gets old. I've always prided myself on my abilities in bed, making sure to leave a partner satisfied. I might have a reputation as a player, but I make sure none of the girls who flit around the edges of the football team wanting a turn with an elite athlete ever have reason to spread around that I'm selfish in bed. I might be selfish in other ways, but never there.

Being with Piper has taken that to the next level. Not only do I not want her to be able to complain about our bedroom activities to anyone, but I don't want to give her reason to suspect she could get better anywhere else. Ever.

It starts as a slow tightening, first her thighs, then her ass. Her belly shrinks as she sucks it in, curling forward a little. And then it crashes over her almost in slow motion, once again starting with her thighs and working its way up her body. Her thighs shake and quiver as her pussy spasms against my tongue, a wave of release flowing over her entire body until she's slumping in my hands, her hands once again on my head. When I don't let up, she starts whimpering, trying to push away.

After one last lick, I let her, helping her off my face. She slumps over sideways on the bed, and I grin as I wipe my chin with one hand and reach for a condom with the other. Rolling onto her back, she looks up at me, her hair wild and spread over the bed, one arm thrown over her head. "I think you're trying to kill me," she says as she watches me shove my gray sweatpants down and off and roll the condom on.

"Why do you say that?" I ask as I climb onto the bed with her, hooking one leg with my hand and making room for me to move between her thighs.

She adjusts, moving down closer to me, welcoming me into the cradle of her body. When I prop myself over her on one arm and use my other hand to run the head of my cock all over her soaked pussy, she gasps, pressing her hips closer to me. "Because ..." she says, her voice barely more than a breathless whisper. "You're trying to fuck me to death."

Chuckling, I slide inside her, holding back my urge to pound into her hard enough that she might think I'm trying to prove her right. When she lifts her knees, her thighs squeezing my hips, I flex deeper into her, making her arch and gasp. "Just trying to make sure you're satisfied, baby," I murmur against the skin of her collarbone.

And even though I desperately need to spend myself inside her, I want this to be more than some oral and a quick fuck. I need her to realize that what we have is different, special. That my desire to leave her satisfied has more to do with her now than it does with my own pride. I want her to want to come back. To come here when she's upset. Or happy. Or horny. Especially horny. But anything in particular she's feeling, I want her to feel comfortable telling me about it.

I don't know how to say any of that without sounding like an idiot, though, so I'm doing my best to show her with my actions and my body that she's safe with me.

That she's desired and cared for and important.

She pulls my face to hers, her tongue delving into my mouth, dueling with mine as her hips press up, meeting me stroke for stroke. I hold myself up on one elbow, my other hand moving constantly over her body, rolling her nipple between my thumb and finger, then sliding between our bodies, my thumb gathering some of her wetness before sliding it in circles over her clit.

"Fuck, Cal," she whispers, and I can't help but grin.

"That's it, baby," I encourage. "You know you love it when I make you come multiple times. You know you want to come for me, milking my cock with your hot little pussy. Don't you?"

"Yessss," she hisses out, her hips moving more, and I move my thumb in tighter circles, feeling her start to clench around me.

I cover her mouth with mine, swallowing her cry when she comes again, her pussy squeezing me in the way I've come to crave. I push through it, moving faster, harder, deeper, until the heat zips down my spine, my orgasm washing over me with her legs circling my hips and her arms around my shoulders, like she can't bear the idea of ever letting me go.

Which works for me, because at this point I have no intention of letting her go, either.

My phone vibrates on my nightstand, then again a second later, ruining the moment. Groaning, I slide to the side, annoyed at whoever decided now was the time to text me. Another alert lights up my phone.

Brows pinched in a frown, I grab it and hold it over my face, intent on figuring out the best way to deal with this distraction. If I can respond quickly and get whoever it is to leave me the fuck alone, I'll do that. If it's something that requires a more detailed response, well, I'll just put my phone on Do Not Disturb and deal with it later. But I've been away from Piper for too long, and I'm not willing to sacrifice my time with her for anything less than a true emergency.

"What are you doing?" Piper asks, and something in her voice has me looking over at her, concerned.

"Figuring out why someone's texting me fifteen times in a row and getting them to stop." I say it slowly, carefully, wondering what the big deal is.

Piper's face is pale, and she's clutching a pillow to her chest. My brows pull together as I take her in. "Are you cold? We can get under the covers. Gimme a sec, and I'll snuggle you and keep you warm." I give her my most charming smile, hoping that'll ease whatever's going on right now.

She licks her lips, her eyes glued to my phone. "Has that been on this whole time?"

Propping myself up on my elbow, I put my phone on Do Not Disturb without even reading the texts. Whoever it is can wait. Because something's going on here, and I definitely need to figure out what it is.

"Yes," I answer in the same careful voice. "Should it not be?"

She shakes her head slowly, her eyes still on my

phone like it's a venomous snake poised to strike.

Clearing my throat, I look between the phone now on my side table and her again, and I think back to every other time we've been together. She's turned off our phones more than once. Always mine first. And now that I think about it, the first time, she didn't seem like she was going to turn off hers until I prompted her to. And she's told me to leave it in the other room more than once too.

"Piper, is there some reason you're not okay with me having my phone while we have sex?"

She stands, still clutching the pillow to her torso, and moves carefully around the room, crouching to gather up her clothes that were strewn around moments ago. When she straightens, clothes in hand, her gaze darts between me, my phone, her clothes, and the pillow, like she's trying to figure out that riddle where you have to take a wolf, a goat, and a cabbage across the river on a boat that can only carry yourself and one other thing. Except it's clear the riddle is how can she get dressed without revealing any part of her naked body to me or my phone.

I pick up my phone again, and she tenses. "Cal," she starts, but I hold up my phone facing her, holding down the button to turn it off so she can see the screen go dark.

"There." I set it down. "It's off. Can you come back to bed, now?"

Her shoulders visibly drop, and the tight lines of her face relax as she climbs back on the bed, still holding the pillow in front of her, but this time more like a comfort object than a shield.

I glance at my phone one more time before moving closer to her. She lets me gather her into my arms, but avoids my gaze.

I kiss her shoulder and stroke her back, waiting until she seems more relaxed before broaching what just happened. Clearing my throat, I settle us so I'm propped up on my pillows against the wall and she's leaning back against me, my arms around her and under the pillow. Her grip on it has relaxed, though, and while it's still on her torso, I could easily pick it up and move it away if I were so inclined.

"So … what was that?" I ask, trying to keep my voice light.

But it does nothing to ease what is clearly something she doesn't want to talk about. She lets out a heavy sigh, her eyes falling closed.

"I just want to understand," I whisper softly, brushing a kiss over her cheek. "If that's a thing that you need, phones off all the time, I'll do it, but you have to tell me. You have to talk to me. Okay?"

She nods, eyes still closed. And when she starts speaking, it's in a flat voice like she's reciting a story that happened to someone else, some random person she doesn't know as she tells me about an ex in California, some douchey fratboy asshole, who took pics of her during sex and shared them with his frat brothers as some kind of … game, I guess.

But her dispassionate recitation does nothing to calm the rage that's strong enough that I have to slide out from behind her and pace the small space at the foot of my bed, staring at the walls and calculating if it's worth the physical pain and cost of repair to punch a hole in one of them, not to mention the shit I'd get from my coaches if I show up tomorrow with scraped up knuckles.

Deciding I can't risk it, I stop, my back to Piper, and force myself to take a deep breath.

"Cal?" she says in a quiet, tentative voice. I've never heard her sound like that before, so uncertain. So worried.

I whirl around, doing my best to master my temper. "I'm sorry, Piper," I say in a quiet voice.

She nods, her face drawn. "Sure. No problem. I understand." Setting the pillow aside, she reaches for her clothes again, but I stop her with my hand on hers, confusion overtaking the rage.

"What are you doing?"

CHAPTER THIRTY-THREE

Piper

My eyes fly to Cal's, unsure what to make of anything that just happened in the last ten minutes or so.

When I heard his phone vibrate, I panicked. In my excitement at seeing him, I didn't even think to make him turn it off. And my eyes were closed for … I don't know how long while we fucked. Could he have taken a picture when I was unaware of what was going on?

I don't think so … he had one hand on me the whole time and his other was occupied holding him up.

But he did want a topless pic while he was gone.

And what if he did snap a pic and send it to his friends, and the texts he was getting were his buddies congratulating him or something? At least that's what was going through my head when I saw the phone, reliving every moment of our encounter from an analytical perspective, trying to decide if he ever had the actual opportunity to take a picture, clutching the pillow over me, the first option to cover myself I had available, just in case he didn't take one before and wanted to rectify the situation.

It doesn't matter that this is Cal. That he's not Brent. I never thought Brent would do something like that to me, either. Though, if I'm honest, if I'd insisted Brent leave his phone in another room or turn it off like I've done with Cal, I doubt Brent would've gone along with it so easily. Especially knowing he was tasked with getting pics of me.

Was he sleeping with other people to get pics of them too?

I hadn't actually considered that before.

"Piper." Cal's deep voice brings me back to the present, his hand holding onto mine as I reach for my clothes.

I just told him everything—what happened with Brent, how the university did nothing, how I decided to take justice into my own hands, how my parents swooped in and withdrew me from school, insisting I move back home and finish college at Marycliff. I didn't bring up Gray and his self-appointed babysitting duties, partly because after last week, I'm still too raw about that and I knew I wouldn't be able to tell Cal the more recent history in the same quiet, emotionless voice I did everything else. It's been nine months. I've had time to cultivate that distance. But not with last week's events.

And now he's angry. So angry he can't even look at me. And when he said he's sorry, I took that as my cue to leave. No one wants to date an angry, untrusting, unhinged woman who suspects everyone of taking covert nudes to send to their friends or post online who then will break into your house and steal your router and video game consoles.

I've seen Cal's setup. It'd probably still be in the realm of petit theft here, because it's just him and Simon, not an entire fraternity's worth of equipment, but still. No point in risking that, right?

I blink up at his hand stopping mine from dragging my clothes closer to me so I can get dressed and leave. Leave and never come back. That brings unexpected tears to my eyes.

"What are you doing?" he repeats. He sits on the bed, his other hand gently circling my wrist as he disentangles my fingers from my clothes. "Please talk to me before you run away."

"Can I please put my clothes on?" I ask quietly, feeling far too exposed.

"Of course." He jerks his hands away, giving me space to stand. I don't bother with my panties or bra, just needing to cover up right now.

He watches me as I sit down on the bed again, holding myself stiffly apart, and part of me wants to be mad at the exquisite care he's showing. He's looking at me with that same careful concern I've been getting from my parents since last year, and I'm tired of everyone looking at me that way.

"That's why you turned off my phone," he says, his gaze level, his blue eyes serious.

I nod, swallowing hard and looking down at my hands in my lap. "I couldn't take the chance."

"The chance that I'd be like that … that …" He puffs up, his shoulders seeming to grow broader as his chest expands. He casts around, but can't seem to come up with a term harsh enough.

A fleeting smile passes over my face. "Yeah. I mean …" Shrugging, I drop my gaze again. "I didn't ever suspect he'd do that, either. Clearly I can't trust myself not to pick that kind of asshole. If I did once, I could do it again, right? But you were determined to get with me, and I'd decided that letting you catch me was the quickest way to put an end to whatever little game you had going. At the very least, I could make sure you couldn't take pictures as easily." I glance around the corners of his room. "I mean, I guess you could have hidden cameras in here, but …" I shrug again.

Horror takes over his expression. It might be comical if we were talking about anything else. He looks away, his Adam's apple bobbing as he swallows, blinking rapidly. "I would *never* do something like that," he says harshly.

"Okay." I mean, what else is there to say?

He meets my eyes, his hand reaching out to cup my face so I can't turn away. "I swear to god, Piper, I want you to tell me that guy's name and what frat he's part of so I can go down there and find him and tear him apart. The fact that anyone would do that at all is …" He shakes his head, letting out a rough breath. "I can't even think of strong enough words to describe how I feel about that. It's despicable. He's despicable." Understanding dawns on his face. "That's why you wouldn't send me pics this weekend?"

Nodding, I pull away from his hand so I can examine my cuticles some more, pushing them down unnecessarily. "Yeah. I can't—I won't—" I shake my head, and he pulls me into his arms, moving back on the bed so he can settle me across his still very much naked lap.

But for the first time maybe ever, his touch is completely unsexual. His goal is simply comfort, and my initial fear that he was upset with me and not *for* me is adequately relieved, and I absorb his heat. His strength. The comfort he's offering so freely.

When he approached me at that party and I shut him down without a second thought, who would've thought we'd end up here?

He brushes his lips over my cheekbone, then tucks my head under his chin, his arms wrapping around me, a soothing weight. His chest rises and falls as he breathes in deep, his heart thumping steadily under my ear. I'm not sure how long we stay like that, silent, each lost in our own thoughts. Though I'm not really thinking so much as just existing, enjoying this moment for however long it lasts.

At length, he sets me away from him for a moment, his thumb brushing away a tear I hadn't even noticed, his gaze level and serious. "Piper, I swear to you that I would never share any pictures you ever decided to send me. But I also won't ask again. That's a firm boundary, obviously, and I get it. And I'll turn off my phone when we're together. I thought it was a fun game where you wanted all my attention with no chance of interruptions, and to be honest, I had no objection to that. When we're together, I don't want interruptions anyway. But now that I know the reason why? I'll do my best to show you it's off or let you turn it off yourself, okay?"

The shell I've been trying to keep around my heart to guard it from Cal cracks open completely at his words. Sniffing, I try not to start blubbering like a ridiculous girl who cries about everything. I've never been that girl, and I don't want to start now. But his solemn promise breaks down my walls in ways I didn't know were possible.

"Okay." And he seals his promise with a kiss.

* * *

I end up staying at Cal's far later than I planned, only extricating myself from his arms and his bed because it's either that or stay the night. And as tempting as staying the night sounds, especially after his promises and the way he once again made love to me, wiping away my tears with the tender attentions of his whole self, body and soul, the knowledge of how early he has to be up for his morning workouts and the fact that all my things are back at the dorm has me heading there.

We settle into an easy routine where we carve out time for each other as much as possible. Cal's busy with classes and practice and workouts, and while I have one paper due by the end of the week plus general studying for finals to get through, my homework schedule is lighter than it's been in weeks. We spend every evening together, usually ending up in his room, muffling our cries of pleasure and just basking in each other's company.

Our relationship has changed on a fundamental level, and while we haven't had an official discussion about it, the daily time together and texts while we're apart make it clear we're a genuine couple. There's nothing casual or temporary about our relationship or the feelings that are sinking their roots deep into me.

In light of all the happy feelings engendered by Cal, I haven't felt at all like listening to the voicemail Gray left days ago to find out what he has to say for himself. But when he texts me on Wednesday afternoon while I'm in the library asking if I want to meet him for dinner that night, I decide I should at least listen to his voicemail to hear his apology before making a decision about dinner.

Except there's no apology. Just further justification for his behavior, and I'm not interested in that. At all.

Why is it that the guy I was only casually sleeping with is the one who wanted to go tear Brent limb from limb, and not my protective big brother? Why is Cal the one who thinks my response to the profound injustice of my situation was mild compared to what everyone deserves and has mentioned several times that once football season is over, we should take a road trip to California. To visit my friend, of course. And, you know, if we just *happen* to stop by the frat house, and Brent's face just *happens* to run into Cal's fist a few times, well, what a crazy coincidence, huh?

He did ask me what frat Brent belongs to, and I answered without thinking anything of it. But then he pulled out his phone, his face set in lines of grim determination, and that's when I found out he knows the president of the local chapter, and apparently he's working to get revenge on Brent through whatever channels he has available.

And yet my brother, the guy who came back here supposedly to help look out for me, doesn't seem to care that I was wronged and taken advantage of. All he cares about is making sure I can't be happy now, throwing my mistakes back in my face as proof I can't be trusted, and that Cal's really just out to use me the same way Brent did.

Fury bubbling in my veins, I delete the voicemail and ignore his text message. Let him figure out I won't be joining him for dinner. And I won't be riding with him to Mom and Dad's tomorrow night either.

I will need to actually talk to Mom and Dad sooner than later, and not just the minimal updates by text I've been giving, because I can only stay in the dorm through next week. Once finals are over, I need somewhere to stay over the break. And while I'm sure I could stay with Cal if it came to that—and I plan on staying there at least some of the time regardless—he'll be going home to Oregon for part of break to see his parents and then they're off to California for the Poppy Bowl.

They'll be gone for almost a week, getting acclimated to being there ahead of the most important game of their season. And considering this is the team's first year as a Division I school, the fact they've made it this far is impressive and a tribute to the new coach's strategy. Though with the way these things work, it's possible his contract included hitting certain success benchmarks in his first year if he wants to continue. But he should be guaranteed to stick around for at least a few years after this, so good for him. At least I should have good football seasons to look forward to while I'm stuck here.

And while part of my goal was originally to leave as soon after Gray as possible, now it's Cal's absence I'm dreading. He only has one more semester, and then he's gone. And if he gets drafted like he's hoping, he'll be off to who knows where, but almost guaranteed it's far away, while I'll be stuck here.

Yet another reason to cultivate Ellie's friendship, I guess, because she'll be stuck in the same boat as me with Simon leaving and her still having at least two years left of school. Though with her waiting over a year to declare a major, will she need longer to finish? We haven't really discussed it. I wonder if she'd be open to the idea of summer classes with me so we can both get out of here faster …

It's with those thoughts buzzing around my head that I get a text from my mom, checking in to find out if she'll see me tomorrow.

Sighing, I gather up my things. With my family members texting me and my swirling thoughts, I'm not going to get any more studying done right now. Might as well go back to my room, have a snack, deal with my mom, and finish the paper due tomorrow before meeting up with Cal tonight. It's mostly done, but there are a couple spots I want to double check before giving the whole thing one more read through and making sure my bibliography and footnotes are all formatted properly. I'm always lazy when doing footnotes and just stick them in with a reference I'll understand and then fix it later. It makes more work on the back end, but it gets me through drafting my papers faster, so I don't mind too much.

Pressing my phone to my ear, I listen to it ring a couple times before my mom picks up. "Piper!" She sounds surprised, but not upset. "I didn't expect you to call back. How are you?"

It's that same overly concerned tone I've come to resent so much, but I grit my teeth and force myself to answer as normally as possible.

"Good. Great, actually. This week is less hectic than

most of the semester's been since we're winding down. I have a paper due tomorrow, and it's almost done. I'm just taking a little break to get some space from it before finishing it up."

"Oh, well, that's good," she says.

"How's work for you?" I ask, hating the stilted quality of the questions and answers, even as she spends a few minutes gushing about her latest project. She's in her favorite part of a project where she gets to spend time picking fabrics and styles, creating the space of the clients' dreams. Normally I love listening to her talk about it, but right now the forced brightness in her voice just serves to illustrate how far from normal we are.

"So," she says, winding down and I know getting down to the real purpose of this conversation. "Tomorrow is Thursday."

"It is."

She sighs at my nonresponse. I know what she's asking. For one, she already asked it in her text message. For another, even if she hadn't, I'd know just based on that. "Will you be coming to dinner tomorrow?" Despite the quiet volume of her voice, there's an edge to it, that special edge that moms everywhere do so well that says I better give her the correct answer.

And we both know I'm not going to. Or at least I know. She should know. If she didn't, she wouldn't even be asking, because she would just expect me to show up.

It's my turn to sigh. "Not this week, Mom."

She's silent for a long moment, and so am I. I stay on

the phone even as I enter my dorm and start walking up the stairs.

"Where will you go for break?" she asks at last, her voice even quieter, that edge completely lacking now.

I really hate this, because right now she just sounds sad. Heartbroken. Worried. And not the overly cautious worried about me breaking again that I've been dealing with for months and months. No, this is a different sort of worry. Like she's afraid I won't ever come home, and she doesn't know how to handle that.

"I'm hoping I can still come home," I say carefully, not missing the way she expels a breath in relief. I'm not sure she'll still feel that way by the time I've said all I have to say, though. "But only if I can be treated with the same trust you give Gray."

I'm tempted to say more, but I'm proceeding with caution. I'm not entirely in a position to give a list of demands and expect them to be met. Especially since I don't have a backup plan at this point. I'm making some assumptions about Cal's willingness to have me around based on how things have been going for the last week, but I haven't exactly asked him yet. I can't handle a month of feeling like I'm essentially grounded, though, with fewer freedoms than I had in high school.

"What does that mean, exactly?"

Pulling out my key, I unlock my door and push through. Dani's not home yet. She has class at this time, so it's not surprising. I drop my bag inside my bedroom door and head over to the couch, flopping down so I can finish this conversation.

"It means that I'll tell you if I'm going to stay out late or spend the night elsewhere as a courtesy, but you don't get to monitor my whereabouts like I'm a child or try to prevent me from seeing anyone in particular."

This sigh is annoyed. "This is about that boy, isn't it?"

"Yes, Mom." My sigh is equally annoyed. No one can ever accuse me of not being my mother's daughter. "It is about that boy. I know Gray has decided he's the worst, and to be honest, Cal's not Gray's biggest fan either, but they're both wrong about each other. And I would appreciate it if you'd trust me to make my own decisions about who I spend time with."

"Piper, you have to understand—"

"That you think my judgment is suspect. I know. I've been operating under the same assumptions since last spring too. I get it. No one has beat me up for my poor choices more than me, I promise you. But Cal is different."

"How?" The single syllable is the first volley in a rapid fire interrogation, short and to the point.

"He's proven himself trustworthy. He won't do to me what Brent did."

"But how can you know that, Piper?"

I let out a choked laugh, trying to choose humor over anger or tears. "How do you know Gray wouldn't do that, Mom?"

"Well," she sputters, "it's Gray, of course he wouldn't—"

"Because you trust him, right?" I push. "You know him. He's done things to show that he's a trustworthy person who wouldn't violate someone's boundaries like that."

She's silent for several beats. "I suppose so."

"Right. So has Cal."

She mulls that over. "Will we get to meet him?"

That question catches me off guard. For some reason, I wasn't expecting that. "Oh, um, maybe? I don't know right now."

This time she lets out a resigned sigh. "We'd like to meet him," she says. "If you're both willing to do that."

I take a minute to think about it before answering. I feel like inviting Cal to a family dinner is like inviting him to eat in a lion's den, but it's not actually a ridiculous request. But if Cal comes to dinner, Gray needs to either agree to be nice or agree to be somewhere else, and I'm not sure which is possible right now.

"I'll talk to him about it," I finally say, deferring the decision until later.

"Alright," Mom says. "I need to go, but, Piper?"

"Yeah, Mom?"

"I love you. And I'm glad you'll be coming home."

Heat and moisture gather behind my eyes. "I love you too, Mom."

CHAPTER THIRTY-FOUR

Coach has given us an easier schedule for finals week. I'm not sure he has much choice since class schedules are all messed up, it's not like we can maintain our normal workout, game tapes, and practice schedule.

Nevertheless, he makes us all gather on Tuesday evening to watch game tape of our opponents for our upcoming game. We have our first postseason game in Arizona this weekend. While everyone else on campus is looking forward to relaxing, our stress levels are only increasing.

We have three more games before we're done, the final one just after the first of the year. Which means our break will be spent in the weight room and on the practice field regardless of the weather or whatever other normal family plans anyone might've made. This is the first year this has been the case, and I know my mom isn't happy about the change. Especially since Ellie's planning on staying at our house for most of the break as well. I think she'll be going home for a few days when Simon and I are gone, but she's driving back up as soon as she can get away.

I wonder what Piper's plans are for Christmas break? We've mostly been focused on one day at a time, only planning the next time we can get together and what we need to accomplish before that can happen each day.

I haven't asked her what her plans are for the break, partly because I'm afraid of the answer. I want her to spend as much time with me as possible, and for her sake, I don't want a repeat of Thanksgiving. I'd much rather just start with the understanding that she belongs with me rather than having her show up on my doorstep crying and dragging a suitcase. I suppose even if she chooses to go home, she knows that's an option now.

Settling into the uncomfortable ancient folding chairs in the tape room, I push aside my worries about Piper and focus on the tape. Sure, the odds of me actually playing are small, but I need to be ready just in case. Now that we're entering the postseason, the odds of scouts showing up at games is even higher. They'll be examining my stats not just from this season but last season as well, which is the only thing keeping me from working harder to trip up

Kilpatrick.

At this point, I've done all I can short of injuring the guy myself, and that's not an option. But I know that Coach Miles has been watching me closely during practices since I've taken Simon's advice and stepped up, buckled down, and worked harder. No more bitching about how unfair it is that I lost my starting spot to a random transfer student the new coach brought along with him. I still *think* that, but I've stopped talking about it.

Which has the added benefit of not pissing off everyone around me, including my coaches.

Coach Reese points out specific things he wants us to pay attention to, certain players and the way they move, their quirks and idiosyncrasies.

"They're a solid team," he says as he switches off the projector, signaling to Coach Bennett to turn on the lights.

A wave of murmuring goes through the team as we all blink, our eyes adjusting to the sudden brightness.

"We can beat them if we keep our head in the game," Coach says, pitching his voice louder to be heard over our noise. "We've all gotta pull our weight. Be ready. That means no slacking off in the weight room or on the practice field, got it?"

Mumbled yesses echo around the room.

"We want to make this first season in Division I something to be proud of. Then you can tell your kids that *you* did this. You changed divisions part way through your college careers and stepped up to the challenge of a tougher schedule and defeated it."

Another round of agreement goes up.

"What was that?" he asks, cupping an ear like he didn't hear us the first time.

We all chorus, "Yessir," louder so that he's satisfied.

Just as he dismisses us and we all reach down to gather our things, a loud groan goes up from one corner of the room.

We all turn to see what the problem is, and Gardner stands up, Piggy in his hand. "Seriously, guys? We're watching game tape. We're not supposed to be passing Piggy around."

A round of laughter goes out.

"He has a point," Coach Reese says, a hint of censure tempering his obvious amusement.

"Coach, I think it's your turn to have Piggy," Gardner says, obviously just trying to get out of finding a legal way to pass Piggy to the next player. He lobs Piggy through the air, and Coach Reese whacks Piggy away with his clipboard like he's playing baseball.

"Wrong sport, Coach," laughs Foster as the coaches file out, picking up Piggy and making a show of dusting him off. Then he turns to Gardner. "That's not how we treat Piggy here. You know better than that. Tell him you're sorry and take care of him until you can pass him to someone else."

"Legally," I stress. "Tossing him across the tape room isn't how you give Piggy to someone else. We all know the rules."

Kilpatrick glares at me. "Shut the fuck up, McAdam. No one's talking to you."

I jerk back, hands up, caught off guard by the wave of anger emanating from him, entirely directed at me. "Whoa, there, man. I wasn't talking to you, for one thing. And what the hell is your problem? What'd I do to you?" I glance around at my teammates, wondering if any of them have any idea what his problem is.

"Dude," Lancaster says, his hand on Kilpatrick's chest as he tries to push past. "He's not worth it, man. Leave it."

I cross my arms and cock my head back, staring Kilpatrick down. He's got a few inches on me, but I have more bulk. If he wants to fight, we can fight. I'm not the one that's gonna be tossed out of a game, though. Not with all these witnesses able to articulate that he started it and I'm acting in self defense.

"I'm not worth it?" I question. "What the fuck did I do? All I said was that we don't throw Piggy at our teammates. The game is that you sneak him into someone else's things. This isn't controversial." I glance around for support.

Several guys nod. Piggy's not new. We all know the rules, including Gardner. Kilpatrick's the only one who might be forgiven for not understanding, at least at the beginning of the season.

I jerk my chin at him. "You feeling left out, man? Did no one give you a turn with Piggy this year?"

"Don't fucking talk to me, asshole," Kilpatrick growls,

and I can't help laughing, because how'm I the asshole here?

"Seriously, dude? You're the one talking to me. You're the one who came in here and took over, but you don't get to tell me I can't talk to my own teammates, who've been my teammates for *years*, about our team game. Why don't *you* stop talking to me?"

He pushes past his friends, getting in my face. "Why don't you stop talking to my sister? We all know why you're sniffing around after her."

My eyes widen, because shit. I didn't even put that together right now. After everything that's happened between Piper and me the last few weeks, I'd completely separated Piper from her brother. They exist in different compartments in my life. She's my girlfriend, and he's my asshole teammate, and I don't even think about them as being connected anymore. Plus Kilpatrick and I have been spending time in the same spaces for the last two weeks without a problem, so for this to start now, so far removed from when she got in a fight with him about something she still won't tell me about …

The penny finally drops.

They fought about *me*.

I shut down all my feelings, though, pasting on my cockiest smirk. Let him suffer. I might not know the details, but he's the reason she showed up at my door in tears. Her parents played a role too, I know, but she's at least talked to her mom once or twice since then. As far as I know, she's still refusing to talk to her brother.

Which makes me think that he's the instigator between them.

"And why am I sniffing around after her?" I ask, making sure my voice is loud enough that everyone listening can hear. He wants to turn this into a show? Then let's make it a full-on production. I had friends in high school who were in theatre. I learned a few things from them about staging a show, and this whole thing feels entirely planned. His goal is to make me look like the bad guy here, but he's the clear aggressor.

"You fucking piece of shit," he spits. "Everyone knows you don't poach your teammates' girlfriends, and little sisters are always off limits."

I make a show of glancing around and finding Simon. "Does everyone know that? Really?" Gesturing at Simon, who grimaces at me—sorry, dude, you brought this on yourself, though—I continue. "Simon, who's both my best friend and my roommate, beyond being my teammate, is currently in a relationship with my little sister. Simon, have we fought over that?"

"Hold up, hold up." Trey reaches Kilpatrick and pulls him back. As our starting center, Trey's got a lot more mass on him, rivaling Simon for size, though I'd put my money on Simon for grappling ability. Either way, these guys have literally covered my ass in the pocket more often than they've done Kilpatrick's, even if he is the starter this year.

"Gray," Trey says, his hands on Kilpatrick's shoulders, forcing him to look at him. "Leave it, man. You get in a fight, Coach will have your ass on a platter. You want to play out the rest of the postseason?"

Jaw obviously grinding, Kilpatrick jerks a nod.

"Great." Trey pounds his shoulders and gives him a gentle shove out of the way, where he turns to face me, hands on his hips. "And Cal. You've spent over half the season being a little bitch." He holds up one hand as though to forestall a protest I'm not making. "Don't try to deny it. We all know it's true." He gestures around the room and the circle of guys still watching. Pointing a finger at me, he levels me with a glare. "Did you or did you not start checking out Gray's little sister only *after* you found out he was related to her. And before you lie," he says when I open my mouth to respond, "remember that I'm well aware she was at football parties and various practices all semester, and you didn't *really* get interested in her until after you knew exactly who she was and you'd found out about Simon and your sister, which we all know you weren't exactly thrilled about."

I grunt in response, which he takes as agreement.

"Fine. I rest my case. Maybe don't do that shit, yeah?"

Grinding my teeth, part of me is tempted to just leave it, because I don't think anyone would believe me, but the part of me that can't stand unfairness in any capacity won't let me stay silent. "It's not like that, man. Not anymore," I say quietly. I don't care about the rest of the team, but Trey and I have been friends as long as Simon and me. We maybe haven't been as close, but I care about his opinion of me.

He stands, hands on his hips again, his eyebrows raised, inviting me to elaborate.

Sighing, I drop my arms. "Fuck, man. She's …" I shake my head. "She's it. Y'know? It's … serious. It's not about her brother, even if maybe I started showing obvious interest in her in an attempt to piss him off. If I were still doing that, don't you think I'd rub it in his face right now? Especially with him coming at me about something unrelated?"

Trey grows thoughtful, rubbing a hand over his chin and nodding. "Yeah, okay. If your goal was to fuck with Kilpatrick, you'd definitely be the one to bring it up. And probably before now."

"Exactly." I'm not entirely comfortable with that assessment of my character, but if it means Trey believes me, then I'll let it go.

Decision made, he purses his lips and nods again, this time more firmly. "Alright, assholes, let's move along. Show's over." He claps his hands together, drawing the attention of the guys still left. Probably half the team has cleared out, including Kilpatrick. Shit. So he didn't hear any of that exchange. Though I'm not really sure it would make much difference. He's decided I'm the bad guy, that I'm the reason his sister won't talk to him.

Simon's in the hall herding people along, reassuring them that he and I are fine, that while I wasn't thrilled about him and Ellie getting together, it had more to do with the fact that they lied to me than anything. Which is a generous interpretation of events, but I appreciate him covering for me.

Trey claps a hand on my shoulder. "Dude. Number one, bad form. I get where you're coming from but, duuuude. That's fucked up." When I open my mouth to protest, he holds up a finger. "*But*. I'm happy for you, man. If you and Piper are really a thing, then you're absolutely right that your relationship is worth fighting for, even over the objections of her brother, who's mostly against the idea because you and he don't get along." He leans in close like he's about to tell me a secret. "Maybe try not being such a dick to him. If you're serious about his sister, you're gonna have to try to get along with him. Those two are pretty close."

Swallowing down my objections and corrections, I nod. "Thanks, man. I hear you."

He pats my shoulder before letting go. "I'll see if I can talk Gray around for you. At least get him to give you a chance." He points at me as he walks backward out of the room, leaving me on my own. "You're lucky we're friends, man. Otherwise I would've let him kick your ass."

Laughing, I shake my head. "No you wouldn't have. Not with a game coming up."

He shrugs. "Sure. Maybe not today. But after the season?" He holds up a fist. "All bets would've been off. You treat that girl right, or we still might have to do that, you got me?"

I laugh again, but this time it's more forced. "I got you."

I guess it's good to know that Piper has more people looking out for her than just me. Even if Trey is threatening to help her brother kick my ass.

CHAPTER THIRTY-FIVE

Piper

Dani pokes her head through my bedroom door after knocking quietly on the doorframe. "Um, Piper?" she says tentatively.

Which is weird. Dani's never tentative. Pushing away my laptop, I rub my eyes and sit up straight. "What's up?"

She steps into the room, tapping her phone into the palm of her other hand. "Um, so, I was texting with Eli."

"Okaaaay." I'm not sure where she's going with this. She and Eli text like every day, so that's not exactly unusual.

Clearing her throat, she glances down at her phone,

back at me, then at her phone again. She sucks in a deep breath, then hands her phone to me, the screen unlocked and open to her text messages. "You should read what he's saying," she says with her eyes closed like she's bracing herself for something terrible.

My brows pull together, because I'm thoroughly confused. But I take the phone from her outstretched hand, blinking at the most recent message. But it doesn't make any sense. Like, I know how to read the words. They're English, and they're all words. But all together like that, they don't make sense. Scrolling a little, I find the beginning of the most recent conversation.

Eli: What's going on between Piper and McAdam?

Dani: They're dating or whatever. She won't actually call him her boyfriend. Says they haven't had the "DTR" talk, but he basically is. Pretty sure you knew that already, though. Why?

Eli: Um, she kinda came up today.

Dani: Why?

Text doesn't communicate tone of voice of course, but I've spent enough time with Dani and Eli together that I can just imagine how this would've played out face to face.

Eli: Apparently McAdam's using Piper. He's only with her to get back at her brother.

The second time I read those words, everything in me freezes. Seizes up.

"I'm so sorry, Piper," Dani whispers, and I blink at her, just realizing that she's still here, still in my room. Witnessing me getting my decisions thrown in my face. Again. It seems everyone was right not to trust my judgment. It clearly can't be trusted.

Numb, I hand back her phone.

"Are you okay?" she asks, clearly unsure what to make of my nonreaction.

I shake my head. No, I'm not okay. I'm not sure I'll ever be okay again.

* * *

Time passes. My phone rings. I turn it off. I don't know who's calling, but I don't want to talk to anyone.

I hear voices outside my door. Dani and someone else. Quiet, like they're trying not to disturb me. Not that it matters. I'm disturbed regardless of their volume.

The sun goes down and my room grows dark since I don't get out from my cocoon of blankets and turn on the lights.

How could I be so stupid? Again?

The questions pound in my head, an incessant drumbeat. Gray tried to warn me. All along, he suspected

Cal's intentions.

He used me.

I thought he cared about me. I thought he wanted *me*.

He just wanted Gray's little sister. So he could use me to screw over my brother.

But he didn't. Gray's still the starting quarterback. Cal's still the backup.

And I'm just screwed.

* * *

"Piper," Dani's voice breaks through my cocoon of numbness. I think I may have slept, but I'm not really sure. Everything's just a timeless, hazy blur. "You need to eat something, at least. I ordered a pizza. Come out and have some food."

I don't respond. Maybe she'll think I'm asleep. But the light clicks on, filtering through the blanket covering my face. The room is so small that the sound of her footsteps barely registers before she's pulling the blankets back, peering down at me with a mixture of concern and sternness on her face. "Come on, Piper. It's been hours. I know ..." She pauses, pursing her lips as she takes a deep breath. "You're better than this. You're upset, and you have every right to be, but you don't get to shut down and quit. You only have to get through two more days. Your boyfriend turning out to be a douche isn't enough of a reason to take an incomplete. And even if they would let you, you'd still have to make up the final later. Do you really want to do that? After how hard you've worked all semester? Seriously?"

I blink up at her as the banked fire behind her words penetrates the fog I've wrapped around myself. But she's right. It would be exceptionally stupid to fuck up this semester too after fucking up the last one. I'd just be proving everyone right, wouldn't I? One thing goes wrong, and I completely self-destruct.

This is exactly why my parents and brother think I can't be trusted. Exactly why they watch me like I might combust at any moment. Because look at me. Apparently this is what I do.

Well, not this time.

Sighing, I sit up and push my hair out of my face.

Dani lets out a relieved breath and steps back. "Good. So, pizza?"

"Yeah, pizza." My voice sounds more croaky than normal, but when I clear my throat, I think it'll be okay. I cried off and on, but I'm done with that now. No more crying over stupid boys.

I push back the blankets and get out of bed, following Dani to our living area. The smell of grease and melted cheese envelops me. She pulls back the lid of the box with a flourish like she's presenting the prize on an old game show. "Ladies first."

I can't help laughing. "You're not a lady?"

Shrugging, she hands me a paper plate from the stack we keep near the sink. "I suppose I am. But I'm more like one of the guys, really, so." She shrugs again.

Pizza on my plate, stray strings of mozzarella pinched off, I lick my fingers and sit on the couch, looking her over with a critical eye. "We could make you into more of one of the girls, you know. Go shopping. Fill out your wardrobe with something other than baggy T-shirts and joggers. Buy some makeup. You could cut your hair if you wanted."

She sinks onto the couch next to me with a snort. "You're the one who just broke up with her boyfriend. Aren't you the one supposed to be getting a haircut?"

I give her a confused look. "I think you have me confused with a forty-something wine mom who's suddenly getting a divorce."

"Touché," she mumbles around a mouthful of pizza.

"No, but seriously," I try to push, but she cuts me off with a shake of her head.

"No, ma'am. I'm not going to become your project to distract you from your pain. I'm perfectly happy with my baggy shirts and joggers, thank you very much. And it's not like I don't *own* nicer clothes. I just see no point in wearing them daily. I'm not trying to impress anyone." Her face clouds. "Besides. I've tried making that effort. Everyone always reacts with shock and awe, looking at me like some strange insect they've never seen before. I feel worse about myself, not better. So I have my slightly dressier versions of my usual outfits I wear for parties and whatever, but for class?" She shakes her head. "I'll stick with my comfy clothes, thanks."

I frown, wanting to find something to latch onto in

that defense. But if she's happy, who am I to try to make her feel bad about herself just to give me something to do? And she's right, I'm only looking for a distraction.

"Besides." She nudges me with her shoulder. "There's no time for a makeover before Christmas break anyway. You'll have to find some other project to distract you. I could take you to the weight room, show you around, get you started." She looks almost hopeful. "Picking up heavy shit is surprisingly cathartic."

Laughing, I shake my head. "So you'll turn me into your project to distract me from my broken heart, huh?"

She flashes me a grin and shrugs. "Worth a shot."

"And there's time for that before break?" I ask, eyebrows raised.

Another shrug. "Well, no. But you could keep working out over the break whether I'm around or not. And then we could work out together next semester." Her face brightens, like she's really getting attached to this idea.

I feel kinda bad letting her down, so I hum noncommittally. "I'll think about it."

"You do that. And we'd time our workouts so we're unlikely to be in the gym the same time as the football players. Then you wouldn't have to worry about …"

"Cal," I finish for her. "We don't have to pretend he doesn't exist. You can say his name."

"Okay." She pauses, picking a piece of pepperoni off her pizza and popping it in her mouth. "So, Ellie came by."

"Did she?" I ask, trying to keep my voice neutral, but the frog in my throat gives me away.

Dani looks at me, sympathy stamped on her face. "She said Cal sent her to check on you since you weren't answering his calls."

Nodding, I stare at my half-eaten slice. "I turned off my phone."

"Makes sense." Another long pause. "I showed her the texts," she says at last. "I thought she should know. I don't think she did before."

That's unsurprising. Ellie seemed to be genuinely rooting for us, and she doesn't strike me as the type who'd go for some kind of twisted revenge plan like helping her brother date a girl just to screw with that girl's brother. Plus, I always got the feeling that she and Cal don't have that kind of relationship anyway.

I nod to show I heard, but don't really have anything to say.

"I'm really sorry, Piper," Dani says quietly. "About everything. I know you really liked him."

Blowing out a breath, I set my pizza down and stand. "Thanks, Dani," I manage to get out, my voice hoarse and clogged with tears. I can't say anything else without completely breaking down, though. So I go back to my room to let it all out without an audience.

When Dani taps on my door a few minutes later and asks if I'm alright, I manage to pull myself together enough to answer her.

"I just need to be alone tonight," I say, my voice

wavering with the strain of projecting through the closed door. "I promise I won't screw up my last two tests, though. I'll take them, and I'll ace them."

I'm not going to let some dumb guy derail me. Not again.

Never again.

CHAPTER THIRTY-SIX

Cal

I pace my bedroom, staring at my phone. Willing Piper to respond to my last text. But she doesn't. She hasn't responded to any of my texts. Every time I've called it goes straight to voicemail with the glaring exception of the first time when it rang three times before getting sent to voicemail.

While it's not unheard of for Piper to take some time to get back to me if she's busy, that hasn't happened in over two weeks. And the last time we talked, I told her I'd be calling as soon as I was home. She was going to come over, we were going to have dinner together, and both finish up studying for our last finals. She has two to go still, and I just have one more tomorrow.

Then I planned to reward our studious efforts with sexy times in my room until she fell asleep, too exhausted and satisfied to keep her eyes open a moment longer. I even bought an extra toothbrush for her to keep here for when she stays over, which I'm hoping will happen more often since classes won't be a thing we have to worry about for a few weeks. And once the break is over and my brutal schedule eases up a bit, she won't have the excuse of not wanting to disrupt my morning workout routine to fall back on either.

Things have been good, on the right track, and I want them to get more serious.

I mean, we haven't discussed all these changes, but I didn't think it was necessary to have a business meeting about it or anything. We've been taking everything as it comes all along. Why should this be any different?

But now she won't respond to my calls or texts.

Worry settles over me, dark and cold, seeping into my skin.

"Hey, Ellie," I call as I head for the living room. Maybe I'm overreacting, and I hope this doesn't make me look like a psycho stalker, but I just have a really bad feeling, and I need to make sure that Piper's okay. Ellie can get me into her dorm, and I can go check on her. Make sure everything's okay. "Can you get me into your dorm? I need to check on Piper."

Ellie looks up from her textbook, her brows wrinkled

together. "Wasn't she coming over later? That's what she told me earlier."

"Yeah, that was the plan. I told her I'd call when I got home, and she was supposed to come over. But it's been almost an hour, and I can't get her on the phone. I have a really bad feeling, and I just want to make sure she's like … I dunno, that she got busy studying and forgot to plug in her phone and it died and she didn't realize it or something."

"Hang on. Lemme check with her roommate. I have her number too." Her fingers fly over the screen, then her eyes narrow, and she glances at me quickly before typing something again.

"What?" I demand. "What's going on?"

Ellie shakes her head and stands. "I'm not sure." She sounds distant, though. Cold. Not the happy, helpful little sister she was just a minute ago.

"Ellie, what's going on? Did something happen?"

She looks down at her phone, types something else, then sticks it in her pocket and holds out her hand. "I need your car."

"What?"

She wiggles her fingers, standing in front of me with her other hand on her hip, her face a mask of impatience. "Come on. You want to know what's going on with Piper? Give me your car keys. Me driving will be faster than walking."

"I'll drive you," I say, my voice brooking no

arguments, but she shakes her head. She never did fall for my bossy older brother routine. Not in years, anyway, and not at all since she and Simon got together. It's like she's grown completely immune.

"Nope," she says, as though her refusal weren't plain as day without her verbalizing it.

Simon wanders in from the kitchen, taking in our standoff. "What's going on?"

"Something's wrong with Piper," I supply, "and Ellie kindly offered to take me to her dorm to investigate."

Ellie shakes her head. "I did not," she says emphatically. "What I did was offer to go find out what's going on myself, but Cal is refusing to let me use his car." With a shrug to show nonchalance that's entirely feigned, she flops back down on the couch. "Fine. Have it your way. I thought you wanted to find out what's going on, though."

She's practically vibrating with tension as she opens her textbook and stares at the pages. I don't think she's actually reading at all, though, because when she reads, she fiddles with things, taps her pen, clicks the cap, rolls the hem of her shirt between her fingers, something. And she's doing none of those things. She's sitting, her back stiff and straight, her shoulders hunched up to her ears, her eyes fixed on the page like that's a believable approximation of reading.

But her tension only ratchets up my concern. If she's this desperate to find out what's going on herself, Piper's roommate told her something. And it's something not good.

"Ellie," I say, infusing every ounce of command I can muster into her name. I'm not in the mood to deal with this shit anymore. I want answers. "What did Piper's roommate say?"

She opens her mouth, looks at Simon, then me, and closes her mouth again. She points at Simon. "He's your best friend, right?"

I give a grudging, "Yeah," in response. Where's she going with this?

"And if something were wrong that he didn't want you to tell other people, would you?"

Crossing my arms over my chest, I stare down my nose at my little sister. "That's different."

She nods. "You're right. Because I'm the one prying. Dani's the one who knows something. And her loyalty is to Piper. Not to you. Not to me. Something's up, which I'm only telling you because you figured out that much on your own. If you want more information, I need to go there and you need to stay here."

"I'll drive you, Ellie," Simon says, already heading back into the hall, presumably to get shoes and a sweatshirt and his keys.

With a sigh, I recognize that I've been defeated. Digging into my pocket, I pull out my keys and toss them to her. "You better tell me everything when you get back."

"I've got Cal's car," she calls to Simon, and I block out their voices as he tells her goodbye, because I don't need to hear or see them being all cute and couple-y right now.

Although, at this moment, having my little sister dating my best friend is working out in my favor. Because if they weren't, I wouldn't have anyone to ask to check on Piper for me. I'd just be left stewing and frustrated until she finally decided to tell me what's wrong herself.

* * *

My bedroom door bangs open, and Ellie stands in the doorway, eyes flashing. "You. Complete. Asshole!"

She throws my keys down, and I'm under no illusion that she'd prefer to throw them directly at my face but is holding herself back only because of years of parental instruction that throwing things at your sibling's face when you're mad at them is not okay.

I blink at her anger, totally lost. "What'd I do?" I ask, bewildered.

She splutters, her rage making her incoherent.

Simon appears behind her in the hallway, his hands landing on her shoulders. "What happened, Ellie?" he asks in a surprisingly soothing voice.

She points a shaking finger at me and whirls on him. "Did you know?" she demands. "Did you know what he was doing?"

He looks at her face. "When?"

Another splutter of incoherent rage. "When he decided to pursue Piper. Did you know the only reason he wanted her was to get back at her brother?"

Simon lets out a sigh, which is all the confirmation Ellie needs. She yanks herself away from him, taking a step back. "You did. You knew."

Running a hand over his face, he shakes his head. "I didn't *know*," he clarifies. "I suspected." He sends a glare my way. "And I told him it was a terrible idea. Didn't I, Cal?"

I squeeze the back of my neck with both hands. "It's not … it's not like that."

"Oh?" Ellie's perfected that expression of profound disbelief, her eyebrow perfectly arched, her face bland and deceptively open, inviting explanation. Inviting me to keep digging my own grave, more like.

Sighing, I drop my hands. "No. It's not. Not anymore."

"So it *was* like that." She purses her lips, looking at me like she expects a response, and how the hell is my little sister managing to make me feel like a chastened kid who's about to be sent to the naughty step? Except I fear the consequences of this fuckup will be much worse than a ten minute time out. "Just not anymore," she finishes when I don't say anything.

"Ellie, come *on*. You've been here. You've seen us together. Did it look like I was using her?"

She softens. Just a smidge. The lines of her face relax,

and her shoulders drop a fraction of an inch as she looks at me, thinking through what she's witnessed of our relationship. "No. It didn't." Her face hardens again, like in a movie when you watch someone literally get turned to stone. "Which is what makes it so much worse. And you, what? Bragged about it in front of the whole team?"

I jerk back. "What? What are you talking about?"

Simon lets out a groan, drawing Ellie's attention. "She's talking about today in the tape room. Gray must've said something to her."

But that doesn't make any sense. I shake my head. "She won't talk to him. Or she hasn't been. Not since Thanksgiving. I'm guessing he tried to convince her of that then." I level a glare at Ellie. "Which wasn't true then, either, in case you care. But why would she believe him now?"

Something in Ellie's face tells me that it's not Kilpatrick who ruined everything. "What do you know, Ellie? You went over there to find out what happened and help me out. So help me out."

Her face turns mutinous, her arms crossing again as she stares me down. "I went over there to find out what was going on with *my friend*. Who also wouldn't answer my texts and my call went straight to voicemail like her phone is off. Which it is. Because she doesn't want to talk to you or anyone else. She's devastated."

I take a step closer. "Ellie." I'm barely holding my temper in check now. She knows exactly what went down, and she's not telling me. How can I fix this if I don't even know whose head to bash in?

Simon holds up a hand to me and turns Ellie to face him, running his hands up and down her arms. "I think I can say with confidence that the last thing Cal wants to do at this point is hurt Piper. Right?" The last word is accompanied by an edge and a meaningful glance in my direction.

"Right," I confirm. At least *someone*'s on my side, even if I did kinda throw him under the bus this afternoon. Still, if he can date *my* sister, and I can get over myself and be more or less okay with it, Kilpatrick should be able to get over himself and not hold me dating his sister against me. Even if nothing about our relationship has gone as I'd planned or hoped.

It's been better.

"See?" he says to Ellie. "Cal just wants a chance to fix what's wrong. He's ..." he hesitates, looking up at me. "He has feelings for her. Serious feelings."

She glances at me too. "It wasn't just an act? Because to Piper it all seems like just an act. And I can't blame her, either. After what—" She clamps her lips shut, cutting off whatever else she was going to say.

"After what?" Simon prompts.

Ellie sags, her eyes closing as she rubs her forehead with one hand. "Her roommate Dani is good friends with some of your teammates."

Simon nods. "Yeah. She's a cool chick. She works out

with us sometimes too."

"Yeah, well, Eli Foster texted Dani that you're using Piper to get at her brother." She looks back and forth between us. "I'm guessing he heard whatever happened in the tape room? I don't know what that means exactly, but Dani showed me the texts. She showed them to Piper too, because who wouldn't if you got a text like that about your friend?"

My fists clench at my side. "Fucking Foster," I mutter under my breath. Nosy little shit butting in where he doesn't belong. Closing my eyes, I shake my head. Frustration at him, at the situation, but mostly at myself bubbles up inside me.

"Thanks for telling us," Simon murmurs to Ellie. They move into the hall, exchanging a few more quiet words, and then my door closes.

But I'm not alone. "What're you gonna do?" Simon asks.

Lifting my hands in a gesture of helplessness, I let them fall back to my sides. "I don't know."

Because what can I do? She won't talk to me. And even if she would, based on Ellie's reaction, I'm not sure, *I was only interested in you to begin with to get back at your brother for stealing my starting spot but I fell in love with you somewhere along the way,* is enough of an explanation or apology. The fact that the part of that statement I'm most worried about isn't the L-word part is also saying something.

But the last guy she trusted used her too. For something far worse, in my opinion, but the fact that I tried to use her at all isn't going to do much for her trust in me or anything else I have to say.

And telling her she was never supposed to find out won't do any good either. How could it? If someone said that to me after screwing me over, it'd feel like a slap in the face, not an apology.

Sitting on my bed, I drop my head in my hands. "I have no fucking clue what to do, man. I'm not sure there's any way to actually fix this."

CHAPTER THIRTY-SEVEN

Piper

True to my word, I get up the next morning and go to my final. I spend the afternoon in my room studying. I'd normally go to the library, but after turning my phone back on and seeing all the calls and texts from Cal and thinking back over how persistent he was in the beginning, the library's dangerous. He knows I tend to go there, so odds are he'll be looking for me there. He clearly wants to talk to me.

But I don't want to talk to him.

I don't want to hear whatever he has to say to try to make something okay that's just not.

I also have another voicemail from my brother. But I

delete that as well. I don't need an *I told you so* any more than I need whatever half-assed apology or explanation I'll get from Cal.

Dani gave me Eli's number last night when I eventually emerged from my room. He filled me in on the conversation he witnessed. There's no disputing the truth. He doesn't have an angle to play and sounded genuinely apologetic to be the one to have to tell me. But he considers me a friend now, and he'd tell any of his friends if someone they were dating was using them like that. Which I really appreciate, even if it guts me. It's hard to find friends who'll stand by you with so much honesty and conviction. Though I guess even if Cal finds out that Eli's the one who told me about his little plan, this is Cal's last season. There's not a lot he can do to Eli in the next month before the postseason is over. And after that, they'll go their separate ways.

Still. I appreciate Eli telling me. He could've decided his loyalty is with his teammates, not some random chick who lives with his best friend.

When I get off the phone with Eli, I tip my head back against the couch and stare at the ceiling, drained. Everything about this is exhausting. All I want to do is go curl up in my bed and stare at the wall until I go to sleep. Just turn off my brain and ignore the world.

But that's impossible.

I still have a final to study for, and then I have to pack up whatever I need for the break. I guess at least it's not the end of spring semester. I don't have to pack up everything in this room and move it somewhere else in the middle of my emotional turmoil.

Last year, when my parents swooped in and took over, they did all that for me, my mom taking charge and packing everything. She's meticulous and organized, so I wasn't worried she'd break anything or forget something, but I resented the intrusion all the same.

I resented everything, though. Absolutely everything.

At least this time no one's taking over and making all my choices for me, even if Dani isn't letting me wallow in grief when there's shit to do. Even that, though … it's not the same. She's informing me she won't let me make more bad decisions, but she's not making my decisions for me. She's just forcefully encouraging me to stay on the path I'd already decided on.

A path that never included Cal in the first place. In fact it was specifically and deliberately devoid of boys and their attached drama.

That was a smart decision. I need to get back to that tough-as-nails chick who decided to take control of her life as best she can, keep her nose to the grindstone so she can get out as soon as possible, and move on.

Cal's going to be moving on. Soon I'm sure I'll be little more than a memory, a joke he tells his NFL friends about how he was so twisted up about losing his starting spot his senior year that he tried to get it back by screwing his teammate's sister in an effort to mess him up.

And they'll all laugh, even harder since it didn't work.

But I won't be the pathetic loser watching him play on

TV and telling people I dated a pro football player once, back when we were in college, before he made it big.

Because I've watched him practice. Gray only barely edges him out of his spot, and that's more because Coach Reese favors passing plays and Gray's passing game is better than Cal's. But Cal's running game is stronger, so it's really a toss-up.

Cal also doesn't get knocked around in the pocket quite as easily. What he lacks in passing finesse and accuracy—which don't get me wrong, that isn't much, and a good coach could bring him up to par in no time, he just hasn't been at a Division I school his whole college career—he more than makes up for in his ability to stay on his feet long enough to get the play running, even if his linemen fail.

But why am I mooning over Cal and reminiscing about his playing ability?

I'm moving on.

He's in the past. And I'm focusing on my future.

Yanking my bag closer, I pull out my folder for my world history class and get out the review sheet. It's been a fairly easy class—mostly lectures, note taking, and Scantron tests—so I'm not worried. But going over the entire semester's worth of information a few times before tomorrow morning is smart in general and a good distraction from my thoughts.

I don't get very far before there's a light knock on the door. Probably someone looking for Dani, wanting to say goodbye or give her a Christmas present before taking off tonight or tomorrow. The dorm is already starting to clear out as people finish their finals, at least the lucky jerks who don't have any tests tomorrow.

I shouldn't complain, though. My English class didn't even have a real final. We turned in a final paper last week and our scheduled "final" was the professor bringing in pastries, juice, and coffee as a farewell party to end the semester.

But when I answer the door, I'm surprised to find Ellie on the other side.

"Oh, good. I was hoping you'd be here," she says on a relieved sigh, wrapping her arms around me in an even more surprising hug.

I pat her back awkwardly, grateful she doesn't do more than give me a quick squeeze. "Um, hey. What's up? Dani's not back from her two o'clock final yet."

With a light laugh, Ellie passes me and comes into my room, waving a hand. "I'm here to see you, silly. Not Dani. I mean, if she were here, that'd be fine too, obviously, but she's going home to Montana for break, and you'll be here still, right?"

"Yeah. I'll be staying with my parents." Where else would I stay, after all? And now that Cal's out of the picture, I can spend all my time moping around the house, which they'll be happy about, I'm sure. The only hitch in that plan is Gray. I'm not sure what his plans are. Normally I'd just ask him, but since I'm not speaking to him at the moment …

Ellie brightens. "I'm going to be here for most of the

break too." She opens her mouth, hesitating for a second before continuing. "I'll be heading home this weekend, but then I'm coming back until right before Christmas Day." Her face turns disgruntled. "My mom won't let me do Christmas with Simon's family." She rolls her eyes. "Says something about if we were getting married, it'd be different. And staying with him for most of break is bad enough, but she draws the line at missing the holiday entirely when it's just a few hours' drive." Leaning in close, her eyes brighten with glee. "Though they're predicting a nasty December, so maybe there'll be a storm and it'll be too dangerous to drive. Wouldn't that be great?"

I can't help chuckling at her strange enthusiasm for a nasty winter storm. "I guess so."

Shrugging, she waves her hand again. "Anyway, I didn't come here to ask you to help me petition the weather gods for a storm or anything. I just wanted to make sure you'd be around so we can make plans to hang out."

"Ellie," I start, but she shakes her head, cutting me off.

"Nope. Don't 'Ellie' me. I know where you're going, and I'm not going to let you. We're friends. I knew you before you ever met my dumb brother. And I'm not going to let him ruin the friendship that we've built."

I open my mouth, wanting to find something to contradict her. Because I'm not sure I'd take my brother's girlfriend's side over him. Ex-girlfriend, I mean. Not that Cal and I ever used those terms. And maybe I would actually take someone else's side against Gray at this particular moment in time.

Shaking my head, I close my mouth and clear my throat. "Why would you choose me over your brother?"

She cocks her head and looks at me, her eyes skating over my face. "Besides the fact that he bullied me into staying away from him for most of the last decade?"

"What?"

She nods. "Oh, yeah. When Simon and I first got together, we hid our relationship from him. He was always big mad if I even so much as happened to show up at the same party he was at. And they weren't even football parties." She throws her hands up, still clearly frustrated by the whole thing. "I would *never* have gone to one of those. These were other people's parties, and he still tried to throw me out every time."

I'm super confused now, because he's never seemed to have a problem with his sister being around that I've noticed. I mean, there was that one time where we were supposed to have the house to ourselves and she came in to get something she'd forgotten and he was annoyed, but I'd be annoyed if someone had promised to give me privacy for a set amount of time and didn't, too. And also, she tried to warn him, but I'd made sure he didn't have his phone because of my issues, so he never got the text.

Other than that time, he's been friendly with his sister. At Friendsgiving, he even sat with her for quite a while. Sure, he stared at me like he could incinerate my clothes with his eyes, but I did the same to him. And I watched him laugh and joke and tease his sister. I thought they had a relationship a lot like mine and Gray's. Or at least the way mine and Gray's used to be.

"Anyway, he's made an effort to not be such a complete dillhole to me anymore, but that's more to do with Simon than with me." She shrugs, acting unaffected. "I'll take it, though."

"So you're not here to like, spy on me and report back to him?"

She sniggers. "No. Much to his dismay."

"Meaning he asked you to."

She shrugs, but doesn't confirm or deny anything. "Do you really want to talk about my brother?"

I press my lips together. No, I don't. But also I do.

With a soft chuckle, she pulls me in for another hug. "Seriously. We can, if you want to. And you can tell me if you want me to answer as your supportive friend or as his little sister who has intel. But I didn't come to talk about him. I came to make sure that you and I are still good."

Nodding, I hug her back. A real hug, not the awkward pat of a few minutes ago. "We're still good."

"Awesome." She steps back and heads for the door, giving me a finger wave as she drops her other hand on the doorknob. "Simon's already waiting for me, so I'm going to leave you to your studying. I'll text when I'm back in town, okay?"

I give her a smile, trying my best not to let the sadness slip in. "Sounds good."

I stare at the door for longer than a sane person would after she leaves. She has intel on Cal. And she basically just offered to tell me what she knows.

Do I want to know?

No, I decide at last, returning to the couch and my review sheet. That's why I've ignored all his calls and deleted all his texts and voicemails.

"No more boys," I say out loud. "No more drama."

CHAPTER THIRTY-EIGHT

Cal

"I hope you're proud of yourself," Kilpatrick grumbles as we switch places, me stepping up to run routes with Martinez.

I toss him a questioning look over my shoulder as Coach Miles tosses me a ball. "I don't know what you're talking about, man. I thought we agreed to stay out of each other's way." I mean, we didn't sit down and have a tea party and discuss our feelings or anything. But I've been steering clear of him. He's been steering clear of me. And when we're forced into these types of situations, we both pretend the other doesn't exist. It's been working since our blow up in the tape room last week that ended with Piper refusing to take my calls.

After trying to get her to talk to me all weekend and trying to bribe my sister to convince her to give me at least one chance to explain myself—which she flat refused—I've mostly come to the conclusion that whatever was between Piper and me is over. The knowledge sits in my belly like a hot, molten ball of anger and disappointment.

I'd honestly love nothing more than to blame Kilpatrick for his part in the situation. Him and Foster. If Kilpatrick hadn't come after me in the locker room that day … If Foster hadn't taken it upon himself to loop Piper in on the conversation he only half heard …

But really, I only have myself to blame. I did approach her with the intention of fucking with her brother.

I just didn't expect to catch real feelings for her in the process. I didn't know she was going to be so awesome. I figured she'd be an arrogant shit like her brother.

Though, I don't know, probably I'm projecting a little there. Everyone else seems to like him. And I probably would too if he hadn't stolen my spot.

Sighing, I wait while Martinez starts running his route, firing off the ball. It goes long, and he has to jump to tip it out of the air before catching it and pulling it close, slowing down and jogging back to his starting position.

"Focus," Coach Miles barks. "For someone who's been bellyaching all season about not starting, your accuracy is shit."

Kilpatrick sniggers, which does nothing to help me feel better. Instead of punching him in the fucking mouth like I'd pay actual money to do right now, I focus my glare on Coach. I should keep my mouth shut. I know it. But I'm feeling way too riled up at this point to do that. "I didn't hear you bitching about my accuracy last year."

Coach Miles moves his toothpick around his mouth, entirely unbothered by my griping. He shrugs, his beefy arms still crossed over his torso. "You weren't on a Division I team last year. You didn't have anyone to compete against forcing you to want to be better. Me bitching doesn't take you very far, and you and I both know it. Now. Get your head out of your ass or I'll have Kilpatrick show you how it's done again."

Kilpatrick snorts again, and I block out whatever he's saying, focusing on Martinez. I envision the route he's going to be running, then give him the signal, planting my feet, cocking my arm, and sending the ball in a perfect spiral … right into Martinez's waiting hands.

He jumps as he turns, cheering. "Yeah! That's what I'm talking about McAdam! That's how you throw me a ball!"

Another snort from Kilpatrick. "I thought the cheer squad practiced later," he grumbles.

"Shut your fucking mouth," I snarl.

"Boys," Coach Miles says, but Kilpatrick ignores the warning, stepping up until his chest brushes mine.

"You gonna make me?" he asks, his breath hot in my face.

I stand my ground, though, not backing down. This asshole wants to come at me? Fine. Please do.

Puffing up, I push back, forcing him to step back instead. He might be taller, but he gets sacked way too fucking easy. I sneer at him. "Ohhh, you don't like it when I push back? What? You worried that if I increase my accuracy, Coach will let me start at the bowl? Awww, poor little Kilpatrick. It'd suck to have someone steal your starting spot, wouldn't it?"

"Fuck you, McAdam," he seethes. "You think this is about a fucking starting spot? It's mine. I earned it. I'm the better player, and we all know it. Which is why *you're* the one constantly working on your accuracy and getting told off for being a crybaby. But I dealt with your shit, ignoring you and letting you whine to whoever was willing to listen. I never said a word to you. Never rubbed it in. Never did anything. And then you go after my *sister?*" His dark eyes flare with unmitigated anger. "I mostly came back here for her. To help her. To protect her from fucking assholes like you. And now she won't even talk to me."

I let out a bitter laugh. "Oh yeah? Pretty sucky, huh? Join the fucking club, man."

He takes a step back, confusion replacing the anger on his face. "What? What are you talking about?"

I throw my hands wide. "What does it sound like? She's not talking to me either. And I have you—well, you and Foster—to thank for that."

He snorts. "How d'you figure I have anything to do with her deciding to drop your sorry ass?"

"Well, she dropped yours too, and I'd say you have a

lot more time invested in that relationship than I do, so maybe look in the mirror before you go around calling me shitty, huh?" I turn back to the coach, holding out my hands for a ball, which he supplies, something of a bemused expression on his face as he watches Kilpatrick and I go at it.

Martinez stares at me with his hands on his hips, his eyebrows high on his forehead.

"We gonna keep practicing, or what?" I yell to him. "We have an important game coming up, don't we?"

Coach Miles gives Martinez the signal to go, and with one last funny look in my direction, he starts his route. Focusing all my frustration and anger into my arm, I fire off the ball, staring at the spot where it should intersect with Martinez. It lands perfectly in his hands. He barely has to reach for it before pulling it tight to his side, weaving like he's dodging defensive players before turning and jogging back to his starting position.

Another throw. Another catch. Rinse and repeat, no more talking except barked instructions from the coach and the minimal encouragement he provides when you do something right until my shoulder burns from throwing so many passes and Martinez's chest is heaving from running so many routes.

Coach signals to me when he notices me rubbing my shoulder. "You're done for today, McAdam. Good work. You too, Martinez. Send Sanders over. Kilpatrick will finish practice with him."

Martinez falls in step beside me, bumping me with his

shoulder. "You were on fire out there, man. Do we need you and Kilpatrick to get in a fight over a chick every day?" He sucks his breath through his teeth. "Hmm. Somehow I think we'll run out of chicks for you to fight over. Might need to find some other way to tap into that."

I shove him in the shoulder. "Shut up," I grumble, but there's no heat in it. Maybe earlier I would've been pissed. But now I'm just tired. And Martinez gives everyone shit. It's his way of showing affection. He cackles, jogging ahead of me to the locker room.

"McAdam." I turn to find Kilpatrick behind me.

Stopping, I wait placidly for whatever he has to say. I'm not interested in fighting with him anymore. I hold up my hands. "Look, man. Can we just bury this? You won, alright? Your sister wants nothing to do with me, and while part of me wants to be mad at you about that, I know it's my own fault. You got it all. You're the starter. You're untouchable. Let's just stay out of each other's way for the remainder of our time here, alright?"

"I don't get it," he says, almost like he didn't hear a word I just said.

"Don't get what?"

He shakes his head. "If she realized you were using her and broke up with you, why won't she talk to me?"

He sounds so lost and bewildered, I have to drop my head to hide my grin. Usually he's all confident and put together, and now his little sister won't take his calls and he's reduced to asking me why. That must grate. Once upon a time I would've rubbed his face in it or smugly withheld any information I might have.

But knowing how it feels to realize your sister—the sister you've done your best to look out for and protect, and if I'm being totally honest, it seems like he's done a better job of that than I ever did—thinks you're a piece of shit, I feel kinda bad for the guy. Of course, I *was* a piece of shit to Ellie. For a long time. I said I was trying to protect her, and to some degree I was, but I also just saw her as my annoying kid sister who followed me around. That hasn't been true in a long time, though, even if I was still acting like it was.

Kilpatrick and Piper seem to actually like each other. Or they did, anyway. And knowing what happened in California, him coming back here to look out for her makes a lot of sense. He saw an opportunity that helped him and put him in a position to be there for his sister.

If I'd been in his shoes, I probably would've taken it for the guaranteed starter spot *despite* it being closer to my sister, not *because* it was closer to her.

Suddenly I have a lot more respect for him. I don't *like* him. But I understand him.

And knowing his sister hates his guts right now, I can't help but feel sorry for him.

"You pissed her off," I finally answer with a shrug. "I don't honestly have a lot of experience with a pissed off Piper, because this is new for me too. But based on what she told me about what happened last year and what happened over Thanksgiving, I think she feels like everyone's just waiting for her to screw up. If you're equating me to that"— I have to stop and think of the most appropriate word for that … guy—"that predator, you made her feel like you don't trust her. And she's nothing if not independent." Crossing my arms, I can't help giving him a quizzical look and saying, "Given that you've known her forever, I can't believe you don't realize that."

He seethes, his shoulders rising and falling as he takes a deep breath, his eyes narrowing like he wants nothing more than to punch me in the face.

Shaking my head, I hold up my hands again. "Hey, man. You asked. I might understand you a little better now, but it's not like we're friends." I make a circle in the air. "Everyone knows I'm a bitchy asshole. Don't be surprised that it gets turned on you when you say something stupid."

Surprisingly, that provokes a bark of laughter. "Fair enough." His face turns thoughtful, and he gives me an appraising look. "You actually care about her, don't you?"

"Yes. I do."

He looks me up and down again. "Huh." He shakes his head and looks away. "Don't think this means I think you're good enough for her."

"I wouldn't dream of it."

Coach Miles's annoyed voice reaches us. "Kilpatrick! This isn't social hour. Get Sanders and get your ass back over here."

I turn away before Kilpatrick gets in any more

trouble, all this talk of Piper making my longing for her rise up something fierce. It's an ever-present thing, but I usually manage to ignore it and distract myself. The fact that I know Ellie has seen and spoken with her but won't tell me anything doesn't help me at all. In fact, I'm pretty sure they had plans this evening. But even when I try to corner Ellie at my house afterward, she just gives me a smug smile and deflects until Simon tells me to leave his girlfriend alone and whisks her into his room.

Our early agreement that they'd only have sex when I'm not around fell by the wayside weeks ago. About the time I started bringing Piper around while they were home. I guess I only have myself to blame for that too, since I broke the rule first.

And any argument that it's not the same since she's not anyone in our house's sister would be quickly laughed out of the room. So I keep my complaints to myself.

But if Gray, who has a much better history with his sister, can't even overcome one fight, how'm I ever going to get Ellie on my side?

And without Ellie's help, what hope do I have of ever winning Piper back?

CHAPTER THIRTY-NINE

Piper

I spend Christmas Break trying to distract myself and not get bored. Because when I'm bored, just sitting around with nothing to occupy me, my thoughts inevitably drift to Cal. And that's not where my brain needs to be spending time.

Ellie is surprisingly a lifesaver in that regard. While she does have to spend part of her time with her parents, the rest of the time she's in town. And whenever Simon is working out or in practice or watching game tapes, she's hanging out with me. At my house, of course, at least most of the time. We go out, getting in our last minute Christmas shopping and catching a movie now and then, but mostly we hang out at my parents'.

Things with my parents are … stable. They're no longer threatening to police my whereabouts or try to force me to move home from the dorms. But the fact that I'm not seeing Cal anymore probably has more to do with that than some newfound trust in me or my decision making skills.

When I came home after my last final on Friday, my mom and I had an extremely brief conversation about that.

"Piper," she said, her voice almost hesitant, but mostly firm. "About this boy—"

"There is no boy," I cut in with a forced smile. "It's over. No need to worry about it anymore."

Mom looked me over, examining the bland face I presented her with. "Are you okay?"

"Fine. Peachy. It's better this way." Another forced smile, and I picked up my things and took them up to my room, effectively ending the conversation.

And my mom took the hint and left it alone. I'm sure she told my dad, because they watched me carefully for a few days, but when I invited Ellie over—see? I can make smart choices, because they finally saw that Ellie is a real person and an actual friend, not someone I made up to cover for time spent with Cal—they relaxed.

The only sore point is Gray. He's stayed away for most of break, but as Christmas Day approaches, I know that reprieve is soon to end.

"Gray's coming over for Christmas Eve," Mom tells

me the day before. "I know you two are still at odds, but I do expect you both to be civil to each other."

Crossing my arms, I stare at her while she moves around the kitchen, cleaning up the last of the dinner dishes. "Did he get this same talk?"

She nods, drying her hands on a dish towel and meeting my eyes. "He did. This afternoon." She holds up her hands. "I don't know what exactly you two said to each other, and I know that the two of you have to work things out yourselves. Gray's chosen to stay away for the break to give you your space. But it's Christmas, and we will be doing our usual Christmas activities, and you two will be polite to each other at the very least. Got it?"

Dropping my arms, I sigh. "Got it."

With a nod, she pours herself a glass of wine and picks up her tablet. Coming around the counter, she kisses me on the cheek. "I'm going to go relax and read. Let me know if you need anything."

"Thanks, Mom." It's a normal thing for her to say, something she's been saying to me since I was a kid. But somehow right now it feels more significant than a rote offer.

She pauses and studies my face, just for a moment, then she gives me a small smile and goes into the living room, where she and Dad exchange words in low voices, and he chuckles about something. Normal domestic sounds, the sounds I grew up listening to every night.

But I feel more disconnected from them than ever, even if they aren't actively rooting for me to fail like I felt like for so long. They care about me. They want what's best for me.

I want that too.

Which is why I need to not dwell on the fact that Cal has already given up on trying to talk to me. I never could bring myself to block him. And now he's not even reaching out.

I should be grateful. If he were still calling or texting, I'd think he was an obsessive creeper or something.

But instead I'm just sad. Because it was two weeks ago today that I got his last message.

Cal: I get that you don't want to talk to me. I don't blame you, so I'll stop. I just want you to know that if you ever change your mind, I'd love to talk to you again. <broken heart emoji>

And as stupid as it sounds, the inclusion of that emoji is what makes a simple text hit so much harder.

Sighing at my own stupidity, I head up to my room and throw myself on the bed, calling Ellie because I need something to get me out of my head. I don't think she'd tell me to stay strong and ignore her brother if I pushed her on it, so we carefully don't talk about Cal. But somehow *not* talking about him at all makes his presence even more tangible.

* * *

I'm in my room when Gray comes home on Christmas Eve, wrapping the last couple of presents. I got something for Ellie—a new set of her favorite brand of brush pens and a new notebook since she'll use them eventually even if she doesn't need them right away—but I'll have to wait until she's back in town to give it to her.

I stall in my room until Mom calls me down for dinner. Normally I would've gone down immediately and given him a hug to welcome him home. That's what I've done the last few years since he went away to college.

But this year … everything's different.

I'm different, at least, and so our relationship is different, even if he's actually the same guy he's always been.

I guess he's always been looking out for me like this, I just didn't notice before. Or didn't find it so stifling and patronizing.

Maybe that's what it is. When you're thirteen or sixteen, you expect your parents and older siblings to protect you and look out for you and you plan on being told what to do all the time. But I turned twenty two months ago. And while I'm aware that I'm not exactly a greatly experienced adult or anything, I'm not a little kid anymore either. How am I supposed to learn from my mistakes if I'm never allowed to make them?

Shaking myself out of my irritated musings, I stare at myself in the mirror above my dresser, pulling my lips into a smile, or at least as close to it as I can manage. It's not great. It's definitely not genuine. But it's the best I've got right now.

I head downstairs before Mom has to call me a second time. That always annoys her, and I promised that I'd at least be polite to Gray. That means coming down for dinner and exchanging pleasantries.

He stares at me when I enter the room like he's not sure how to act. Like he wants to say something, but isn't sure if I'm willing to talk to him.

I give him the same fakey-fake smile I practiced in the mirror.

His answering smile is pained as he lifts a hand in a limp wave. "Hey, Pipes. How you been?"

"Fine." I wave back, painfully aware that he didn't call me Monkey or Monkey Butt like he normally does. "You?" We don't address each other by name. Not when we're our usual selves, anyway. But that went out the window when he decided to throw Brent in my face and made me responsible for his choices. Like I begged Gray to transfer.

I won't lie, I was grateful to have him around as a buffer with Mom and Dad at first. But when he became as bad as them? Nah. I don't need that. So we're reduced to this.

"Good. Fine."

I look at Mom, who's looking between Gray and me, a hopeful expression on her face. But when we don't say anything more to each other than that, her mouth turns down at the corners. Clearly she was hoping that putting us in the same room would magically make everything okay.

Dinner is largely made up of separate conversations. My parents and Gray have a conversation. Then Mom turns to me and asks a question, and she and I talk for a few minutes. But Gray and I don't talk to each other.

He makes an effort once, asking how finals went. But when all I say is, "Fine," he takes the hint and stops, though the wounded look that flashes across his face gives me a pang of guilt. Just a little, though. Because I'm not over what he said and how he's acted or the voicemails spent justifying his behavior instead of apologizing. Asking about finals isn't enough to make up for any of that.

Yes, we have to get through at least another twenty-four hours of this, because he'll be here through Christmas Day, but I'm content with this arrangement for that amount of time.

The tone of conversation changes, however, when Mom sets down her fork and starts talking about the flights they've booked. I'd been zoning out because they'd been talking to Gray about something, but when she mentions my name in conjunction with a plane ticket, I perk up.

"Wait, what? Where am I going?"

Dad sighs loudly, but I ignore him. Mom presses her lips together and looks at me. "Haven't you been listening, Piper? I was talking to both of you. Gray's playing in the Poppy Bowl. We're going to support him. I bought you a ticket too. I told you about it the other day, and you said it was fine."

I did? I think back over our conversations this last week. I don't remember anything about that, but my dad has clearly reached the end of his patience with my disconnection from Gray and the family at large, so I clear my throat and duck my head. "Right. Sorry. I was just … thinking about something else and I missed what you were talking about."

Shit. It's too late to back out now. Mom and Dad have already bought tickets. But the thought of being stuck in a hotel with them for days is … unappealing. The game will be fine, because I don't mind cheering for my school's team even if I am mad at two of the players. The team is bigger than the two of them, after all. Plus, I have other football player friends. I can cheer for *them*.

Maybe Ellie will be going. If not, maybe I can convince her to come …

That makes me feel better.

Clearing my throat, I wait for Mom to turn back to me. "Sorry. I know you've said already, but I forgot. Where is the game again?"

"Estrando." Gray supplies the answer, meeting my eyes.

Great. The home of SCU. The city where my life blew up the first time. And now I get to drag the shrapnel of my current life back there for a tour.

This should be fun.

I really hope Ellie's planning on coming, because I need someone to distract me and keep me sane.

Maybe I can get in touch with Shelby. If the three of us went out one night, that would be a lot of fun.

The deeper that thought takes hold, the more I can't help thinking it's a great idea. Maybe this trip won't be so bad after all.

CHAPTER FORTY

Cal

"Alright, men," Coach Reese says from his spot at the center of the unfamiliar locker room. "Tomorrow's a light day before our game the following day. I know it's New Year's, so the urge to celebrate is strong. But take it easy tonight. Save the celebration for after the game."

A murmur of assent goes up from the guys, and we start moving around, stripping out of sweaty gear after today's practice. We have the visitor's locker room since we're the lower seeded team for this game, which means it's not as nice as ours back home, and I'm sure the home team locker room here is way better than this too. Old, dented metal lockers bearing flaking blue paint, scarred wooden benches full of semipornographic graffiti, showers with shower heads so crusted over with lime scale that the water does little more than dribble out, the ripe smell of sweaty socks permeating everything.

I've been in worse locker rooms, for sure. But not in a while.

We at least make an effort to make our visitor's room clean, if basic.

Even our home lockers were not much fancier than this for the first few years. Over the summer the athletics department gave it a facelift in honor of our first season as a Division I team, replacing the basic metal lockers with much nicer wooden ones, our benches replaced and upgraded, the showers power washed and repainted, brand new shower heads installed, the works.

While this might feel like a slap in the face to some, the fact that we've made it this far our first season as a Division I team is a victory in its own right, and Coach is right that the urge to celebrate is strong.

Guys are already debating the best place to go once we're all cleaned up, and what time we should head out. I catch Simon's eye, and he shakes his head at the loud-mouthed antics of some of our younger teammates. As one of the captains, it's his job to deal with their nonsense.

I grin at him. "Better you than me, man."

He flips me off and wraps a towel around his hips. "You heard Coach," he barks at the underclassmen. "No clubs. You're underage anyway."

"Psssh. Like that matters. I have a—" His buddy

smacks him in the chest, and Alvarez looks around and lowers his voice before continuing. "I have a fake ID. So does Hunter. We can go clubbing if we want."

"No you can't," Simon barks. "Not if you want to still be on the team tomorrow."

"Aw, c'mon, Hindley," Hunter whines. "You'd really rat us out and get us kicked off the team?"

Simon shrugs one big shoulder as he heads for the showers. "You wanna find out?"

They grumble but turn their attention to more age-appropriate venues.

When I return from the showers, a consensus seems to have been reached. There's a steakhouse with a back room big enough for the team, and Trey is going to act as the cruise director and call them to see if they can fit us in. If not, they've apparently got backup options in mind. While there's a bar in the restaurant and we could get drinks if we want, this close to a game, we're all supposed to be abstaining.

Tomorrow is meant to recover from travel and today's workout and practice so we're fresh for the game, not recovering from a hangover and putting our bodies through more stress than they need.

Usually that's not a problem, but the excitement of this final game seems to have a few guys losing their heads. Especially Mitchell, who just turned twenty-one the day we flew down, so he hasn't even had the opportunity to use his freshly-minted ability to buy alcohol legally.

I nudge Simon where he sits next to me on the bench, rubbing a towel over his head. "We better keep an eye on those guys," I say quietly, nodding at the group in question. They might try to cause trouble regardless.

Simon gives me a surprised look. "You're suddenly a stickler for the rules now?"

I shrug. "For this game? Yeah, I guess I am. Like Coach said, we'll have plenty of opportunity to blow off steam after the game. We don't need any minor in possession charges away from home right before our first bowl game."

With an approving nod, Simon grunts, which for him passes as unqualified agreement.

We're a loud and enthusiastic crew when we get to the restaurant. But we're all good boys and no one orders any alcohol, filling up instead on specialty sodas, steaks, and the best kinds of carbs.

When we settle up the bill and make our way out into the night, the air cool but so much warmer than we're used to back home that it feels like an early spring, a minor argument breaks out about what to do next. The older, stodgier contingent is in favor of going back to the hotel.

The younger, rowdier group wants to explore.

Sighing, Simon nudges me and nods at the underclassmen who are clearly not amenable to listen to reason. "As captain, it's my job to make sure these guys don't do anything too stupid. Come with me and help out, will you?"

With a chuckle, I nod and shrug. "Sure." It's not like I have anything exciting to do in the hotel. Simon probably wants to talk to Ellie, but if I'm not mistaken, he was texting her at dinner quite a bit.

She's here for the game, jumping at the chance to come hang out with Piper and her family. They've been spending time together all break, and Ellie still won't give me any information on Piper and how she's doing. I get an eye roll and, "She's fine, Cal. That's all I'm going to say, no matter how much you badger me."

I've stopped asking. Mostly.

Except Simon pulls out his phone and taps out a message. Craning my neck, I try to see his screen. Maybe Ellie sent some selfies of her and Piper together … "What's she up to?"

Glaring at me, Simon turns his phone so I can't see it. "Dude. Ask her yourself if you want to know that bad. Trust me, you don't want to look at our texts."

"Gross, dude. I didn't need to know that."

"You're the one being a creeper," he grumbles, shoving his phone in his pocket bumping my shoulder with a closed fist. "Besides, I wasn't even texting her. I was updating Coach about the boneheads we're accompanying." He gestures at the guys in front of us who've started down the sidewalk.

We're in a busy part of town full of restaurants and bars, and I'm not sure what the end goal is here. Most of these guys are underage, and the no alcohol rule is in effect anyway, so it's not like it matters how old anyone is. Some of us could go into a bar and hang out I guess, but most of these places have clear signs that say no one under twenty-one is allowed inside.

Fortunately, it's not just Simon and I along as the dubious voices of reason. Kilpatrick and Lancaster are here too. And while I might not be Kilpatrick's greatest fan, our absence of hostilities in the last couple of weeks has been a relief. We can both be in the same group without worrying the other one will make it uncomfortable, at least.

Another large group of guys, bigger than ours, comes down the street from the other direction. They're loud, singing something together, and when I get a better view of them it's clear they're from a frat. Not surprising. This part of town was chosen because it tends to be a favorite for local university students.

But when they mention Alpha Nu, my ears perk up. Because that's the name of the frat that asshole who hurt Piper was a member of. My attempts at getting him sanctioned or kicked out or *something* through the local chapter at Marycliff went nowhere.

I'm apparently not the only one who's noticed, because Kilpatrick takes the lead and steers us closer to the frat guys.

As we approach, his cheerful voice calls out to them. "Brothers of Alpha Nu!" he yells, like he's one of them. They let out a big cheer and welcome him into their group, holding out their hands for some kind of weird handshake.

Laughing, Kilpatrick kind of slaps at their hands, clearly having no clue what's expected.

That puts a damper on their acceptance. One guy wearing an Alpha Nu hat jerks his chin at Kilpatrick. "You're not a brother. What gives?"

Kilpatrick lets out a chuckle, all affable goofiness. "You caught me. I've been too busy to pledge. But you know I would've picked Alpha Nu if I could've!"

A few half hearted cheers go up from the other guys, probably more just in reaction to hearing the frat name than any real understanding of what's going on.

Kilpatrick leans in close. "Hey, I got a buddy who's a member here, though. You guys know him? His name's Brent Hughes."

A guy with dark hair and a scruffy shadow along his jaw steps forward. He's tall and lean, similar to Kilpatrick, but not quite as filled out. Maybe an inch or two taller than me, but I've got a lot more muscle over him.

I clench everywhere as he approaches Kilpatrick and gives him a nod, confusion on his face. "I'm Brent." He looks Kilpatrick up and down. "Don't think I know you, though."

Almost without thinking, I edge my way through my teammates, getting closer to the front where Kilpatrick is facing off with this jackass. No one else knows the significance here, but I sure as hell do, and I'm not about to stand on the sidelines and let Kilpatrick get revenge on his own. If he's going to deliver a beatdown, then I am in.

A harsh edge to his voice, Kilpatrick draws up to his full height, looking down at this asshole. "You're right. You don't know me. Word is you know my sister, though."

A loud, "Ooohh," goes up from the guys around him, some of them covering their mouths with their hands.

Kilpatrick ignores them, even when Brent sticks out his tongue and accepts fives from the guys around him. He jerks his chin at Kilpatrick. "Oh yeah? I probably know lots of guys' sisters. Which one's yours?"

I'm amazed by Kilpatrick's restraint, because I'm about to punch this douche in the face right now. If he were in my face talking about Ellie like that, I would've.

But Kilpatrick leans in close, a savage smile on his face, and says, "Piper Kilpatrick."

Brent's brow creases in confusion as he flips through what's apparently a mental contact list.

Then one of his buddies slaps him on the chest and says, "C'mon, man, you remember her. She was that bitch that freaked out and stole a bunch of shit after you fucked her last semester." He turns to Kilpatrick. "She got kicked out of school or something, right? You here to steal more stuff or something?"

From my spot behind him I can see Kilpatrick's jaw clenching and the muscles in his arms popping as he flexes his fist. The only thing standing between these assholes and a throat punch is Kilpatrick's masterful self control. Hell, mine too. Because rage flows down my spine like scalding lava.

It's only the fact that Kilpatrick has a greater right to avenge Piper than I do that I'm staying back. She's his sister. And she's my … ex, I guess. I haven't been able to bring myself to say the word yet, partly because I never even called her my girlfriend. Can you be someone's ex if you were never officially dating?

But this asshole is definitely Piper's ex, and as shitty as my behavior may have been, his was definitely worse. And I blame him for the fact that she now won't talk to me. I might've been able to apologize and earn her trust again if he hadn't shattered it so badly first.

Now she's not even willing to give me a second chance. And who can blame her with these kinds of douchebags running around, free from the consequences of their actions? I deserve consequences, and I'm getting them.

This jackass deserves consequences, too. And I'm just waiting for someone else to throw the first punch so I can deliver them.

Kilpatrick leans in close, his teeth bared, and I'm afraid he's just going to, I dunno, grab the guy's face and slam it into his knee or something. But he doesn't. Instead, he speaks quietly into the guy's ear so that no one else can hear him.

Whatever he says pisses off the guy, and he shoves Kilpatrick. Triumph lights up Kilpatrick's face, and I realize that this was his plan, to get the other guy to lay hands on him first. And with someone like that, it seems reasonable to think he wouldn't be too difficult to provoke.

Quicker than anyone can react, Kilpatrick grabs the guy's shoulder and delivers a sharp jab to his gut.

With a roar, the guy doubles over, then charges Kilpatrick, head down. At that point, all hell breaks loose. I grab the guy's shirt and yank him off Kilpatrick, turning him so I can punch him in the face. It's a glancing blow off his cheek that seems like it pisses him off more than it hurts, but he should at least have a bruise tomorrow, and that's satisfying.

One of his buddies grabs me, and I swat him away in time to see Kilpatrick grappling with Brent, neatly shoving his foot into the spot behind the guy's knee, driving him to the ground.

Simon's voice eventually makes it through the sound of my own heart pounding in my ears with the rush of adrenaline and the desire to fight.

He blocks me from getting involved further, his hands on my shoulders shoving me back toward my teammates, then he inserts himself between Kilpatrick and Brent, shrugging off the attempts to attack him like they're little more than annoying gnats. He pulls Kilpatrick close and growls in his face before shoving him in my direction, then he turns to face the frat guys, his hands held up almost like he's surrendering but I also know that he's ready to grab these guys and toss them aside if necessary. That's his defensive grappling posture. I've seen it enough times on the field to recognize it.

But before any of that becomes necessary, we're

approached by two guys in tight T-shirts as packed with muscle as Simon, one of them maybe even bigger. Obviously bouncers from a nearby bar.

"Hey!" the bigger one barks, his bald head shining in the lights from the bars and restaurants surrounding us. "Break it up and move it along before we call the cops."

A couple of the frat guys start to protest, but quickly fall silent in the face of the bouncer's flat stare. "I don't give a fuck," he says in a no-nonsense voice. "Get out of here."

Simon takes a few steps back, keeping his eyes on the frat guys, but they turn and start meandering back the other direction under the weight of the bouncer's glare.

Even the most vocal about staying out later are silent when Simon directs us back toward the hotel. But before we get there, we're met with Coach Reese's thunderous glare.

He's sweeping down the street, coming for us like a man on a mission to punish. "You got into a fight?" he shouts when we're close enough for it to have the desired impact.

We collectively flinch, silent under the force of his anger.

He paces in front of us, his arms crossed. When he finally speaks again, his voice is quiet, but no less furious. "Kilpatrick, I understand you were the leader of this little altercation?" He pauses, but no one answers, which is close enough to agreement for Coach. "You know the rules on fighting."

"It was me," I jump in, drawing surprised glares from the guys next to me, Kilpatrick most of all. But I ignore them, focusing on Coach.

He stops his pacing to stare at me, his anger focused enough that it feels like it might burn a hole right through my skull.

"He was talking shit about my girlfriend," I say by way of explanation. Kilpatrick grunts next to me.

Coach crosses his arms and stares me down, waiting for me to say more or to break under the weight of his glare, I guess. When I don't, he sighs and points between Kilpatrick and me. "This the same girlfriend you two were shouting about a few weeks ago?"

I jerk my chin in a nod. Coach heard all that? Or did he just hear about it? Who's the rat who keeps telling Coach about shit like this?

Coach stares at me another long moment, though his anger seems to be dissipating. Some. "I guess I should be grateful I don't have to bench my starting quarterback," he grumbles, then tips his head back to stare at the sky. "But suspending my backup for our most important game isn't exactly a great feeling either."

Shaking his head, he gestures at the hotel entrance. "Go inside. If I hear about any of you even stepping a toe outside of your rooms before it's time to leave tomorrow, you'll sit out the game, even if we have to forfeit, and the start of next season will be spent running sprints until you puke the first few weeks. Are we clear?" When no one moves or responds, Coach lifts his eyebrows. "Are we clear?" he repeats more loudly and more slowly.

"Yessir," we all grumble, filing into the hotel and heading straight for the elevators.

Kilpatrick hangs back with Simon and me, catching me before I follow Simon into our room. "Hey. McAdam."

I turn, holding the door open with one hand. "Yeah?"

He looks up and down the hall like he's uncomfortable talking to me like this. "Why'd you do that?" he finally asks.

"Do what? Punch that guy in the face? Same reason you did, I imagine."

He blows out a breath and shakes his head. "Well, that too, but that's not what I meant." He looks me up and down. "She told you? What happened last spring?"

I nod.

"All of it?" he clarifies.

I nod again, and he rocks back on his heels, looking down and shaking his head. "Huh. I didn't realize you guys had gotten that close. It's not something she talks about. Ever." He lifts his eyes to mine again. "But why take the fall? You would've started. Isn't that what you were going for all along?"

Shrugging, I'm not sure how to answer that question. Because, yeah, it is. "I wanted to earn the spot," I say at length. "Not because you were suspended for fighting with a douchebag who deserved far worse than the couple of punches we got in. And if anyone did to my sister what he did to yours? I don't know if I could've waited for him to shove me first. I might've just started pounding his face in once I realized he was in front of me." I shrug again. "I would've started the fight if you hadn't been blocking my way like usual." He doesn't crack a smile at my lame attempt at a joke. "Might as well take credit for it, right?"

CHAPTER FORTY-ONE

Piper

Ellie leans over as the football teams take the field. "I have to confess. I don't really like football all that much."

I look over at her, surprised, and she shrugs, a little grin on her face. "I know, right? It's a sacrilege." She reaches behind her and tugs on her ponytail, looking at the sea of people around us, everyone settling in and focusing on the field where they're getting ready to do the coin toss. She leans on her arm rest closer to me. "Honestly? It's been kind of a relief that most of the games since Simon and I officially got together were away games. That way I wasn't expected to go. Autumn would come with me to the home games, which made them not so bad." She squints at me. "You're a fan, though, aren't you? Didn't I hear someone say you used to go watch practices for fun?"

Chuckling to cover my flare of embarrassment, I nod. "Yeah. I'm a fan. And yeah. I did." I shrug. "I had a hard time making friends at first"—because I made no effort to make friends, but we won't get into that—"and it was something to do other than studying. Plus, I'd grab dinner with Gray and his friends after, so it wasn't as pathetic as it sounds."

"I don't think it sounds pathetic," Ellie says lightly. "You and your brother are pretty close, huh?"

At my nod, she sighs wistfully, then wrinkles her nose. "Cal and I were close when we were little, but that all changed once he got to high school. Then I became, like, the worst human to walk the planet. Having me at the same school was so *awful* if you asked him. Sadly for him, our parents are Marycliff alums and they'd always said they'd cover college if we went there." She spreads her hands, palms up. "So here we are at the same school again." She shakes her head in mock sympathy. "Poor Cal."

I can't help laughing. She hasn't talked much about her brother with me—a fact I appreciate for obvious reasons—but this isn't so much about him specifically as it is contrasting their relationship with mine and Gray's. "You guys seem to get along better now, though. You come to all the football stuff and everything. And I mean, you're here watching the game."

She shrugs. "Yeah. Because you invited me to stay with you if I could fund my ticket. And because of Simon. He's the only reason Cal's *kinda* okay with me being around. He wasn't given much of a choice in the matter." She tilts her head back and forth. "And I mean, to be fair, he did help smooth things over with Simon and me when we'd broken up. If not for Cal, I don't know that Simon and I would be together at all. So I guess I have to give him credit for that."

"Wait, what? I haven't heard this story. I thought he wasn't happy about you dating his friend. Isn't that what you said before?"

She laughs, filling me in on the details about her secret relationship with Simon and how the stress of it staying a secret caused problems serious enough that Simon broke up with her. I get the feeling there are *a lot* of details she's glossing over, but I don't push, because while I am interested, the game is starting. "Anyway," she says quickly, "when the truth came out, Cal blamed himself for our breakup and everyone's unhappiness and decided it was his job to fix it."

I grab her wrist, sitting up as tall as I can in my seat and peering down at the sidelines. "Speaking of Cal, why isn't he dressed to play?"

"Huh? What do you mean?" She peers down at the sidelines as well. We're about halfway up on the Marycliff forty-yard line, so we have a pretty good view of the whole field, but picking out distinct players in the crowd by the bench is tricky.

I point him out, dressed in his jersey and jeans, a headset over the red Marycliff hat on his head where he paces along the sidelines by the bench watching the field. Marycliff is kicking off. "There. Did he get hurt?"

"Oh," she says, her voice unsurprised. "Yeah. Um, not exactly? I mean, I think his knuckles got a little bruised, but nothing serious."

"His knuckles?" I practically shriek, drawing the attention of my parents.

"Girls? Is everything alright?" my mom asks.

"Yes, sorry, fine. Ellie was just telling me something surprising. I didn't mean to be so loud." I turn back to Ellie and lower my voice. "Was he in a fight?"

"Oh, ummm ..." She looks all around. Good thing that Ellie's terrible at coming up with believable stories on the spot.

"Ellie. What. Happened?"

Sighing, she deflates, slumping in her seat. "I *said* I wasn't going to be the go-between for you two. I promised myself I'd just be your friend and stay out of it." She nods to herself, forestalling my protest that telling me what happened when she clearly knows *is* being a friend. "But you should probably know." She peeks past me, checking my parents. Satisfied, she refocuses on me. "I don't know all the details, just what I got out of Simon, and he's not exactly a Chatty Cathy."

"Ellie, please, for the love of god, just tell me what happened."

The words spill out in a rapid stream, her eyes constantly darting around and her voice as hushed as possible so that no one overhears us. "The guys went out for dinner the other night and they apparently bumped into some frat? I dunno exactly what happened, but one of the other guys shoved Gray, Gray punched him in the gut, and when he charged him, Cal yanked the guy off and punched him in the face. There probably would've been more, but a bouncer came out and broke it up and they went their separate ways, but someone told the Coach. He was about to yank Gray from the game for fighting, which is against their code of conduct, and Cal said he was the one who started it or something. So Cal is suspended from the game instead."

I blink at her, trying to make her words make sense. Because it sounds like she just said … "Cal took the fall for Gray?"

Ellie nods, eyes wide, face solemn.

"But why?"

She shrugs.

Looking around like Ellie did, I make sure no one is listening in and lower my voice as well for good measure. "But he started dating me to try to mess with Gray so he could have the starting spot."

Ellie nods.

"This would've been his chance to start. In the biggest game of the season. The biggest game of his career to date."

She nods again. "Yup."

"So why would he do that? And who were they fighting? And why? They all know the code of conduct. They know the coach is serious about that. Why would any of them, especially Gray and Cal, risk the consequences?"

"Why do *you* think they would risk all that?" Ellie asks, with that annoying patronizing quality certain teachers give you when they know the answer but are waiting for you to figure it out for yourself.

"If you know more, you better tell me right now."

She holds up her hands. "I don't *know* anything in particular. Just that you used to go to school here. You've refused to go to parties held by a specific frat at Marycliff who also has a chapter at your old school which just so happens to be located not too far away. And the only thing that both your brother and my brother have in common enough to fight over is ..." She hesitates, meeting my eyes, her mouth twisting for a second before finishing. "You."

I sit in my seat, stunned, my mind flitting through the various possibilities. They encountered a frat. Gray provoked one of them into shoving him so he'd have an excuse to punch back. Cal joined the fray.

It could just be a coincidence. It could've been a different frat or a different guy. But deep in my gut, I know Ellie's right. Anyone else, even if some guy were mouthing off, neither of them would've gotten into an actual fight. Not with a huge game looming. Not with everything they'd stand to lose.

I've watched an angry Cal hold back so he wouldn't do anything to injure himself or risk his spot in a game—his pacing when I told him about Brent comes to mind—and that's with just the off chance of seeing time on the field. And I know Gray well enough to know that he doesn't fight. I've literally never heard of my brother getting in anything worse than a verbal confrontation with someone, and even that's rare. He's not a hothead. Usually if someone's being stupid, he just leaves.

I'm barely aware of the game, not paying any attention until a cheer goes up around me. Marycliff has forced a turnover and now has possession of the ball. But now I don't care about the game. Because the need to talk to Cal, to confirm that what Ellie suspects is true, is nearly overwhelming. I want to run down the stairs and hop the railing so I can stand on the sidelines and drag him somewhere to talk. But I know that's not possible. For one thing, security would probably drag *me* off to talk before I even got to Cal. And for another, no one down there needs me as more of a distraction than I apparently already am, if Gray and Cal actually punched Brent on my behalf.

I can't deny that the thought of Brent gasping from a punch to the gut only to have it followed up by a black eye from Cal is immensely satisfying. I only wish I could've gotten a knee to the balls in myself.

Sadly, I don't think that'll ever happen. I'll have to be content with this sort of secondhand justice and the hope that karma will catch up to him eventually.

Questions swirl through my head in a never-ending loop. Were they fighting with Brent? Did Gray or Cal throw the first punch? If it was Gray, why did Cal take the fall? He could've gotten exactly what he's been working for all season. Will this hurt his chances of getting into the NFL draft?

At halftime, I dig out my phone to text Cal, determined to get answers. He won't be able to talk until after the game, of course. But this is something I can do right now.

Me: Call me

I stare at the terse message for long moments, only coming out of my daze when my mom leans over and asks if I want Dad to get me a snack from concessions.

I blink at her, forcing a smile. "Yes. A hotdog and a pretzel please. And a Dr. Pepper."

Mom squeezes my hand and smiles back before asking Ellie the same question.

I only sent Cal two words, and part of me wants to modify it somehow, though I'm not sure if I want to up the intensity or tone it down, but I eventually just decide to let it go. I've done what I can for now. The only thing left to do is wait.

CHAPTER FORTY-TWO

Cal

We file into the locker room quiet and slightly dejected. It was a close game, hard fought on both sides, but in the end we couldn't quite manage the last touchdown that would've secured our win.

I stand off to the side, feeling disconnected from my team. I'm part of the team, but I didn't get to play today. Me not playing isn't exactly unusual, but it wasn't even on the table today. Instead I helped the offensive coaching staff. Kilpatrick played the whole game, firing off his signature long-range passes again and again. There's no chance I would've played even if I'd been suited up.

Disappointment at our loss, at this being the end of

my college football career, wells up inside me as I look around the locker room and watch my friends and teammates slump on the benches.

Coach Reese makes his way to the center of the room, crossing his arms over his clipboard and taking a moment to survey the team as the few murmurs of conversation quiet down. "I know this wasn't the outcome we hoped for," he says, provoking a round of grumbles of agreement.

A small smile curves his mouth as he looks at everyone, his eyes making contact briefly with each player. "It always feels better to end on a win. There's no denying that. But you played your best out there, and that's all I've ever asked for. It's been an honor to be your coach this year, and to take you to your first bowl game. And as much as the coach gets credit from the administration, we all know that it's you"—he points a finger, moving it around the room, turning to encompass everyone—"it's you who do the work. Who come in day after day and push yourselves to work harder, run faster, be better. And that work has paid off. Look at us, making it all the way to a bowl game in our first season as a Division I school. That's nothing to be ashamed of. So go home with your heads held high. Have some fun tonight." He holds up a finger. "No fighting." He has to wait for a few chuckles to die down. "I'm serious. No more calls giving me a heart attack about my players, even if my time as your coach is quickly coming to an end for you seniors. Thank you for your hard work this season. And those of you who are returning, I look forward to seeing how far we can go next year."

A smattering of applause fills the room, and I head to my locker to get my things, bittersweet emotions filling me. For as much as I complained about Coach Hanson being forced to retire at the end of last year, Coach Reese is a good coach. And he's pushed all of us to be our best. I can't say I've always given him my best, and I regret starting off the season on such a crappy note. And now that I've finally pulled my head out of my ass, it's too late to do anything about it.

One of the assistant coaches taps my shoulder. "Coach Reese wants to talk to you."

Swallowing hard, I nod, shoulder my duffle bag, and head to the small office Coach Reese was assigned during our time here. With my hands in my pockets, I stand in the doorway and clear my throat, waiting for his acknowledgment.

He looks up from his clipboard and gestures me inside. "Close the door, please."

Uh-oh. I figured the lecture I got about fighting yesterday would've been the end of it, especially now that the game is over. Is he going to ream me out some more?

But he doesn't have his angry face on. Confused, I take one of the chairs he indicates, setting my bag on the floor.

Coach stares at me for a moment. Then, "I heard what actually happened."

"What?" I croak, not following.

"The other day. With the fight. I know it was Kilpatrick that started it and not you." He stares at me for a beat, and I shift in my seat.

"It wasn't Kilpatrick. It was the other guy."

Coach Reese dismisses that with a shrug. "Regardless, it wasn't you." He pauses, studying me. "I know you weren't my biggest fan at the beginning of the season, and I know you resented me bringing a new starting quarterback along when that position had been yours. I gave you a lot of leeway—more than I normally would—because I recognize that it felt crappy to you. But the last couple of months, you seem to have turned a corner. I've been glad to see you dig in and work hard and give Kilpatrick a run for his money. If I'd benched Kilpatrick and had you starting, I would've been just as happy with our chances of winning. Your passes have gotten better, and your blitz game has always been top notch." He taps his fingers on the desk. "All this to say, when the NFL recruiters contacted me, your name was on the short list for evaluation by the NFL committee, and they've predicted you should get picked in the second or third round if you apply for the draft."

My eyes widen and my breath freezes in my chest. I open my mouth, but no sound comes out.

He holds up a hand. "Now, I know everyone wants to hear they're first round pick material, but that's just not realistic. Still, it sounds like you have a solid chance, and you not getting much playing time this season—and none in this game—hasn't hurt your chances any. It's been an honor being your coach, and I'll be watching to see what you end up doing."

He extends his hand across the desk, and I grip it in a firm shake. "Thank you," I croak out, clearing my throat and trying again. "Thanks, Coach. I appreciate the vote of confidence."

He gives my hand another firm shake. "My pleasure." He jerks his chin at the door. "Go tell Kilpatrick to come see me when he's dressed."

After delivering Coach's message, I sit on the bench to wait for Simon to see what he's planning, even though I'm sure it'll involve meeting up with my sister, and dig out my phone. My breath freezes when I see the text from Piper. It's been almost two hours since she sent the text, which means she sent it during the game.

Immediately, I unlock my phone, press on her name, and hold the phone to my ear. It rings and rings and eventually goes to voicemail, her cheerful recorded voice filling my ear for the first time in weeks, telling me to leave a message if I want but that text is a better choice. Clearing my throat, I leave a message anyway. "Hey. Piper. It's Cal. Uh, you said to call, so I am." I clear my throat again. "You're probably still stuck trying to get back to your hotel or wherever. So, um, call me back. Or I'll try you again later. I … I'm really glad you texted. Talk soon. Bye."

Closing my eyes at my stupid voicemail, I hit end and shove my phone back in my bag. Then immediately pull it back out so I don't risk missing her calling me back.

Simon gets pulled in to talk to Coach Reese—probably to have a version of the conversation I just had with him—so I end up waiting longer than normal, my leg bouncing out of control, the desire to run out of here and find Piper immediately almost too much to bear.

She wants to talk to me.

I have no idea what prompted the sudden change, because it's been abundantly clear that she hasn't wanted to talk to me for weeks, and I'm dying to find out what she wants. Dying to tell her how sorry I am for trying to use her, how all of that changed as I got to know her, how I've only wanted her for longer than I can remember. I don't even remember what it feels like to want anyone else. That while I might eventually recover and get over her, it won't be any time soon, and that she's indelibly changed me regardless. That I'll have to shift and grow around the hole she's left, that it isn't something that can just be filled by anyone else.

But I can't do that until I get the fuck out of here and figure out where she's staying.

When Simon finally comes back from talking to Coach, he gives me a concerned look, and I can only imagine what a picture I make. "What's up?" he asks.

I hold up my phone. "Piper texted me, but didn't answer when I called."

Simon grins. "Awesome. Let's get back to the hotel. Ellie and Piper can come over, and Ellie and I'll go somewhere else so you two can talk."

He picks up his bag and starts walking, and

apparently I'm supposed to follow him because it's as simple as that. He'll get Piper to me, and then it's up to me to talk.

So why do I feel like puking?

CHAPTER FORTY-THREE

"You're sure this is okay?" I ask Ellie for the third or fourth time as we exit the elevator and walk down the nice but nondescript hotel hallway, looking for room 1134.

Ellie tosses a look at me over her shoulder, and it's a testament to her patience that she's not rolling her eyes. "It's fine. I promise. It was Simon's idea." She grins at me, and I grunt in acknowledgment, not really sure how I feel about her boyfriend getting involved in my relationship with Cal, even if they are friends and roommates and teammates. *I* don't know Simon very well, and having yet another person involved in my love life in any capacity feels weird.

I've always been private about that sort of thing, and after what happened with Brent, that need for privacy dialed up to an eleven. Which is why Ellie's determination to act more as a distraction than someone to talk to and give advice about my relationship has been so welcome. She knows she's not a disinterested third party. She has definite opinions. And I suppose that her deciding to spend time with me at all could be taken as her choosing my side over her brother's anyway, which is kind of hilarious, but less so in light of the new information she gave me at the game about their relationship.

Then we're in front of the door, and she's knocking, and it opens to reveal the giant slab of man that is Simon. He gives Ellie a tender smile and pulls her in close, bending to plant a kiss on her lips. Straightening, he looks at me and jerks his head behind him. "He's waiting for you," he says in that low, rumbly voice of his.

He steps back, pulling Ellie with him, and holds the door open for me to enter. "We'll see you guys later," Ellie calls out, and I turn in time to see the door close behind them.

When I turn back around, Cal is standing next to one of the beds, his hands in his pockets, his eyes intent on me.

I take a few steps closer, drawing even with the bed I assume is Simon's, and stop. "Hey," I say, feeling like I need to start this conversation.

"Hey," he says back, his voice soft and hoarse. He looks me up and down like he's devouring the sight of me, like he needs to imprint this on his memory so he'll have something to look back on later.

His chest rises on a deep breath, and he pulls a hand from his pocket to run it through his hair. "I know that nothing I can say will make anything right. I know you feel used and betrayed, and I don't blame you. I just … I'm sorry. My motives when I started pursuing you were selfish, and I didn't think about you or your feelings at all." He turns the hand that was in his hair palm up in front of him. "But at some point, and I can't even pinpoint when, it became about you, about spending time with you, and not about anyone or anything else." His Adam's apple bobs as he swallows, and I bite my tongue to keep from saying anything, because he's clearly not done yet.

"I miss you," he continues, a gruff edge to his voice. He clears his throat, but it doesn't do anything but call attention to the emotion ringing in his voice. "I miss you so fucking bad, Piper. I haven't wanted anyone but you in ages. And I don't see that changing anytime soon. I'm so fucking sorry I hurt you, because hurting you is the last thing I ever want to do. I hope …" he clears his throat again. "I hope you can forgive me, and I'd love it if you'd be willing to give me a second chance. But if not"—a deep breath, and his eyes fall closed like what he's saying pains him deeply—"if not, I understand," he finishes on a whisper.

If I weren't already poised to forgive him based on the fight and him taking the fall for my brother—a clear demonstration that he's not the selfish asshole who came up with the idea of using me to mess with Gray anymore if ever there was one—that speech would push me over the edge.

Still, I came here because I want some answers, and I don't want to be distracted by accepting his apology and the makeup sex that would surely follow and forget to ask my questions. I really want to know why he took the fall for Gray before we end this conversation. Don't he and Gray hate each other?

I clear my throat, mostly to fill the silence, because now that he's here in front of me looking devastatingly sexy with his hair mussed from running his hands through it, those gorgeous blue eyes staring at me full of longing and hope, his broad shoulders still draped in the red Marycliff jersey that's tucked in at his narrow waist, it's hard not to just throw myself at him.

"Ellie said you got in a fight." My voice comes out just as hoarse as his. I clear my throat again.

He nods slowly. "That's a bit of an overstatement. I punched a guy in the face. But he started it."

"Brent. You punched Brent in the face."

He shrugs. That's it. He fucking shrugs.

"What happened?"

Sighing, he looks away from me, his jaw clenching as

he runs his hand through his hair again and pauses with it resting on the back of his neck. "There was a big group of us who went out to dinner, and some of the guys weren't ready to go back to the hotel, so we were exploring a bit. There were these guys singing some dumb song, and I recognized them saying the name of the frat that …" he gestures lamely at me.

"The frat Brent belongs to," I supply.

He nods, his face pained. "Your brother made his way to the front of the group, and I followed behind him." He shakes his head. "I'm not sure exactly what he and Brent said to each other, but Brent shoved him, he punched Brent in the gut, and when the guy went to tackle your brother, I grabbed him and yanked him off." He shrugs again. "I punched him too."

"In the face."

He flexes his right hand. "Yeah. It was just a glancing blow off his cheek. I was hoping to break his nose."

The bald statement provokes an unexpected bark of laughter from me. "Too bad you didn't."

He gives me a crooked smile. "That's what I thought too."

"How come you took the blame for starting the fight?" That's the real question I want answered. Much as I like the idea of Brent puking and bleeding from my brother and my … Cal taking their revenge on him when presented with the opportunity, the biggest thing I don't understand is why he wouldn't take advantage of the opportunity to start in the game.

He sighs like this question is too heavy for him to hold. "Because," he says, lifting his hands and letting them drop back to his sides.

"Because why?"

"Because he didn't deserve to get suspended for defending his sister."

"But you deserve to get suspended for defending your girlfriend?"

He freezes, staring at me. "I didn't think you were still my girlfriend," he whispers.

"But you only cared because I was. You only cared because you care about me. Why do you care about Gray, though? I thought you hated Gray."

He looks away. "I never hated him. I resented him, yeah. But I never hated him."

"But you wanted to date me so he'd get mad and mess up. So you could have your spot back. You had that chance. Why not take it?"

"I didn't want it that way," he says, all gruff hesitation gone now, replaced by laser-focused determination. "I wanted it because I deserved it. Because I was better. Not because he got in trouble for provoking the asshole who abused his sister. If anyone treated Ellie that way—" He cuts himself off, his chest puffing out and his shoulders appearing to get more broad. Shaking his head, he continues, "Let's just say, if anyone did that to Ellie, I'd want to do a lot more than punch them in the gut. And I dare anyone to tell me that that douchebag didn't deserve more than a gut punch and a bruised cheek."

I hold up my hands. "You won't hear any argument from me."

His shoulders fall, and he seems to resume his normal size, that crooked smile coming back to his face. "I just didn't think Gray should suffer for something anyone would do in his shoes. Besides, the other guy laid hands on him first. It's dumb he'd get in trouble for defending himself in the first place. My punch was arguably gratuitous. It made more sense for me to get in trouble for it. And all I got was suspended from one game. I'll still be applying to the draft in the spring. No long-term harm done."

"Good. I'm glad." I stare at him. He stares at me. I've had my questions answered. He's apologized. But I still feel like there's this gulf between us, and while I want to cross it, I don't know how.

He takes a tentative step in my direction, his eyes falling to my lips. "I really am sorry, Piper," he whispers. "I wish you could forgive me."

"I can," I whisper back. "I do."

His eyes jerk up to mine. "You do?" His voice is so achingly full of hope, it almost makes me want to cry.

When I nod, he closes the remaining distance between us, his hands moving up and down, outlining my shape like he wants to touch me but isn't sure where. "God, that's all I've wanted to hear since you stopped talking to me." When I put out my hands and twine my fingers through his, he sighs and takes a deep breath. "I wasn't out bragging about how I'd bagged you in an effort to fuck with your brother," he says. "I want you to know that. And for real, that was my plan. But I couldn't do it. Your brother was yelling at me, though, saying that was the only reason I ever got with you, and I didn't deny it, even though by then that wasn't what being with you was about at all. I explained that to Trey, but Foster must've left before that part."

He removes one of his hands from mine, reaching up to brush a strand of hair off my forehead and tuck it behind my ear, his fingers trailing along my jaw. "I've wanted you for you since the first time I saw you. But when I found out you were Kilpatrick's sister, I convinced myself there was no way you'd go for me. And then I thought maybe you would and I could use that to my advantage."

Hearing him lay out his entire thought process and motivations is a lot. But it's the kind of honesty that just makes his apology feel even more genuine. He could lie or downplay things. But he doesn't. Not even to spare my feelings.

"I could tell you were attracted to me, even if you refused to acknowledge it. So I bet you that you couldn't kiss me and not enjoy it." A smile touches his lips, and he tips my chin up and brushes a kiss across my lips. "And oh, did you enjoy it," he whispers, his voice all husky and full of promise. "So did I. I was so hard just from one fucking kiss. I wanted to pick you up and carry you to a bedroom then and there and have my way with you. But I think it was our date that really pulled me all the way under your spell. That was when I was lost to you, and no matter how much I tried to remind myself of the reason I was supposedly dating you, the real reason was that I wanted you. I only wanted you. Always."

I can't take anymore of his sweet, whispered declarations. Having him this close, touching me, telling me he wants me and no one else, and not kissing me? It's too much.

Wrapping my hand behind his neck, I pull his mouth to mine. And then he takes over, one arm yanking me against his chest, hard, his other hand gripping my ass, tilting my hips and sliding down to lift my leg so he can grind against my center.

When I let out a desperate groan, he drops my leg and pivots us, backing me up until the backs of my knees hit the bed. Sitting, I grip his jersey and pull him down with me.

With that smirk I've come to love on his face, he follows, climbing on the bed as I kick off my shoes and scoot back. He yanks the jersey out of his waistband and pulls it off, but holds himself up and over me, tantalizingly out of reach as he looks me over, something like reverence on his face.

"This is for real?" he asks, like he can't quite believe

his good fortune, even though I already said it. "You forgive me?"

Reaching up, I cup his face with my hands, and he brings himself closer. "This is for real," I confirm. "I forgive you."

His eyelids fall closed, like he's soaking in the words.

"Now make love to me," I whisper.

His eyes open, full of tenderness and affection. "My pleasure."

CHAPTER FORTY-FOUR

Cal

My breath shudders as I release it slowly, trying my best to maintain my control and my composure as Piper looks up at me with love in her eyes. I don't even have the words to express how I feel right now. Amazed. Overwhelmed. Grateful.

Fortunately she doesn't want words from me. Not anymore. Apparently what I said before, my rambling, stupid explanation somehow did the trick. After weeks of no contact, of mentally rehearsing what I would say if she ever gave me the chance, I'd given up hope that she'd ever not be mad at me. And who could blame her? Especially after what happened with the last guy. He used her to score points with his frat brothers. And I started out using her, too. While my actions may not have violated her physically in the same way, it was no less of a betrayal.

Of course, by the time I found out about that asshole, I was already in over my head with her.

And now she's back, pulling me in for another kiss. Her soft lips part under mine, pliant and willing, welcoming me back to her, and it's everything I could hope for. As I deepen the kiss, it turns more passionate, and I layer my body over hers, the fabric of her sweatshirt cool against my overheated skin. Her hands roam my back, exploring like it's our first time. In a way, it kinda is. It's our first time with no ulterior motives, no subterfuge, no distractions. Just us, what we have and what we want.

I slip my hands under her top, and she pushes on my shoulders so she can sit up, letting me take her clothes off. As I'm tossing aside her sweatshirt and whatever she had on underneath that I took off all at once, she's already reaching behind her to undo the clasp of her bra.

The cups loosen, then she pulls the straps down, and my hands cup her soft flesh, my thumbs moving in circles around her nipples so they pull up into tight peaks. Rolling one between my thumb and finger, I bend to take the other into my mouth.

She arches into me, her fingers sliding into my hair to hold me in place.

This. Fucking hell, this is what I've missed so much.

Her skin. Her soft sighs. *Her.* The way she makes me feel. The things she does to me without even trying. She's turned me from a serial hook-up guy who only cares about himself to a one-woman man who's willing to sacrifice his desires for someone else's benefit. If you'd told me I'd end up here a few months ago, I would've laughed and laughed.

But I don't feel like laughing now.

I feel like stripping off the rest of our clothes and sliding inside Piper's sweet little pussy and losing myself there so I can find us both on the other side.

She whimpers in protest when I pull away, but when I stand and undo my jeans, shoving them and my boxer briefs down and off, she sits up, devouring my naked body with her eyes.

I make a show of rubbing my chest, then dragging my hand down my belly to fist my cock, giving it a few slow strokes while she watches. My breath hisses between my teeth when she crawls closer and reaches for me, her hand nudging mine out of the way so she can take over. When she swipes her tongue over the crown, my eyes practically roll back in my head, and I have to force my legs to keep holding me up.

"Condom," I grit out as she closes her lips around me and gives a gentle suck, followed by another swirl of her wicked tongue. "I was gonna get a condom."

She looks up at me, her lips tightening in a smile around my dick, and fuck me, that's hot. "In a minute," she pulls off and whispers before diving back on, bobbing her head over me a few times.

I groan, because I fucking love blow jobs, and I haven't had one in way too long. But I also really want to be inside her. It's the worst kind of dilemma.

After a moment, she releases me, wiping her bottom lip with her thumb, a seductive grin on her face. "You get the condom. I'll finish getting undressed."

I'm distracted from the condom by her standing and shimmying out of her pants, though.

Her husky laugh pulls me out of my trance, and I turn to start digging through Simon's stuff. I didn't bring condoms, because I wasn't planning on getting laid. I know he did, though—which, gross, but I'm not thinking about that now. I'll buy some to replace them later.

I find his stash in the inside pocket of his duffle bag and make quick work of covering myself. Piper's already back on the bed, lying on her side like she's posing for a painting, her head propped up on her hand as she watches me, her eyes dark with lust and sparkling with happiness.

She rolls onto her back as I approach, her thighs parting to make room for me to kneel between them. I rub my cock all over her pussy, loving the way her lips part on a tiny gasp as I spread her wetness all around. Her hips move, and I'm not sure if she's trying to rub herself on me more or get me inside her, but either way, I'm happy to give her what she wants.

"Say it, baby." It comes out as more of a dark command than I intend, but her pupils dilate even more.

"Fuck me," she says.

Positioning my cock at her opening, I drive into her in one flex of my hips. She arches up to meet me, her eyes closing and her head falling to the side.

With one hand, I move her face so I can kiss her. "I thought you wanted me to make love to you," I whisper against her lips.

Her eyes open. "Yessss," she hisses, her hands gripping my ass and her hips moving against me. She's as ready for this as I am. "Both."

"You want me to fuck you hard and slow?" I ask.

Biting her lip, her eyes closed again, she nods.

"My pleasure," I grind out, sitting back on my knees so I can give her what she wants, my hands under her back to pull her with me.

She's sitting on my lap, impaled on my dick, her arms and legs wrapped around me, her face level with mine. Her eyelids flutter open, and a small smile tugs at her lips as she rotates her hips on me. "This is gonna be hard and slow?" she asks.

I nod. "Yeah, baby. All you ever have to do is tell me what you need, and it's yours."

"Really?" she asks, one eyebrow arched.

I nod again.

She sighs when my hands grip her ass and lift her up, letting gravity carry her back down. When she bottoms out on me, she gasps. "Fuck, yeah," she whispers.

"See? Told you I'd give you what you ask for." I capture her lips with mine, swallowing her groans as I make good on my promise.

Gasping, she throws her head back, and I nip and kiss and suck on the skin of her neck and shoulder, loving the way she feels moving up and coming down hard. It's so good. So hot. So perfect. Just like her.

Everything with her is good and perfect and beautiful. When she meets my eyes, a smile touching her lips again, I realize I must've said that out loud.

"You're good and perfect and beautiful too," she murmurs, her head lolling to my shoulder. "Why are you so good to me?"

I'm not sure if it's a real question or a rhetorical one, but I answer anyway, honestly, because I've promised myself I'll never be less than that with her again.

"Because …" I lick my lips, hesitating slightly, but then dive forward as she drops down on me again. "I love you."

She stills, leaning back so she can look at me, the lust-drunk haze gone from her eyes as she examines my face. Whatever she sees must be what she's looking for, because she melts into me again, moving herself up and down slowly a few times until I take over again, lifting and dropping her like I've been doing.

"Fuck," she says on a low groan. "That feels amazing."

"Yeah? You gonna come like this?"

She shakes her head. "I dunno. Maybe?" Pulling herself closer, she seals her lips to mine again, her tongue filling my mouth, and I can't think of anything better than this at this moment—the woman I love in my arms, surrounding me, giving me everything.

I don't even care that she didn't say it back.

Maybe she's not ready. Maybe she thinks it's just a sex-fueled declaration. That's okay. I'll just have to spend however long it takes proving to her that I'm serious. That I mean it whether we're having sex or not.

This slow pace is killing me, though, and as much as I want to keep going for as long as she needs, I don't think I can. My biceps are starting to burn from lifting her, and when she puts her knees under her and starts moving, I know she needs more too.

"Hold on," I tell her, holding her tight to me so I can lay her down.

She keeps her ankles crossed just above my ass when her back hits the sheets, only loosening her grip when my hand slides between us, my thumb circling her clit. Her feet slide down my hamstrings to land on my calves, giving me the room I need to work her over.

I keep my thrusts slow and steady until I feel her pussy fluttering around me. She arches and undulates, a beautiful sinuous wave of sexual energy, and it's the most gorgeous thing I've ever fucking seen.

Her heels dig into my legs and her thighs grip my hips as she gets closer to her peak. I let myself move faster now, working her clit with my thumb and pumping into her with a determined ferocity. I need her to come. And then I think I might lose my fucking mind from the pleasure of it all.

She cries out, her whole body shuddering with the force of her orgasm, and I plant both hands on either side of her, fucking her hard through her orgasm and into my own. Slumping over, I take her with me onto my side, burying my face in her neck.

She strokes my neck and shoulders as I come down from the high, and when I look up at her face, she gives me a gentle smile. "I love you too," she says.

Happiness lights me up from the inside, and I kiss her, unable to do anything else. "I'll make you so happy, baby," I promise when I pull back. "Whatever you want, if I'm able to give it to you, it's yours."

Laughing, she kisses me again. "All I want is you."

CHAPTER FORTY-FIVE

Piper

Cal groans as I reach for my phone, which sits on his nightstand, vibrating with an alert. "I think I liked it better when you had your phones-off rule," he grumbles, wrapping himself around my naked body, caressing my breasts like he didn't just feast on them a few minutes ago to our mutual satisfaction, and placing a kiss between my shoulder blades.

I let him pull me back against him as I look at my phone. "It's not like I'm looking at it during sex. I don't know what you're complaining about. Besides, it's Gray asking if we're free for dinner tonight." Classes started last week for spring semester, and I've barely seen him.

I'm not sure if it was the way Cal jumped in and punched Brent in the face before the game a couple weeks ago, Cal taking the fall so Gray could play, or something else entirely, but Gray doesn't seem to have a problem with me being with Cal anymore. They'll never be best friends, but they're at least capable of being in the same room without trading glares or wanting to punch each other, so I'll take it. I hated being at odds with my brother, and now that I don't have to be, I'm grateful.

Cal growls against my shoulder. "I thought we were going to spend the night here."

Glancing at him over my shoulder, I raise my eyebrows. "You weren't planning on stopping for dinner?"

Just then his stomach growls, prompting a laugh from me.

He makes another grumbly noise and drops a kiss on my shoulder. "Fine. We can have dinner with your brother. Where? His place, or do you want to invite him over here?"

I send off a quick text relaying Cal's questions, then set my phone down and roll so I'm facing Cal, tangling my legs with his.

A small smile pulls up the corners of his mouth. "Much better," he says, pulling me tighter against him and kissing me. He's already hardening and lengthening against my thigh. When I try to pull back to express my surprise that he's already ready for round two, he won't let me, instead thrusting his tongue farther into my mouth, rolling us so I'm beneath him, reaching for my hands and pinning them above my head.

He lifts his head, his eyes sparkling with mischief as he rocks against me. "Yes," he answers my unspoken question. "You should know by now that when you're naked in my bed, it doesn't take me long to get ready for another round." Releasing me, he pulls out a fresh condom and rolls it on, pinning my hands again with one of his before I even have time to try to escape.

With his free hand, he lines himself up and sinks inside me, dipping his head to nip at the top of my breast with the sharp edge of his teeth. The contrast of that sharp burst of pain with the slow, pleasurable slide has me moaning immediately and arching up to meet him.

"I fucking love the sounds you make," he says, his eyes boring into mine. "I love the way you react to everything I do to you. The way you're always willing to try new things. I've never had so much fun fucking before I met you."

Such crass words shouldn't sound so sweet, but they melt my heart all the same. I tug against his hold, and he releases my wrists so I can wrap my arms around him and pull him close. I brush a light kiss over his lips as he moves slowly inside me. "I've never had so much fun fucking before you either."

He lowers himself to his elbows, his forearms going under my shoulders, holding me chest to chest as he holds my gaze. "I love you, Piper."

"I love you too, Cal."

The words come so easy now, like we've been saying them forever and not just a few weeks. When he first said it, I wasn't sure if he was serious, but nothing in his face or his behavior made it seem like it wasn't true. And even though he said it first during sex, all his actions outside the bedroom only make it obvious that he means it.

He starts moving faster. "This is gonna be quick, baby. Can you come for me again before I'm done?" Without waiting for an answer, he reaches between us to rub my clit, sending me barreling toward my orgasm in no time at all.

Minutes later we both lay panting and spent, still wrapped around each other. A few months ago, I didn't want anything like this. I thought I had no time, no room in my life for a relationship. Really, I didn't trust myself to pick someone worth having a relationship with.

Cal has proven me wrong over and over in the best ways—wrong about him, wrong about me, wrong about us. I thought he was nothing more than a player looking for a challenge and a quick fling. I thought he'd discard me as soon as he grew tired of me, and so I did my best to keep him at a distance. But Thanksgiving weekend changed all of that, showing me that he was genuine and caring and kind under his brash, arrogant, pretty boy exterior.

He's not perfect, but he's pretty perfect for me.

EPILOGUE

"Tiffany, you seem like you'd make a great group leader," says Autumn, one of my new group mates for our scene in our Theatre class that we have to perform in a few weeks. I give her a bemused look, because it seems like she's taking charge, so wouldn't that make her the best group leader? But as I'm opening my mouth to point that out, she thrusts a piece of paper into my hands. "Here's my number. Text me with possible meeting times. I gotta run!" And with that, she walks quickly out of the room.

The tall guy next to me, Jackson, clears his throat. "Umm, I guess that means you're in charge of picking times," he says to me, amusement tinging his voice.

"Guess so," I say, looking down at her number then up at Jackson. I hand him the paper. "Why don't you write your number down too, and I'll start a group text so we can plan our next meeting time."

Jackson takes the paper and lays it on the desk in front of me, pulling a pen out of his pocket and clicking it before writing his name and number down. I stare at his shoulders, broad, draped in soft gray cotton, the long sleeves pushed up to his forearms. He's a cute boy, but I think he's a bit younger than me. And anyway, I don't have time for cute boys. Not anymore. Not at all the last several years.

Having a baby right after graduation puts a damper on your dating prospects in high school, and guys my age aren't really interested in diaper duty or hearing about cracked nipples during the baby phase or daycare and preschool decisions now that Ben is older.

"I need to get going too," I say as I take the paper back, checking the time on my phone. With Autumn delegating responsibility to me right off the bat and rushing off, I'm a bit concerned about how this project is going to go. Jackson seems stable enough, or at least used to following directions, but Autumn seems like a wildcard. How are we going to pull off this scene if we can't all get together to rehearse, though? It might just be a fine arts credit gen ed, but I don't need it tanking my GPA.

"I'll walk you out," Jackson says. "Where are you headed?" He shoulders his bag and gestures for me to precede him. Feeling ultra self conscious of my messy bun and secret pajamas mom-style of oversized tee and joggers—cute joggers, but still joggers—I walk in front of him, pulling my jacket on as I go. His long fingers wrap around the strap of my bag, and he lifts it off my shoulder, making it easier for me to get my jacket all the way on.

I give him a quick smile as I take my bag back. "Thanks."

He shrugs, following me to the exit. "No problem. What class do you have next?"

"Oh, um …" Might as well just be straightforward. "I don't have class. I have to pick up my son. He's going to the preschool on campus, and they get out at one, then I have to take him home to my parents' before coming back for my evening class." I shake my head, thinking over my schedule and letting out a breath. "I have a seminar class on Tuesday evenings, which means one day a week I won't be home to put him to bed. It's going to be weird. I've never missed bedtime before."

Jackson glances at me out of the corner of his eye, his eyebrows rising the only outward sign of surprise before they crinkle together as he looks me over. "How old are you?"

I laugh. "Didn't your mom teach you it wasn't polite to ask a lady her age?"

His cheeks turn a little pink. "Sorry," he mumbles, "I didn't mean—"

"It's fine," I cut in. "I'm not upset. It's just funny that's where you went first. Most guys …" I clear my throat.

"Never mind. I'm twenty-two. I had Ben, my son, when I was eighteen. He'll be four in August"

His face smooths out, and I brace myself for the careful reaction of people who don't know what to make of a teen mom. It's a weird combo of slut shaming while trying to be polite that somehow feels worse than a direct insult. Like I have to apologize for making them uncomfortable in the face of their obvious judgment. It's ridiculous and stupid, but that's not what I end up getting from Jackson.

"My sister had a baby at nineteen," he says, surprising me. "My niece. Gina." He grins. "She's in first grade now, and a little hell-raiser. I helped out a lot when she was a baby, so I know it's not easy being …" He hesitates, his mouth open like he's just realizing he might be making a big assumption.

"A single mom?" I supply for him.

He nods, another blush on his cheeks.

I can't help smiling. This guy is almost too adorable. "Yes, I'm a single mom."

Just then someone calls his name, and he turns, lifting a hand in a wave. When I turn to see who he's waving at, more out of idle curiosity than because I expect to recognize them, I freeze.

Because walking toward us is the reason I'm a single mom. The guy responsible for Ben's creation. The guy I haven't spoken to since that night over four years ago.

Somehow he looks even better than he did back when he was the star quarterback of the rival high school's football team. He's taller. Broader. Older. The hard planes of his face devoid of the remnants of baby fat that clung to them at seventeen. Despite that, I'd recognize him anywhere. Such a stark contrast to the adorable boy standing next to me, Grayson Kilpatrick is all man.

I knew he was back. I heard all the fanfare about him transferring to Marycliff now that we were a Division I school. But it's a big enough school and campus that our paths didn't cross at all during fall semester. A fact I'd begun to take for granted.

It appears my good luck is at an end.

Jackson's saying something, but the only thing I can hear is the blood whooshing in my ears and the alarm bells going off in my head screaming at me to run.

I'm not in contact with Grayson Kilpatrick for a reason. A very good reason. And I'm not about to break that rule now.

Acknowledgements

It's time for the thank yous!

To Deb who helped me figure out how Cal would eventually redeem himself and also is the reason this book is as girth as it is. If you're a sucker for long stories, you have her to thank as well.

To Leslie for making me think about my metaphors and keeping me from overusing whatever the word of the book is. (This time it was "get" if you're curious.) And for cheering me on with every single book. I'm not sure I would've made it this far without you. You're the best! Muah!

To Danielle for booking the writing weekend that got me through over a quarter of this book.

To my Book Club members and my Book Junkies. I have so much fun sharing updates with you and getting your feedback. Never stop being awesome!

To Grey's Promotions for your assistance with this release. You've made a stressful part of the process a little less stressful this time around.

To all the bloggers, bookstagrammers, and reviewers who took the time to read this book. Thank you for giving Cal and Piper a chance (especially if you read Off Limits first lol). I appreciate you!

And last but not least, thank you, dear reader, for taking the time to read my books. Without you, none of this would be possible. Thank you.

Jerica MacMillan has been reading romance since she stumbled into the paperback section of the library as a middle schooler. And it's been an ongoing love affair ever since!

You can frequently find her sipping coffee out of snarky mugs while dreaming up stories and trying to bring them to life on the page. Join her Book Club at www.jericamacmillan.com/book-club and get a free book!

Marycliff Football
Off Limits
Trick Play

Players of Marycliff University
Summer Fling
Close Quarters
Always You
Unsaid Things
Coping Skills
False Assumptions
A Very Marycliff Christmas

Cataclysm
Anything You Need
Shouldn't Want You
Everything I Want
Just For Now
Anyone But You

Songs and Sonatas Series
Double Exposition
Development
Recapitulation
Broken Chords
Counterpoint and Harmony
Overtones
Reverb
The Arrangement

www.ingramcontent.com/pod-product-compliance
Lightning Source LLC
Chambersburg PA
CBHW030659190726
48286CB00001B/95